Who could have guessed
would made my life so co

Despite my determination to think about everything later, thoughts swirled around in my head. Maybe I should look at this as my chance to really date some guys, as in multiple. Why did I keep thinking everything was such a disaster? So some incredible, beautiful men wanted me. I could think of several women who'd love to be in my shoes. Yeah, the whole cousin-best-friend-sucked-into-mirror-hell, homicidal monsters, smitten magicians, and accidental familiars put a crimp in the positive side of things, but a girl's got to look at the silver lining, you know?

To my support network, my parents Joyce and Norman Jackson who had faith in me, husband Gary who understood when I put the "Do Not Disturb the Writer" sign on the door, my son David who is the light and joy of my life, and my writing groups. I also have to mention my three furry cheerleaders (I'm talking about my dogs, in case anyone had strange ideas pop into their minds). I also have to thank my editor Linda Kichline whose hard work, patience, expertise, and humanity made this first book a reality.

Syn in the City
A Synemancer Novel

✻✻✻

Mertianna Georgia

ImaJinn
Books

Syn in the City
A Synemancer Novel
Published by ImaJinn Books

ISBN: 978-1-61026-000-8

10 9 8 7 6 5 4 3 2 1

PUBLISHER'S NOTE:
This book is a work of fiction. Names, characters, places and incidents are products of the author's imagination or are used fictitiously. Any resemblance to actual events or locales or persons, living or dead, is entirely coincidental.

Books are available at quantity discounts when used to promote products or services. For information please write to: Marketing Division, ImaJinn Books, Inc. P.O. Box 74274, Phoenix, AZ, 85087, or call toll free 1-877-625-3592.

Cover design by Patricia Lazarus
Cover credits:
BranislavOstojic Dreamstime-sorceress
NataliaBratslovsky Dreamstime-skyline

ImaJinn Books, Inc.
P.O. Box 74274, Phoenix, AZ 85087
Toll Free: 1-877-625-3592
http://www.imajinnbooks.com

Chapter One
Warlock Moon

"Come on, Cara. It's our birthday! Don't be an old witch-in-the-mud!"

I watched my Cousin Evika toss her long red hair over her shoulder. My eyes lingered on the shining length of scarlet with long-held envy as I watched her pace up and down in front of me. She'd always liked being the center of attention, and with her vivid beauty and outgoing personality that wasn't a problem. I looked like her dark-haired kid sister even though we were born on the same day. Men were attracted to her like dragons to gold, while all I seemed to attract was trouble.

Evika stopped pacing to stand in front of me. She impatiently placed a manicured hand on her hip, fixing her emerald green eyes on me. "You've turned into such a homebody! It'll be good for you to get out of the house. Why don't you want to go?"

She reached up to stroke her necklace, a thin crystalline snake the same shade of green as her eyes. It rippled gently under her touch. The deadly stone snake, her familiar, could come alive at her bidding. I felt another stab of guilty envy at the thought of her incredibly exotic familiar. It would probably scare a human, even these days, hundreds of years after Portalkind traveled to this dimension during the Great Purge to prevent humans from wiping out all of earth's magic users.

Not every witch had a familiar because it had to come to you. You couldn't just pick one up at the local animal shelter. Maybe one in five witches had enough power to attract one. I'd always wanted a familiar, a companion, some little thing I could call my own. With my meager abilities, I couldn't even dream of having an ordinary familiar, like a housecat, much less one from a demon dimension. Probably why I volunteered for FAR—Familiars-At-Risk—so I could at least be with the poor sad creatures that had lost their witch.

I pushed away my self-pitying thoughts to focus on Evika's question. "I don't know, maybe it's because I had a bad dream last night and it threw off my whole day." I couldn't really explain it because there wasn't a definite "why." Just like I didn't know why trouble followed me around like a lovesick puppy. It's not like I *try* to get into trouble. It just happens, like bad hair days and astral projection. I could feel trouble the way Grandmother used to know a storm was coming, in my gut, in my buzzing head. I'd started awake last night, dread covering my body in cold sweat, but I lost the details of the dream almost immediately. I almost told her about my nightmare but knew she'd dismiss it. I never had prophetic dreams. Why would last night be any different? I tried to reason with her instead.

"Evika quit hounding me! Besides, you know what happens when we go out. You hook up with a guy and I end up going home in a taxi." I tossed my hands in the air. "That's after I've spilled something or accidently set someone on fire. Remember last year? You *know* putting me into a crowd of strangers is like tying a steak around my neck and poking a Hellhound with a stick!"

I sat back on the sofa, arms folded. I was currently on an extended visit with Sonya, my other cousin, in her Berkeley hills home. She'd left earlier on some kind of urgent errand that she'd said would take all night. I only caught a glimpse of her as she raced out the door, calling over her shoulder, "I have to go. My mother had a vision and she's got the whole house in an uproar. I'll fill you guys in later."

Celebrating our birthdays without Sonya seemed wrong. For as long as I could remember, we three cousins, born minutes apart, had always managed to celebrate together. I loved my cousins. They accepted me when everyone else, even my parents, ignored me after my powers never manifested. Apparently my mother blamed my father's side of the family for this embarrassing turn of events. The two people who should have loved me pretended I didn't exist most of the time. I lived off the small trust fund Grandmother had set up for me and just wandered from home to Cousins Sonya's or Evika's to college and back around again.

"Let's go out tomorrow when Sonya gets back, then we can celebrate together, like usual," I offered hopefully.

Evika smoothed the front of her form-fitting dark green dress while exhaling an exasperated breath, "Cara, you need to get a life, girl! I'm tired of you moping around since what's-his-face broke up with you last year. And wear something decent for a change."

I frowned, suddenly feeling frumpy in my jeans and plain gray t-shirt.

Evika grabbed my hand and pulled me into Sonya's guest bedroom. I flopped onto the twin bed while she reached into the closet and took out a little black dress and patent leather stiletto heels, which incidentally were the birthday presents she'd given me earlier in the day. She silently held the dress and shoes out to me with raised eyebrows and waited.

With a capitulating sigh, I reached for them. "Evika, it's not fair. And just for the record, *I* broke up with Deccan because he got too serious. I'm not ready for any kind of long-term commitment. What's so wrong with going out in my t-shirt and jeans? It's not as if anyone will pay attention to me anyway," I muttered while wriggling into the tight dress and slipped into the heels as I spoke.

Brushing aside my complaint, Evika looked me over with a satisfied nod and said, "Well at least you don't look like jail bait with that dress on. You've got great hair, a nice figure, and gorgeous eyes, so unusual with the blue and gold together."

"You mean 'funny eyes' don't you? Who has bicolored eyes besides me? No one," I groused.

Evika pursed her lips in disapproval, "Would you quit putting yourself down? Here's a lipstick, put some color on those pouty lips. I won't leave your side tonight. We'll be like conjoined twins."

"Promise?" I asked.

"I promise. Don't I always look out for you?" she replied.

I shot her a skeptical look and said, "No." She'd always thought of ways to get us into trouble when we were kids, and I always got caught, not her. I gave her back the lipstick, which she threw in her purse next to a golden compact, my gift to her this year.

She ignored my comment, linking her arm through mine. We walked out of the house arm in arm, with Evika beaming because she'd gotten her way again.

I climbed into her new sports car, a birthday surprise from her doting father. Shiny red with white leather interior, sleek and expensive-looking, just like her. I still felt grumpy.

Evika looked over and, seeing my expression, laughed, loud and full-throated, filled with life and amusement. "Oh Cara, lighten up! We're turning twenty-one tonight! Let's order champagne and have a good time."

I couldn't help smiling fondly at my best friend and cousin. Once again, I let my love for her override my own instincts.

"I'll try. Hey, maybe I'll have fun. I wouldn't mind meeting a nice guy, maybe even get back into dating." I looked up at the moonless night sky through the passenger window. Witches call it a warlock moon, making the world dark with mystery. I could almost feel the night close around me like a living being, pulling at me, making promises I couldn't understand.

"Isn't having a warlock moon on your birthday good luck?" I asked.

She turned the key in the ignition and replied dismissively, "No, it's the other way around, but that's just an old witch's tale." My stomach tightened, almost making me nauseous. I wanted to run back into the house. My hand was on the door handle just as she revved the engine, backing quickly out of the driveway. I made myself loosen my white-knuckled grip on it as we raced towards the City.

Chapter Two
The Mystery

I inhaled sharply, causing myself to cough. My mouth tasted of stale champagne. Strange images grew faint and began to fade into a twilight place between vanishing dreams and reality, where thoughts crowded around like curious children . . . who were banging painfully on the inside of my head.

Lying in bed with a major headache, I felt the old familiar sensation of being in trouble. I cautiously cracked open my eyes. I might as well see what I'd gotten myself into this time. I tried to settle into a more comfortable position and encountered something solid and person-sized beside me. I inwardly rolled my eyes as that *oh no* feeling of trouble playfully jumped on my stomach, knocking the wind out of me.

I opened my eyes another crack. The room looked unfamiliar, and with a high ceiling shrouded in darkness, it felt immense. The chilly air felt strangely like the regulated coolness of a well-kept wine cellar. I sat up, pulling silky sheets up to my neck, as I blearily took in my surroundings. This was definitely not my cousin's guest bedroom.

Several lit candles where scattered around the room in crystal holders. I took another deep breath and let it out slowly in an effort to calm myself. A scent permeated the air. I couldn't put my finger on it, but underneath the candle's sandalwood fragrance, the room smelled *male*. A rich mélange of aged woods, furniture polish, leather, and some musky, exotically spicy tang I might normally have liked, but now made me faintly nauseous.

I warily turned my head toward my sleeping partner. In the soft golden light of the candles I could just make out his features. He lay on his back, his head partially turned, as if he had fallen asleep while looking at me. His utterly pale skin seemed to softly glow in the dim candlelight, his long dark hair a startling contrast against it. I studied his face—extraordinarily handsome, lean, with a straight nose and soft-looking lips, the lower one fuller than the upper. I'm a pushover for nice lips, which might explain my current circumstances.

I glanced down at the bare swell of his smooth chest and farther down to a well-shaped leg which had escaped the covers. Ah . . . well . . . Here was trouble with a capital "T" if

I'd ever seen it. I only wished I could remember him. I don't
do casual hookups. I must have had way too much to drink last
night.

I'll never drink champagne again, I thought irritably.
My rational mind laughed derisively at yet another impractical
remorse-fueled resolution.

I muttered under my breath, "Where in *Hades* is Evika?"
She'd pleaded with me to go out last night and I also recalled
that she'd ordered the third bottle of champagne. I couldn't
believe she would have let me go off with this stranger. Evika
swore she wouldn't let me get into trouble, that she'd stick
with me all night, like "conjoined twins" she'd said, for *Hade's*
sake.

I clutched the sheet tighter to me. I didn't like this at all.
My trouble-indicators were flashing and alarms were ringing
in my head. This felt incredibly *wrong*. I remembered most of
last night, but nothing about this person lying next to me. I also
had no desire to get to know him, to talk over coffee or whatever
people did in these types of situations.

At the thought of coffee I almost reconsidered. Almost. I
couldn't wait to get my hands on my cousin and so-called best
friend. I decided to leave, as stealthily as possible, before he
woke up. I'd just have to hope I'd had a good time and chalk it
up to an embarrassing birthday story. But . . . I couldn't help
being curious. Against my better judgment, which hardly ever
wins an argument anyway, I leaned in to get a closer look. The
room immediately began to spin. I caught myself on his still,
cold, bare chest.

I let out a small, involuntary, high-pitched squeak as I
scrambled backwards as fast as I could to get away from his
frigid, possibly dead, body. The bedcovers tangled up with my
legs and I fell hard to the floor, landing painfully on my side.
Quickly turning over, I crawled on my hands and knees until I
hit my head on a wall. Shaking as I sat on the thick carpet, all
I could see for several seconds where sparkly little motes
dancing in front of my eyes. I glanced down and, through the
sparkles, noticed I only had on a pair of panties. Pushing my
back against the wall, I pulled my knees up against my chest
and lifted both hands to push my thick tangle of hair out of my
eyes.

"Ow!" Something on my left hand caught in my hair and
painfully pulled out several strands. I untangled my hand and

squinted down at my outstretched fingers—and saw a huge diamond ring. It glittered dazzlingly, even in the dim light of the flickering candles.

Zul's horns, am I *engaged* to the dead stranger?

As I tried to think, my head pounded, so I had to close my eyes. A couple of stray motes chased each other across my inner eyelids. What happened? I had to force myself to do something. Making decisions hurt my head at the best of times. This caused the excruciating band of pain around my head to tighten even more.

Sitting on the floor, in a quiet desperate panic, I started to get flashes of memory from last night. *Evika and I going out to celebrate in San Francisco . . . ordering champagne . . . laughing . . . telling everyone it's our birthday . . . a tall devastatingly beautiful dark-haired man approaching our table . . . I notice his silvery gray eyes rimmed in black, making them unusual . . . sexy . . . strangely familiar . . .*

I opened my eyes and glanced over at the bed. He looked like the man, but it was hard to tell without looking at his eyes.

Then what happened? How did I get from there to here? Focused on my memories, I almost didn't hear a light tapping on the bedroom door. When I did notice, the panic kicked in full force. What should I do? If people found me here, they might get the wrong impression, like I might have had something to do with this guy's death.

The knocking grew a little more insistent, and a nice baritone voice called out, "Madam Cara? Are you awake? May I enter?"

"Uh, who is it?" I called back in an almost calm voice.

"It's Roland, Madam. The Master gave me instructions to see to your comfort while he is, ahem, indisposed for the day."

Indisposed? He had no idea how "indisposed" the Master was. I quickly scanned the room for my clothes and my purse. With neither in sight, I hesitantly called out, "Roland?"

"Yes, Madam?" he answered. His voice now emanated from the old-fashioned keyhole below the door's ornate brass knob. A thin slice of light from under the door barely penetrated into the room. I wished this room had more light so I could find my clothes.

Suddenly, all the candle flames leapt higher, burning brighter, revealing more of the room. I lifted my brows in faint surprise, but shrugged. They were probably charmed. I looked around at my surroundings. My impression of a large room turned out to be true. It exuded wealth, with richly furnished, carved dark wood furniture and thick rugs placed strategically on top of a marble floor. There were numerous art pieces tastefully displayed about the room and what looked like original paintings on the walls.

Despite the opulence, something about the room struck me as odd, and then I realized there were no windows. *That's why it's so dark in here.* I took one more calming breath and looked at the closed bedroom door with, Roland presumably waiting on the other side. I called out in an admirably steady voice, "I can't seem to find my clothes and we, um, have kind of a situation in here with, uh, 'the Master.'" I could feel my face grow hot and my heartbeat start to climb again, making my head pound harder.

"Madam, if I may enter. I have your garments and your breakfast," Roland patiently called through the keyhole. I inched closer to the door, quickly grabbing a pillow off the bed, while avoiding looking at the occupant. Using it like a shield in front of my body, I leaned over to position my mouth in front of the keyhole. "How would you like to call 9-1-1 for me?" Unwillingly, I glanced over at the man in the bed. The occupant hadn't moved. I'd hoped I'd been wrong about his condition. In the increased light he looked like he merely slept. His lips weren't blue; in fact, his face had a little color instead of the ashen gray I expected. Maybe I should have tried CPR . . .

Oh, great Zul's horns, I was a newt! I threw down the pillow, ran and jumped on the man in the bed while yelling out, "Get in here, Roland. Now!"

I tried to remember CPR from the class I took five years ago at the Red Pentagram center. Let's see, ask if the victim is okay, listen for breath, plug nose, tilt head back, blow in mouth, push on chest, okay, and ready, and go. I shook his muscular and unyielding shoulders and yelled, "Are you okay?"

No, I'm not okay, I'm dead, his body said to me.

I had my mouth clamped over the man's lips and was in the process of trying to inflate his lungs when Roland opened the door and walked in. I rolled my eyes up to look at him while continuing to hold the "the Master's" nose and blow into his mouth. Roland turned out to be a tall, slim man maybe in his sixties, with thick graying hair. He wore a dark suit, a white shirt and a burgundy tie. He held a large tray with covered silver platters in both hands and my dress from last night neatly draped over one arm. I had no idea how he could have opened the door while holding everything.

His eyebrows shot up in alarm as he took in my semi-naked CPR efforts. "Madam! Your efforts are quite unnecessary, I assure you!" He hurriedly set the tray down on a small table and carefully but quickly laid my dress over the back of a wing chair.

I pushed on the good-looking man's chest while yelling, "Call emergency, it might not be too late!" Roland had hurried over to the bed and gazed at the beautiful wooden headboard, politely avoiding looking at my bouncing body parts as I continued pushing.

"Madam, I must insist you cease this activity at once. The Master is quite well and has no need of your, er, resuscitation efforts." His voice sounded firm, yet had just the right amount of something to not make it sound like a command but more of an urgent request. Like he would never dream of ordering me to do something, but would definitely be willing to make sure I would take his request under immediate advisement.

I stopped my actions as his words sank in past the guilty panic. "What?" I blinked at him.

Roland waved a hand vaguely towards the man on the bed and said, "The Master is in his resting state for the day and will be up and about at sunset. *Surely*, he explained this to you last evening?" He glanced down at my hands on the dead guy's chest, looking pointedly at the ring on my finger, still trailing dark strands of my hair.

I gave him a completely blank look. I had no idea what he was talking about. Up at sunset? Then, understanding dawned in the foggy morning of my mind. I said, "So, what you're saying is 'the Master' is one of the Nightkind? I'm engaged . . ." I held up my left hand and looked at the pretty shiny expensive diamond ring. ". . . to a *Nightkind*?" Nightkinds came from a demon-dimension and had what humans might call vampire-like tendencies. I recalled stories about their retractable fangs that could inject a chemical agent to create a sense of bonding to them. They also had to ingest some blood on a regular basis for their metabolisms to be able to live in this world, but didn't live totally on it like the vampires of myth. Magicians were the Nightkind's ruling class, the only ones who were capable of making the chemical.

Roland grimaced. "I believe the term used now is 'daylight-challenged,' Madam."

I sat back on my haunches, stunned. I stared at the gray-haired Roland and then back down to my "fiancé," at which point I suddenly remembered I needed clothes. I grabbed the top sheet to fashion a makeshift wrap.

"I need to get dressed now," I said hastily, grabbing at the sheet and slowly climbing out of the bed, holding the silky material in front of me. As I backed away, I noticed the covers sliding slowly off the man in bed. I took a second to notice—and admire—his incredible physique, my eyebrows lifting in inappropriate appreciation. I'd feel ashamed of myself later, but right now, the only thing I could think about was escape.

Roland quickly turned and walked towards the door. His back to me, he pointed to his left and said, "The bath and dressing room are through that door, Madam. I'll return shortly for the tray." Then, back straight, he made a dignified but hasty exit and shut the door behind him.

I grabbed my dress off the back of the chair, dropped the sheet, and ran to the door Roland had indicated. I threw it open and quickly shut it behind me. The bathroom was pitch black and cold. I fumbled along the wall until I found a switch and flipped it on. Suddenly, I stood in a bathroom of incredible splendor. Discreet sconces located around the room illuminated a dream bath. It had marble tiles on the floor inset with intricate mosaics of multicolored stones. The double sinks stood on beautifully carved wooden vanities. The sinks themselves were large bowls of thick, hand-blown art glass. Silver dragonheads came out of the wall above each sink, open mouths serving as faucets. I used the facilities and washed my hands and face in one of the gorgeous sinks, watching as illuminated water poured from a silver dragon's mouth.

Grabbing one of the black hand towels piled near the sink, I looked around for the dressing room Roland had mentioned. I noticed another door, slightly ajar. I went in and turned on the light to discover an enormous closet with floor to ceiling built-in wooden cabinets. Hanging from gleaming brass-colored rods were what looked like the entire contents of a high-end men's clothing store. In one corner sat a large, square, black leather ottoman directly in front of a full-length three-way mirror.

I looked down at the ring on my finger, sighed and reluctantly slid it off. I admired the way the smaller side diamonds set off the extraordinarily large central diamond and how the whole thing sparkled so beautifully. The hell of it was, I just loved it. I loved gems in general, always had, anything crystalline, they *called* to me. Evika used to say I acted like a magpie, attracted to shiny objects. I never had a comeback because, well, it's hard to argue with the truth.

It seemed monumentally unfair that circumstances forced me to return this gorgeous ring to the handsome "daylight-challenged" person. I should just keep it to teach him he couldn't take advantage of a drink-impaired witch to become engaged to her. But I discovered, after a short internal struggle, my exceedingly bratty conscience wouldn't let me keep the jewelry.

I reverently placed the ring in the center of the ottoman, confident he would see it as soon as he picked out his outfit for the day and came over to the mirror to check it out. Silently snorting as I imagined the scenario, I got dressed quickly, finally getting the courage to look at myself in the large mirrors. I gasped. I appeared almost as pale as the man in the other room, and my hair looked as if it I had been in a fight, in the rain. My pupils were dilated; I looked hung-over and a little shocky. I tried to smooth my hair with my fingers, getting the worst of the tangles out. Then I straightened my back, ran my hands down the front of my dress and prepared to go out and either face the music or run like hell. I put my bet on the running option.

I walked back out into the bedroom barefoot because Roland hadn't given me my shoes. I shot one last glance towards the bed and the beautiful man of Nightkind persuasion and very short acquaintance. Quickly striding to the door, I opened it a crack and poked my head out slowly into the hallway. I looked around for Roland and, not seeing him, decided to keep on going down the hall where I found a wide carpeted stairway leading up to what I hoped would be the way out of this house.

I climbed up the incredibly long stairway two steps at a time in my bare feet. Was this floor of the house deep underground like a bomb shelter? Panting a bit at the landing, I had to wait to catch my breath. I looked around again, spotted the front door and ran-walked towards it in a, hopefully, nonchalant manner.

Before I could make my escape, Roland came around a corner from another hallway. He spotted me and quickly started walking in my direction, concern and alarm written all over his face. He held my shoes and handbag in his hands.

I lifted my eyebrows, looked down at my feet, made a quick decision and walked towards him cautiously. "Hey there, Roland. I see you found my shoes and purse, uh, thanks," I said as I reached for them.

Roland instinctively pulled back. "Forgive me Madam, but I am reluctant to release your possessions. I have my instructions to make you comfortable while we wait for the Master to rise."

I lunged at him and grabbed my shoes and purse in a death grip. We engaged in a silently polite, yet intense, game of tug-of-war. After a few anxious moments he reluctantly ceded the battle. He was likely still under the mistaken impression I would soon become his future employer.

He tried to talk me into staying all the way out the door, but stopped at the end of the walkway. He might have been afraid of what the neighbors might think. Everyone knew the Nightkind were absolute sticklers for fitting in with human society. Most of them were obsessed with etiquette and clothes. It's common knowledge that the ones who had integrated into society took great pains to determine the occasion and the weather for any given day so they could wear the correct type of clothing. I guess not feeling the heat and cold like we do, they took extra care not to look out of place. And probably being so long-lived, they had to keep up with fashion changes.

I took in my surroundings which looked to be in Pacific Heights, an upper-end residential area of San Francisco. At least I had decent weather. Maybe a little too chilly for my short dress, but it couldn't compare with how I felt about this whole incident.

The house sat at the top of a hill. No way I could walk up and down the steep San Francisco streets in my mile-high stiletto heels. But I did make myself gingerly walk down another block, tottering slightly, periodically checking behind me to see if Roland had followed me. He hadn't. I wished I had a pair of sunglasses as I took my cell phone out of my purse and called a taxi. I sat down on a low stone wall, looked at the street signs to tell the cab company my location and waited for my ride.

When the taxi arrived, I gave the driver Sonya's address across the Bay. He dropped me off in front of my cousin's house about a half-hour later, and I hurried up the front walkway, eager to forget this morning ever happened.

With a sigh of relief, I opened the front door and was immediately set upon by enormous, slavering Hellhounds.

Chapter Three
Cousin Sonya

There were two of them, enormous beasts with pure black fur and eyes, except for red flames where their pupils should have been. I held out my hands defensively as they closed in, knowing my puny efforts would be useless. The first of them leapt up, and I felt its hot breath, smelling faintly of sulfur, right before it reached out with a head at least twice the size of my own, and started licking my face.

"Get down Jupiter," I gasped while laughing. The other Hound joined the first and also started licking me. They pushed me to the floor where I felt in serious danger of drowning in Hound drool. I pushed at their big muscular bodies, "Jupiter! Archer! Down, now!" They continued their onslaught, tails wagging.

I heard Sonya's voice telling them to "sit." The two of them sat simultaneously with a whoop, mouths open, tongues hanging out in doggie grins.

"Geez, you guys. Go. Go on now." They stood and bounded off into the house, Jupiter bouncing halfway up a wall before disappearing around a corner. I started wiping their gunk off my face when Cousin Sonya appeared with a dishtowel in her hand.

"Here, use this," she said, looking down at me where I still lay on the floor, and handed me the towel. Sonya is my height but with a more slender, boyish figure, and her short blue-black hair is cut in a smooth, straight pageboy. The bangs and sides of her hair frame a sweet oval face with large brown eyes.

"Thanks." I said as I stood, rubbing the towel over my face and neck.

I started walking towards the kitchen with the thought of having a whole pot of coffee. I felt so thirsty and my head wasn't feeling much better, despite the warm welcome I'd received from Sonya's "babies." Sonya walked beside me, looking at me worriedly, but not saying anything until we got to the kitchen.

Sonya's kitchen is large and sunny, with modern appliances and dark granite countertops. A special island had a protection circle carved right into the granite around the potion brewing area. She'd remodeled this room last year. The kitchen is located at the back of the house, and a rounded bank of tall windows looked out over the hills. You could glimpse a glint of blue-gray water from the Bay over the tops of the trees. She had placed an oval wooden table with four chairs in front of the windows so she could sip tea and look out over the tree-studded view. A door off to the side led to a deck with stairs leading down to her backyard. The entire lower half of the door had been cut out and had a flap of thick clear plastic fastened to the top of the opening—the Hound door. I could see them cavorting out in the yard. In the daylight they looked like giant, short-haired, black dogs, instead of their normal dog-panther-indescribable selves. They usually only took on their true aspects at night or while hunting.

The Hounds had been a gift from Sonya's father, a half-demon, even though the general witch community frowned upon having them as pets. He thought a young woman living alone should have protection and company. He also knew Sonya wouldn't be able to resist the two small, squirming black puppies he had brought over. They were so adorable back then. We used to play with them after they had dinner, big bowls of blood, still warm from the animal. Rounded little bellies full, tails wagging, the fires in their eyes would go from red to orange and eventually to yellow as they fell asleep. They grew incredibly fast over the next year. The first year they had grown to their full heights, shoulders taller than my waist, but they'd had the lanky leanness of youth. Over the next few years they filled out to the muscular brutes they were today. They were usually very well-behaved unless they sensed danger to Sonya or me. I think they bonded with both of us, not just Sonya, probably because I stayed with them when they were pups. As adorable as I thought they were, I knew their potential to turn deadly with an unearthly ferocity. "Hello? Have you heard a word I've said?" Sonya waved a hand in front of my face. I snapped out of my reverie and focused on her.

"What? Oh, sorry. Um, thinking about the Hounds when they were puppies." I gave her a weak smile. "Hey, got any coffee left?" I looked over my shoulder towards the coffee maker, and Blessed-be-the-Portal, saw a half carafe left.

I walked over, got my big thermal cup from the cupboard and filled it with coffee, then went through my routine of adding hot cocoa and milk. I saw Sonya wrinkle her nose; the purist that she is just took it black, "the way nature had intended." I didn't give a flying newt about nature, I liked my coffee rich and sweet, just like the man I hoped to meet someday.

I chuckled to myself, couldn't hurt to wish since I hadn't had a real date in months—I was *not* counting last night. Sonya had set me up with my last one, a disastrous blind date. At least he put out the fire before it caused any real damage. Never let a part-demon cousin set you up on a blind date. That's my advice for the day.

"Okay, enough already. Spill it. What happened last night? Where were you? Where's Evika? What kind of trouble did you two get into this time?" Sonya stood with her arms akimbo, an impatient look on her face. Then she softened as she saw my expression, "Are you alright? Did something bad happen?" She dropped her arms and came over to me, pulling out a chair so we could sit side by side.

I looked down at my coffee, now half gone, and told her about my "morning after" adventure. She went from concerned to wide-eyed as I finished.

"A Nightkind? Are you sure? How big a diamond? Where's Evika?" She kept staring at me like I had grown horns. That's her side of the family, not mine. "We have to call your mother. She'll know what to do."

"No!" I looked at her, panic rising. Zul's horns, I didn't need my mother to know I'd screwed things up again. "I can't tell her what happened. No one can know. I left the ring and we'll just forget it ever happened."

Sonya shook her head, "No way he'll forget about it. He chose you. He'll try to get you back. You've heard how they are about this sort of thing. He obviously didn't want you for a one-night stand. He gave you an *engagement ring.*"

I forgot my thoughts when we heard a sudden swell of sound, like a large choir had decided to sing a single discordant note at the top of their lungs. The house vibrated slightly. Alarmed, I looked at Sonya and said "Earthquake?"

She looked back with a resigned expression, "No, it's my Dad."

She ran into her living room and I followed. We took up positions side by side in front of the huge floor to ceiling mirror she had on one wall. I always liked her mirror with its heavy gilt frame carved with fanciful creatures. In all the years I've been visiting my cousin, I'd never seen anyone use it as a doorway. The glass seemed to waver and shimmer as a small figure grew rapidly larger until I saw Uncle Max looking out at me where my reflection should have been.

He turned to Sonya and said, "May I come in?" in the deep dark voice I knew so well. She nodded and he stepped through the looking glass.

Sonya got her straight black hair from her father. He stood six feet tall with hair that hung in one shining length from the widow's peak on his forehead down past his shoulders. Sunlight from a window opposite the mirror brought out the blue highlights even more than usual in his fall of thick hair. His eyes were pure black so you couldn't tell where his irises ended and his pupils began. He wore all black clothing, his only adornment a large ruby pin at his throat instead of a tie, and a matching earring in one ear. I thought he might be almost a century old but looked to be in his early forties. Uncle Max. is one of my favorite Uncles. He's usually fun to be around, showing us girls how to cast cool spells and throw low-level hexes, although mine tended to have embarrassingly unexpected results, unlike the perfect ones my cousins threw. At the moment, however, he had a frown on his face. It didn't look like we were going to have much fun on this visit.

Uncle Max walked into Sonya's living room and sat in one of her comfortable upholstered chairs. He motioned for us to sit on the couch. We sat and looked at him expectantly. He leaned forward and rested both of his forearms on his knees and looked at me intently. I looked back, puzzled.

"What did you and Evika do last night?" he asked.

"Well, um, we went out to dinner." I said, my gaze roaming to the ceiling, which suddenly became very interesting, then back to Uncle Max.

He continued to look at me, patiently waiting for more information.

"Uh, I'm not really sure after that." I looked over at Sonya for help. She looked back and shook her head apologetically, the message clear. I was on my own. "I mean, I remember we went out for dinner in the City and then things are a little hazy. I think we may have had too much to drink . . ." My voice trailed off towards the end. I felt like a little girl having to confess to a grown-up.

Uncle Max stood and started pacing. "Evika is missing. I got a call from her mother who waited for her to show up for their weekly lunch. Apparently, after waiting for half an hour,

Marissa tried to call her at her apartment and then her cell phone and got voice mail both times. She then tried to crystal-scry for her on a map of the City with no success. As you can imagine, she's very worried. You were with her last night. What happened?" He looked at me and the pure black of his eyes seemed fathomless.

"I don't know!" My stomach dropped as concern for my cousin suddenly overcame me. In a rush of words I told Uncle Max an abbreviated version of what had happened this morning, leaving out some details like lack of clothing and diamond engagement rings. The gist of it being I woke up in a stranger's house, couldn't remember where I was or what had happened, and I immediately left and came to Sonya's house.

Uncle Max's brows came together when I got to the part about the Nightkind. "Are you alright? Did this Nightkind hurt you?" I could see him getting worked up, his protective instincts fueling his anger and concern. His small black horns started to poke through his hair, a sure sign of agitation, and he had balled his hands into fists like he wanted to hit something. He held my chin and looked into my eyes, as if he could see in them some clue as to my state of well-being.

"I think I'm okay, Uncle Max." I said, as I gently pushed his hands away.

"Who is this person? Where does he live?" he demanded, his voice growing louder. "How dare he take advantage of a girl who did not have her full faculties. Shades of Hades, he should be taught a lesson!" He looked at our surprised expressions and sighed, "Sorry for shouting girls."

He took one of my hands, saying, "Can you remember anything about what happened? What's the name of the restaurant where you two had dinner? How did you get to the Nightkind's house? Was Evika with you?" His hands were getting almost too hot to touch.

I slid mine out slowly, not wanting to offend him. Thinking hard, I shook my head. "I'm sorry but I just can't remember." I closed my eyes wearily and felt something bump against my leg. The Hounds had come back into the house through their doggie door. Sensing agitation in the air, Jupiter tried to get his head under my hand for a pet. I obliged him, running my hand across his velvety soft, dense fur. I looked at my Uncle. He had started pacing.

Sonya had moved from the couch to the floor. As she

rubbed Archer's tummy, he rolled onto his back, long legs pawing the air in bliss. "I should have gone with you last night." Her voice barely above a whisper, she looked at the Hound and not at us, as she made the statement.

"What would you have done? I don't mean it in bad way, Sonya. You *and* Evika might be missing now instead of just Evika. Don't beat yourself up over this," I said.

She looked up, anger coloring her pale cheeks with two spots of pink, "Hey I can take care of myself, unlike some people I know." She glared at me pointedly.

I straightened my back, offended. I may not have much power, but one way or another I can usually hold my own.

Before I could say anything in response, Uncle Max held up his hands in a placating gesture. "Girls, girls, don't pick at each other. I know you're upset. We have to figure out what happened so we can find Evika."

Silently, Sonya continued petting Archer, whose tongue hung out in rapture over all her attention. I could smell the occasional waft of Hound sulfur-breath from where I sat, but the sunlight masked the red glow of his eyes. Not to be ignored, Jupiter wriggled under my hand again, angling for more scratches behind his little flopped-over ears.

"Uncle Max, don't tell my mother just yet, okay?" I widened my eyes and looked at him pleadingly while continuing to scratch Jupiter's ears.

He looked at me a long minute, as if weighing the risks, and finally said, "For now. I don't want to worry her, but as head of House Augustine, she'll need to know what's going on and soon. If she finds out before we tell her, there will be *Hades* to pay."

Relieved, I said, "I think I know where we went last night. I'll go there today to see if anyone remembers us." I had my right hand behind my back, fingers crossed. I didn't have the slightest clue which nightclub or restaurant we went to, but we had a handful of favorites I could check out. Uncle Max nodded and said, "Be very careful. Only go to the restaurant. Keep to public places and come home before dark."

He went over to Sonya and kissed her on the cheek. I got a quick hug. He then made a gesture with his fingers. An arcane symbol glowed red in the air for a moment and the mirror again began to shimmer. "I have to contact some people and make some plans. I'll be in touch with you girls. In the meantime,

Cara, if you remember anything else, make sure to let me know."

I said I would, and he walked into the mirror and disappeared; it became just a mirror once more. Apparently there were no sound effects when he left, only when arriving.

I sighed and looked at Sonya. "If I can't find the restaurant, there's one more place I can try." She lifted her eyebrows at me, eyes wide as realization dawned.

"What do you mean if you can't find the restaurant? You said you knew it. And you're not going back to the Nightkind's house! It's too dangerous, Cara." Sonya, typically the more cautious one of the three of us, stayed true to form.

"I may have to if the restaurant doesn't pan out."

"I'll go with you." She quickly offered.

I shook my head, "I don't want to put you in danger. Besides, I don't think I could stand losing *both* my favorite cousins. I'll be okay." I pointed to myself, "*Chosen* person, Remember?"

I sat next to her on the floor and gave her a hug, then added, "I'll just take a shower and grab something to eat before I go." My head felt marginally better after the coffee, but I really needed more sleep. Zul's horns! I resigned myself to the fact I'd have to go back to City, and I was *so* not looking forward to it.

Chapter Four
The Nightkind Magician

Trying to find the restaurant in San Francisco proved fruitless. None of our usual places remembered us being there last night. I'm sure they would have noticed two young women whooping it up and getting sloshed, especially if one of us happened to be a beautiful redheaded witch.

I drove around awhile, looking at the seemingly endless choices of eateries available in the City, trying to see if any of them struck a familiar chord. None of them did. I checked out the few night spots I knew with no success there, either. My frustration mounted as I drove down street after street, getting lost, driving around in circles. I loved the City but hated driving around in it, with all the steep hills, one-way streets and no left turns allowed.

I somehow ended up at the Nightkind's house and parked across the street. I *really* did not want to face him—or Roland, for that matter. When a man has seen your kibbles and bits it's just embarrassing, especially since I couldn't remember what "the Master's" bits and my bits may have done together.

I sat in my car, an older model BMW convertible, procrastinating. I loved putting the top down on nice days like today had been. It messed up my hair, but what the heck. It was worth it. The sun started setting, the few clouds above me glowed orange and red, floating like bright islands in the azure expanse of the sky. The evening had a particular beauty that blesses the California coastline. Cool, fresh air, tinged with saltiness from the Bay, blew across my face. I closed my eyes and inhaled deeply, letting my head fall back against the headrest.

I thought of Evika and gathered my courage. I *had* to talk to him. He might be my only possible lead to finding my cousin. I took another deep breath and sat up straight. I still didn't feel my best, residual effects from last night making my head feel muzzy.

The sky darkened and it got cooler. I felt glad I'd thrown on my favorite blue cashmere sweater, the one matching the outer rim of my bicolored eyes. With my jeans and boots, I felt comfortable. The brilliant colors which had dominated the sky a few moments ago had now narrowed down to a single bright stripe of neon orange close to the horizon. I could almost feel the soothing, deep, black of night slowly envelop the City.

Lights turned on in the house. A shadow moved in front of a downstairs window. I got out of my car and walked across the street. I stood on the sidewalk, caught between going forward and turning around and making a run for my car. I almost started to turn tail and run when the front door opened. Roland stood there peering out at me, squinting a little in the fading light. I saw a flash of recognition. He looked absolutely delighted to see me. I wished I could feel the same.

He started towards me then seemed to think better of it. He leaned a bit forward from the waist and said gently, "Madam Cara, please do come in." His tone was softly cautious and coaxing, one usually reserved for talking to timid forest creatures.

I straightened my shoulders and walked up to him, then past him and into the house. I nodded as I went by, saying, "Hi Roland. Is 'the Master' up yet? I need to talk with him."

Roland quickly stepped out of my way, eyebrows raised. He managed to recover his decorum and take on the role of manservant once more as he closed the door.

I gathered my courage and held up my head, working furiously to overcome the need to blush and look at the floor. Rather than face Roland, I glanced around the entryway and noticed the lush surroundings. Antiques and objects d'art were displayed even here in the foyer. I really hadn't paid attention the last time I stood here, having more on my mind, like making a quick getaway.

"Please allow me to escort you to the library. The Master is most anxious to see you. He was beside himself when he awoke and found you had gone." This last bit Roland said in a rush. He looked at me aghast and clamped his lips together, apparently appalled at what he'd just revealed. He frowned and gestured for me to follow him. We walked down the hall together in silence.

Roland led me down a hallway and into a wondrous library, an inside room with no windows. Three walls were lined with built-in wooden bookcases, full to almost overflowing with books, and took up what I estimated to be two full stories of the house. An artificially backlit stained glass skylight was displayed in the center of the ceiling. A narrow walkway vertically separated the bookcases where I assumed the second floor would have been. Towards the back of the room, a metalwork spiral stairway connected the levels. Ladders on two sides of the room hooked onto a metal railing that ran around the room, anchored to the walls.

I spotted a leather-upholstered chair and nervously sat down to wait. After a few minutes, I saw a movement on the spiral stairway that made me start and leap to my feet. A shadow materialized into a man holding a book in his hand. Definitely the same man in bed with me this morning. He radiated power and sex as he walked towards me in a sensuous glide. Silent, and deeply affecting, the Nightkind frightened and thrilled me at the same time. He stood tall and broad shouldered, and as extraordinarily beautiful as I remembered.

I felt my face start to grow warm as he got closer. Damn. He smiled and flicked the book away, where it just disappeared. He held out his arms as if for a hug. Yeah, right.

I stepped back quickly, looked at his left shoulder, and said, "Uh, Hello." I held out my hand for a shake. He dropped his arms and looked at my hand. After a moment, I dropped it, saying, "This is really awkward, but I, uh, kinda forgot your name. I guess the drinks and everything last night . . ."

He frowned and still managed to look delicious as he said, "Excuse me?" He had a deep hypnotic voice, rich and smooth. I thought of my morning coffee. Zul's horns, why would I think of such a thing at a time like this?

"I, um, don't remember you, okay?" I started to get angry at the blank space in my head where my memories should have been. I started to pace as I continued to talk, "I woke up this morning in bed with you and I don't have the slightest clue how I got there." My face felt hot and I knew I'd started blushing. I hated when I did that.

He quickly closed the distance between us and took my hand. "Let's sit and talk about this," he said, leading me to the leather sofa. I let him, but I slid over to the far end of the sofa as soon as we sat. Twisting my body so my back pressed mostly against the armrest, I folded up one leg on the seat and looked at him. He had dressed in casual chic, black trousers and a dark gray silk sweater that complemented his lighter gray eyes with their black coronas. Something about him seemed maddeningly familiar.

"Can I tell you how pleased I am you returned? Now, why would you come here if you didn't remember me?" With an intense look he reached for my hand, but I pulled it away and awkwardly folded my arms. I never could pull off the crossed arms bit very comfortably with my full breasts getting in the way. He sat back and looked at me patiently. I felt a tendril of dark power coming from him. It oh so gently curled around my mind. His eyes looked so beautiful and shiny, like little silver mirrors. He seemed so *kind* and *concerned* for me. It felt so *nice* here with him . . .

What? Hey! I shook my head and glared at him. "Cut out the mind tricks, Mister." He'd tried to capture me with his eyes. Damn these magicians anyway, I heard they always try to pull this stuff.

"Please forgive me, but I wanted to see for myself what you remembered." He didn't look the least bit sorry. He smiled. He had dimples. Damned if I couldn't help returning his smile. I warned myself to be careful of this totally delectable, potentially dangerous, man.

"You really don't remember me?" he said.

"No, I really don't." I replied.

"Well then, that's very unfortunate. I believe you're telling the truth. Why would you come here with such an odd story? After our reintroductions we'll have to solve this mystery. And, of course, allow you to feel more comfortable with me. After all, we are engaged." He just had to throw that in, didn't he? He then placed a hand on his chest and made a little bow from his seated position beside me, "My name is Roman Balthazar."

Surprised, I remembered the name as the youngest son of the Head of House Balthazar, currently located in Paris. I vaguely recalled, perhaps from a magazine article, he was maybe tenth in line for being head of his House. If he wanted to marry me as a political maneuver to gain power from my House, it seemed pretty farfetched. House Augustine would only accept a female witch as Head of House. Any male attachment would be considered a consort. With a *Nightkind* consort I could envision a more concentrated effort to restrict any possible influence he might have on me.

"Okay Roman, help me out here. What happened last night? Did you do something to my memory? Do you know what happened to my cousin?" I gave him a determined look.

He held up a hand. "Let's take this one question at a time. Last night I happened to be at a nightclub called *Après Soleil* conducting some House business when I saw you. You were sitting at a table with a rather boisterous red-haired woman."

I nodded, "My Cousin Evika, go on."

"You were laughing and drinking champagne. These things first got my attention, but then I sensed something more about you that . . . intrigued me. I wanted to meet you, so I came over to your table and introduced myself." The way he spoke sounded vaguely old-fashioned, like he'd never bothered to bring himself totally up-to-date with the modern way of speaking. It sounded a little off, marking him as long-lived, although I couldn't even venture to guess how long.

He'd been inching closer to me on the sofa. I could feel his power intensify, darken, expand. A struggle between desire and control flashed across his face so fast I might have imagined it. He lifted a hand and stroked my cheek, barely touching my skin with his fingertips. Goosebumps formed on my arms and my stomach got a little fluttery feeling.

I pulled back against the arm of the sofa, "I don't think you should . . ." He stopped my protestation by leaning forward and brushing his lips lightly against mine.

He murmured against my lips, "You're so exquisite, Cara. I've waited so long to taste you. I have to, just a little . . ."

His lips were soft and cool. They sensually slid across mine as his tongue licked at the seam of my lips, asking permission to enter. I knew I shouldn't, but I opened my mouth and allowed his kiss to deepen. He smelled wonderful, all male muskiness with a hint of expensive fragrance and a strange spicy tang further beneath it all. I recognized it from this morning. An aching need began to grow and grow as his kiss grew deeper. I couldn't help sliding my hands up into his silky hair, holding his head to mine. Oh, this felt so good. No one had ever kissed me like this. I made a little sound. He tensed his body and then he pulled me onto his lap and slowly pushed up my sweater, his mouth never leaving mine. His thumb played with my nipples through the fabric of my bra, sending small waves of pleasure through my body.

I moaned again. He deepened the kiss even more, his hand slid lower, pressing against the core of my ache. I could feel the hardness of his erection against the side of my thigh. I wanted him inside me so bad it almost hurt. He pressed his hand against my jeans and rotated his palm in delicious circles at the juncture of my legs. I struggled to remember the reason I'd come here.

When his hand moved to slide over my stomach towards the top of my jeans, I pulled away from him and climbed off his lap and back onto the coach. It felt like one of the hardest things I had ever done.

"No. I can't do this," I told him, my voice more quavering than firm.

He tried to pull me back, but I put a hand up against his chest. I had meant to only give him a little push to show I was serious, but an unbidden surge of power came up through my arm and into my hand. He just had time to look surprised when he flew off the sofa and kept going until he hit a section of the bookcase with a thud and a crack, as one of the shelves broke. He sat on the floor while books cascaded off the shelves on top of him.

Just as surprised as he was, I raised a hand to my mouth and just stared at him while he sat on the floor wearing an ancient-looking grimoire as a hat. I dropped my hand, and as I pulled my sweater back down, I started to laugh. I couldn't stop. I tried to control it, but every time I looked at him, I laughed harder.

He scowled and stood, brushing the books off of him, as he asked, "Was that really necessary? I'm not a monster, no matter what you may have heard about our kind. I had you in my bed last night and did nothing, as you were in no condition to give consent."

Well, that answered one question. It made me think better of him. "How did I get from the restaurant to your house in the first place?" I asked, now more serious. And then as an afterthought, "Oh, uh, sorry," I gestured towards the bookcase. "I didn't mean to give you that big a push."

He had no idea that I had *never* been able to do that before. It gave me one more thing to think about, but that would have to be later.

Luckily, the bookcase incident cooled my libido enough to let me think more clearly. I got up and went to sit in one of the armchairs. A much safer place psychologically, if not in reality.

He opened his mouth as if to answer my question, but we turned simultaneously at the sound of a loud crash coming from the direction of the front door. We heard a man scream in pain and then heavy footsteps pounding rapidly up the hallway to the closed library door. Before I knew what was happening, Roman hurled his body at me, knocking me and the chair I sat in to the floor just as the library door tore off its hinges and came crashing into the room. It hit right about where I had been sitting. I ended up face down on the floor with Roman on top of me. I pushed my head out from under his arm and looked around the side of the overturned chair and towards the door to see what had happened. I found it difficult to breathe with a heavy magician pressing the air out of my lungs. My head now buzzed with my familiar trouble signal, only much louder and more persistent. Great. It wasn't telling me something I couldn't have figured out on my own this time.

A huge manlike beast stood in the doorway. It had vaguely humanoid features, but with an elongated jaw like a short muzzle, and coarse brown hair covered the upper half of its body, the bottom half had thick, greenish brown reptilian skin extending to a long tail that whipped back and forth. It stood at least seven feet tall, and its hairy half looked seriously buffed out. A strange-looking symbol had been branded into the middle of its chest. It looked around the room. The chair must have hidden us from the beast because its dirty yellow eyes kept sweeping over us without stopping.

"Zul's horns, what is it?" I whispered to Roman.

He looked down at me and said, "A sub-demon. It somehow breached my house wards. Stay here."

The beast swung its misshapen head towards Roman as he stood. It roared, its inhuman voice unnervingly high pitched and low at the same time. Then it lunged at him.

Roman leapt at the man-thing almost faster than I could visually track. He landed behind the beast and whipped his arm around its throat, locking it in a stranglehold no human would have been able to break. Roman muttered a spell under his breath. The beast roared again as it clawed at its back. Roman's hands started to glow blue as he hung on and kept squeezing, even as his clothes shredded and turned wet with his blood. The beast stumbled forward a few steps before jumping straight up into the air, all the way to the stained glass skylight and crashing through it, using Roman as a battering ram. Razor sharp shards of colored glass, with clinging bits of lead, rained down on me. I tried to use the chair as a shield, but my legs were partially exposed and I could feel dozens of sharp pains where glass imbedded in my flesh. I should have stayed under the chair, but I had to see what had happened.

As soon as the glass stopped falling, my whole body was

shaking with fear and pain as I dragged myself around so I could get a better view. The shards in my legs dug deeper as I moved, wringing gasps of pain and a little whining sound I'd probably be embarrassed about later.

Roman had lost his hold at the impact, jumped away from the beast and grabbed onto one of the second-story bookshelves. He clung there snarling, lethal looking. Hairy-lizard-thing had crashed to the floor, greenish-yellow blood dripped off its face, one eye a ruined mess, the other covered in its blood, essentially rendering it blind. It now stood about three feet from me sniffing the air. I froze, hoping it wouldn't notice me, but it did. The misshapen head swung right towards me, using its sense of smell to zero in. I guessed the scent of my blood gave me away.

As it reached out for me with huge hairy hands I quickly grabbed a long shard of rose-colored glass and slashed at the thing, yelling "Get away from me!"

One hairy hand brushed my arm but I managed to cut it with the glass shard. At the beast's touch, a vision filled my head. A dark cave and torches, human sacrifice to an ancient demon-god. They were raising living darkness, a thing of power, drawn to blood and greed. I inwardly recoiled from the vision in revulsion, but unfortunately, I couldn't pull away in reality. I saw a man-shaped shadow staring into the cave's darkness, its glowing eyes casting yellow shadows on the walls. It snarled in fear and anger as it looked directly at me. I screamed.

I came back to the room from the vision place to see the sub-demon had pulled back just for a second before it reached forward again. I hunched up under the chair, held up my makeshift weapon, the sides cutting into my palm, and steeled myself to fight.

The beast bent over, trying to get to me. Why it didn't just flip the chair off me, I'd never know. Probably not the brightest bulb on the Solstice tree, more muscle than brains.

"No! Cara!" Roman growled as he leapt from the bookcase and landed on its back once more. He pounded the beast's head with his fist, lightning fast punches backed with inhuman strength. It roared, fighting back. I heard a bone snap, a wet sharp sound, and I didn't know which of the combatants it came from. I crawled out from under the chair ignoring the burning pain in my legs.

Swallowing a lump of fear that had formed in my throat, I

stood, glass shard in hand, planning to plunge it into the beast. I felt power inside me rising. I felt my hair stir and rise, crackling with power as I focused on the monster. Pieces of glass started floating up into the air all around me. I let go of the shard in my hand. It, too, floated up until it was level with my line of sight. The shard had turned so that the dagger-like point was aimed directly at the lizard-man. I felt each of the dozens of pieces as if they were physical extensions of me as they waited for my will to turn them into weapons. The beast had thrown Roman against a wall. It had to be *now*.

As quick as my thought, the razor sharp glass flew towards the roaring beast. They all hit at once cutting deeply into the right side of its body from shoulder to thigh. It yowled in pain, turning towards this new source of torment, and blindly charged towards me. From where he lay on the floor, Roman desperately reached towards the beast and managed to grab onto one of its legs.

It jumped and spun, anchored by one leg and lashed out towards me with its tail. It made contact. I should have dodged but was too stunned by what I'd done with the glass to think fast enough. The impact knocked me across the room. I fell onto a wooden table hitting my head on a large bronze statue. The room smelled of blood and ochre and slowly faded to black. I barely noticed when a new voice shouted out a word of power. I heard a sizzle of energy and saw a blindingly bright flash of green light through my closed eyelids. I struggled to stay conscious. Again, I heard the word and another sizzling flash of light. This time I recognized the voice and felt a sense of overwhelming relief. Uncle Max. I could now let myself pass out. And I did.

Chapter Five
Santa Lacuna

I awoke with a start from a strange, frightening dream, the details immediately eluded me. I glanced around the room and recognized Sonya's guest bedroom. I blinked a couple of times, getting my dry eyes to produce some lubricating tears. I wanted a glass of water, a really big one. My throat felt as dry as my eyes.

On the nightstand next to the bed sat a pitcher of water and a glass. Blessed-be-the-Portal. I reached over to pour a glass and felt a tight band around my ribs, and my legs had been bandaged from the knees down. I remembered the falling glass and my brief flight across Roman's library, and just like that I started feeling the pain. It wasn't as bad as I thought it would be, but my head had the stuffed-with-cotton feel of a medicinal potion. Someone had probably given me something for the pain. No wonder I felt so thirsty. As I reached for the pitcher I saw my right hand had also been bandaged. I wondered if I had needed any stitches.

Uncle Max walked in, saw my attempts to grab the pitcher, and poured the water for me. I smiled at him, croaked out a thank you and gulped down the water, only sloshing a little on myself.

I cleared my throat, and asked him "What happened? Is Roman okay? Is Roland okay?"

My uncle pulled up a chair to the side of the bed and sat next to me. "I destroyed the sub-demon, but, unfortunately, the Nightkind survived. A servant sustained an injury, a broken arm I think, but he'll live."

He looked at me and scowled. "Great Zul's horns, young lady, you took too great a risk already. What were you thinking?" He got up and strode to the foot of the bed. "I had to tell your mother about this. You were injured and she had to be informed. If Sonya hadn't started getting worried about you and called me, I might not have arrived in time. Fortunately, I managed to track down your car. The broken door and rampaging sub-demon told me which house you had to be in."

I inwardly cringed, knowing what Mom's reaction would be the next time she saw me. "Did you tell Dad?"

Uncle Max folded his arms, his black gaze directed

towards the ceiling, "He is still away on some kind of mysterious assignment for your mother. I have no idea where he is or what he's doing." He looked back at me. "Your father usually lets me know how to contact him." He shrugged, "Ah well, don't worry, I'm sure he's fine."

He said the latter almost more to himself than to me. My father and Uncle Max were half-brothers, sharing the same mother. My grandfather was a witch, and Sonya's was a demon lord. Grandmother Cho must have been a very busy witch.

"What time is it?" A breeze from the window gently stirred the curtains, and I saw daylight. I must have slept through the night. "How did I get back here?"

"I brought you through a mirror in the Nightkind's house and called a doctor to attend you."

"The mirror in his closet?" I asked, sitting up straighter in the bed, trying to find a comfortable spot against the wooden headboard.

"Yes, as a matter of fact. How did you know about the mirror?" He gave me The Look. You know, the kind that said he knew the answer but wanted to hear it from me anyway.

"Hey is there any coffee left?" My version of let's change the subject, shall we?

Uncle Max decided to take the hint. "I'll check." He started to leave the room.

"Wait. Did Roman tell you what happened to me and Evika on our birthday?" I called out to him.

He turned and looked at me, his black eyes expressionless. "No. I didn't have time to talk, with you bleeding and unconscious. But I plan to make a trip back there very soon and have a nice long chat with him."

He'd practically snarled the last sentence as he left. Oh boy. Roman was in for it now. But at least I might get some answers.

* * * *

Two days after the sub-demon attack, I could get out of bed on my own. I healed rapidly. Actually a lot faster than I thought I would. Everyone made sure I had the best of care. Mom sent witch healers with charms and potions. Uncle Max, who always thought it never hurt to cover all the bases, had his personal human physician come check on me. It looked as if I would have full use of my hand and no scars. The cracked ribs were healing fine too. Magic and science, what a combo. Gotta love it.

I started wearing sweaters, as the soft, cool, morning fog rolled in from the ocean. Sonya kept me informed of what had happened since the sub-demon attack in San Francisco. House Augustine had used considerable resources to try to find Evika without success. Oh, there were clues, but they only led to dead ends. One way or another, I had to find out what had happened that night.

Uncle Max told me Roman had refused to meet with him, instead demanding to see his fiancé. He was becoming a persistent nuisance. House Balthazar had been in contact with my mother over the matter. She had told them House Augustine did not recognize any formal betrothal agreements between the two Houses given the young witch in question did not remember anything about it. This rendered the engagement null and void, no matter what the aggrieved petitioner may have thought or said about the agreement. I silently thanked the ancient covenants. Who would have guessed this sort of thing had been a common enough occurrence in the past that someone thought it warranted a covenant?

This morning Uncle Max sat down at the breakfast table with me and handed me a large white envelope. Inside were an airplane ticket and a wad of cash big enough to choke a Hellhound. "What's this for?" I asked.

"We, your mother and I, think it would be good for you to get away for awhile. House Balthazar is not giving up and it's possible they may try get to you by fair means or foul."

"You mean kidnap me?" I asked, surprised by the thought.

"Yes, I think that's a distinct possibility. The Hounds caught a couple of Nightkinds lurking around the house last week. They were persuaded to leave."

"What? Roman wasn't one of them, was he?" I had a sudden knot in the middle of my stomach. I didn't really know him, but I didn't want him to become Hound chow either. Besides, I thought about his soft, cool lips. Even now, his seductive kiss made me squeeze my thighs together in reaction.

Uncle Max shook his head in reply. "Roman wouldn't have come himself, nor would I expect a high ranking magician to do his own dirty work. But it became a deciding factor in our decision to send you to your Aunt Amelia in Southern California. The cash is so you won't have to use your credit cards. They can be traced." He nodded towards the envelope on the table,

"You'd better get ready. Your plane leaves this afternoon."

"What? Today?" I jumped up. "I have to pack my stuff!"

"I already told Sonya to pack up your things. She sent them on ahead to Amelia's. You don't have to do anything except get on the plane here, and Amelia will meet you at the airport at the other end. We'd better get going so you don't miss your flight. Security at the airports is messy, and I know you have a certain reputation in the family for not getting to your appointments on time."

I rolled my eyes but didn't argue. I had gained an unfair reputation by virtue of my reluctance to go to family gatherings. I hated being the subject of conversations, usually starting with something like, "Isn't it a shame about Cara . . ."

I hadn't seen Aunt Amelia in a long time. She's my mother's older sister and a powerful witch. Based on family stories, she apparently could be a bit off-the-wall at times. Hmmm, interesting. So Uncle Max and my mother decided it safer for me to go visit with wacky Aunt Amelia than to stick around here? Well, at least it probably won't be boring.

We got to the airport and I boarded the plane on time. I had an aisle seat next to a handsome wizard. He held the latest copy of *TechnoMage* a magazine for non-technologically challenged practitioners. He looked a little older than me, but it's often hard to tell age with us. The wizard looked up as I sat next to him. He smiled and nodded. I smiled and nodded back. He had dark hair, cut short, and nice blue eyes with a few laugh lines at the corners.

I looked over at his magazine. "So you can work with technology? I guess it's safe being on the plane with you." I kept smiling to show him I wasn't really worried. Some wizards just naturally disrupted the electrical flow of energy. Around technology it caused all kinds of unpleasant and potentially dangerous things to happen. Others can use it just fine, even to the point of using a piece of technology as a magical focus. No one knew why, but it seemed more recent generations had fewer techno-challenged wizards than in the past. Witches had always gotten along fine with technology. My mother used her food processor as much as her mortar and pestle for making potions.

We pleasantly chatted while we flew to Southern California. He had a melodious British accent, and he could have read me the emergency exit instructions and I would have loved listening to him. He also happened to live in Santa Lacuna where my Aunt lived. He owned an art gallery there. I told him I had always been interested in art, having been an art major my first couple of years of college. He offered to show me his gallery. We agreed to get together during the next week. I looked forward to seeing him again.

When the plane landed and we stood, I saw he towered over me at least a foot. I guess his knees scrunched up against the back of the seat in front of him should have tipped me off. He had a strong aura that seemed to resonate well with mine. Important if it worked out and we became more than friends. Simpatico auras are essential for good, um, physical compatibility.

We walked out to the baggage area together. I looked out the glass doors towards the passenger pickup area and saw an older woman, dressed in a flowing multicolored caftan, waving wildly in my direction. She looked quite a bit like my mother except she had very short, spiked white-blond hair and a different fashion sensibility. My mother wouldn't have been caught dead in a bohemian dress like my aunt's. Amelia had a man with her. She stopped waving when she saw she had my attention, and they both walked towards us. The man wore faded blue jeans, a worn t-shirt and flip-flops. He had one of those slim-hipped glides some really athletically graceful guys have. He seemed oblivious to how sexy he looked which, of course, made him all the more appealing. As they got closer I realized he was in his early twenties, and his tanned skin told me spent a lot of time outdoors. He had pulled his shoulder length, sun-streaked blond hair into a loose ponytail. He looked like a quintessential Southern California surfer.

Smiling as he held out a hand, he said, "Hi. I'm Tom. I drove your aunt to pick you up." His teeth were very white against his tanned face. I smiled back and shook his hand.

"Whoa. Your Aunt didn't tell me you were *hot!*" Tom grinned, appreciation lighting his eyes. He wasn't a witch or wizard, but I did feel a warm energy from his aura and wondered what type of being he was, because he wasn't completely human. Paul stood by my side somewhat possessively inspecting these newest arrivals.

Paul frowned at him and stepped closer to me, nodding to them as he said, "Hello."

"Oh, where are my manners?" I gasped, embarrassed at

forgetting to make introductions.

"Aunt Amelia, this is Paul—we met on the plane. He owns an art gallery in Santa Lacuna." I looked at Paul. "Paul, this is my aunt, Amelia Augustine."

Paul smiled warmly and made a little, old-fashioned bow. It reminded me that most practitioners seldom shook hands— too many things could potentially happen with a touch. Since I never came into any powers, I've never had to worry much about it.

"Yes," Paul said to my Aunt. "I know you by reputation. I'm honored to meet the Shadow-hunter Pack's *Shaman*."

I looked at Paul, puzzled. My Aunt, a *Shaman*? News to me. Geez, why didn't anyone ever tell me the really good stuff about my relatives? Apparently, Amelia was part of a werewolf clan—or pack—and acted as their spiritual guide and protector. I realized now that the energy I felt coming from Tom was due to his lycanthropy. I'd never met a *were* before, so I looked at him a little closer. His aura shone a hot, golden yellow, and animal energy rippled off him like heat from an open fire. How did I not notice his muscles moving under his skin like rippling fur? I could feel my eyelids get heavy as I felt his aura envelop me, pull at me, making me want to roll around in his heat.

"Cara?" Paul looked from me to Tom.

I blinked a couple of times and looked at Tom. He became a good-looking, young surfer once more. But his smile said he knew he had affected me. It looked a little too knowing for my taste. We'd just met, for *Zul's* sake.

Paul left our group to get his suitcase, but returned quickly, and now stood beside me, looking reluctant to leave me with Tom. He definitely had an "I saw her first" expression. Men. I inwardly rolled my eyes.

Aunt Amelia took it all in, smiling. She then said to me, "You must be tired, dear. I know Maximillian probably rushed you out of the house this morning." She tilted her head towards Paul. "You'll excuse us? I'd like to get my niece settled in. Nice meeting you."

Tom grinned. "Yeah, nice."

Paul ignored him and looked at Aunt Amelia "The pleasure was all mine." Then, turning to me, he leaned in closer and lowered his voice, as he said, "Cara, I look forward to seeing you soon." He got Aunt Amelia's address and phone number and left.

Tom acted as tour guide as we drove into town. "Santa

Lacuna's pretty secluded—well, as secluded as a seaside community can be in Southern California. We get some tourists in the summer, but they don't stay long because we don't have any hotels or motels."

"Really? Does the town have *any* accommodations for visitors?" I asked, curious.

"Yeah, there's a row of summer cottages for rent along a dirt road leading to a small beach," Tom replied.

Amelia turned around in the front seat to look at me. "The cottages are mostly rented by visiting werewolves attending annual festivities hosted by the local pack. This is a good place for *were* families to take a safe vacation. They can just be themselves here without humans getting upset and worried. Old misconceptions about the two-natured die hard, you know."

Just be themselves? I silently wondered if they even bothered to fire up the barbecues or just slapped raw hamburger on their buns. Was that one of those "misconceptions" Amelia referred to? We chatted for a while about the family, then sat in silence for the remainder of the drive as I gazed out the window at the passing scenery.

Soon we pulled up to a beautiful Victorian house sitting only one street up from an oceanside park. Amelia's house looked like a large gingerbread confection. One front corner of the house was a rounded, two-story turret. There were scalloped and lacy wooden do-dads all over the place. The backyard extended into the lot behind it where a rather incongruous, modern, gleaming glass greenhouse stood.

The interior of the house surprised me. Where I had expected fancy, uncomfortable Victorian furniture and lots of crocheted doilies, there were thick Persian rugs, big pillows in earthy colors scattered all over the floors, and several low, mother-of-pearl inlaid wooden tables. The rooms were expansive and open. It looked like the walls had been removed to allow for free flow between the living spaces.

Aunt Amelia took me upstairs to a bedroom in the turret section. She had beautifully decorated the room in soft blues, greens, and cream, with watercolor paintings of beaches on the walls and a scattering of seashells throughout. The furniture consisted of a four-poster bed, with matching dresser, armoire, and nightstand. Tom followed us in, carrying my bags. They must have weighed a ton, but he handled them easily.

"Thanks for bringing my stuff up," I said to Tom.

"Hey, no problem-o," he replied with a smile.

Aunt Amelia started towards the door, saying over her shoulder, "Make yourself at home, dear. I'm running late for an appointment. I'll be back this evening."

A minute later I heard the front door close. Moving aside the curtains, I watched her hurry down the sidewalk with a big basket of herbs and cobalt blue potion bottles. When I turned back to the room, Tom lay on the bed. He had stretched out on his side, his head propped up on one hand. He also had a gleam in his eye that bothered me.

"So, Cara, while you're here I could show you around town. See the sights. We have great beaches. The surfing is awesome." He tried to look innocent as he pulled the rubber band out of his ponytail and shook out his hair, causing it to fall in a shining blond wave over his shoulder.

As I watched him, I became very aware that we were alone in the house, and I could feel his aura radiating out from his body. He patted the bed with his free hand. "Why don't you have a seat? Relax. I won't bite."

I looked around the room for a chair, but there wasn't one. Oh, what the heck. He hadn't done anything to make me kick him out. Yet. I shrugged and sat beside him. Immediately, I felt enveloped in the warmth of his golden yellow aura. It felt good.

He started to lightly stroke my back as he talked. "In a couple of days the pack is having a casual get-together. You should come. Be my guest."

Our auras were touching, blending together at the edges. I felt warm, protected, and languid. I didn't get any frightening vibes from him, besides him being overly familiar for someone I'd just met. I relaxed as he pulled me closer until I was using his stomach as a backrest. I let myself relax against him. Through his aura, I felt his wolf move. Curious about me, it brushed against my aura, back and forth, like it was getting my scent, trying to figure me out. Tom lay still, looking at me through half-closed lids. He had a little smile on his face as his wolf investigated.

I felt something in me rise, responding to his wolf's touch. I'd never felt anything like it before, but then I'd never been in contact with a werewolf before, either. A strange energy started to build inside me and it felt wonderful. I wasn't even alarmed, as I should have been at such a thing happening. It felt *right* somehow.

I closed my eyes and slid my hands out to either side of me. My left hand stroked up his jean-covered thigh, and my right hand slipped under his t-shirt, sliding over his warm back. I heard him take a quick, inhaled breath.

The power in me wrapped itself around Tom's aura. It reached out in sensuous tendrils and entwined with the wolf energy. With a groan, he grabbed me firmly but gently, twisting until he had me under him on the bed. He lay full-length on top of me, as he brought his mouth down to mine and kissed me almost desperately. He was good at kissing. Then he started to move his hips, pushing the now tightly stretched crotch of his jeans against me at the exact right place at the juncture of my thighs. As our energies started to build so too did my pleasure.

One last little shred of my sanity felt appalled that I was doing this with a stranger. Everything else was having the time of its life and told sanity to go to its room as Tom began moving in ways that sent waves of intense, exquisite pleasure flowing through my body. Each time he rocked against me, the pleasure grew stronger, and his tongue echoed his movements as we kissed.

Then he stopped kissing me and pressed his face against my neck as he inhaled my scent, my arousal. He growled low and bit me lightly on the shoulder while pressing and grinding his crotch against mine. My energy burst out and melded with his inner wolf as I climaxed, my back arching. I felt the formless presence radiating from within me subsume Tom's beast as it mutated into a defined shape. It became a great gray-white she-wolf, and she became a part of me. He shouted out and pressed hard against me one last time, head thrown back, neck straining, then collapsed on top of me, panting. As my energy pulled back, it took a piece of his wolf with it and, in its place, left a tiny piece of itself.

Tom kissed me on the cheek and rolled over onto his back beside me. He reached for my hand and held it. I looked over at him, stunned by what had just happened. We were connected now on a metaphysical level and I didn't know if he knew it. I had never done this before, but I realized I had inadvertently made the werewolf my familiar.

Tom took a deep breath and looked at me, "Wow. That was the most fun I've ever had with all my clothes on. Good thing I have an extra pair of jeans in the car."

I gave him a sick little half-smile and thought, how am I going to explain this to Aunt Amelia?

Chapter Six
The Familiar

I spent the next morning avoiding Tom and Aunt Amelia. I had to have time to think, to be by myself for a while. Glad Sonya had packed my small backpack, I went downstairs to the kitchen and threw a bottle of water, some cheese and crackers, and an apple into it. The weather had turned cool, so I had dressed in jeans, a sweater, walking shoes, baseball cap and sunglasses. I pulled my hair back into a ponytail secured with the rubber band Tom had left behind yesterday. Just thinking about Tom made me feel embarrassed and confused. I definitely needed time to think.

The sun's rays seemed to gild everything with a soft golden light. The air was full of rich scents: the spiciness of autumn foliage, the salty tang of the ocean, a few late-blooming flowers, and someone was baking a pumpkin pie. Mmmmm.

I took a deep breath and immediately my worries didn't feel as bad. There were good things in life to enjoy, even amid the not-so-good stuff. I walked swiftly to the beach and started following the shoreline. The sound of waves lapping over the sand soothed me.

The usual piles of seaweed littered the beach, along with bits of things that once were probably man-made but were now sand-polished into unrecognizable lumps with rounded edges. I walked around a large jumble of boulders near the edge of the tide line and hopped up and over some rocks, trying to keep my shoes dry. Spotting a small tidal pool on the other side of the rocks, I squatted down to investigate. Small crabs, startled by my presence, scuttled into rock crevices and hid among sea anemones.

I held still, watching, and soon the crabs crept out again. There were more in there than I thought at first. A lot more. One brave crustacean even came out of the water doing its sideways walk right to my shoe. Then onto my shoe. I let out a little yip, stood and shook it off. It fell with a plop back into the tide pool. Okay. Time to continue my walk. I hopped off the rocks, back onto the beach.

I looked up as a couple of gulls swooped through the air near the shore. Suddenly, a hoard of flies surrounded me. The odor of salty decay, so strong it stung my nose, choked my throat. I'd stepped into a large mass of seaweed, disturbing the dozens of flies which had settled there. Waving my hands in front of my face, I quickly ran clear of the pile. The flies disbursed and went back to their seaweed mound. Out of the corner of my eye, I'd have sworn I saw the seaweed move. No, it must have been my imagination, because of all the flies. I looked closer, and then jumped back when something crawled out from under a piece of seaweed. I laughed at myself when I saw one of the little tide pool crabs with an oddly familiar pattern on its shell. Where had I seen that pattern before? I couldn't remember.

As I watched, more crabs started appearing from beneath the tangle of vegetation. Strangely, they were crawling on top of each other, dragging pieces of seaweed with them. I watched in fascination as the whole pile seemed to move, and with the crabs' activities it grew taller. What in *Hades* was going on?

In a matter of seconds the jumble of seaweed, crabs, and flies grew taller than my head, the hollow seaweed tubes were twisting around in the air by themselves, like tentacles, all around the main "body" of the mass. The tentacles started waving in my direction.

Great Zul's horns! I turned to run, but fell flat on my face in the sand, as a seaweed tentacle wrapped itself around my ankle. Spitting sand out of my mouth, I grabbed the leathery hose-like appendage and ripped it off, but more of them whipped out from the mass and snaked around both my arms and legs. It dragged me toward the seaweed thing. A big hole had appeared in its center, like a gaping maw. Hundreds of small crabs lined it like living teeth, all their claws snapping and mouth parts moving. I wrenched off my backpack and threw it into the opening. The "mouth" closed on it and I heard the sound of cloth tearing, things being crunched. The opening appeared again, and I saw my backpack shred into little pieces, some of which were still in the mouths and claws of the crabs.

I yelled for help and yanked frantically at the seaweed. As fast as I broke free of tentacles, new ones took their place. I didn't want to know what being eaten alive by crabs felt like, but it looked as if I might not have a choice. My feet were almost to the seaweed monster's mouth. I clawed uselessly at the sand, trying to grab onto something, anything, to pull myself away from the hideous thing.

As I was dragged even closer to it, I let out a girly scream that would have done a horror movie proud. Seaweed wormed into my open mouth, choking off the scream and my air supply. I kicked and struggled, gagging as seaweed slithered down my throat. I heard muffled running footsteps and someone shouting my name. Then, hands pulled me away from the seaweed monster with incredible strength. After yesterday, I'd know that aura anywhere. Tom!

He ripped the tentacles off me as I pulled salty, rubbery stuff out of my mouth. Then he dragged me away from the writing mass and looked me over intently, apparently checking for injuries.

"I'm okay," I gasped, then looking behind him, yelled, "Look out!"

The seaweed monster had re-formed and began reaching out towards Tom. He turned to face it, face fierce, and his hands turned into claws. Then he ran straight towards it, letting out a battle cry of a howl.

Suddenly, I felt my own power rising. Oh sure, *now* it shows up. As I watched, Tom attacked the mass with huge sweeps of his claws. Pieces of seaweed and crab parts where flying all over the place.

I concentrated on the center of the creature and thought, *Boil!* My power gathered, and a part reached out to Tom's power and connected. I felt as if I were a vessel filling up to its brim with power, felt near to overflowing with power when it released and rammed into the animate mass. The thing started writhing frantically, and steam billowed out of it in great white clouds.

I yelled at Tom, "Get away from it, now!"

He turned to look at me, then back at the steaming creature. He ran back towards me just as the whole mass boiled dry and burst into a fireball of flame.

We watched it burn down to a pile of blackened vegetation and crab shells. It smelled like a seafood restaurant. I swallowed a couple of times, trying not to throw up. I wouldn't be ordering a crab entrée anytime soon.

I heard shouts and footsteps, and I saw Aunt Amelia leading a group of about half a dozen people. They scrambled over the rocks and ran towards us.

Aunt Amelia ran up to us, face red, breathing hard. "Cara. Tom. Are you alright? We heard Tom howl . . ."

As soon as everyone knew we were safe, I told them

what had happened with the seaweed creature. I was thankful Tom could back up my story because a couple of the people looked a bit skeptical about the "monster."

Tom introduced me to the men and women who had been coming to our rescue. They were members of his pack. While introductions were made, Aunt Amelia stood over the still smoldering pile, looking at it thoughtfully. As I smiled and talked with people, I saw her pick up a few of the charred pieces from the pile and put them into a plastic bag she took out of a pocket in her skirt. She wiped her fingers on a tissue and then joined the group.

Tom's hands looked normal again, and he tried to put his arm around me. I moved away under the pretence of yucky crab stuff all over him. I wasn't ready to think of us as a couple or have his pack think we were. Besides, I never did get to have my thinking time to try to sort things out, and I really needed to figure out if it was possible to unmake Tom my familiar.

Back at the house I let Tom use the shower first. I practically threw him out of the bathroom as soon as I heard him turn off the water. By the time everyone arrived, my skin was still stinging from the hot water and fierce scrubbing I gave myself to get rid of the crab stink. The entire group, came in, and sat on the floor pillows. Everyone looked comfortable, like they had done this many times before. I imagined the pillows would work for a wolf as well as a person. As I envisioned one of the people plopped on a pillow in wolf form, I wondered if werewolves shed. Tom sat next to me, his arm draped protectively around my shoulders.

Aunt Amelia had made herbal tea and poured it into small ceramic cups for everyone. She gave me a larger mug into which she dropped three lumps of sugar. When I looked at her questioningly, she said, "Drink up, it's good for you. You must have expended a lot of energy fighting the *animorphia*."

Oh! *That's* what you called living seaweed monsters.

* * * *

That night I dreamed of Roman. I lay in his bed again, but the room and all of its contents had been replaced by thick white mist. I looked beside me, expecting to see him lying there, but he wasn't.

Cara, I heard Roman's voice call me from somewhere in the mist. *Cara, come to me.* I looked around but couldn't see him, as his voice urged, *Come to me, my sweet.*

I wanted to see him, to find out about our birthday night, about Evika and what had happened to her, about him and me. I flung back the covers and swung my legs over side of the bed, and, glancing down, realized I wore a long, red silk-and-lace negligee that clung to my curves.

I looked up and called into the mist, "Roman, where are you?"

I saw something move, a dark figure coming towards me, mist swirling, obscuring face and feet. Then I saw Roman. He didn't walk so much as glide towards me, mist parting as he grew nearer. This began to look like a bad B-movie and his next words solidified my opinion. He held out his arms and said, "I've been searching for you, my bride. We must not part again."

I didn't like the sound of that, but I needed answers from him. I stood and walked towards him. "Now, Roman, I just want some information. I did *not* agree to be your bride or anything else of yours." He stood a couple of feet away, wearing an unbuttoned black silk shirt, black slacks, and black boots. His shirt billowed out behind him as he moved, revealing a smooth, pale, well-muscled chest and sculpted abs. Oh yeah, just like I remembered. My mouth watered and I had to swallow. This dream seemed far too real.

His dark hair looked tousled, actually a bit unkempt, as if he had been running his hands through it, but he still looked delicious. Oh man, this was so unfair. No guy should look this gorgeous. His eyes were intense and focused totally on me. His mouth, with that lusciously full bottom lip, smiled just a little. The distance between us melted and I found myself in his arms.

"Cara," he breathed into my hair. I tried halfheartedly to push him away, but his arms were like steel bands that gently, but firmly, kept my body pressed against his. He moved his mouth down to my neck, trailing kisses. Before I could panic, he moved to my jaw line and then to my mouth. His lips were soft as they slid over mine. I could feel my nipples harden against the red silk as they brushed against his bare chest.

"I've found you and I'm coming to claim you," he murmured against my lips.

"No, you're not," I said as I closed my eyes. He deepened the kiss, his tongue sliding in and doing incredible things to my mouth. I could feel an exquisite ache growing between my legs. He shifted his arms and picked me up, our mouths still locked together, and carried me to the bed. Oh, I liked this dream—a lot. Too much. I forced myself to break off the kiss.

"Roman, we need to talk," I protested when he tried to kiss me again.

"Later," he growled. He looked fierce, his need raw, on the surface and unstoppable.

At this point I wasn't sure I wanted him to stop. Our clothes had disappeared. I could feel the hard length of his erection against my thigh. He felt huge. My body felt very happy about the discovery. I tried to look down, but he caught my mouth in a soul-stealing kiss as he rubbed himself against me. His fingers brushed down my stomach, around my navel, and into the curls below. His fingers found my pleasure spot and started moving in little circles. My back arched with the pleasure.

My last shred of resistance disappeared. I couldn't stand it any longer, "Oh, great Zul! *Now*, Roman." I almost pleaded.

He looked down at me, his expression unreadable. "Yes, now," he said and repositioned himself between my legs. I breathed in his complex scent of subtle cologne, musky male and tangy magician. I felt oh-so-ready for the next step when something changed. I smelled . . . wolf.

Roman looked up into the mist and snarled, "No! She's mine!" His face darkened with frustration and rage. "NO!"

* * * *

"Cara, wake up." Someone shook me, yelling into my ear. I opened my eyes and focused on Tom, sitting beside me on the bed. He looked worried. When he realized I was awake, he stopped shaking my shoulders, and asked, "Hey, babe, you okay?"

I glanced around, momentarily confused. I wasn't at Roman's house, but in my room at Aunt Amelia's. I looked at Tom. "What are you doing here? Why did you wake me up? And don't call me 'babe.'"

He looked at me and distractedly ran a hand through his hair. "I don't exactly know why I'm here. I suddenly felt like you were in danger, like yesterday with the weird-ass seaweed thing."

I raised an eyebrow and sat up. I wore the long-sleeve t-shirt and boxer shorts I'd put on last night, not a red silk negligee. "*Animorphia*," I said. My mouth felt cottony.

"What?" Tom frowned, as though confused.

"*Animorphia*. The seaweed thing. That's what Amelia called it. I think it's a witch thing."

"Oh. Well, anyway, babe, I got this like tingling sensation and I just *knew* you needed me. It was strange but cool, you know? So I ran over to find out what was going on. You were sleeping so heavy duty that I thought I'd need to get Amelia to help me wake you up."

He looked all sweetly concerned, so I had to forgive him for waking me. "I had a dream about this Nightkind I met in San Francisco." I looked at the piece of bedspread I'd twisted between my hands, a little embarrassed. I was surprised to see it was morning already. The sun was shining brightly through the window.

"Well, it must have been some dream. Like I said, I'd have to grab Amelia to help out 'cause I couldn't wake you up." Then he smiled and sniffed. "Was it a sex dream? You smell primed."

He started to pull the covers back. I grabbed at them. *The man is always sniffing me,* I thought irritably.

"None of your business! Out. I want to get dressed." I pushed him off the bed, which he allowed me to do, laughing as he left via the window. It must have been how he got into my room.

After he left I flopped back down on the bed and took a deep breath. Was it just a dream? Or did Roman actually contact me? I had heard Nightkinds could visit people through their dreams. He said he would come to "claim" me, but he couldn't know my whereabouts, could he?

Somewhere in the house a telephone rang. I heard a muffled voice that sounded like my Aunt's, then footsteps coming up the stairs. There was a knock on the door and Aunt Amelia asked, "Cara dear, are you awake? You have a phone call. It's the nice wizard you met on the plane."

"I'll be right there. Thanks." I got out of bed, threw on my warm fleece robe and went to answer the phone. I felt a little thrill at the thought of talking to Paul as I padded into the kitchen in my bare feet. He'd invited me to take a tour of his art gallery and said he'd pick me up at one o'clock today. I hung up the phone and smiled. The old adage, *when it rains it pours,* was true. With Roman, Tom, and now Paul, this was the most attention I'd ever had from men at the same time. I tried to see my reflection in the chrome toaster on the kitchen counter. Did I look different lately? I still looked the same as far as I could see.

I searched the cupboards, found a box of hot cocoa and went about making my morning mocha. Sitting down at the old fashioned Formica-topped table, I savored my chocolaty drink. Roman posed a dangerous problem. I was definitely attracted to him, but how much was real and how much Nightkind seduction? And this whole bizarre Evika disappearance. . . You'd think with all of House Augustine's resources being thrown into finding her, something would have turned up by now. And where were my parents? Mom hadn't seen me once since this whole thing started. Granted, as Head of a Witch House, she was always busy, but she usually managed to make it to major milestones like graduations and monster maulings. Yet I hadn't even had a phone call. Huh.

My feelings were close to being hurt, and I grumbled to myself for a while, then finished my mocha and went upstairs to get ready for my date with Paul.

After a long, hot shower, I slathered on moisturizer. My hair looked shiny clean after I blew it dry, and I grabbed my small travel case and pulled out a cosmetics bag. I usually didn't bother with much makeup, just mascara and lip gloss, but today I added eye shadow, blush, and face powder. Not much but enough to enhance my features a little bit more. I knew I could look halfway decent when I put in the effort.

I slipped on a pair of snug, baby-blue leather pants—the ones Evika had talked me into buying—and a cream-colored cashmere sweater. Then I put on a pair of pearl drop earrings and slid my feet into pearlized-beige, high heel ankle boots. One last touch, a few dabs of my favorite perfume. It cost me a small fortune to have it custom-made in France, but I loved it.

I heard a knock at the door. I looked at my watch and saw it was a quarter to one. "Come in," I called out.

Tom walked in and sniffed the air. Zul's horns. What was with the man and his wolf-nose anyway?

"Mmmm. You smell good. Sexy good." He looked me up and down. "You look good too. Like a creamy dessert. I could eat you up." He smiled, walked over and leaned in for a kiss.

"Whoa there, partner. We need to talk about what happened between us." I put a hand on his chest. I felt our connection click together like magnetic puzzle pieces. He felt it too. I could tell by the expression on his face.

"What about us? We're good together. Can't you feel it?" He sat on the bed and patted the spot beside him. "Come on, babe, have a seat. We can talk, if you really want to."

I backed away. "Oh no, you're not pulling that one on me again."

He just looked at me, and I quickly said, "Tom. You're a nice guy, and I know we had that, um, moment together the other day. But about that, it didn't feel like a normal make-out kind of thing. Something else happened that I need to tell you about."

Tom just gazed at me with those big, brown, puppy-dog eyes and I faltered. How do you tell a guy he's now your familiar and you don't think romance will be a part of the relationship?

I heard the doorbell peal, and then Paul's voice and my Aunt inviting him in. Blessed-be-the-Portal, saved by the bell. "Tom, I have to go now, but let's talk tonight, okay?"

He turned towards the voices. "That's the guy from the airport," he said accusingly. "I thought we were together now."

"I promised Paul I'd go with him to see his gallery," I said, trying not to sound apologetic. I did not have to explain myself to him—at least I kept telling myself that.

Tom looked angry but didn't say anything else as I raced down the stairs, thinking I was a cowardly newt.

Chapter Seven
The Wizard

The small downtown area of Santa Lacuna was quaint. I tried to think of another word to describe it, but quaint seemed accurate. The shops were all small and had a European-village-meets-artsy-conclave look about them. There were trees everywhere along the gently sloping sidewalks. A good number of the buildings had ivy clinging to walls and roofs. The town had installed old-fashioned looking streetlights along the main street, and some workmen were stringing them with holiday lights for Winter Solstice.

Paul's gallery stood snuggled between a store selling glass objects d'art and a café. We headed towards the café. As we stepped through the door, a slim, gray-haired woman greeted us warmly. Paul introduced us. Her name was Jenny. It was obvious she and Paul knew each other well, as they talked about her grown kids and upcoming town events. She kept glancing over at me with a puzzled expression, but she didn't say anything as she led us to a booth and handed us menus.

I looked at the menu and saw it was a work of art in and of itself. The menu selections were listed in beautiful calligraphy, accented with hand-painted vines and blooming flowers across the parchment-like paper. Paul told me the menus changed monthly to reflect the freshest ingredients available. One of the local "starving" artists traded producing the menus for food. At least the artist wouldn't starve with this deal.

As we ordered, Jenny stared into my eyes a bit too long for comfort. I stared back a bit defiantly, "Did you want to ask me something?"

She blinked a couple of times and smiled. "Oh, I'm so sorry I stared at you! But we haven't seen your kind here since, well, never." Her words seemed to fall out of her mouth of their own accord, without internal editing. She looked around quickly as if to make sure no one had heard her.

I raised my eyebrows. "My kind? What kind of 'kind' do you think I am?" Okay, I wasn't offended by her words as much as curious. Witch burning has been illegal for a long time now so I didn't think the townsfolk would rise up, brandishing sharpened paintbrushes, to hunt me down, particularly since nearly all the townsfolk were werewolves.

I glanced toward Paul whose expression was both surprised and a bit appalled as he stared at his friend. He opened his mouth as if to say something when Jenny responded with, "You mean you don't *know*? Zul's horns! Excuse my language, but you don't know, do you?" Without waiting for me to reply, she leaned down close to my ear and whispered, "You're a Synemancer." Then she straightened up with a satisfied look on her face.

I know I had a "Duh?" look on my face, but Paul looked alarmed. "Jenny, what are you talking about? Cara is no such thing," Paul whispered to us both.

"Yes she is. I *know* she is. Paul, I've known you for most of your life, and I wouldn't lie to you. It's been a long time since I've even heard of one, but here she is, sitting in my restaurant, and I tell you that's what she is." Jenny nodded emphatically, as if agreeing with her own conclusion.

"Will one of you tell me what you think I am because this is getting really annoying." I sat back and crossed by arms beneath my breasts and then crossed my legs for good measure.

Head cocked to one side, Jenny looked at me for a long time, then finally said, "Honey, your body language is looking a little closed. Are you sure you're ready to be open to what I'm going to tell you?"

I felt like screaming, even though it would make a bad impression on people I'd just met, but Shades of Hades, I was beyond irritated.

I uncrossed my arms and did a palms-up gesture. "See, I'm open. So what's a Synemancer and why is it something you have to whisper about?" I whispered.

Jenny pulled a chair from an adjacent table and sat down with us. "Okay Cara, in order to understand this, I have to tell you that although I'm human, I'm also a sensitive—you know, sensitive to mystical energies. I can pretty much tell what a person is from the moment I lay eyes on them. Like Paul here. I knew he had to be a wizard the day he pedaled by my restaurant on his little tricycle."

She glanced at Paul and smiled fondly, then turned back to me. "Anyway, like I started to say, I can tell what a person is, you know, witch, wizard, fae, werewolf, and the like, and I can also tell if they have anything special about them. My ability is sort of like someone who can tell which spice someone added to a dish just by tasting it. People with strong energy fields have a, I don't know, flavor I guess is the best word. Your flavor is Synemancer."

I had uncrossed my legs and leaned forward with my elbows on the table. "I still have no idea what a Synemancer is. I've never heard the term before, and I grew up in a house full of witches." My lips twitched to the side as a thought occurred to me, "Did you make up the word?"

Paul shook his head, "No Cara, it's a more modern word, granted, but it's only a new word for a very old kind of practitioner. I'm sure you have heard about the Mages who opened the Portal?"

"Sure, I took Portal History in my freshman year in college."

He nodded. "Almost every one of those Mages were Synemancers. That's the reason they were able to open the portal. The mystical dynamics of inter-dimensional physics are so overwhelmingly complex only a group with a common focus and incredible power, such as the synemancers, could have performed such a feat. No one has been able to duplicate it since, although many have died trying." Paul had been leaning forward across the table as he spoke. Now he sat back in his chair.

"So where are all the Mages?" I looked back and forth between Jenny and Paul.

Jenny looked at Paul, then at me. "As you probably learned in school, many of the earth's practitioners were killed during the Great Purge. After the few Mages left had opened the portal, they disappeared. Probably killed in battles before the Truce of Paris. Once in a while a witch or even a wizard is born with the power to draw energies from multiple sources and manipulate that energy so it becomes greater than the sum of its parts. The term *Synemancy* was coined from the modern word *Synergy* and a combining term *–mancy* to describe this ability to manipulate and expand energies. It is a rare ability."

I laughed. "No offense, but I can barely perform basic magic, much less all the stuff you're talking about. Maybe my 'spiciness' is due to something else?" I winked at Paul.

Jenny didn't look amused. "I'm never wrong. Sometimes I wish I were, but I always turn out to be right." She shrugged, "Well, to give your statement credit, I sense your ability has just started to manifest. It's a tiny glimmer of what you will become. Your power will reach out and pull in others with powers that can help it mature, so you need to be careful that you don't accidentally attract negative forces. The magic wants to attain its potential, but it doesn't have the kind of discernment and judgment a person has. It'll just sense what you need and try to get it. You are like a fledgling bird—you're beginning to grow your adult feathers, but you can't fly yet."

"I guess I better not order poultry for lunch then." I said.

Paul smiled and said, "Very funny. But seriously, Cara, I'd listen to Jenny. I felt an immediate attraction to you on the plane. I mean, even more than I normally would for a beautiful young woman," he hastily added.

I took a deep breath, trying to decide whether or not to be insulted. But just a few hours ago I'd been wondering about my sudden femme fatale status, so it didn't seem fair to be irritated with Paul over the same thing. "I guess that might explain some things that have been happening in my life lately." I looked at Paul. "So my magic thinks you have something I need?"

His smile widened and there was a lusty gleam in his eye, "I certainly hope so. I'll take any excuse to be in your company. And now that you mention it, I think I feel the pull of your power. Yes, it's demanding we go out on another date very soon."

This time all three of us laughed. Jenny got up and moved her chair back to its original table. "All right you two, I think I need to get some food into you to keep up your strength. Forget the menu. Today's lunch is the owner's special surprise."

An hour later I picked my napkin off my lap and dabbed at my lips. My taste buds were in a state of bliss. The lunch amazed me with fabulous flavors and gorgeous presentations. I just wished I could remember half of what I ate, but my mind still reeled from what Jenny had said about me. Could I believe her? Paul seemed to take her assertion at face value, but it was ridiculous, I wasn't a *Mage*. To even think was just, well, absurd. Jenny was a very nice nut case and Paul was . . . what? Just humoring an old friend?

My head started to hurt with all the thoughts and new information running in circles in my mind. I needed someone I trusted to talk to, like Sonya or maybe Aunt Amelia. No, it had to be Sonya. Some of the events of the past few weeks were too embarrassing to reveal to my Aunt even though I knew she converted to Druccanism several years ago. Most mainstream witches these days were members, and they tended to be pretty open-minded about peoples' thoughts on the gender or nature of God, other members' sexual practices or preferences, that sort of thing. Druccan is one of the newer religions combining Druid, Wiccan, Zul, and even some Christian teachings.

But no matter how open-minded she might be, she is my mother's sister. She'd probably feel obligated to share information. I didn't want Mom to know about my situation, at least not yet.

After lunch Paul took me on a tour of his gallery. It currently featured the works of three local artists, two painters and a sculptor, but also displayed an eclectic mix of other artists' pieces as well. The interior of the gallery consisted of a contemporary blend of woods, metals, and stone that belied the "quaint" exterior of the building. It looked surprisingly expansive, the mix of natural and electric lighting professionally arranged to enhance and highlight each piece's color, texture and form. I was totally impressed.

We sat down on a sofa in one of the viewing rooms with a large abstract painting on one wall. I turned to Paul. "So what do you think about what your friend Jenny said about me?"

He thought for a moment, looking at the painting. "Frankly, I'm not sure what to think. I believe Jenny because I've known her a long time and she's always been right on the mark with her readings. But this is a new one." He turned to look at me. "If you're what she says you are . . . you have the potential of becoming very powerful. What you do with the power, how you use it, will be incredibly important. You know our history, how the general human population tends to look askance at magical powers. In the Dark Ages, during the days of the Great Purge, they hunted down magic users and systematically killed them off by deception, ambush, and sometimes sheer numbers."

"But that's ancient history. In this day and age I can't believe I'd be in any danger. Do you?" I asked, practically begging for reassurance.

He shrugged, "Old fears and prejudices die hard." I must have had a stricken look on my face because he smiled at me and gave me a hug. "Don't look so worried. People around you will protect you, and besides, I'm probably just being overly dramatic. You certainly don't look like a stereotypical Mage with a long gray beard and peaked hat."

I smiled back, "Hey, if I start growing whiskers I'd better have some pretty good powers to compensate."

He leaned in and kissed me on the cheek, then said, "No whiskers yet."

I laughed. "Are you sure? Maybe you should try again." I looked into his sky blue eyes and could almost see his pupils dilate at my words. But he shook his head and took my hand, standing.

"Cara, you're a temptation, but I have an appointment this afternoon with a buyer that I can't put off. If I kissed you the way I'd like to, I know I'd never make it on time. Let's go. I have just enough time to take you home and make it to my meeting."

As we walked to his car, he held my hand. I liked the way his hand felt, warm and dry, his grip on my hand just right.

"I'd like to see you again soon," he said.

"I'd like to see you again, too," I replied, meaning it.

We drove back to my Aunt's house, filling the time with chitchat, neither of us bringing up Jenny by silent mutual consent.

As he walked me up to the door I turned to him. "I had a great time. I loved your gallery, and thank you for lunch. It was interesting, to say the least."

"Thank you for coming. I enjoyed spending the afternoon with you, but next time I think I want you all to myself. No café owners or the public anywhere around. Are you free for dinner on Friday night? I'll cook at my place. I'm told I make a very passable pasta Pomodoro. I'll toss a salad, pour some red wine. What do you say?"

"Sounds wonderful. I love pasta. And a man who cooks, what could be better? I'll bring the wine." We stood close together, not wanting to say good-bye. He put both hands on either side of my face and gently but thoroughly kissed me. I felt a little dizzy as I waved at him when he sped off down the road.

"Shades of Hades," I muttered under my breath. I couldn't shake the thought that Paul was only attracted to me because of my power. It could be making him think he likes me. Guilt surged through me, dampening the happy little high I had from Paul's kiss. Would I ever know, for the rest of my life, if men were genuinely interested in me or if they had been brainwashed by my power?

Chapter Eight
Confession

I called Sonya after dinner and extracted a promise from her to visit me. Unfortunately, that visit wouldn't happen as quickly as I needed to. She was worried about leaving her "babies," the Hellhounds. She couldn't leave them alone. Who knows what kind of trouble they'd get into? She couldn't take them to a normal kennel for obvious reasons. Her Dad was her only real option—one of the downsides of having exotic pets, I guess—and he wouldn't be able to take them until next week.

I hung up the phone with a resigned sigh. I needed to talk to Aunt Amelia. I just couldn't wait a whole week for Sonya to visit, and this type of conversation was too sensitive to take place by telephone. I was on my own, as usual. I had asked Sonya if she could do her Dad's mirror travel trick, but she didn't know how. Apparently, it required demon magic and that was dangerous. Well, the two things *were* practically synonymous, you know—dangerous demon-magic? Might as well be one word. Given that I didn't want Sonya to go missing in some strange mirror dimension, I resigned myself to waiting for her to fly out here by mundane means.

I went in search of my aunt. I found her in the backyard picking herbs to use for dinner. Tom had joined us for dinner, and he was carefully piling chocolate-covered cookies on a plate for dessert. He stood at the counter, intent on his task. His long, blond hair was loose and flowed down his back. He wore a gray Henley-style thermal top and jeans. I leaned against the kitchen door jamb and admired the way his muscles pulled the top snug across his back and shoulders. He suddenly looked over at me, apparently knowing I stood there, although I'm sure I didn't make a sound.

He gestured to the mound of cookies on the plate and asked, "Think that's enough?"

"Definitely. Probably more than enough, even if they do have chocolate on them," I answered. He smiled and I noticed he had dimples. Damn, he looked adorable.

A little voice in my head said, *He's mine, my familiar.* A little wave of warm delight infused my being at the thought.

Tom looked surprised as he put down the plastic storage

container of cookies to turn and look at me. "What was *that*?" he asked, wonder in his voice.

I took a step back and shook my head. "I, I was just thinking good thoughts about you," I stammered, too startled to even pretend I didn't know what he was talking about.

"Those must've been bodacious thoughts. I got this, like, warm buzz all over and I knew it came from you." He walked over to me and whispered in my ear, "Think some more good thoughts, babe. Just say the word, and I can climb in your window tonight and return the favor. I could make you feel good too." He held me close and nuzzled my neck, inhaling my scent.

"Oh, excuse me!" Aunt Amelia said as she walked into the kitchen carrying a small basket of herbs. Tom straightened, hands going behind his back like a naughty schoolboy. "Well, you two have hit if off quickly." She smiled and made a shooing motion with her hands, "Let's go into the living room and have our tea and cookies. I think I'd like to have some chocolate now."

I took a deep breath, reaching for my courage. This seemed as good a time as any to talk to them both about the Tom situation. I just had to figure out a way to break it to them gently.

We settled onto the big floor pillows with our tea and cookies. The room was warmly lit with a row of lights shining from punched metal sconces mounted on the walls.

I looked down at my tea mug, drew in a deep breath and said, "Aunt Amelia. Tom. I need to tell you both something." They looked at me expectantly. Aunt Amelia took a sip of tea, keeping eye contact over the rim of her cup, and Tom popped a whole cookie in his mouth while staring at me. I took another deep breath and blurted, "I accidentally made Tom my familiar." So much for breaking it to them gently.

Aunt Amelia looked like she was about to spew her tea. She swallowed quickly, the wrong way, and started coughing, amber tea dribbling down her chin. She held her napkin to her mouth as I jumped up and started patting her on the back. I've never known it to actually help someone stop coughing, but it gave me something to do instead of just watching her choke. I glanced over at Tom who sat looking thoughtful as he munched on another cookie.

Finally she waved me away so I'd stop thumping on her

back. "Oh, dear. For goodness sake, child, you've only been here three days! When did this happen? *How* did this happen?"

"I'll answer the 'when' question first. The day I arrived." I grabbed a cookie and stuffed it into my mouth.

Tom looked at me, "You mean when we . . ."

"Yes, when we . . ." I confirmed quickly, cookie crumbs escaping my mouth. I took a sip of tea.

Aunt Amelia's eyebrows had shot up, "You mean you two, er, got together the first day?"

I hastened to correct, "We just kissed—well, kind of made out, you know? Not real sex or anything. It just happened accidentally." I could feel my face heating up as I said it.

Tom looked like he wanted to say something about the "not real sex" part, but he stuffed another cookie into his mouth when I glared at him.

"Are you sure about this, dear?" she asked.

Tom said, "Yeah, we really made out. I mean really, really made out. Oh, man."

Aunt Amelia's face colored as she looked at him. "No, no, I didn't mean if she was sure about *that* part. I wanted to know if she was sure about making you her familiar." She turned to look at me.

"Well, I've never had a familiar, but I know the basics. I always thought it would be a cat or dog or something common, if I ever did attract one. I didn't even know a *person* could be a familiar." I threw my hands up in a helpless gesture.

She looked thoughtful. "Tell me why you think Tom is your familiar. Can you describe what the connection feels like?"

Tom looked up from polishing off another cookie. "I can tell you that since we made out, I can kinda feel Cara's emotions. So far it's mostly strong emotions, like fear. When the seaweed thing attacked her, I knew she was in danger. And I knew where to find her, like I had a homing signal to go by or something. But it's not only bad stuff. Just now in the kitchen she thought something good about me and it felt really awesome."

"When we were together I felt our auras meld together for a moment," I explained. "I could feel us exchange a tiny piece of ourselves with each other. I couldn't stop it from happening." I added.

Aunt Amelia looked at me intently. "Now, this is very important. When this *exchange* happened, did you sense the bond was with the human or wolf aspect of Tom?"

I nodded, "Definitely the wolf aspect. As a matter of fact, we were just sitting together at first, and then I felt his wolf and things started happening."

She looked relieved. "Yes, yes, I see how it's possible. You know it's forbidden to make a human being a familiar, but a wolf is another matter entirely. It could be explained. Not easily, but defensibly. You two need to be very careful. You were drawn together and are now connected to each other for life."

"What?" I gasped, feeling stricken. "Tom is bound to me for life? Oh Tom, I am so sorry." I buried my face in my hands as my stomach churned.

Tom came over and put his arm around my shoulders. "Hey, I don't think it's so bad. So, I have this magical connection to a radically hot witch? Worse things could happen to a dude, you know? I don't know what a familiar does, but I can learn."

His kindness was the tipping point. I started to cry. "You don't understand!" A crushing wave of guilt and fear came flooding through me. I wanted to run and hide and make it all go away.

Aunt Amelia came over and sat on the other side of me and put her arms around me. "There, there, dear. We'll work this all out somehow."

With the two of them hugging me, I started feeling better. Sitting there enveloped in their warm embraces, my guilt and fear receded to a place where I could handle them a little bit better. I sniffed.

"Thank you. I feel better." Aunt Amelia tightened her hug for a moment, then unwound her arms and sat back. Tom lowered his arms from my shoulders, but wrapped one arm around my waist. It should've seemed too intimate, but it felt so right I couldn't tell him to stop.

I wiped at the tears on my face. I needed to blow my nose badly. As if reading my mind, Tom twisted in his seat and grabbed at something behind him. He placed a box of tissues on my lap, pulled out a couple of sheets and started dabbing at my face. I smiled my thanks and, grabbing a tissue from the box, blew my nose.

I took a deep breath, and thought, *in for the puppy, in for the hound*. "Okay, I hate to tell you this, but there's more I need to share with you."

Aunt Amelia patted my knee, "Not just yet, dear. There are some things both of you will have to know in order to, well, deal with your special relationship." She looked at Tom. "Tom, I believe you've already discovered you're in tune with Cara's emotions. This is important for a familiar to fulfill his role in a witch's life. Her fear will make you want to protect her; her pleasure will become your pleasure. You will derive intense satisfaction in carrying out her will. You will not want to be parted from her for very long, and you'll feel a great need to not only be in her presence, but to touch her and be with her. If you were a true animal familiar, this wouldn't be a problem. The cat that brushes her legs or climbs onto her lap or the dog that follows her around the house, these things are expected and accepted. A man with these desires will channel his need for closeness and touching into something men and women want from each other."

I said, "You mean sex?"

Tom had been absently rubbing my back in little circular motions while my aunt spoke. He seemed to realize what he was doing and moved his hand back to my waist.

She nodded, "Quite likely, given both of you are young, attractive, single and heterosexual. If this had happened with, oh say, a much older witch or a male witch, the bond might be something like a beloved nephew or a very close friend. Now, I'm not saying there would be anything intrinsically *wrong* with having a physical relationship with each other, but I'm cautioning you to be careful. Make sure you don't confuse the natural affection between a witch and her familiar with something more."

Tom straightened his back, "Hey, I just thought of something. We're going to have to tell my pack leader about this, and he isn't going to like it."

Aunt Amelia tightened her lips together for a moment before saying, "Yes, I thought of that, too. Whatever his feelings about it, he'll have to accept it in the end. It's done and can't be undone. We'll have to come up with a plan to present it to him."

A clock chimed once from somewhere in the house. It was one o'clock in the morning. I suddenly remembered my long day, and a deep weariness washed over me. I leaned my head on Tom's shoulder. My eyelids felt very heavy as they started to droop.

Aunt Amelia exclaimed, "Goodness, look at the time! Cara
looks exhausted. Tom, take her up to her room, would you?
We can talk more tomorrow."

I wanted to protest, to tell them about the Nightkind magician,
but my eyes had closed and refused to open. I felt Tom cradle
me in his arms and stand up smoothly, as if I didn't weight an
ounce. Muzzily, I thought I rather liked it. I especially liked not
having to walk up the stairs to my room. I felt so tired I might
not have been able to muster up the energy to make the trip.

Half asleep, nestled against Tom's warm solid chest, I felt
us ascend the stairs. I listened to the comforting sound of his
heart beating steadily as he climbed. He laid me on the bed
and pulled the comforter over me. Then, he lay down next to
me on top of the comforter. I turned on my side so he could
spoon my back. As he slipped his arm around me. I fell into a
deep sleep.

Chapter Nine
Roman

Roman came to me in my dreams as I feared, or maybe hoped, he would. He lounged on his bed in that misty place, chest bare, silver eyes full of dark promise. I stood at the foot of the bed, dressed in red lace and silk, as before. He held out a hand and beckoned me to come to him.

I shook my head. "No. Answer my questions, damn it."

He lowered his hand and sighed. "Very well. Come sit by me and I'll tell you what I know."

"Promise you'll behave yourself if I sit there?" I asked warily.

He looked feral, predatory, for an instant, and then he smiled. "Of course, but only if you promise me you'll stay after I tell you what I know."

I stood silent in indecision. He waited patiently, as if he could wait an eternity for my answer. I knew what staying with him would involve. The thought of us coming together, the feel of his cool skin gliding over mine, made my body feel things that almost made me forget about my questions. Oh yes. I wanted to stay.

"I'll stay," I said.

He stood next to me in an instant, and he took my hand and led me to the bed. We sat down side by side, using the headboard as a backrest.

"So tell me," I said.

"Let me start by saying I'd seen you before that night in the restaurant. As you know, we Nightkind are very long lived. I met your grandmother when she was a young woman. I found her to be a fascinating, powerful, beautiful and deadly but, oddly enough, compassionate woman. I grew to admire her. I kept track of her life, her family. I knew you were her pride and joy. As a small child you played at my feet when I visited her." He stopped talking for a moment, eyes unfocused, remembering the past. He came to himself and smiled at me. "Those were good days."

"My grandmother never mentioned you," I said, eyebrows raised.

"No. I'm sure she didn't. She cut herself off from me when you started growing older. I don't know why. She never told me." A flash of sorrow came and went across his face. "You look very much like her, you know, except for the eyes."

"Everyone in the family tells me that," I replied.

"Ah, yes, well they would, wouldn't they? It's rather remarkable."

He ran the tip of a finger along my jaw line to my lips and dipped inside my mouth, just a little. I pulled back, startled, it felt like his finger had found my most intimate parts. He placed the finger into his mouth and closed his eyes, as if savoring the flavor. When his eyes opened his pupils had dilated so only a narrow band of silver was visible.

"Tell me about that night at the restaurant," I urged, afraid he would get distracted and I still wouldn't learn what had happened.

He looked at me with his nearly black eyes. I held my breath. He leaned back and I slowly exhaled.

"The night I saw you sitting in the nightclub with the redheaded witch, I thought you were your grandmother for an instant. But then I realized you were her granddaughter. You looked so full of life, laughing, your head thrown back at some comment from your loud companion. To me it seemed as if every man there coveted you. I think you could've asked any man there to do anything, and they would have done it."

He paused at my skeptical look, but then he ignored me and went on. "You captivated me and I walked to your table to introduce myself, to be closer to you. I asked if I could join you and you agreed. The three of us sat and talked and laughed into the night. We toasted your birthday more times than I can remember. The waiters kept appearing with bottles of champagne, offerings from the other patrons, mostly men, I might add. Neither of you could have safely driven home, so I offered to give you both a ride. I practically had to fight off several others who wanted the honor, even your waiter," he added wryly.

He had lapsed into his old-fashioned way of speaking. I'd noticed he did that when he focused more on his thoughts than how he articulated them. I also knew that the only woman the men would have fought over to drive home was my cousin.

"Okay, say I believe you up to this point. What happened to Evika, and why don't I remember all this?" I asked.

"I have a theory, but I'll get to it in a moment. Late in the night, a man joined us at the table. You two appeared to know him and welcomed him with open arms. Although I could see immediately he was demon-tainted, so I was on my guard."

"What did he look like?" I asked urgently.

"Dark eyes and hair, skin as pale as mine, you called him 'Uncle.' When he recognized me for Nightkind, he dared to show disdain and ordered me to leave your side. Of course, I chose to stay. Normally, I would've been more active in dealing with his rudeness, but I decided not to do so that night because you seemed to like him."

"Uncle Max?" I said almost to myself. If it was Uncle Max there that night, why did he act as if he didn't know what had happened? "Then what happened?" I asked.

Roman seemed to search his memory, "At this point the restaurant started to close. We sat at the last occupied table. The serving staff had disappeared. This Uncle creature took your hand and urged you and the other witch to go with him. Naturally, I couldn't let you go, having just found you." He said it like it was the most natural thing in the world. I wondered what Uncle Max's reaction had been to a strange Nightkind attaching himself to us.

"The red-haired witch had been using a small mirror to apply some lipstick. She screamed and dropped the mirror on the floor where it cracked in two. We all stopped talking to see what had happened. I noticed that the crack in the mirror started to seep a thick blackish-red liquid. The substance continued to flow from the mirror until a large puddle had formed on the floor. The puddle began to pulsate with glowing red lines, like radiating arteries and veins growing out from a central point that started to beat like an aberrant heart."

He continued, "The Uncle placed himself between this ooze and the two of you. He told me to get you both out of the restaurant. A tentacle-like rope of ooze shot out of the puddle and wrapped around his leg where it started spreading itself like another skin over his lower body. The red-haired witch screamed again and tried to pull it off of him. At her touch the tentacle split in two, and the second one wrapped around her arm. The ooze on the floor flowed up through the tentacles to fuel its spread across their bodies. The pulsating veins grew brighter the more of its victims it touched. You slipped out of my grasp and ran towards them. The spawn, your Uncle, uttered an incantation and shot demon fire into the ooze. The tentacle holding him drew back only to turn and attach itself to your

friend. With two of the tentacles spreading over her, her body
was almost completely covered; just her head and part of one
shoulder remained free. You threw yourself onto her, tearing
at the ooze covering her."

I gasped, "Shades of Hades preserve me. I can't believe
this story! Why didn't the ooze latch onto me?"

He looked at me, his face a mask as he shrugged. "The
ooze recoiled from you instead of attaching itself to you as it
did to the others. I have no idea why it reacted to you that
way."

"Go on." I said.

"The Uncle uttered the same incantation, and another gout
of demon fire hit the ooze. This time when it withdrew, it took
the witch with it, disappearing into the mirror."

"My cousin got pulled into a *compact* mirror by *living
ooze?"* I yelled.

I knelt on the bed with my hands on his bare shoulders,
shaking him. This had to be a real dream, not a Nightkind
visitation. The story sounded too bizarre.

Roman grabbed my arms and pulled me onto his chest,
wrapping his arms around me. "Listen, to me. There's more.
Do you want to hear it?" I stopped struggling and nodded, and
he said, "The Uncle cried out and tried to follow, but when he
stooped to pick up the mirror, it exploded in his hands. He
must've been killed instantly. I tried to shield you with my body,
but the concussion of the blast knocked us both to the floor.
We were covered in blood and flesh and noisome things. I
checked to see if you were hurt and saw you were unconscious.
I didn't know if the cause was the blast or the horror or both.
So much blood covered you I couldn't tell if any of it was
yours. I had parked my car at the back of the building. I couldn't
do anything for the Uncle or your friend, so I took you to my
house, cleaned off the blood, arranged to have your clothes
cleaned, and put you in my bed. By then, it was close to dawn
and I couldn't do any more."

I closed my eyes, stunned into silence. How could the person
he talked about be Uncle Max? It sounded like Uncle Max, but
Uncle Max was alive and didn't seem to know anything about
all this. And how could anyone have lived after sustaining that
type of damage at the restaurant? I couldn't wrap my mind
around it.

Then a thought occurred to me, and I asked, "Was the

man in the restaurant the same person who helped us fight the lizard-ape?"

He frowned and then shrugged. "They looked a lot alike, but the man at the restaurant was destroyed, so how could they be the same person? If I'd spoken to him at my house, I might have been able to tell if they were one and the same, but I was injured and he whisked you away before I could stop him"

I raked by hands through my hair, mystified, but I did manage to have the presence of mind to ask about the other mystery. "What about the engagement ring?"

"Ah. Yes. After I bathed you and lay you in my bed, I realized I didn't want to let you go. I wanted you. Your blood sang to me, your soft body was a temptation, and the promise of your power bespelled me. I knew we were meant to be together. Like a bolt, understanding came to me. *This* was why your grandmother shut me out of her life. She understood what you would become to me. She knew you were destined to be by my side, and she tried to prevent it. But destiny isn't so easily thwarted; the Fates will have their way. They brought us to the same location so I could find you. When I realized this, I took out the ring I had saved for many years, waiting for my chosen, and placed it on your finger. It fit perfectly. Another sign it was meant to be."

Uh, oh. He talked like a lunatic stalker. This couldn't be good. "Roman, thanks so much for filling me in on what happened that night. There's a lot I need to think about and some people I need to talk to. Er, can I take a rain check on staying with you right now?"

I started trying to edge away, but he held me close and uttered one word before he kissed me. "No."

I wanted to fight. Really, I did. But he kissed me until his passion consumed me. It drove all thought from my mind. The only thing I could think about was the rising heat between us. His mouth and tongue did things to me I could feel all the way to my core. My reservations about him dissolved under his sensual onslaught and I kissed him back. He moaned as I explored his mouth.

Suddenly, our clothes were gone. I could feel him down the length of my body. The now oh-so-familiar pulse and hardness of his desire lay against my thigh and drove me to whimper helplessly as I envisioned the length of him inside of

me. He broke off our kiss to move his mouth down my neck
and to my breasts. He sucked and licked my nipples while his
hand did delicious things down below. I threw back my head
as the sensations grew and grew. I could feel my power pour
out of me in ever increasing waves as my pleasure became a
pulsing, all-consuming feeling that left no room for other
thoughts.

My power enveloped us in a golden cocoon. It hungered
for Roman, reached out to surround him and pull him into itself.
The white mist around us became charged with a sparkling
glow. Roman let out a low growl as he sought my mouth again
for a hard kiss, then dragged me off the bed. He positioned me
so I stood on the floor, my back to him. Bent at the waist, I
braced my elbows on the bed. From behind me he reached
around and continued to stroke between my legs until I begged
him to enter me. He rubbed the tip of his cock against my
wetness and then slowly slid inside me. He felt huge, long and
thick, stretching me almost to the point of pain, but he knew
how to make me accommodate him. He moved back and forth
by inches, slowing going deeper, making me take more of him
with each stroke until I could feel him bumping up against the
very entrance to my womb. I rose up on my hands, the feeling
of being so completely filled almost overwhelming. Then he
started moving his entire length in and out, slowly at first, then
more quickly as my wetness eased his passage.

He had found the perfect spot inside me and slid over and
over it. I felt delirious with pleasure, almost as if I could die
from the ecstasy. My power closed around us, the pressure of
it mirroring the pressure inside my body. I could feel my bright
aura wrap around Roman's cold, dark one, and the two of
them melded into something both terrible and beautiful. It built
upon itself as our bodies came together until I reached the
point of no return, that pinnacle where the pleasure peaked
and spilled over me in wave after wave. I cried out, inarticulate
sounds coming from me, as I thrashed in frenzied rapture.

Roman held me against him as he increased his pace, now
pounding into me as fast as he could. Then he too cried out his
pleasure. As he climaxed, my aura pulled back into me, taking
with it a piece of Roman's aura, but unlike with Tom, it did not
leave any part of me behind.

I realized too late what had happened when I felt that piece
of Roman break free to join to me. I opened my mouth to tell

Roman what had happened, but another wave of pleasure started to build and I couldn't get the words out. Then, without warning, the misty place faded as Roman called my name.

I woke up in my bed, but the pleasure didn't disappear. I was disoriented, but I could feel the slide of male hardness going in and out of me. I glanced down and recognized the strong, tanned arms around me as Tom's. He cradled me in the same spooning position we'd fallen asleep in, but he was now inside of me and I could feel my climax about to wash over me. I instinctively curled my knees up to allow him deeper access and he complied. It pushed me over the edge and I cried out into my pillow. He immediately did the same. We continued to lie spooned, panting.

Finally, I turned over to look at him, and asked bewilderedly, "Tom, what are you doing?" Realizing how stupid that question sounded, I said, "Forget that! I know *what* you were doing. Were you wearing protection?"

His face was beaded with sweat, blond tendrils sticking to his forehead, and he grinned at me. "Of course. I always have a spare in my wallet. I got it when you were begging me to . . . well, you know. Who am I to turn down a request like that? As your willing familiar, I live to serve."

I stared at him appalled. I must have been talking in my sleep. When Roman and I came together it spilled into my physical world, and Tom picked up where Roman left off.

I pulled my pillow over my face and groaned. This whole mess kept getting more and more complicated and I had no idea what to do about it I couldn't tell Tom to leave me because we were inextricably bonded. Roman did what he wanted to regardless of what I said to him. And I didn't even want to factor Paul into the equation, but I couldn't ignore our attraction to each other. Before I had powers my life had been simple, uncomplicated, but admittedly boring. Now there were so many things to wrap my head around that I thought my brain would implode if one more thing complicated my life.

Chapter Ten
The Pack

Tom left via the window, after making me promise to come with him to the werewolf shindig the next day—or today, to be exact. I said yes just to get him to leave. Zul's horns, what was I going to do with him now? I told him he shouldn't expect this type of thing as a side bonus to being my familiar, which only made him laugh and kiss my nose. Like, wasn't I being just too silly?

I decided to deal with it later, and I rolled over and slept in until noon with no dreams or Nightkind visitations to disturb me. I woke up feeling fuzzy-headed and cranky. The lupine social event was scheduled for two o'clock at Oceanside Park, just down the street, so I had time to drink a couple of cups of stale coffee and get dressed. Tom came by at one-thirty and we walked to the park together. I carried a freshly baked apple pie Aunt Amelia made for us to take. She had left early in the morning to run some errands, and had left me a note saying she'd meet us at the event.

California weather on the coast makes it possible to have outdoor barbecues in November. What a place to live! The day felt chilly but it was sunny, and if you stood directly in the bright rays of the sun with your eyes closed, face turned up until you saw a red glow through your eyelids, you could almost believe it's warm. I wore thick corduroy pants, a soft chamois shirt, sneakers, and a lightweight jacket. I could take the jacket off later if I didn't need it. Tom looked happy. He seemed to be basking in the afterglow of our bedroom encounter. I just couldn't shatter his bubble about what had happened between us. Not yet, anyway. I was determined to enjoy myself. Maybe eat too much barbeque, drink one too many beers, and win the egg toss or the deer toss, whatever these folks did at get-togethers.

Despite my determination to think about everything later, thoughts swirled around in my head. Maybe I should look at this as my chance to really date some guys, as in multiple. Why did I keep thinking everything was such a disaster? So some incredible, beautiful men wanted me. I could think of several women who'd love to be in my shoes. Yeah, the whole cousin-best-friend-sucked-into-mirror-hell, homicidal monsters, smitten magicians, and accidental familiars put a crimp in the positive side of things, but a girl's got to look at the silver lining, you know? I refused to even think about what my mother would say about Nightkinds and werewolves "dating" her daughter. Nuh uh, not going there.

I hooked my arm through Tom's and gave him a radiant smile. He looked bemused but accepting of my good mood. Maybe I felt some afterglow too.

As we approached the park, I could see a large crowd of people milling around a circle of tables. My good mood faded as anxiety butterflies started fluttering around in my stomach, making me feel slightly queasy. I never liked butterflies. Meeting strangers was daunting enough, but what would the pack leader say about the whole familiar thing? I told myself to settle down, Tom seemed okay with it, and Aunt Amelia would help smooth things over. The pack leader would have to listen to their spiritual advisor, right?

As we got closer to the group I saw many of them wore shorts and t-shirts. I asked Tom, "Aren't they cold dressed like that?"

He shook his head, "Nah, we have high metabolisms. It would have to be colder than this for us to want to put more clothes on. The less clothes the better is our motto."

Several people looked up and waved at us. Tom waved back. I slowed down. The nearer we got, the slower I walked until we were standing still at the edge of the park lawn.

Tom frowned, "Come on, babe. What's the matter?"

I shrugged, embarrassed to put my fears into words. "I'm just nervous about meeting your pack. But I'm okay. Really. Let's go." I started forward.

Tom put his arm around my shoulders. "Don't worry. They'll love you. Just don't get any barbeque sauce on you."

I shot him a puzzled look, "Why?"

"Because you're such a juicy morsel and I don't want anyone getting any ideas about having you for lunch." At my shocked expression he started to laugh. "Kidding, just kidding."

I tried to punch his shoulder, but he dodged my fist and ran ahead of me to his friends, still laughing.

He stood talking to the knot of people who had waved to us earlier when I walked up to them with my best nice-to-meet-you-I'm-harmless smile plastered on my face. Tom took me around and made introductions. Apparently *weres* had a different definition of personal space. They all stood way too close for my comfort and seemed to want to get close enough to smell me. I looked around and saw similar greetings happening around us, sometimes with people nuzzling each others' necks, just behind the ears. As we walked from one group to another, a man brushed past us, bumping into Tom hard enough to make him almost lose his balance.

Tom turned around, irritated. "Hey, watch it."

The man turned around to face him and just stared at him. He turned his gaze to me and looked me over from feet to hair in a purposely slow and frankly sexual manner, lingering on my breasts and lips.

Tom growled and grabbed the other man's arm. "What do you think you're doing, Etienne? This isn't your pack. You don't have rights here."

I stared back at the stranger. He stood at average height, slender, but you could see the bunching of muscles under his long-sleeve, black t-shirt. Dark hair and eyes, a thin predatory face I supposed some women would find attractive. His eyes seemed to glow with an inner light as he leered at me from under dark eyebrows.

He smiled and licked his lips. "I like your woman. I'll challenge you for her." He had a touch of an accent that told me his origins were in central Europe.

I felt Tom stiffen beside me, and I watched the man stiffen, also. Just when I thought Tom and the man would actually fight over me, a deep voice rang out, "Tom. Could you come over here and bring your friend with you? Now."

The man called Etienne suddenly turned around and melted into the crowd without another word.

I turned to see who had called out. A tall, powerfully built older man with short, military-style salt and pepper hair stood over a huge grill covered with thick steaks. His face looked rugged, mature, seasoned by the elements. He wore a red-and-white checked apron that said "Grillers Do It With Heat." He looked up from the glowing coals, face flushed from the heat, and motioned with his tongs for Tom to come over.

Tom turned to me, "That's Bart, our alpha. He wants to meet you."

I looked around desperately for Aunt Amelia. I wanted her with me when I met the pack leader. Unfortunately, I didn't see her. "Tom, can we wait until my aunt gets here? And what happened with that guy? Did he really want to fight with you?" I asked.

He shook his head. "Sorry, babe. I'll explain pack rules later. We have the royal summons. Not good to keep the big Kahuna waiting."

As we approached the leader, the group who had been around him casually thinned out so that by the time we stood next to him, a circular clearing had formed around us. I noticed Tom kept his eyes averted, careful not to look directly at Bart. I remembered direct eye contact can be construed as a challenge among wolves. I guess it was the same for *weres*, or maybe it was just respect.

Bart flipped over a couple of steaks, then called another man over and handed him the tongs. He looked at me with intense pale blue eyes. The irises seemed a little too large to be entirely human. I thought of Little Red Riding Hood—What big eyes you have, Grandma.

He walked over to a picnic bench without even glancing our way, confident we would follow. The people sitting at the bench got up when they saw Bart approaching and wandered away, acting as if they had meant to leave just at that very moment. Bart used the tabletop as a seat and planted his feet solidly on the bench. He wore hiking boots. Tom and I stood in front of him. Tom looked silently at Bart's shoes. Guessing this was *were* protocol, I followed his lead.

Bart reached out with a hand big enough to have engulfed most of my head and gently lifted my chin. "Let's have a look at you, girl. So you're the one who's got our Tom all in a dither," he said, not unkindly. He had a natural commander's power and force in his voice. A good general's tone, the kind that made you want to obey and trust his orders were right. He had a hot, bright gold aura radiating out from him. It felt similar to Tom's but *more*. I shivered, but not from the cold, as his aura touched mine. Our energies immediately roiled together, knew each other, his wolf and mine brushing against each other, accepting each other as equals.

He withdrew his hand and looked a bit shaken, like he had encountered something he hadn't expected. "You're not one of us, but you're like us." He leaned forward, forearms on his knees, and sniffed in my direction. "You smell like pack and like Tom, but there's something else underneath, witch and something more that I don't recognize. What are you?" He frowned.

Okay. I did not want to answer his question because I wasn't sure what the answer was. I wished Aunt Amelia was here. I needed backup. I looked at Tom. His lips were pressed together in a tight line, like he wanted to say or do something but held himself back. I let out a breath I didn't realize I held when I saw my Aunt hurrying across the lawn. She looked worried when she spied Bart sitting on the bench in front of us.

As I glanced around, I noticed we had a considerable audience who tried hard not to look like an audience. About half of the pack had casually wandered closer, not looking at us, but definitely curious. I could almost see their ears perked up trying to catch what we were saying. Some were chewing on their steaks, which they picked up whole, dripping juices, and bit into. The steaks looked really rare. Most of the men had two or three on a plate. Suddenly, my mouth started watering and my stomach reminded me I hadn't eaten anything today. My reaction surprised me. I tended to eat more along vegetarian lines with occasional eggs and fish. But the smell of the cooking steaks was heavenly. I wiped a little drool from the corner of my mouth with the back of my hand. What had gotten into me?

"Cara." Tom said, apparently trying to get my attention.

"What? Oh, sorry." I turned back to our little group and found my aunt had joined us. Bart looked at me with an odd expression which included a certain covetousness—well, at least a good dollop of personal interest. Shades of Hades. Not another one.

I took a half step back but Amelia hooked her arm through mine as if she feared I'd run. She wasn't completely off the mark.

"Bart, I see you've met my niece. I wanted to introduce her to you myself, but I got tied up at the Fortson's house with their youngest girl. Her first canines are coming in early." She smiled calmly at the werewolf leader.

"Yes, Amelia. I just wanted to meet your niece on an informal basis. I got a taste of her power. Intoxicating, to say the least, like an alpha female." Bart looked directly at me as he said it. Beside me, Tom started to bristle. If he had hackles they'd probably be puffing out.

Bart glanced at Tom and sighed. "Calm down boy. I'm not going to challenge you for your witch."

Tom visibly relaxed his tense muscles, but he still watched Bart warily.

A male voice shouted out from the circle of people. "I have challenged him for the female."

I turned and saw it was Etienne, the guy who had purposely bumped into Tom earlier. He sauntered confidently up to our picnic table, staring at me as he approached. It wasn't the leer he'd given me earlier, but close. Okay, this was getting way out of hand.

"Don't I get a say in this? What is this 'challenge' stuff anyway?" I didn't give anyone a chance to answer as I said, "Let's get this straight. I'm not going off with some stranger no matter what happens." I crossed my arms and stood with my feet apart to show I meant business.

The men totally ignored me. Amelia squeezed my arm and gave me a warning look as she whispered, "Cara, let me take care of this. You don't know how things work in a pack."

I nodded, but it had better turn out that I wasn't some horny wolf's prize for beating up my familiar. I looked at Tom who now had changed his stance and demeanor. He wasn't the cute surfer dude anymore. He looked dangerous, wild. He stood in a slight crouch, arms tense, fingers facing outward and curved into claws, staring at his challenger. His eyes had changed to a burning amber color, spreading to cover nearly all the white so they now looked more wolf than human.

Before my aunt could even open her mouth to speak, Bart leapt off the table and stood between the two men. "I will not allow this! Stand down, both of you." The last part came out a low growl, as if his human throat had lost the ability to speak properly. I could feel waves of energy radiating off Bart like heat from a hot sidewalk in summer. It touched the entire assemblage, and I heard a few whines coming from the group. Here stood a man a little past his prime but still filled with power.

"Etienne, you are a visitor from the *Gevaudan* pack," he said in the growly, nonhuman voice. You cannot challenge one of mine. The ground rules for a multi-pack gathering apply, even for an informal event. There will be no challenges unless it's for leadership." He stared directly into Etienne's eyes. "Do you challenge me for pack leader?"

Etienne's eyes widened in fear and he quickly looked down. He shook his head and kneeled on the grass. "No, I do not challenge you. I wanted the woman only. I will obey the ground rules."

Bart nodded and seemed satisfied, but when he turned to look at Tom, the kneeling man pulled back his lips in a soundless snarl. A couple of men that I guessed were his friends came up behind Etienne and pulled him to his feet, urging him to go with them. They left together, but not before I got a scorching look from the departing would-be challenger.

Bart walked over to us and good-naturedly put an arm around both Tom's shoulders and mine as he said, "So, do you two want your steaks now? Let's eat."

Half an hour later Bart was gripping the edge of a picnic table so hard it started to crack under the strain, and his eyes and the veins in his neck bulged alarmingly. He hadn't taken the news about Tom's new status as my familiar very well.

To my aunt, he said surprisingly softly, considering how he looked, "Only *animals* are familiars, *not people*. We may be werewolves, but we are people first and foremost. It's illegal, and frankly immoral, for anyone to bind another person to them. You know that."

Aunt Amelia bravely put her hand over one of his and talked to him in a low, urgent tone. I couldn't hear what she said, but whatever it was seemed to be working. Bart let go of the table. He nodded and looked at Tom, then looked at me and nodded some more. His facial coloring had returned to a more natural hue, and his veins had decided to retreat back into his muscular neck. He might be calming down, but I felt wound up. I couldn't take just sitting and waiting.

"Tom, let's go for a walk," I said.

He looked uncertain, stealing a glance at his pack leader's back. "I don't know, Cara. We should stick around, just in case."

"I have to do something. Besides, this is nerve-racking." I poked at my cold, half-eaten steak with a plastic fork, then pushed the plate away. I jumped up from the bench, grabbed his hand and pulled. "Come on. Please? Just a quick, super-short walk." I opened my eyes wide, pursed my lips in just a hint of pout and gave him my best cajoling look, the one I'd learned from Evika. "Pretty please?"

He chuckled. "We really shouldn't, but I just can't say no to you, babe. Okay. A really short walk, and not too far."

With one more glance towards Bart and Amelia, we started

walking towards the trailhead marker. Tom had pointed it out earlier, telling me it led to a nice one-mile loop with great views. It sounded perfect to get out some of my nervous energy, but it wouldn't take us too far from the others.

We walked hand-in-hand down the trail. Tom seemed to be on the alert; he kept scanning the sides of the trail, lifting his head and sniffing the air every so often. Then he suddenly said, "Did you know our kind, werewolves, came through the portal as servants and slaves for Nightkinds and witches?"

I nodded, "My professor in Portal History mentioned it briefly, but that's ancient history."

"*Weres* had to fight for their independence as people. The Houses didn't want to give up all the free labor. You know, farmhand by day, security wolf by night. Sweet deal for the House, but bogus for the werewolf."

"A lot of the Houses have *were* security these days. It's almost a status symbol."

"Yeah, and the *weres* get paid a bundle to do it. It's a career, not slavery."

"I see your point. So, is that why Bart got so angry? Because he thought I was treating you like an animal and a slave by making you my familiar?"

Probably. I mean, I can't read his mind or anything, but I'll bet it's a big part of why he reacted badly. It took a long time for others to really see us as people with a special condition instead of just animals."

"Hmmm." I hadn't realized *were* feelings about their past were still sensitive, still so close to the surface, like a wound just starting to heal. I guess I should have realized it, but all this was so far out of my everyday realm of existence it just hadn't occurred to me. In this country and others there have been, probably still are, similar situations between different races of humans. I'd been pretty sheltered growing up, and it occurred to me that I'd really had very limited contact with other types of beings until recently. Until now, I'd never met a Nightkind or werewolf in person. I had a few wizard acquaintances in college, but I was homeschooled through high school because I couldn't keep up with use-of-power classes like the other young witches. The only demons I knew were Uncle Max and Cousin Sonya, and they were only part demon and family. I didn't know a thing about the fae, except they were extremely reclusive and, in many ways, just as dangerous as demons.

We walked along the trail in silence as I digested this information. I felt a little ashamed of my naiveté, but there was no going back. I had made Tom my familiar. According to Aunt Amelia, no matter how I felt about it, or even how Tom or his pack leader felt about it, it was a done deal. No rewind button or do-over allowed. I'd inadvertently made Tom my familiar and we both had to live with the fact, whether we liked it or not. I hoped we could both learn to like it; otherwise, life was going to be a little slice of *Hades*.

I took a deep breath of the cold, fresh, salty sea air and looked around. We had walked to the halfway point of the trail, and I spotted a small fenced area on the edge of a cliff overlooking the ocean. We looked over the fence. Below us I saw a small white crescent of beach, Piles of seaweed had washed up to the shore. I shivered, thinking about the anamorphous attack.

Tom wrapped his arms around me. I snuggled against his chest, listened to his heart beat, and felt his warmth. His wolf brushed gently against my aura, and my wolf responded, the two energies settling into each other like old friends, curling around us in a protective circle. For a moment I forgot everything, luxuriating. I felt warm, protected, and this felt more like home to me than my own home ever did.

I wanted more, greedy little thing that I am, and I unbuttoned the top of Tom's shirt so I could feel his skin. I ran my hand over the smooth muscles of his chest, rubbed my face against his skin where my hands had been, and inhaled the male scent of him, with its musky wolf undertone. I licked the skin nearest my mouth to taste the salty-sweetness of him, and he tightened his hold on me, letting me drink him into my senses.

"Oh, babe, you're killing me," he groaned as he caught my head in his hands and brought his mouth down on mine.

As our kiss deepened, our energies swirled and grew, and our beasts rolled in and over each other, sending waves of hot pleasure through us both. Suddenly, in unison, our wolves turned their heads and snarled, sensing an intruder.

Tom and I quickly broke apart to face whatever had alarmed our beasts. It was Etienne. His eyelids were half-closed as he rubbed his hands over his arms, like he was bathing in something.

He looked at me with naked lust. "I knew you were special the moment I saw you. I followed you downwind so you wouldn't smell my presence. I felt your passion and had to come closer. It is like nothing I have experienced before." His handsome face twisted as he emitted a deep growl. "I must have you, to be inside that hot energy."

Tom stepped in front of me, "You touch her and I'll rip you apart."

Etienne grinned savagely, little more than a baring of his teeth. "You could try, *mon ami*."

I grabbed Tom's arm. Our beasts were still connected and ready to fight this impudent outsider. Before I could say anything I felt the wolf-energies leap out from us and crash into Etienne. He looked surprised as he flew through the air. He plowed through a thick strand of poison oak and flailed wildly as he tumbled downhill, coming to rest on a small rock outcropping.

Tom and I looked at each other and ran over to the side of the trail. Etienne crawled through the poisonous shrubs back to the trail, his face red with anger. I figured it would be red with a nice itchy rash pretty soon. I grabbed Tom's hand. "Come on. Run!"

We ran side by side toward the picnic area as we heard Etienne cursing at us in French, and we didn't stop until we were back at the picnic grounds. We were laughing like children, fueled by adrenaline and the wonder of the manifestation of our combined power.

But the laughter died on our lips as we noticed the palpable tension in the people around us. I looked around for Amelia, finally spotting her sitting alone on a large rock at the edge of the picnic area. She didn't look happy.

Bart stood on the other side of the area with a small group of men who were all frowning and murmuring amongst themselves. This didn't look good. When we left for our walk it seemed like the conversation between my aunt and the pack leader was going well. What had happened?

I looked at Tom, "Divide and conquer? I'll talk to Amelia; you find out what's happening with the pack?" Tom nodded and loped towards the knot of men while I went to Amelia.

Aunt Amelia looked up as I approached. I could see she'd been crying—her eyelashes were wet and her eyes were red. Oh no! I just knew I didn't want to hear what had happened between her and Bart. The pesky little voice in the back of my head started telling me to think of people I could go visit for a while, how long it would take to pack my bags, and the best way to ask if my werewolf familiar could come along, too. Zul's horns! I should've known this wasn't going to turn out okay.

Amelia slowly got to her feet when I walked up to her. She took both my hands in hers, "Dear, I have some bad news." I noticed she looked tired, her true age showing for the first time since I'd met her.

"Bart refuses to acknowledge Tom as your familiar. He has ordered us to 'undo it.' I kept trying to tell him it can't be undone, but he won't listen to me." We both turned to look in Bart's direction as we heard a commotion. Etienne had come stumbling out from the trailhead, covered in poison oak leaves, his eyes blazing in fury. He ran straight for Bart's group, yelling and pointing at Tom the whole way.

Bart broke away from the other men to deal with the situation. I noticed his mouth tweak up at one corner, like he was trying not to laugh as he listened to the wildly gesturing, disheveled *were*.

I started forward to join them, but Amelia grabbed my arm. "No, don't interfere. This is pack business."

"But I'm part of it. I have to explain what that guy tried to do." My voice rose as I watched Bart's expression turn dark.

I heard the pack leader shout out Tom's name. Now Bart, Tom and Etienne were shouting at each other until Bart, roaring for silence, reached out with his both hands and cuffed each of the younger *weres* on the sides of their heads. The two men fell to the ground and stayed there, eyes downcast.

"Amelia, come here please. Bring your niece with you," Bart called to us.

The other pack members had retreated so just the five of us were standing together, but I noticed plenty of bright eyes looking curiously in our direction.

Bart looked only at Amelia as he spoke. "This pup—" He pointed at Etienne. "—claims your niece and Tom attacked him on the trail."

Etienne snarled at the word "pup." I guess it was considered derogatory in *were* culture.

"He followed us and tried to get to Cara!" Tom burst out.

"Silence!" Bart glared at him. "See? He doesn't deny what happened, just tries to justify it. Amelia, you know I will not have this kind of hostility between packs in my territory. When I took over as pack leader, I swore to maintain peace between the Shadow-hunters and the other packs while continuing my efforts to lobby for *were* equality. Your niece has been here for what? A couple of days? She has managed to bind a member of my pack to her like a common dog, and caused two members of different packs to fight each other over her."

"Now, Bart, you know that isn't being fair to Cara, and . . ." my aunt began in a placating tone.

"Stop right there, Amelia. You fix it and soon, or you are no longer our Shaman. Until Tom is freed, your niece is no longer welcome here." Bart looked down at Tom. "Tom, I order you to stay away from these witches from now on."

At his words I felt a heavy weight on my chest. I could barely breathe around the intense and sudden grief I felt at the possibility of losing Tom.

Tom looked up at me and thinned his lips. His eyes were glistening with unshed tears. "No. I won't stay away. I want to be with Cara."

"If you do, you will no longer be a member of this pack and will be considered an outcast, a rogue wolf. I'll give you twenty-four hours to reconsider." Bart looked sorry, regretful, but stubbornly determined to carry out the sentence.

Tom looked stricken. I walked over, knelt down beside him on the cold, wet grass and put my arms around him as Aunt Amelia pleaded, "Bart, please don't do this to the boy. The pack is his only family."

Bart ignored her. He held up an arm and pointed to the street, "Etienne, go back to your own pack. You've caused enough trouble here."

Etienne gave us all a menacing look but said nothing as he got up and walked away. But after a few paces he turned around, as if he couldn't help himself, and spat, "This is not the end. I shall tell the *Gevaudan* pack of my mistreatment by the Shadow-Hunters, and they will not be pleased. You say you want peace? Now you have caused a war!"

Other than clenched fists, Bart gave no indication he was affected by the threat. He held up his hand as a few of the men looked as if they wanted to stop Etienne from leaving. At Bart's signal they stood still, looking unhappy.

Despite the icy moisture soaking into the knees of my pants, Tom and I leaned against each other, foreheads touching. Our hair merged together to form a shimmering curtain around our faces. I whispered, "I'm so sorry. I can't let you leave your pack for me."

He whispered back, "It's okay, babe, as long as I can be with you."

I shut my eyes and wondered, not for the first time, if I had ruined his life.

* * * *

Aunt Amelia hung up the kitchen phone, "Well, you can't go back to Sonya's house or to your parents' house right now. The Nightkinds have them under constant surveillance. We haven't been able to persuade Roman to stop this nonsense. He's obsessed with you, Cara, and apparently has convinced his higher-ups to support him in his foolishness. If only your grandmother were alive. She knew the ways of the Nightkinds better than anyone, even forged a temporary alliance in her early years as Head of the House."

I arched a brow at this. It fit in with what Roman had told me during his visitation.

The three of us were sitting at the kitchen table sipping tea. We'd left the park and walked home right after Bart's ultimatum.

"Who were you talking to?" I asked my aunt.

"Maximillian," she replied.

My stomach briefly clenched, but I didn't say anything. After all, I didn't have any proof it was Uncle Max at the restaurant the night of my birthday. All I had was Roman's vague description and the fact we called the person "Uncle." I wasn't inclined to fully trust anything Roman said to me. I wished again that I could remember what had happened that night, but there was still a gaping hole in my head where those memories should've been. I started getting a headache just trying to think about it.

The phone rang; Amelia answered it, and then held the receiver out to me. "It's Paul." I glanced at Tom's scowl as I walked over to the phone.

"Hi, Paul."

"Cara. Good to hear your voice. You know, I haven't been able to stop thinking about you over the last few days. What time shall I pick you up tomorrow night for our dinner date? Jenny is 'whipping up the ultimate chocolate dessert' for us. Her words, not mine."

"Oh, Paul it sounds wonderful, but I won't be able to keep our date. There's been some, um, complications with the local *were* pack, and I have to leave town right away."

"Complications? What kind of complications?" He sounded both surprised and concerned.

"I really don't want to go into it, but I've basically been told to get out of town. It was great meeting you. I'm sorry it didn't work out."

"Stay there. I'm coming over."

"Paul, no. You don't have to do that. Paul?" He had hung up.

A short time later the four of us sat on Amelia's floor pillows in the living room, discussing what had happened. Paul had come striding in wearing a long, black, cashmere coat, unbuttoned so it billowed out behind him as he walked. Underneath he wore gray wool pants and a burgundy sweater. His chiseled cheeks were flushed from the cold, with just a little shadow of beard showing, like he'd forgotten to shave this morning. He looked adorably serious and seriously sexy. I had a moment when I thought he'd have problems with sitting on the floor, being so tall, but he just eyed the pillows, gracefully folded up his long legs and lounged back like he always sat on floor pillows. Didn't everyone?

By the time the night had ended, Paul had convinced me to stay at his Lake Tahoe cabin. He assured us the cabin was quasi-isolated, warded and safe because he would join me there. When I expressed concern about his gallery business, he explained that his assistant could look after it, just as she would if Paul were to go off on an extended buying trip, and it would not be any trouble at all. The big issue was Tom. Paul made it clear he didn't want Tom to join us in his lake-side retreat without actually coming out and saying it. I hoped he didn't have visions of cozy, romantic dinners by the fire.

Amelia and I explained the whole familiar thing to him. In the back of my mind I thought he would withdraw his offer when he found out, but ever the gentleman, he didn't like it but he accepted it with raised eyebrows and no condemnation. What a guy. I liked him more every time I saw him. He even extended the invitation to Amelia.

She reluctantly refused and explained she had to stay behind to try to talk some sense into Bart and, just as important, to continue to take care of the *were* and witch community with her herbs and potions. She was the closest thing to a doctor some of them would trust with their illnesses. Some so-called "real" human doctors still refused to treat a patient with lycanthropy for fear of contamination. Amelia considered those doctors ignorant fools and refused to abandon her pack, even if their leader acted like a "bullheaded idiot." We would leave tomorrow. Paul would make all the travel arrangements, and Aunt Amelia would contact the family to give them an update. I was on the move again, but this time I had my familiar with me—a big, blond, lusty one I didn't know how to deal with— and a charming wizard for company. Could my life get any more complicated? I didn't even want an answer to that question because I was afraid of what it would be.

Chapter Eleven
Tahoe

We said our good-byes to Aunt Amelia with lots of hugs and assurances of keeping in touch. She said she had a game plan for convincing Bart to accept Tom as my familiar and averting a pack war with the *Gevaudan* clan. We sincerely wished her luck. Tom gave her an extra hug.

Paul had arranged for a shuttle bus to take us to the airport. He didn't want to leave his car in the parking garage. We loaded our luggage into a small private airplane owned by a longtime client turned good friend of Paul's. The rocky ride, due to air turbulence was only slightly scary, mostly exhilarating. Tom excitedly pressed his nose against his window, making comments about every interesting cloud and land feature. Paul sat up front in the copilots seat, keeping his friend company. I just tried to relax and not think about anything overly much. I only roused to make some noncommittal noise when Tom wanted to know if I thought a particular cloud looked like a wolf or how swimming pools looked like turquoise stones thrown across the drab housing developments. Then there was the dizzying dip into the airport, over the tops of tall trees. The aircraft seemed to skim too close for comfort to the steep mountainsides right before we landed.

Paul had rented a good sized SUV and arranged to have it waiting for us at the airport. We all piled in after transferring the luggage from the plane to the back compartment of the vehicle. Tom only brought a beat-up looking duffle bag, Paul had a medium-sized roller bag, and I had my two large matching suitcases with an overnight case. Hey, a girl had to have clothing options for changing weather conditions. Right?

The lake looked picture beautiful with incredible bright blue water, snow-covered mountains, and evergreen trees everywhere. Paul drove while doing the host thing by talking about available activities, if we were careful to stay incognito. There were casinos shows, restaurants, skiing and snowboarding, and hiking. Tom wanted to go "boarding." I told them I was really more a snow-bunny type, preferring to sip hot cocoa by a lodge fireplace to being on the slopes. I'd tried skiing a long time ago and basically turned into a human-shaped cannonball, wreaking havoc on my fellow skiers and leaving a trail of destruction in my wake. Besides, I usually spent more time on my backside than on my feet, which left me cold, sore, and cranky. The guys looked at each other in silent male communication. I just knew they were making fun of me.

After stopping in at a grocery store to load up on provisions, we continued for a ways until finally taking a hard left off the main road and traveling another mile or so along a narrow, barely-paved road to emerge into a clearing. I saw a modest, wooden, two-story house with a peaked roof located at the far end of a circular patch of gravel. It nestled between a strand of pine trees and a tumble of massive boulders; white-frosted mountain peaks showcased in the distance. I grabbed the car door handle and jumped out almost before Paul came to a complete stop. I gratefully stretched my cramped muscles, walking around in front of the house, snow crunching beneath my feet. The flight to Tahoe together with the car ride, had made me stiff. I felt a little guilty letting the men carry in my luggage, but not overly so. I picked up my overnight case and walked up the stairs and into the house.

Paul had decorated the inside of his cabin in rustic chic, with big, man-sized furniture made out of leather and wood. The bottom floor consisted of one big room, with sofas, chairs, and tables defining each area's usage. A sofa and a couple of overstuffed chairs were positioned in front of a beautiful stone fireplace. A long dining table with a bench sat on one side of a large picture window, and wooden dining chairs sat on the other side. Native American style rugs hung on the walls and carpeted the floors. A pile of cut wood stood waiting by the fireplace.

Paul pointed to a doorway by the dining table, "There's the kitchen and a bathroom. The bedrooms are upstairs."

I looked at the stairs, "Which one is mine?"

"You can have my room. It has an attached bath so you don't have to walk down the hall in the middle of the night if you need to use the facilities."

"I can't take your room," I objected. "I'll just take one of the other rooms."

"Cara, no arguing. It would be much better this way. Please."

How could I refuse? "Well, okay. Thanks. That's very considerate."

"Tom and I will take the rooms on either side of you. We'll

be able to get to you fast, just in case anything happens."

"I like the getting to you fast part, anyway," Tom said, grinning.

Paul looked annoyed but said nothing. Awkward.

We settled in at last, as the sun started to set. I would have normally enjoyed watching as the colors of sunset painted the tops of the mountain ranges, but something made me jumpy, nervous, like too much caffeine. There was going to be a full moon tonight. The moment I thought it, I felt my wolf moving just under my skin. The wolf that had formed when I bonded with Tom. I thought it was just the way his wolf had become my familiar, of my power identifying with him. Now, a deep fear welled up inside me that hadn't been present when Tom and I first bonded. I couldn't be a *were*, Tom hadn't attacked me in his wolf form. This couldn't be happening! Yet, the smooth brush of her fur made me scratch at my arms. My skin had an itch, a tickle, and a painful pleasure. All those feelings rolled into one and left me feeling like she would soon burst out of me. No! This . . . couldn't . . . be . . . happening! I doubled over as a wave of nausea hit me. Dizzy, I stumbled drunkenly to the bathroom to dry heave into the toilet. I hadn't had anything to eat since breakfast, which consisted of half a cup of coffee and two bites of wheat toast. I felt both happy about my stomach being empty and sorry I was going through all this with nothing to show for it.

I felt hands holding my hair, rubbing my back. "Cara, what's wrong?" Tom's voice.

The sensations inside me got worse, made me want to tear off my skin to make it stop. I could feel my she-wolf rise out of me, snarling. I couldn't form words. This impudent male comes too close; he hadn't earned the right to touch me. I whipped my head to the side. My teeth were sharp and drew blood as I snapped at his hand holding my hair. A cold, little part of me thought his blood tasted like ambrosia and wanted more. With an effort of sheer will, I stopped myself from grabbing his wrist to get at the sweet hot blood flowing just under the surface.

Footsteps. Paul's voice. "Zul's horns! Is she infected? Did you infect her, you son-of-a-bitch?"

Tom was wretched away from me. The males were shouting, growling at each other. Good. They should fight to see who wins me. Only the strong are deserving of Her.

I lifted my head, looking for escape. The moon called to

me, an achingly beautiful siren song telling me to run, to be free, to hunt, to leave this place far behind. The males' voices distracted me. Words floated in the air, tinged with anger. They glowed hot red then cooled to black ash like embers. *Not infected . . . why is she changing? She can't . . . I'm changing . . . what do I do . . . .I don't know . . . have to leave . . . NOW . . .*

The change started coming on the younger male. He smelled like pack, but his blood smelled like food. My stomach cramped with hunger, the nausea gone, replaced with craving. The other male turned to me, blue eyes calm but wary. He had a stick in his hand; it radiated power. Symbols carved into the wood glowed white. Not a stick, a wand. I sensed an almost solid outer layer of energy form around him, one I couldn't see but knew existed. He talked to me in calming tones; it sounded like gibberish. I needed to run, to hunt, to sing to the goddess moon. He barred my way. How dare he! Fury rose in me. I leapt at him, wanting to bite and rend flesh. I came upon his barrier and it threw me backwards.

I fell hard against the sink, pain shooting up my arm, momentarily clearing my head. "Paul? What's happening?"

"Cara, let me help you. You're not yourself. Trust me. Please."

He held out his hand tentatively through his protective shield. My she-wolf sniffed at it, thoughts crafty. I lifted my uninjured arm and clasped his hand with mine, then yanked hard to pull him to me. My teeth clamped on his forearm drawing blood. Oh, he tasted like liquid lightening, this wizard! I let go to scream in triumph and ecstasy as his blood was absorbed into me.

He took the opportunity to touch me with his wand. Suddenly I couldn't move. Ropes of light held me tight as he lifted me off the bathroom floor and carried me into the big room. I struggled against the light, howling my rage. I looked around wildly for escape. The other wolf had left. The door stood wide open, icy wind blowing into the room, carrying the forest scents of deer, rabbit, wolf, and blood. I struggled more fiercely, I needed to go, be free, to catch the soft warm thing in my mouth, taste its blood searing my throat and filling my belly.

The male's annoying voice interrupted my thoughts, "Cara, please. Come back. I know you're in there somewhere."

I stopped thrashing to look at him. Something in me liked

his power, assessing him with a strange logic amidst the pull of the moon madness. I felt the powers shift. My wolf was unhappy, whining as she lay down. I felt another power rise, felt it take Her energy to use as fuel, take the blood of the *were* and the wizard to rise and build on itself. My hunger for blood changed into hunger of another kind. Paul. My power reached out to caress him.

His eyes widened then closed halfway in pleasure, and he took a ragged breath. "No, Cara. You don't know what you're doing."

I felt his power, connected to it by his blood, pulled it out, wrapped around it, twining his and mine together like sweet taffy. The bonds around me melted as his will dissolved, and we reached for each other. Our energies merged, flowing in and out of each other, so bright we cast shadows on the walls. We tore off our clothes, impatient with the obstacles prohibiting us from feeling skin against skin. We fell to the floor, limbs entwined, mingled auras forming a brilliant nimbus surrounding us.

He lay outstretched on top of me, holding my hands above my head, as if afraid I'd tear at him with my nails.

"Let me touch you," I stated hoarsely.

He hesitated a moment, then let go, trusting or, perhaps, hoping I wouldn't harm him. I ran my hands over his shoulders, down his arms. He began kissing my neck, my breasts, the soft curls between my legs, licking, sucking, nipping until I felt desperate for more. I reached down and grabbed handfuls of his hair, pulling him up for a kiss wet with the taste of me.

The energy around us felt heavier, pulsating. I heard an unearthly howl in the woods as I urged Paul to sink into me. He rubbed himself against me, wetting the tip of him, and pushed in slowly, pushed until he was completely sheathed. He looked down at me once, then he started to move. I grabbed at his back, bucking beneath him from the incredible pleasure. From our joined bodies, rays of power arched into the air like solar flares. Each slide of him inside me became exquisite torture, so incredible it was almost unbearable. I could feel the familiar, heavy build of sensation between my legs. The power pushed at us, a crushing weight, but I didn't care. I was so close, so close. And then it crashed over me in wave after wave of pleasure. I cried out. Paul pushed up on his arms, his spine bowed, head thrown back, eyes shut as he pushed one more time and spilled himself inside me. A bright flash of power burst out from our solar plexuses, engulfing us for an instant, then drawing back into us, like film going in reverse, until it vanished completely and we were left utterly spent and breathless on the cold floor.

Paul pushed himself off of me and slowly slid his arm across my stomach. It seemed a monumental effort for him to do so. I stared at the exposed beam ceiling, not thinking of anything. A flash of fur darted across my peripheral vision, but when I turned my head, it vanished. Then another flash. Gone again. I struggled to sit up but lay trapped under the weight of Paul's arm.

Another flash of white-gray fur, tall ears, cottontail, and I ran through the snow. I pursued my prey, four legs running, claws gripping the icy ground, breath steaming. I could smell the little warm thing's fear and it excited me. I ran and changed direction, weaving through brush and rocks, following the scent trail like a ribbon of color in the night air. And then it zigged when it should have zagged, and I had it by the back of the neck. It screamed and I thought that sounded good. It sounded like triumph and eating. I held its body with a paw and bit down, felt the rapture of hot blood gushing into my mouth. I wanted to devour my prize in one bite, to take its life into myself in the eternal way of the predator. I heard something, someone, calling. I lifted my head, licking my muzzle with a swipe of my long tongue, ears swiveling to locate and identify the source. My vision faded to gray, and when it cleared, I found myself on the floor of the cabin, Paul calling my name.

"I—I was outside. I was a wolf and I caught a rabbit," I told him. It sounded so mundane to explain such an experience.

"Are you alright? Your eyes were glazed and you seemed to be in a trance. I couldn't snap you out of it. I think you may have been seeing through Tom's eyes. It's one of the connections which can be made with a familiar." As he spoke, Paul grabbed an afghan off the sofa and covered us.

"But it wasn't just seeing. It felt like I *was* him—feeling and doing everything he did. It seemed so real." I looked at Paul, suddenly uncomfortable. "Uh . . . I guess we'd better get dressed."

He pulled me closer to his body, throwing one of his long limbs over my legs. The course hairs on his calf brushed pleasantly along my skin. His warm breath was against my neck as he said, "Cara? Are you okay about what we just did? I don't want you to think I took advantage of you. Zul knows I've wanted to be with you since the moment you sat down next to me on the plane. I didn't want to stop. I couldn't stop. I lost all judgment, rationality, the instant your power touched me. I think it would have killed me if you had said anything to make me think you didn't want to." He propped his head on his hand, elbow resting on the carpet, and looked at me. "The power—you were amazing. I've never experienced anything even remotely like that before."

"Uh, thanks. You were great, too. Don't worry, I wanted to do this just as much as you did, maybe more. I think being with you saved me from something very bad."

"In the heat of the moment, I didn't think to use protection," Tom said, looking at me with his forehead wrinkled in a frown.

"Don't worry, I'm fine, protected," I told him. His forehead smoothed as he visibly relaxed.

Blessed-be-the-portal, I had asked Amelia to work a birth control charm on me before we left. It looked like a small tattoo-like mark on my hip, a diamond shape with a line through the middle to prevent the male and female essences from becoming fertile.

I struggled to extricate myself from Paul's leg and the afghan. I was looking around for my clothes when I noticed the oozing teeth marks on Paul's arm. "Zul's horns, did I do that to you?" I gasped.

He glanced down at the wound and shrugged. "It's nothing. I'll heal. I don't think you have lycanthropy, so I'm not overly concerned. At first I thought Tom had infected you, but when you didn't change I knew it couldn't have been that. If you were infected you would have changed, and nothing you or anyone else did would have been able to stop it. But something did happen, and it seemed definitely *were*-like. I think it's because of your connection with Tom. You're going to have to learn to control the connection, get your—I guess I'd call it your working relationship with him—going smoothly."

I stood, taking the afghan with me and leaving Paul naked on the floor. "Sorry, but I'm taking the blanket."

He laughed, standing up in all his glory, and went to close the front door. He looked like he worked out, but not too much. I saw definite muscle definition on his lean frame.

"The blanket is yours. Throw me my jeans, would you?"

He easily caught them in one hand and slipped them on. I had a cringe moment when he zipped them, but apparently he knew how to handle going commando. We moved around the room in comfortable silence, putting furniture back where it belonged. How did those chairs get turned over and stacked on top of each other? I decided I didn't want to know.

Paul made some soup to eat by the fire and we settled in for the night. We agreed to not talk about the nights' events until tomorrow. Unfortunately, I knew tomorrow would have an irritating way of showing up sooner than I'd like.

At dawn the next morning, the front door banged open, waking us up. Paul and I were sleeping in the master bedroom, having decided that after what happened it would be silly to sleep in separate beds. Besides, it had been cold and I'd decided he was better than an extra blanket. Thankfully, he hadn't tried for a repeat performance. I'd been too wiped out to do much more than take his hand, walk up the stairs and crawl into bed with him.

We ran downstairs and saw wet footprints on the wood flooring between the rugs. They led from the front door to the kitchen. Tom came out the kitchen door, holding a carton of orange juice and staggering slightly. He was naked and shivering, wet hair plastered to his head. I grabbed the handy afghan and threw it over his shoulders as he chugged from the container. He pulled the blanket closer around him with his free hand as he finished the juice.

Then he collapsed on a chair, leaned his head back and closed his eyes. "Oh, man. It always feels like I have a hangover the day after a full moon." He sniffed at the afghan, "I see you two didn't waste any time hooking up." He looked sharply at Paul, "I expected to see your bloody remains after Cara finished with you, but you managed to get laid instead. Pretty good, wiz, how did that happen?"

I saw a flash of anger on Paul's face. I put a hand on his arm to let him know we should cut Tom some slack as I said, "I was in really bad shape when you left last night. I think my connection with you made it seem like I was going to change, *were*-out, you know? Paul did what he had to do to redirect my power."

Tom glared at us, stood, threw off the afghan, and stalked upstairs without a word. Paul and I looked at each other, and I shrugged. Tom would just have to get over it. What happened had happened. I hadn't made any romantic commitments to either of them. I didn't have any reason to feel bad about hurt male pride. That's my story and I'm sticking to it, although I did feel an annoying twinge of guilt, which I quickly kicked down the cellar stairs and, for good measure, slammed the denial door shut on it.

* * * *

"Control is not willpower. It's more a matter of focusing on the right thing," Paul said. "You know those computer optical illusion pictures that look like blobs of color until you focus your eyes just right and suddenly you see a three-dimensional picture? It's like that. You need to find what you want inside of you and coax it out. Trying to reach in and grab it will only make it more elusive."

I nodded at Paul. Okay, I could do this.

"Alright, let's try it again," he said. "This time, don't try so hard. Just let yourself relax, get into your Zen state, for lack of a better term. Ask the power in you to come out and play."

I took a deep breath, held it a couple of seconds, then let it out slowly, just like we had been practicing. *Come out, come out, wherever you are,* I called to my power.

Paul stood behind me and started gently massaging my shoulders. I felt my muscles relax. I hadn't even realized I'd tensed them. Then he pulled my hair to the side and started kissing the nape of my neck.

"Paul, I'm trying to concentrate here." I groused.

"Go ahead. Don't pay any attention to me." I bent my head forward to give him better access. His warm lips were oh-so-soft and nice. The power I had been seeking rose up to the surface, made itself available to me. As it flowed through my body, I carefully raised my hand and pointed to one of the overstuffed leather chairs by the fireplace. It started moving, rocking back and forth. I did a little palm up lifting gesture and the chair flipped into the air, landed on one front leg and balanced there. I did a little circular motion with my raised hand and the chair started spinning like a top on its leg.

Paul whispered, "Good, good. Now keep your focus."

I nodded, trying to push down my elation and keep the chair spinning.

"Whoa!" Tom said as he came down the stairs.

I turned my head toward him, and the chair spun up into the air, crashed into the wall, then fell to the floor with a thud and a crack as one of the legs broke on impact.

"Tom, you made me lose it, "I said, exasperated.

"I happened to be quite fond of that chair," Paul muttered as he walked over to assess the damage. He squatted and studied it. "Looks fixable. Just needs a new leg. Frame is still intact." He stood and dusted his hands off on his jeans. "Well then, let's do our next practice session outdoors, shall we?"

Tom came over and gave me a quick kiss. "I'm going to hit the slopes. Want to go with?"

I shook my head, "No thanks. I have enough to worry about without breaking my leg or someone else's. Anyway, my shoulder's still sore from last night. I hit it on the sink." A thought occurred to me, "If you take the car, we're stuck here."

Paul spoke up. "I have a snow mobile in the shed out back. We can use it in an emergency."

Tom looked out the living room window, "Dude, I'm still not talking to you, but that's cool about the snow mobile. I'll take the car." He turned to look at me. "See ya later, babe. I'll be back before it gets dark. It's still close to the full moon so I don't want to be in public places after sunset."

I shook my head, but smiled fondly at Tom's back as he left the cabin. "You know, I feel like I've been on a roller coaster since this whole Synemancer thing started happening to me."

"What do you mean?"

"I was just living my life, you know? Going along, minding my own business, no worries or responsibilities, when WHAM, I'm suddenly an irresistible sex goddess with a contract out on her head."

"Sex goddess?" He burst into laughter.

"Hey, quit laughing. I'm serious."

"I know," he said around guffaws.

"I mean it, stop laughing." Men! Can't live with 'em, can't kill 'em.

As if in response to my bruised ego, various small objects around the room started hovering in the air. Paul looked around with mock alarm. "Now, Cara. I was only joshing you."

"Josh this, Mister Wizard." He ducked as pillows, tissue boxes, socks, pinecones, and candles started pelting him. Now I laughed as I searched for more things to throw at him. I didn't want to really hurt him, so I looked at, but dismissed the woodpile by the fireplace. Apparently my power clicked onto autopilot because just looking at the wood made the pile start moving. The cut logs lined up like soldiers in a row before flying towards him one after the other. I kind of marveled at my growing ability while another part of me panicked. "Paul, look out! I can't stop it!"

His eyes widened as he ran, stopping briefly to pick up a dining room chair to use as a shield over his head. "Cara, listen to me. You *can* stop this. Focus!"

I watched in horror as the first of the logs smashed into the chair he held. He had somehow managed to get his wand between his teeth and started to chant something out of the side of his mouth. Three more logs hit the chair, knocking it to the floor. He couldn't dodge the next one completely; it grazed his forehead leaving a long, shallow cut. As soon as I saw the blood I knew what to do. I felt an immediate sense of calm come over me. Everything in the air dropped to the floor as I cut off the power. I ran over to Paul.

"Are you okay? I'm so sorry!"

"I'm fine. I see you found your focus." He held his hand over the cut on his head, but smiled.

I had an ugly suspicion. "You did that on purpose, didn't you? You goaded me into getting mad at you."

"It worked, didn't it?" He gestured to the room littered with wood and the other odds and ends I had thrown at him.

"I could have hurt you."

"But you didn't because you didn't *want* to hurt me. As a matter of fact, I was quite counting on that fact. Now, let's see if you can use your power to straighten up this mess. It'll be good practice. While you're at it, I'll see if I can find the first aid kit."

As he walked out of the room, I acknowledge that he was right. I had found my focus, at least for moving smallish objects around. One power down, but way too many to go.

After putting everything back in their proper places, with lots of encouragement from Paul, I was exhausted. I had to have food and maybe a nap, not necessarily in that order. And definitely something sweet. I had an intense craving for sugar, chocolate, anything sweet.

Paul walked out of the kitchen with a tray of sandwiches, a teapot, and a couple of mugs. He set the tray on the dining table, and I sat, grabbed a mug, filled it with steaming hot tea, and then put five cubes of sugar in it.

Paul cocked an eyebrow at me but didn't say a word until I had finished the tea, drinking it too fast and burning the roof of my mouth in the process. "Some witches carry candy or other snacks with them for energy. You'll have to be careful not to drain yourself too much without recharging, so to speak."

I nodded. "Yeah, my Cousin Evika used to always have chocolate in her purse. Her 'emergency stash' she called it." The thought of my cousin made me sad. "I miss her. I hope she's alright wherever she is. With all this stuff going on, I haven't been thinking about her as much as I should. We have to find her."

"Your family is working on it. It's not all up to you, you know."

"I know. But I can't help feeling her kidnapping is somehow because of me."

"You don't know that."

"Yeah, I know, but my gut tells me it's true."

Paul's cell phone rang. While he answered it, I picked up a cucumber sandwich and nibbled at it. Who makes cucumber sandwiches, anyway? Must be an English thing.

Paul handed the phone to me, "It's your Cousin Sonya. Your Aunt gave her my number."

I took the phone and smiled at him in thanks as I put it up to my ear. "Hey, girl. How are you and the boys?"

That's all it took for her to launch into her latest Hound story. Apparently Jupiter and Archer had caught and ate a Nightkind who got too close to her house last night. Now the two of them were hacking up little piles of goopy ash on her carpet. She'd been vacuuming with a wet/dry Shop-Vac all morning, worried her babies had gotten their tummies upset from their nasty Nightkind snack. I brought her up-to-date on what had happened since we'd last talked, leaving out some of the juicier bits in case Paul could hear me. By the time I hung up, an hour had passed. She always had an uncanny ability to call just as I thought of her or Evika. I hadn't brought up the subject of her Dad possibly being at the restaurant the night Evika disappeared. I'd have to think about how to approach her with that information.

I closed the small flip-phone and put it down on the dining table. At some point during my conversation with Sonya, Paul had gestured that he getting more firewood. While I waited for him to return, I idly picked up a magazine we had purchased along with the groceries, sat on the sofa and started reading.

As I flipped through the pages, my mind wandered to Tom, wondering if he was having fun on the slopes. Abruptly, I felt a falling sensation and then *I* was on the ski slope, going downhill at breakneck speed. Cold wind blew back my hair and made my eyes water. I jumped up onto a metal rail sideways, spun around and went up a steeply curved bunker of snow, the world tilting crazily. I saw and felt everything Tom did, and it scared the daylights out of me.

I shook my head and I found myself back in the cabin with a white-knuckled death grip on the arm of the sofa. Okay. Note to self. Be careful when you start thinking about your familiar.

As evening approached, I allowed Paul to bind me with his energy cords before sunset, just in case I tried to give a repeat performance of last night. This time I made sure to get comfortably settled in my bed, and he made sure he was better prepared than last time.

Tom had returned from his boarding excursion and now stood watching the process, looking unhappy. Jealousy, worry, guilt, and a certain regretful wistfulness chased each other across his expressive face. Maybe someone else wouldn't have been able to discern all those emotions, but I could almost smell them radiating off of him like strange cologne.

"You know, I kinda wish you were able to change," Tom said. "I mean, I don't wish lycanthropy on you, but I'm used to running with the pack at full moon. It was a whole group thing. We'd all be excited, and we'd go to the meeting spot just before sunset. Amelia would say a blessing over us as the sun went down. Then we'd strip, throw our clothes into a storage shed and run off into the hills to change. It's like totally the most fun thing to do."

Tom came over and sat on the edge of the bed looking down at me, his eyes shining with good memories. He had taken off most of his clothes to prepare for his change and now wore only a pair of blue boxers dotted with little yellow happy faces.

"Be careful out there tonight," I said.

"I will." He bent down and kissed my forehead, and then he glanced at Paul, "Take good care of her, dude."

"Don't worry about Cara. She'll be fine," Paul replied.

The sky darkened. The bedroom had two large windows

facing west, so we watched the bright glowing colors start to paint the clouds. Tom closed his eyes, his lips moving as if in prayer, then he got up, gave me a big, happy grin, and ran out of the room. I heard his footsteps pound down the stairs, then the front door slamming.

I took a deep breath. Paul came over and sat at the foot of the bed. "Well, what now?" I asked.

"Now we wait to see what happens. We don't know if there will be a repeat of last night or not. If so, we are as prepared as we can be. Although I must say the latter part of last evening is well worth repeating." He looked at me with that certain heated male glint I'd begun to recognize so well.

I quirked my lips in a crooked smile, "Well, you do have me tied up in a bed."

He actually looked shocked for a moment. "I would never take advantage of a lady in that manner," he huffed.

I chuckled. "It's not taking advantage if the lady is willing."

He searched my face for a moment, then smiled. "Cara, my darling, you *are* a sex goddess. A beautiful, tempting goddess, lying there so enticingly in your naughty baggy sweat clothes."

I started to laugh, but stopped as an intense cramp of nausea hit me. "Paul, its starting again." I looked out the window and saw the moon rising over the ridge. He had his wand out and appeared by my side in an instant. "Oh, Zul's horns, I think I'm going to throw up. Let me sit up. Please!"

"We can't risk it, darling. Here use this." He held an empty garbage can up to my head.

I couldn't think clearly, and the garbage can suddenly looked like a trap. *No, I'm not going in there. Get away!* I looked wildly around the room. I couldn't move. He'd trapped me. The walls started closing in on me. I couldn't breathe. My she-wolf came charging out, teeth bared and ready to fight.

Paul dropped the can and jumped back. "Shades of Hades," he whispered.

As I struggled against the bonds, I saw Paul back into a corner of the room, wand held firmly in front of his body, its carved runes glowing white. Beads of sweat broke out on his forehead, and I knew it was from the effort of holding the binding spell.

I tore an arm loose and clawed at the mattress, uselessly trying to free myself. I heard the ripping and tearing of cloth as

I mindlessly savaged the fabric and padding underneath. A part of me wondered how my puny nails could be doing this. I reached out towards Paul and saw my hand. It remained human, but formed around it, like a phantom skin, was a translucent animallike appendage. It had long fingers covered in cream-colored fur, tipped with two-inch claws that looked lethally sharp. The phantom hand flexed when I flexed, moved when I moved. I looked at my arm; it too looked to be encased in spectral pelt, twice as thick as my own, with heavy bunched muscles beneath cream fur. My she-wolf was manifesting.

I heard Paul yelling my name. He had dropped to his knees, still holding his wand. He looked exhausted. The strain of holding me bound was wearing him down. I heard a howl in the distance, too far away for human hears to detect, but I knew it was Tom. I lifted my head and howled a reply. *Come to me. Free me. We can run and hunt this night.* Minutes later I heard another howl, closer. Tom was coming.

Paul jerked up his head, now able to hear Tom, although he was still miles away. "Oh, bloody hell. Cara! Focus! You *can* control your wolf energy. Do it now!"

So many thoughts raced through my head—wolf thoughts, human thoughts. It became too hard to think. Then I heard a sound—footsteps . . . on the roof?

Paul and I both looked up as it grew louder. Could Tom have gotten here that fast? An explosion tore a hole in the ceiling above us. And I used my freed arm to cover my head as plaster, wood, insulation, and snow poured down. Dark figures, dressed in black military-style clothes, dropped into the room through the jagged opening. Before Paul or I could do anything, the first figure held up a gun and shot Paul once and then me twice. I felt a sharp sting in my arm and shoulder. I turned my head to see a metal cylinder, tipped with red fibers, sticking out of my upper arm. A tranquilizer gun.

The world started swimming, which actually felt pretty trippy, but plunged me into blackness before I could really enjoy it.

Chapter Twelve
Back in SF

I gained consciousness slowly, like a bubble rising to the top of a bottle of thick syrup. My head pounded. I lay on something soft. Familiarly soft, in fact. With a sinking feeling I cracked open my eyes. Yup, just as I feared. Lavish surroundings. Check. Beautiful paintings. Check. Scented candles. Check. Killer hangover-type headache. Check and mate. I had been carried back to Roman's house in San Francisco. Specifically, back to his bedroom. That son-of-a-Hellhound had tracked me down and had me kidnapped.

A cold lump of fear settled in my stomach as I thought about Paul and Tom. What had happened to them? I hoped Roman's commando guys didn't hurt them. I tried to force my brain to work, to seek out Tom. My mind saw only darkness.

I looked next to me on the bed. No one there. Good move on Roman's part because I was ready to murder him. I pushed back the covers, stood, sat back down, stood again, swayed a little and staggered to the bathroom. At least I knew the location from the last time I stayed here.

I felt relieved to see I still had on the sweatshirt and pants I'd worn at the cabin. After using the facilities, washing my face and drinking some water, I felt much better. I searched the cabinets for aspirin or a reasonable facsimile but came up empty. Apparently Nightkinds didn't get headaches. I drank more water from a dragonhead faucet. It seemed to be doing the trick. Probably dehydration on top of the aftereffects of the tranquilizer dart had contributed to my discomfort.

I leaned my hands on the edge of the counter and looked into the mirror over the sink. My hair looked like a disaster, sticking out in some areas, mashed flat in others, and bits of plaster clung to the tangled mess.

I stood undecided, torn between taking a shower and trying to escape. Well, twenty more minutes here probably wouldn't hurt. If I ran out looking like a homeless person, good luck trying to get someone to help me.

I walked over to the marble-tiled shower. Someone had stocked it with my favorite shampoo, conditioner, and shower gel. I looked over to the vanity area and saw an assortment of expensive skin care products and cosmetics. I picked up an exquisite art glass perfume bottle, lifted the long glass stopper and held it to my nose. It smelled like my perfume—my custom-made French perfume. How did he get it? For that matter, how could he know all this about me? Humph. Well, he wasn't going to soften me up with this stuff. But since it was here, I decided I might as well use it.

After maybe the best shower ever, I grabbed one of the many big black towels and wrapped it around me, tucking in the top corner to make a terry sarong. Black towels. Huh. Live the stereotype, why don't you, Roman old buddy. Then it occurred to me black wouldn't show blood like a lighter color.

Okay. Time to get out of here. I looked at my discarded sweats and panties, loath to put them back on. Maybe I could find something in Roman's closet.

I padded in my bare feet into his clothing store of a closet and looked around. There was something new that wasn't in here last time—a whole section had been cleared of his clothes and replaced with women's clothing. I looked through them and noticed they were my size. Most still had the price tags attached, like they were hastily hung up without time to take the tags off. And shoes, lots of beautiful shoes, also in my size. I opened a drawer. Rows of undergarments, like a rainbow of silk and lace flowers, filled the entire drawer. He even had my bra size right. Damn him. Damn that sweet—no, terrible—thoughtful, kidnapping vermin. I really tried to dampen my excitement, but it felt too much like a childhood winter solstice morning.

Well, I couldn't fault the man on his taste in clothes, if he had picked these out. I pulled out a pair of dark wool gabardine slacks and a black silk sweater with gold thread embroidery around the low neckline, set them on a handy chair, put on a matching set of La Perla underwear, and picked out a pair of comfortable, heeled Italian leather boots. I went back into the bathroom, found a blow dryer and started to pull myself together.

Half an hour later I walked into the bedroom dressed, groomed, and ready to tackle Roman head on. The wonderful smells of fresh hot coffee, cocoa, and cinnamon greeted me. Someone must have come in while I was in the bathroom. I noticed a silver tray on a small table piled with covered dishes, two small thermal carafes, coffee cup, crystal vase with red roses, and a small Tiffany blue box with a white bow. That monster! I ran over and picked up the box. Then put it back down. I would not be bought, bribed, or whatever.

I poured a cup of coffee, discovered the second carafe had hot cocoa in it and topped off my coffee with it. Oh, blessed-be-the-portal, it tasted good. The dishes held French toast—my favorite—and fresh fruit. I didn't even try to fight it. I might as well keep up my strength. So, with a shrug I sat in the wing chair by the table and started eating. My eyes kept going to the little blue box, no matter how many times I told them to ignore it.

I soon became pleasantly stuffed with French toast and mocha. I should have been on my way out the door just about now, but my curiosity about the box had me tied to a torture rack that increasingly tightened every second I didn't open it. Maybe I'd just take a quick peek, that couldn't hurt. I reverently untied the ribbon, opened the box, and pulled out the little case inside. I flipped it open and gasped. Sitting there were the most gorgeous diamond earrings I'd ever seen. Not too big to be gaudy; not so small they couldn't be seen with my long hair. They were perfect. I snapped the case shut and closed my eyes. Too late. The beauty of the jewelry sang to me, a haunting song of longing and extreme covetousness. My lifelong affinity with crystals and gems surged past my ethics, while thumbing its nose at my better judgment, which should have known better by now than to even try. I had to put on the earrings and see what they looked like on me.

Even knowing I'd fallen for Roman's nefarious scheme, I went into the bathroom to look at myself in the mirror. The earrings glinted hypnotically in the light. They seemed to brighten my face, enhance the shininess of my hair. I absolutely *loved* them. I pounded my fists on the counter. I hated that generous bloodsucking fiend! How dare he be so wonderful to me? I couldn't fall for this. I couldn't! For pity's sake, he'd sent paramilitary ninjas to kidnap me! I didn't know what had happened to my friends. And he wanted to *marry* me for criminey's sake!

I reached up to take off the earrings, but I couldn't do it. I called myself a superficial, diamond-grubbing witch, and I still couldn't do it. I sat on the vanity stool and slumped over, chin in hand. I needed to change the way I looked at this situation. Maybe I deserved them and he deserved to lose them for all the trouble he'd put me through. Yeah. I liked the sound of that. Serves him right, throwing diamonds at a kidnap victim.

Damn straight.

Fortified with my justification I stomped out of the bathroom, through the bedroom, to the door. I twisted the brass knob and found it unlocked. A bit surprised, I opened the door a crack and looked into the hallway. No one there. I bet he thinks he's lulled me into a false sense of security, surrounding me with all my favorite things and giving me fancy gifts. I reached up and lovingly fingered an earring. Ha! He didn't know me very well, did he? I threw open the door and walked to the staircase as quickly as my full stomach would let me.

I marched up the stairs and opened the door at the top with some difficulty which turned out to be because of the crush of people in the way. It looked like a party in progress. I wondered what his guests would think if they knew I was a kidnap victim on the run? I knew better than to ask these people for help. They were obviously his friends.

I pushed my way through the throng of champagne-sipping, beautifully dressed people. They turned and smiled at me. I looked, but they had no fangs that I could see. I smiled back, thinking, *I'm just another partygoer like you; don't pay any attention to me.* To reinforce that image, I snagged a glass of champagne from a passing waiter and slowly headed for the front door.

I almost made it to the foyer when I heard a familiar voice. "Ah, madam, you are up and about. I shall inform the master."

Roland had apparently snuck up behind me and now stood between me and freedom. His usual spot. I turned around and nearly smacked into him. A white cast covered his left arm which rested in a black sling fastened around his neck. "Roland! How are you?"

"Quite well, madam. Thank you for asking," he replied with a very small smile.

"Did you break your arm during the lizard-thing attack?" I nodded towards his cast. "I was worried about you."

"Quite so, madam. A trifle inconvenient. May I be so bold as to say I am glad you are unharmed from the incident?" He made a little bow.

"Thanks, Roland. Now please, let me leave before Roman finds me."

"Too late, my sweet," a deep voice said from right beside me. I gave a little yip as Roman took my arm and said, "Roland, thank you. That will be all."

Roland bowed again and walked away.

"Roman! Let me go." I tied to yank my arm away, but he held it in a gentle, yet steely, grip.

"Why would I want to do such a thing when I've gone through so much trouble to be reunited with you? I'm glad to see you're wearing my engagement gift to you. They become you very nicely."

He reached up to hold an earring briefly on his fingertip, letting it swing back into place when he pulled his hand away. He slid his finger from my earlobe down my neck to the top of my collar bone. I felt goosebumps rise on both my arms. He bent down and whispered, "I love your reaction to me. What else can I make your body do for me?"

"Stop it, Roman, or I'll scream in front of all your party guests. And where are my friends? What happened to them?"

"Do you mean the wizard and the werewolf?"

"You know perfectly well that's who I'm talking about, so quit playing games."

"But, my sweet, where would the fun be in that?" At my expression he sighed and added, "They're fine, Cara. I wouldn't hurt those for whom my fiancée holds such affection."

"The operative word being 'fiancée' I suppose?"

"Of course." He looked at me as if I were a simpleton for having to verify that fact out loud. His version of, *Duh,* I suppose. He reached into his jacket pocket and pulled out the accursed engagement ring. "May I?"

"Will you tell me where my friends are if I wear that thing?"

He simply gave me a little, crooked smile, making an unexpected dimple in one of his handsome cheeks.

A richly dressed, middle-aged woman, with jewelry too big for her outfit, walked up to us as he put the ring on my finger. "Roman! Don't tell me you're engaged! The single women of San Francisco will be heartbroken!" She appraised the ring with an expert eye, then turned her gaze to Roman expectantly.

"Ah yes, where are my manners? Mrs. Ottermeyer, this is my fiancée . . ."

I stuck out my hand. "Jane Doe. Pleased to meet you."

Mrs. Ottermeyer raised her eyebrows. Roman squeezed my other hand in warning. "Please excuse her; she has a rather odd sense of humor. This is Cara Augustine."

I wrenched my hand from Roman's grip and smiled at the

woman as she asked, "Of the House Augustines?"

Roman smiled ruefully, managing to convey false humility with a charmingly boyish delight. "Precisely."

"Oh my goodness—I mean congratulations!" She leaned in so close to me that I could smell her perfume and the champagne on her breath. "We must have lunch sometime soon, just us girls, so you can tell me all about how you two met."

She shook my hand warmly while surreptitiously scanning the crowd. "There's Anna Worthington. I promised to talk to her about a, uh, charity auction. I'll call Roman next week to get your phone number. It was a pleasure to meet you, Cara. Fabulous party Roman . . . Oh, there she goes, but I think I can just catch her. We'll talk soon." She hurried off across the room and was soon out of sight, swallowed by the crowd.

Roman looked way too pleased with himself. He put his arm around me and gave me a chaste kiss on the cheek. "By tomorrow everyone in the City will know we're engaged. Dear Mrs. Ottermeyer is the biggest gossip in San Francisco."

I snorted, "Do you think I give a flying newt what these people think?"

Roman frowned. "I've worked very hard to secure my place in society here." He grabbed my arm and pulled me towards the library, smiling and making introductions all the way. His hand felt as unyielding as an iron shackle; any attempt to pull away tightened his grip. My arm would have bruises tomorrow.

As we reached the library door, he turned to talk to a tall young man who was dressed like a guest but had eyes like a predator. With a tight smile, Roman told him to not let anyone in the room. So the man was security.

I scanned the room, now that I knew what to look for, and saw at least half a dozen men and women with those same sharp eyes. They were positioned strategically at all points of egress. I wondered why there was so much muscle at a gathering of polite, froufrou people. No wonder the downstairs bedroom area hadn't had a guard. It would have been a challenge to escape once I made it up here.

I felt almost glad when the library door closed behind us. The sounds of all those people talking and laughing, not to mention the smells of dozens of perfumes, alcohol, and food, brought back my headache and made me wish I hadn't eaten so much French toast earlier.

He marched me farther into the book-lined room I remembered from my last visit. The memory made me look up at the skylight. I expected to see a hole where the shattered glass had fallen. I saw, instead, a new stained glass art piece. The design depicted a lovely young woman in a flowing red gown with a cloud of dark hair and blue eyes, the pupils rimmed in metallic gold. *Hey! That's me up there!*

I turned to Roman to say something about his presumptuousness, but couldn't because he immediately wrapped both his arms around me and brought his mouth down on mine. I'll give him one thing; the man knows how to kiss. Every coherent thought, every objection, melted under his sensual onslaught. I felt each thrust of his tongue with my entire body—my breasts and my most intimate parts. The intensity there made me squeeze my thighs together and shudder. A little high-pitched moan kept escaping from the back of my throat that I couldn't seem to stop.

He brought one arm down under my bottom and lifted me up so he wouldn't have to bend over. Instead of letting my legs dangle, it seemed the most natural thing in the world to wrap them around his waist. His mouth, still joined to mine, did so many delicious things I never wanted him to stop. I barely noticed that we were moving. He walked to the one wall without a bookshelf and I felt the cool hardness of it against my back.

With me braced against the wall and my legs around his waist, his hands were free. He reached around to the back waistband of my slacks. He pulled in opposite directions with both hands and I heard—and felt—the fabric rip apart. I couldn't imagine the strength it took to do such a thing. So help me, it excited me even more to be held and caressed by those deadly strong hands. He broke off the kiss to set me down. More cloth ripped, and I felt the cool air of the room for the briefest of moments before he lifted me again. My legs found their place around his waist once more, but I felt smooth skin there instead of clothes. His erection rubbed lightly against my most intimate parts as he kissed me again. This time the sensations intensified between my legs. I could feel his talented tongue as if he were actually kissing me there. I had to breathe.

I broke off the kiss and leaned my head back against the wall as the exquisite pleasure built higher. I breathed in little pants as his thumbs stroked my nipples under my sweater. My bra had somehow been pushed up, leaving my sensitive breasts vulnerable to his touch. I didn't want him to stop.

I felt my power start to come to life, curling around the piece of his energy I had taken inside me during our dream. The dark and the light merged and grew. Tendrils, delicate as spider's silk, flowed out from me and into him, connecting us. At the first touch of the strands he threw back his head in ecstasy or pain or maybe both. He seized my hips with a fierceness that should have frightened me, but instead filled me with savage anticipation. He lifted me up, and I reached down to guide him, felt the large, smooth head of his penis at my opening. I wrapped both arms around his neck as he slowly sank home. He was so large, so careful, even though the effort showed in the fine tremors of his legs. He kept going, like his dream visitation, but this was so much better. I felt stretched and full and aching. He stilled and kissed me, allowing me to accommodate him fully.

"Move," I whispered in his ear. And he did.

With each long stroke, the incredible pleasure pressure spiraled tighter and higher. The gossamer threads of energy bound us so very closely that I started to feel a shadow of what he felt. His need was raw, desperate, and all-consuming. He could smell my blood under the sex, and his Nightkind nature craved its taste, almost wild with the desire to join our bodies, our essences, by taking my blood inside him. I echoed his desire.

I had no thought of tomorrow; there was only now, and now was the time to join. "Do it," I moaned.

He held the back of my head in one hand and looked at me, eyes almost all black, pupils dilated to cover the silver of his irises. "Are you sure?"

"Yes, do it now!" I was reaching a point of no return, where the pleasure rose to almost excruciating intensity.

His hips flexed as he drove himself deeper and faster, and his lips fastened on my neck. There was a slight pain, after which all I could see was white light as Nightkind chemicals from the glands connected to his retractable fangs flowed into my bloodstream. I felt as if my entire body was made of pleasure as wave upon wave of orgasm swept over me. I cried out. His lips left my neck and he let out a low, guttural moan of pleasure. This had to be why I hadn't left a part of my energy behind when we came together last time. He had to take my blood in order to make this bond complete. He now had a part of me in him, just as I held a part of him. As the strands of energy flowed back into me, they felt thicker, saturated with power. If I'd had a mirror, I would have checked to see if I glowed in the dark.

We slid down the wall to the floor; he lay on his back with me on top of him. My breathing slowed back to normal. Now it just felt weird to have our naked bottoms and clothed tops together. I pulled off my sweater and bra and unbuttoned his shirt, then lay back down, resting my head on his chest. We were skin to skin, and I breathed in his scent. This felt better.

He rubbed my back gently with one hand as we recovered, and I murmured, "You know this doesn't solve anything."

I felt his voice rumble through his chest. "Yes, it does. It solves everything for me."

* * * *

The library had a secret door built into one of the bookshelves. I think I would have been disappointed if it hadn't. I wore Roman's shirt like a dress, which came down to the tops of my knees, and used his tie as a belt. He said I looked charming, but he was a man who'd just had sex.

A well-lit, carpeted passageway forked after a while into two narrow corridors. We took the right hand one which took us down a flight of stairs. We emerged from behind a section of wall in his bedroom that was covered by a large painting— a depiction of souls being taken across the river Styx. Yeah, I got it. Bet he thought it was clever or funny or both that the passage took us to his bedroom like souls being taken to Hades.

I rounded on him as soon as we entered the room. "Roman, you can't keep me here as a prisoner. The gossip lady is probably alerting the media as we speak that I'm your fiancée. My family will know I'm here."

"Whatever gave you the idea that you are a prisoner, my sweet? This is your house now as much as mine. We have confirmed our engagement in front of a witness."

"I can leave if I want to?" I asked warily.

"Of course."

"Then why do you have security here? I don't remember you having any last time you brought me to your house."

"I felt the need to bring on security after the sub-demon attack. They are not specifically here for you or for your *friends.*" I didn't care for the animosity in his tone when he said "friends."

"Speaking of them, just where are my friends?" My
stomach tightened in anxiety as I thought of them.

"Well, there's the rub, you see. I'd only feel comfortable
giving my fiancée that type of information, or keeping my
fiancée's friends safe. I wouldn't dream of divulging such
strategic intelligence to just anyone." He crossed his arms and
gave me a small smile, one eyebrow raised as he waited for
the threat to sink in.

"You son-of-a-Hellhound!"

His smile grew irritatingly broader. "I can see how you
might have drawn that conclusion, but the dear lady looked
quite human, I assure you. I doubt our offspring will have any
hound-like qualities at all."

I refused to acknowledge that he'd said the word
"offspring." I waved the back of my left hand in front of his
face, flashing the diamond. "I'm wearing the ring. You said if I
wore it, you'd tell me where my friends are."

"As a matter of fact, one of your friends is here in the
house. Just down the hall. The wolfman, unfortunately, chose
not to accompany my retrieval consultants. His whereabouts
are currently unknown." I brightened at the knowledge that at
least Tom was free.

"Paul's here? I want to see him," I demanded.

"Did the wizard become your lover?" He reached out and
held my arm as he stared into my eyes, all traces of amusement
gone.

"That's none of your business," I twisted from his grip,
turning my face away. Why did his accusation make me feel a
little guilty? Our engagement was a sham. I was free to do
whatever I wanted with whomever I wanted.

"I see, so the answer is yes." He said anger made his
voice low and menacing.

"Why do you have to know?" My own anger at his
presumption started to rise.

"I'm a bit old-fashioned in that regard, I'm afraid. Perhaps
in a century or two I won't feel like dismembering a romantic
rival, but right now, I'm rather possessive where you are
concerned, my sweet."

For the first time tonight I felt a cold lump of fear form in
my stomach. Fear for Paul. "He's just a friend. He's teaching
me how to control my powers."

Roman arched an eyebrow. "Really? Why would you need that type of training, and from a wizard? Aren't witches taught such things at an early age?"

I waved my hand dismissively. "It's a long story. Can I see him now?"

He stood looking at me in silence, apparently considering my request. "Very well, but I must insist you put on some more appropriate clothing, as much as I like your current ensemble."

I looked down at my makeshift cover-up. "Oh, right. Okay. I'll be ready in a minute." I practically ran into the bathroom to wash up and pick out a new outfit.

As I stood at the sink, I checked my neck where Roman had bitten me. There were two pinkish dots that looked almost healed. I ran a brush through my hair and made sure I didn't have makeup smeared under my eyes or around my mouth. I actually looked surprisingly fresh, considering.

I went into the closet. Most of the clothes looked too formal, but I pulled out a white knit top and matching jeans with silver studded "V's" on the back pockets that not only looked comfortable, but would allow running, if necessary. The top had long sleeves and an off-the-shoulder neckline that was connected in the middle to a tasseled rope halter that tied around my neck at the back. The tie hid one of the marks so it was less noticeable as a bite. I'd hoped to find a pair of running shoes, but I had to settle for a pair of beige lace-up oxfords. Underneath I wore a strapless bra and beige lace panties.

I dressed as fast as I could and went back in the bedroom. Roman sat in the wingback chair reading a newspaper. He looked up as I came in. "Very nice, I thought Versace would suit you."

"Did you pick out the clothes?" I couldn't help asking, my curiosity getting the best of me.

"In a manner of speaking. I gave specific instructions to a personal shopper regarding sizes, designers, and styles."

"He or she did a pretty good job."

"I'm glad you like them," he said, looking pleased.

"Just because I like them doesn't mean you're off the hook for kidnapping me. Okay, let's go see Paul." I ignored his bid to bribe me with designer clothes or that he seemed glad I liked the selection. Instead, I walked to the door and motioned for him to follow me.

Roman just smiled as he rose from his seat.

We walked down the hallway in the opposite direction from the staircase until we stopped in front of the last door. Roman took a key from his pocket and unlocked it. The room was completely devoid of furniture except for one small, chintz-covered chair, a bit worse for wear, a footstool, and a little table. A diminutive wizened old man with skin the color and texture of a walnut shell sat in the chair. His long wispy white hair moved, as if stirred by a gentle breeze. He wore a somewhat threadbare tan cardigan over a dress shirt and plaid pants. His slippered feet were propped on the footstool, and he had a pair of glasses perched on the end of his nose. He held an enormous ancient-looking book, and a cone of light hovered over it in midair, acting like a reading lamp. The room smelled like the air during a lightning storm—ozone, power, and electricity suspended in the very molecules of space.

The little man looked up from his book as we walked towards him. His eyes were pale green and sharp as broken glass. The book rose in the air, closed itself, and floated over to the table where it actually started purring.

The man lifted a gnarled hand and petted the book like you would a cat, as he nodded towards us, "Hello Master Roman. See your bride-to-be is with you today."

"Yes, Chester. This is Cara. Cara, this is Chester."

I smiled at the old man, "Hi Chester, nice to meet you, even under these circumstances." I turned to Roman, "Okay, where's Paul?"

Roman said conspiratorially to Chester, "The young have no patience, do they, old friend?"

"No sir, Master Roman, don't believe they do. Television and the Internet are what to blame. Not that old Chester's been able to get near enough to the gadgets to use 'em." He turned his bright eyes on me. It felt as if I were being x-rayed, like he could see every atom of my being. My power instinctively leaped out defensively and formed a shield around my body, surprising me. I'd never done that before.

"Oh ho! Good girl! Gotta protect yourself. You don't know old Chester from Adam, do you?" He glanced at Roman, "She's got power as well as looks, this one." He winked at me.

"Chester, would you be so kind as to open the door for us so we can pay our new wizard guest a visit?" Roman asked the wizard.

Chester reached into his cardigan and pulled out a wand

that looked suspiciously like one of those cheap, wooden, break-apart chopsticks you get at restaurants. It was covered with runes written with what looked like a marking pen.

He glanced at me over his glasses. "I see what you're looking at girl. Yep, it's a chopstick. I went to these after I kept misplacing my good wands. Bad as reading glasses; never can find those either. Friend of mine in Chinatown sends over a box every few months. Disposable wands. Use 'em a couple of times then eat dinner with 'em later. 'Course, the trouble is that when you do that, sometimes you end up with dinner or something else altogether."

He waved the wand toward the far wall. A glowing rectangle the size of a door appeared. The glow subsided in a few seconds, to be replaced by a white mist. "Okay, you can go in now. Nice meeting you young lady. You'll make a fine bride for Master Roman down the road a bit, or he could make a fine consort for you eventually. Depends on which way you want to go. Your powers are still green as grass, but at least you got most of the folks you need gathered 'round you now."

"How do you know about me?" I asked, startled by his comment.

"Why, you've got the Eyes of Dominion, of course. Old Chester'd known you for an Augustine mage without anyone saying a word about you."

Before I could ask him what he meant by Eyes of Dominion, Roman grabbed my hand and pulled me towards the door. When he opened it, the mist cleared to reveal a sumptuous apartment. It looked like the penthouse suite of a fancy hotel, except outside the big windows there was an expanse of dark water instead of sky. I jumped when a shark swam by, dead, round, doll eyes black and unblinking.

"Where are we?" I asked Roman as I looked around.

Roman smiled faintly, "Let's just say it's a wizard-proof guest house."

Paul came out of a room, dressed in a white terrycloth bathrobe, drying his hair with a towel. He looked up, startled, and his eyes widened as he spotted us.

Dropping the towel on the floor, he ran towards us. "Cara! Are you alright, darling?"

Roman stepped between us, blocking Paul's attempt to get to me. He looked over his shoulder at me, dark brows pulled into an angry frown. "So do 'just friends' call each other darling these days?"

"Get out of my way, Nightkind." Paul stood in front of Roman, eye to eye. I'd never noticed they were the same height. Roman had greater muscle mass, while Paul was all elegant, slender lines. Roman's fangs had started to descend and I could feel Paul's energy building. They were practically growling at each other.

I heaved an impatient sigh. "Will you two just stop with the male posturing? Roman, tell me where the hell we are. Paul, are you okay?"

Without taking his eyes off of Roman, Paul answered, "I'm fine except for a headache. I woke up in Captain Nemo's hideout and have been trying to get out ever since. From the sea life I've seen, I'd say we're in the Pacific Ocean, somewhere not too far from the California coast. Also, this place is heavily and professionally warded against magic."

"Yes, Chester was quite amused when you tried to break his wards on the windows," Roman drawled. "I believe he said you were a damn fool who would get himself drowned or eaten by sharks."

A soft chiming sound interrupted us. Roman looked around expectantly. A small orb of blue light, no bigger than a marble, floated out of the misty doorway and landed in his outstretched hand. He nodded his head, then closed his hand. The orb disappeared.

"Come, Cara. Your wolfman has been spotted making his way towards the city. He has apparently been tracking you. Frankly, I'd be impressed, if I didn't have a house full of social contacts who now need to be sent home. What kind of host would I be if I let my guests be eaten by a werewolf?"

I had skirted around Roman during his orb-call and now stood by Paul. We looked at each other. Tom was coming, but he didn't know what he he'd be getting into.

Paul took my arm and pulled me aside whispering, "Try to contact Tom. He's your familiar. Warn him."

Suddenly Paul disappeared. It took me a moment to realize Roman had thrown him across the room. He hit the wall and slid down to the floor, looking dazed.

I rounded on Roman, who looked furious. "You will not touch my fiancée. You will not address her with terms of endearment. You're only alive because your death would upset her. If you overstep your bounds again, I'll risk her displeasure by devising an excruciatingly uncomfortable situation for you. Do you understand?"

Paul glared at him and swiped at a trickle of blood running down the corner of his mouth. "I'll find a way to get out of here and save Cara. Do *you* understand?"

Roman actually smiled as if he admired Paul's bravado. "Yes, I think we understand each other quite well, actually."

Before I could squeak out a word, Roman put his arm around my waist and walked us through the misty doorway. Paul jumped up and ran after us, calling my name. I looked back, twisting in Roman's grip. Paul pounded on an invisible barrier, yelling, but now I couldn't hear him. It looked as if he was behind glass, trapped in the underwater apartment, and something suddenly occurred to me.

"Roman, what does Paul see when the door closes?"

"He sees a mirror. Why?"

"Just curious," I said with a shrug, tamping down my excitement. I had to speak with Chester alone. It looked as if he knew how to move through the mirror dimension. Unfortunately, I didn't get the chance to speak with the old man because, instead of coming back into the room with Chester, we emerged from Roman's closet through his three-way wardrobe mirror. Did that mean Roman knew how to travel that way, too?

Roman turned to me, "Stay in the room. I must see to my guests."

With that, he strode quickly out of the closet. I heard the bedroom door close and lock as I followed after him. *Damn!* Well, at least I didn't have to leave here to try to contact Tom.

I went over to the freshly made bed. Huh. Roman's house ran like a well-oiled machine. Must be Roland's doing. I kicked off my shoes and lay on the cool, smooth, silk spread. I closed my eyes and thought about Tom. I wanted to talk with him, not just see what he saw. I wondered if I'd be able to do it. I'd only been able to see what he saw, not communicate with him. If this didn't work, he'd walk into a trap.

I took a couple of deep, relaxing breaths, pushing other thoughts aside as best I could. I concentrated on Tom while reaching for my wolf energy. Just like that, I was in Tom's head. He stood in a terminal of some kind, and he bought a ticket out of a machine. BART was written on the ticket. He walked though a turnstile, after sliding the ticket into a metal slot, then plucked it out of another slot when the barrier retracted. He stood in one of the Bay Area's Rapid Transit stations. He looked up at an electronic sign with destinations flashing across it and stood waiting for the San Francisco bound train.

Why had he decided to take BART? What happened to the car? I didn't know, and now was not the time to find out. I had to warn him that Roman knew he was coming.

Tom? Tom, can you hear me?

I felt a sense of vertigo as he spun around. "Cara?"

Tom! I'm here with you. In your head. "

In my bed? Oh man, I must be tripping out."

I'm in your head, head, like full of lead!

"Head? I'm definitely tripping out."

Tom, listen to me. You are not crazy. You're my familiar, so we can talk to each other like this.

"Whoa! This is radically awesome!" I saw a couple standing next to Tom smile at him and slowly move several feet away.

Tom. Don't talk too loud. Just listen. I'm being held a prisoner in Roman's house . . . well kind of a prisoner slash fiancée—oh never mind that, I said when I felt anger surge through him at the word fiancée. Geez, this jealousy thing was becoming really tiresome. *The thing is, Roman knows you're coming for me. I don't know how he knows, but he does. You have to be very careful. I want you to go to my Cousin Sonya's house in Berkeley. She'll be able to get people to help you. My family needs to know what's happening. Just let everyone know that I'm okay for now.*

I gave him Sonya's address, warning him about the Hellhounds. I had no idea how Jupiter and Archer would react to a werewolf. I asked him how he'd gotten here, and he told me dawn had broken and he'd changed back to human form by the time he returned to the cabin Paul and I had already been taken and someone had disabled the car. Fortunately, he'd remembered Paul saying he had a snowmobile, so he took it as far as he could, then hitchhiked and walked the rest of the way here. His internal 'Cara-compass,' as he called it, had kept him coming towards me ever since.

I'll try to get to a phone to tell Sonya you're coming. Maybe she can pick you up. But just in case I can't call her, start going to her house now, and . . .

"Cara . . . what? Wait . . . you're fading. I can't . . ."

The connection abruptly ended. I opened my eyes and found myself back in Roman's bedroom. I felt exhausted, and the ceiling seemed to be spinning slowly. I closed my eyes again. I had to get to a phone to call Sonya. Maybe I could just lie here for another minute while the dizziness went away.

When I opened my eyes again, the clock on the bedside table told me an hour had passed. Oh no! Tom! I got up too quickly from the bed, and the room tilted to the right as I staggered to the door. It was still locked.

I looked around in frustration, and then my gaze landed on the Styx painting. Of course! I could use the secret door. I just had to figure out how to get it open. I staggered towards that wall, stubbing my bare toe hard in the process. Letting out a string of swear words, I bent down to grab my hurt toe and felt myself start to fall. I reached out for the nearest object to stop myself and grabbed onto a wall-mounted candle holder. It hinged sideways, slipping out of my hand. I fell hard on my side in front of the painting. The door opened slowly until it used my forehead as a doorstop.

I got to my feet, rubbing my forehead, which throbbed almost as badly as my toe, and limped into the passageway. I thought about trying to talk to Chester about the mirrors, but shook my head. First things first. Tom was probably close to Sonya's house, if he wasn't there already. At the thought of him, I saw glimpses of houses set on a steep hill. Oh, good. He hadn't arrived yet. Apparently I could see through Tom's eyes with no problem, but talking to him quickly drained my energy. Okay, good to know.

I climbed the stairs to the fork in the passage. I knew one led to the library, which wasn't too far from the front door, but probably had a lot of people in the way. I had no idea where the other one went. If I had a secret passageway in my house, I'd want to make sure I'd be able to use it as an escape route out of the house, so maybe it led to the outside. Using that logic as my decision-maker, I limped down the unknown corridor.

I'd gone about twenty feet or so when the lights started flickering. Now what? I walked faster, but my toe hurt so much I barely managed to keep up the pace. I clenched my teeth against the pain and started breathing in fast, short pants. If I managed to get outside I'd need to have shoes. Why didn't I put my shoes back on before doing this? Too late now. I walked on the heel of my injured foot, not making much progress. The lights flickered again, then went out altogether. I was now in complete darkness, the kind you encountered in lava tunnels where the very absence of any light whatsoever is like a palpable presence in itself.

I stopped walking in the hope the lights would come back on. I waited a few minutes that seemed much longer. In this utter absence of light, my primitive brain started asserting itself. It said I was vulnerable to bad things with great big teeth. They wanted to have me for dinner, and not as a guest. I knew I was alone, inside a house, in a narrow corridor that would eventually lead somewhere with light. The rational part of me put my hand on the wall, and I started moving forward again. The primitive part of me wished it knew how to invent fire or hide somewhere until dawn. But that was silly because dawn would never show itself inside this man-made cave.

I kept moving until I heard a faint hissing sound. And then several more. I became very conscious of my bare feet as I stood frozen, hoping those sounds weren't what I thought they were. My inner cavewitch screamed inside my head, Runrunrunrun! Snakessnakessnakessnakes!

Chapter Thirteen
The Darkness

Blind panic seized me, froze my mind, I had to run. I turned around, stumbling over my own feet, stubbing my injured toe on the carpeting. Tears of pain ran down my face. I ran head-on into a solid object in the dark. I let out a scream, hitting the thing that was wrapping thick something's around my body. I heard my name through my haze of fear. It called my name. It sounded like a man's voice.

"Roman?"

"Cara, what are you doing in here? The electricity has gone out in the neighborhood. What a bother."

I started crying with relief and babbling about snakes. I felt myself being lifted, carried back the way I'd come. Roman made little shushing noises, comforting murmurs whispered close to my ear, as I hung onto his neck for dear life. The irony of the situation would haunt me later, but for now I felt safe. My big, bad, Nightkind magician wouldn't let the snakes eat me, wouldn't let the darkness swallow me whole. Tom would just have to fend for himself this time.

Roman carried me back to his bedroom and lay me on the bed. He pulled a handkerchief out of his pocket and started dabbing at my face. The candles were lit throughout the room, their soft golden lights a joy and relief. "You're safe. It's just a temporary power outage. I'm here. I won't let anything hurt you."

I took the handkerchief, swiped it under my eyes and then blew my nose. Okay that's better. The panic had receded, leaving embarrassment, then anger at being embarrassed. Anger I could do something about.

I slapped away Roman's hand on my shoulder. "Why do you have snakes in your house? What kind are they? Are they poisonous? I didn't have any shoes on. They could have bitten me!"

Roman looked at me completely puzzled, "Snakes? Cara, I have no idea what you are talking about. Did you hit your head? Your forehead looks red. And *why* aren't you wearing shoes?"

"The door hit me, but not hard because I stubbed my toe. That's not the point. When the lights went out, I heard hissing in there. Lots of hissing. It sounded like snakes."

Roman looked at my head, then my feet. He frowned when he saw my toe. He picked up my foot to look at it more closely. "This looks rather painful, sweetheart. You might lose this toenail. And rest assured, there are no snakes in the passageway."

"Then what made those hissing sounds?" I had struggled up to my elbows to look at him. It was awkward with my leg being held in the air.

"I'll get Chester to perform a healing spell for you," he said. "As for the hissing sounds? Let's see. Well, the passage leads to the kitchen, so it may have been from something cooking. The caterers are working back there for the party."

I lay back on the bed, anger gone and embarrassment back in full force. "Oh. Well, it sounded like snakes, but I couldn't see anything." I waved my hand, dismissing that subject, and said, "I'd really like Chester to perform a healing spell. My toe is killing me."

Roman sat on the edge of the bed and looked at me with concern. "Cara, I'll get Chester in a moment. You have to know that I don't want to lock you up or threaten your friends. I just want you here with me. Don't try to run from me. We were meant to be together. I've lived a very long time and I have to tell you, I want you more than anything I have ever wanted in all that time.

"If you really mean that, then don't treat me like a prisoner or let me think you'll hurt my friends if I don't do what you want," I said.

"If you promise not to try to run again, you may have the freedom of the house. That's all I can give you until we can trust each other," he conceded.

I just stared at him in disbelief. He's talking to me about trust? He kidnapped me and Paul. His people blew a hole in Paul's cabin. He's been a total pain in the ass, making me travel all over the place to get away from him. And he wants to talk about *trust?* I looked at his handsome, deceitful face and, mentally crossing my fingers, said "That sounds wonderful, Roman. I won't run. Now, could you have Chester do something for my foot?"

Roman smiled at me. "I'm not an idiot, Cara. I know it's too soon for you to trust me, but I'll take you at your word anyway, at least for now. However, you should know that even though I initially hired security in case any more rampaging sub-demons showed up, they also have orders to stop you if you try to leave or to stop your misguided family should they try to take you from me." He smiled again and patted my leg. "I'll fetch Chester for your healing."

As he rose and walked towards the door, my anger flared, and I grabbed a clock off the nightstand and threw it at him, "You son-of-a-Hellhound!"

He turned and caught the clock easily, setting it down on another table. "You should be more careful. This is a valuable antique. And I thought we settled the issue of my parentage earlier."

I lay back on the bed with a "Humph" and folded my arms. Stupid Nightkind reflexes.

A few minutes later Chester floated into the room, sitting cross-legged on top of his pet book and tamping something into a carved bone pipe. His reading glasses were perched on his head at a precarious angle, as if he had been in a hurry.

"Hello again, young lady. Master Roman says you hurt your toe." He and his book floated over to the bed and hovered by my feet. "Ah, not too bad. Got just the thing to fix you right up."

He pulled one of his chopstick wands out of his cardigan and murmured a word under his breath. The tip of the wand caught fire. He used it to light his pipe, then blew out the flame.

I sat up, eager to talk with him. "Chester, you know how to use the mirror dimension. Can you tell me about it? I think someone very dear to me is trapped in there somewhere."

He puffed on his pipe for a moment while giving me a contemplative look. "Mirror dimension, hmm? You don't have the training to go there. Dangerous place for the inexperienced. It's a demon dimension, and there are things in there that'd snap up a tender little witch like you in a heartbeat. No, best you don't even think about it. Sorry about your friend."

"Please, Chester. Please help me," I pleaded, putting everything I could in my voice and face.

"Now, don't go looking at Chester with those big blue eyes." He frowned and shook his head, causing his white hair to swirl around like a dandelion puff in a breeze. "Maybe if I told you what happened to her you'd be able to tell me what to do," I said, hope rising as I saw his sympathetic look.

"Guess it couldn't hurt none to listen to your story whilst

your toe gets fixed up. Breathe deep. This'll help the pain."

He took another puff on his pipe, then blew a thin stream of smoke in my face. The candlelight must have been playing tricks on my eyesight because I swore the smoke coming towards me looked pink, and when I inhaled it, it smelled like ripe strawberries.

The pain immediately lessened and soon disappeared. I floated on a cotton candy cloud. Everything glowed with a rosy light, softly out of focus, lovely as could be. I felt wonderful. "Oh, Chester. You have to tell me where you get your tobacco," I said dreamily.

Chester chuckled, "No tobacco in this pipe, girl. Don't believe in it. Now, you go ahead with your story while old Chester works on you."

I watched him wave his wand over my foot. He chanted something as a shower of fine, pink sparkles fell from the tip of his wand onto my foot. The sparkles felt tickly on my skin. I started to chuckle.

Chester smiled at me. "Go on with your story."

I lay back on the pillows and told him Roman's story about that night in the restaurant, the compact mirror, and the mysterious, exploding Uncle Max. I let out all my feelings during the telling—the guilt, sorrow, anger, horror, and frustration. My words came tumbling out of me in a jumbled mess. It felt so good to tell someone, especially someone who might be able to help. When I finished my story, I looked expectantly at Chester. His wand had stopped producing the pink sparkles, and he sat on his book, looking thoughtful.

"Wiggle your toe now and tell Chester how it feels."

I did and it felt pain free. I looked down at my feet and my toe looked completely healed. "Wow, that's great! Thank you."

"You should be good as new. That was some story, girl."

"Can you help me? Give any me information?" I asked hopefully.

"Got to do some snooping to see what's what. Should take a couple of days. Don't you go running off now. You give old Chester time to do some things and we'll see about your friend."

"Oh, thank you, Chester!" I jumped out of the bed to give him a happy hug. He wobbled a bit on his book, taken aback, but then put his frail arms around me giving me little pats on my back.

"Okay now, girl, take it easy. You're squeezing the breath

out of a body."

I let go alarmed, but he smiled so I knew I hadn't hurt him. He had felt slight and fragile as a bird, the skin on his cheek as soft and beardless as a child's. I wondered how old he was or if he was even a human wizard. But it didn't matter. A few more days and I might know where Evika was being held and how to get her back. I smiled hugely. I could hang out here a few more days. Roman wasn't being completely awful.

"Hey, Chester, think I could get another hit of the pink stuff? Maybe you could tell me a story this time. How did you get involved with Roman? And I have some questions about what you said to me earlier."

Chester turned out to be a treasure trove of information. He and I ended up sitting on the bed, his book purring by his side, and we passed the pipe back and forth while he told me fascinating stories about Roman and House Balthazar. As I listened to his tales of heroism and valor during the wars of the Great Purge, I began to feel a sense of pride in the thought that I was to become part of such a noble House. Then I looked at the engagement ring on my finger. This was temporary. Roman had coerced me into wearing it. But as I sat there in a fragrant cloud of pink smoke, I had to admit it looked dazzlingly beautiful. The facets reflected the ambient light like a constellation of living stars. Geez, I really was no better than a raven or a magpie, fascinated by shiny bright things.

I felt Chester's sharp eyes focused on me. I looked up, embarrassed that he'd caught me looking at the ring. The pale green of his irises appeared to turn liquid, and I saw rainbow lights, like those in my ring, swirling in their depths.

They made me dizzy, and I started laughing. "You've got whirly eyes, Chester. How did you do that?"

He gave me a wink. "Well now, old Chester suspects you've had just about enough medicinal treatment for today. Got things to do and can't stay here all day with you, young lady, as nice as it's been."

I leaned towards him and said pleadingly, "No, don't go. Could you teach me how to do things like the floating reading light? It would have come in handy when the electricity went out."

"I most certainly can, but some other time. You want to know about your friend don't you? Only so many hours in the day."

"Okay. Can we talk tomorrow?"

"Looking forward to it. Now you be careful and don't go stubbing any more toes, you hear?" He hesitated a beat, then added, "And you better not try to go working any machines for a while. Medicinal smoke can be a bit discombobulating."

I laughed. "I promise to try to be careful, and thanks again for fixing my toe. I especially liked the anesthetic part of the treatment."

"Helps with the rheumatism, too." He looked down at his book which had, at some point, opened itself and was gently fanning its pages front to back, back to front. It almost seemed like the smoke had affected it, too.

"Looks like your book also likes your anesthesia." I said.

Chester chuckled. "Yep, she sure does. Showed me the recipe for the potion one day when my bones were aching, didn't you, girl?" The book closed and moved itself under his hand for a pet, which he did. "Come on, gal, let's get back to our duties."

The book slid itself under Chester's bottom and rose in the air with him sitting on top of it. He waved at me distractedly as he floated out of the room, talking to his book.

I thought of something and called after him, "Chester! Make sure Paul doesn't hurt himself, and don't let anything hurt him, okay?"

Chester nodded in what I hoped was an acknowledgment of my request, not a response to something the book had relayed to him.

By the time Chester left it was well into the early morning hours, according to the clock I'd thrown at Roman earlier. I drifted happily in a rosy haze, not yet sleepy. I thought I would like to share this nice feeling with Tom one day and waited for the connection I usually got when I thought about him. It didn't happen. Was the smoke blocking my ability to contact my familiar? I shrugged. Oh, well, he's a big wolfy guy, I'm sure he'll figure it out. I started laughing because I'd called him "wolfy guy." Oh yeah, feeling no pain, thanks to good old Chester.

I walked around the room looking at all the objects d'art, finding each one incredibly beautiful and fascinating. I ran my hands over the sculptures and carvings, cool smooth stone and precious metals, warmer woods still resonating with echoes of life. My feet luxuriated in the feel of the thick carpets while I carefully avoided chair and table legs. I wandered into the bathroom, glimpsing myself in the mirror. My face looked relaxed with a dreamy little smile. My eyes were so dilated the black of my pupils covered all the gold, with only a sliver of bright blue peeking out. I gathered my hair on top of my head, posing.

As I laughed at myself, another face swam into view, superimposing itself over my own. I knew that face. "Evika! Hi Cuz! Don't worry I'll be coming for you soon!" I merrily waved at her.

Her mouth moved like she was talking to me, trying to tell me something. "I can't hear you. You're *in a mirror*." I laughed. She turned her head as if looking behind her, then she disappeared. I saw only my face in the mirror again. "Bye! Hang in there!"

I jumped up and down clapping my hands. "Yippee! Evika's alive!" I couldn't wait to tell Chester I'd seen her.

I did a little happy dance around the room, stopping in front of the closet. Oooo, my new clothes were in there. Might as well see what they looked like. I skipped into the closet to my section, as I'd started thinking of it, and skimmed my hand down the rows of outfits, coming to a stop at the end where two long black zippered bags were hung. I unzipped them to find two evening gowns. They were absolutely gorgeous. Designed to show off cleavage, make waists look tiny, and present a woman as if she were a priceless jewel. I wanted to try them on, but on closer inspection I saw getting into them might be a two-person job. One dress had dozens of tiny hooks up the back instead of a zipper, and the other one had a complex system of hidden buttons my fuzzy brain couldn't figure out. Did the people who wear these things have people on staff just to dress them? Or maybe they just had help come in as needed. I wanted to wear them out somewhere. These were meant to be seen. Wait, what was I thinking? Go out with Roman as if we were really a couple? I stuffed the dresses back in the bags and ran out of the closet into the bedroom.

I discovered Roman lounging on the bed. He wore black silk pajama bottoms, and the bedside lamp illuminated his smooth, bare chest as he sat reading a thick sheaf of papers.

Looking up as I ran in, he smiled. "I see Chester healed your toe. I thought I smelled his medicinal pipe smoke. Rather strongly, in fact."

"Oh." I had forgotten this was Roman's room. He probably assumed I'd sleep here with him, the rat. I sat in the wingback chair. He shook his head, patting the bed beside him.

"Time for bed, sweetheart. Dawn is almost here."

I stubbornly stayed in the chair.

He lowered the document to his lap with a sigh. "Cara, I just want you beside me. I won't do anything you don't want me to do."

"Oh sure, easy for you to say *now*, after what we did in the library," I folded my arms, "I want my own bedroom."

"No."

"No? Just like that? I'm used to my independence. I need my own space. Your high-handed ways are not getting us off to a good start here, you know."

He gave me a stern look. "I am not used to explaining myself or having my orders, I mean requests, questioned."

"Ha! You said 'orders!' I can tell you right now you will have one totally ticked off fiancée with that attitude, Mr. Balthazar. And you wouldn't like living with a ticked off witch, believe me."

"Unfortunately, I do believe you, but I'm willing to take the chance. I want you in my home and in my bed."

"And I don't want to wake up next to a corpse every day," I blurted out in frustration.

Thunder crossed his face, and before I could protest, he had carried me to the bed. He tossed me onto the soft surface, quickly throwing an arm around my waist before I could scramble off. He pulled me to him and gave me a kiss that stole my breath and curled my toes. My body thought he felt like a wonderful corpse and wanted more of him touching more of me.

"You are a spoiled little witch. I'll have my hands full with you. I can see that clearly, sweetheart."

"Stop calling me things like 'sweetheart.' My name is Cara."

"Very well, *cara mia*. Ah, it takes me back to my time in Italy. I like that very much. Now I'd like to show you I'm far from being a 'corpse' as you put it."

I didn't like the glint in his eye as he said it. "That's not what I . . ."

He silenced me with another kiss, a deeper kiss, the kind that stole my thoughts and made me ache for him.

Well, hell. I reached up to grab his hair, giving back as well as receiving. He groaned, a deep rumble in his chest, his hand roaming over my body, unzipping and pulling clothes aside. His talented fingers stroked the exact right places in a way that arched my back, made me dig my fingers into his shoulders. He broke off the kiss to explore my breasts with his mouth, going lower, slowly, until his head was cradled between my legs. I heard him whisper, *"Cara mia, come sei bella,"* as he lowered his head. The intimate kiss forced little mewling sounds from my throat, made my head thrash on the pillow. He kept going and going until I thought I couldn't stand it anymore. Then he slipped in two fingers and found that spot inside sending me over the edge.

He let me rest, just for a moment, while I panted, and then started again. His hands were like clamps on my thighs, keeping my bottom half still and open to his sensual onslaught. I lost count of how many times he brought me over that shining edge. In fact, I lost track of time. All I know is he finally stopped, saying something about the dawn. He went into the bathroom and I heard the water running. He came back, drying his face and hands with one of his black towels. I didn't think I could move. I felt boneless, my limbs leaden, and an incredible lethargy suffused me. I closed my eyes, utterly exhausted and satiated, and fell into a deep sleep.

I awoke from a nightmare involving humans having their living hearts cut out by a demon wearing a feathered headdress. My forehead beaded with sweat. I sat up in bed, rubbing my face with both my hands. I was alone. Either Roman had "slept" somewhere else, or it was sunset and he'd left before I woke up. I felt a twinge of guilt, thinking about my "corpse" comment. Then I berated myself for that. I wanted him to leave, right? Then I thought about what he'd done to me before I fell asleep and felt the heat of a blush start at my neck and creep up to my face. Confused by my thoughts about Roman, disturbed from the nightmare, and annoyed at myself for everything, I threw back the covers and stomped to the bathroom.

I thought about Tom while in the shower, worried about my dream. Plus, I didn't know if he'd made it to Sonya's house or if he'd had trouble with the Hounds. In the middle of lathering up my hair, I caught a glimpse of Sonya laughing, drinking tea. Shampoo dripped into my eyes, stinging like crazy, but I smiled anyway because it looked like Tom was okay for now.

Humming under my breath, I wrapped a towel around me

and walked into the closet. I came out wearing a light blue sweater, navy slacks, and black Italian leather shoes with two-inch heels. I wouldn't want to jog in this outfit, but it would work. I blew my hair dry, put on moisturizer, mascara, lip gloss, and a dab of perfume. I was ready to face the day, or rather night. This whole sleeping through the day and staying awake all night thing would get really old after a while. I love the sun. I'm a California girl, after all. I had to convince Roman his notions about me and him together just wouldn't work.

I hoped Paul was doing okay in the underwater guest house. It gave the phrase *sleeping with the fishes* a whole new twist. Despite the strange location, the suite looked comfortable enough. I didn't worry too much about him. But a prison was still a prison, no matter how comfortable it was. I should know. Maybe Chester would have some news for me about Evika so I could finally escape this gilded cage.

I walked to the bedroom door, intent on finding the kitchen, my stomach growling. I hadn't eaten anything since breakfast yesterday. I opened the door and nearly ran into Roland, who was holding a tray.

"Roland! Hi. I didn't mean to run you over."

"Not at all, Madam. I brought your breakfast. I took the liberty of ordering eggs Benedict."

"It's my second favorite splurge breakfast," I asked, eyeing the tray with both mouth-watering delight and suspicion. "Where are you getting all this information about me? The French Toast yesterday, and now this?"

Roland lifted his eyebrows a notch. "Why, from you, I presumed, Madam. The Master presented me with a list of your preferred foods and beverages so you would feel comfortable in your new home. We even have a new chef on staff to see to your culinary needs."

"Really?" I said doubtfully.

"I'm being quite truthful, Madam."

"Of course you are, Roland. Thanks. You can put down the tray. Uh, how many people does the Master have on staff?"

"We have four house staff, the chef, the housekeeper, the gardener, and myself. I'll make arrangements to introduce them to you. I have been quite remiss in my duties, Madam. My apologies for not arranging a formal greeting sooner." He looked flustered and a little embarrassed at having fallen down on the job.

I quickly put a hand on the sleeve of his uninjured arm. How he carried the tray one-handed remained a mystery. "Oh, please don't worry about it! There was the party, and I guess my arrival was unexpected, given I was newly kidnapped and all."

"You are too kind, Madam. Enjoy your breakfast."

I looked at him curiously. "Did you hear me say I was kidnapped?"

"Quite so, Madam."

"And that doesn't bother you?"

"It's not my place to question the Master. Although it is a bit unorthodox in these modern times to have a reluctant bride, it is not unheard of in Master Roman's family history. It's well known the brides inevitably settle in very nicely."

"You do know it's illegal to hold me here? You could be an accessory to kidnapping."

Roland chuckled, "Quite amusing, Madam. You are a breath of fresh air, if I may be so bold to say."

I just stared at him in confusion. Did Roman have everyone around him brainwashed? Did he hypnotize his staff using evil magician powers?

Roland handed me a simple little silver metal clicker. "You have but to click this device if you need my services at any time."

I looked at it and couldn't imagine how he'd be able to hear it more than a few feet away. "How does it work?" I asked, puzzled.

Roland reached into his jacket pocket and pulled out a key chain with several little rectangles and half a dozen keys attached. The rectangles were colored gold, silver, red, green, and black. "If you'll permit me, I'll demonstrate. Please press your clicker, Madam."

I pushed down and heard the expected *click-click* sound. The silver rectangle on Roland's key chain immediately chimed and lit up like a small bulb had turned on.

"That's cool," I said, "who did the spell?"

"Wizard Chester is the House Wizard for Master Roman."

"Oh, right. I've met Chester."

"Just click once for service, twice for immediate assistance, and three times in an emergency. Will that be all, Madam?"

"Sure, thanks. I guess I'll see you around."

"Yes, Madam. Please don't hesitate to click if you require

anything at all. And may I add, the staff is very pleased you are back with Master Roman."

"Are you sure you don't want to call the police? I don't think you'd like the duties your cellmates might have in mind for you when they throw everyone in jail."

"Yes, very amusing, Madam." He shook his head and chuckled again. "Good evening." He made a little bow and left the room.

Huh. I looked at the quarter-sized clicker in my hand. It consisted of two pieces of flat silver metal fused together, with a raised bump in the middle of the top piece making a clicking sound when pressed. It was not as if witches couldn't make these kinds of charms, but we preferred to live simply. Each time magic is used it expends our energy. Every charm has a tiny bit of you locked inside of it. Wizards can more easily tap into other energies, outside of their own, channeling it through their wands or other objects to take the impact of the raw, untamed power, but that, too, had a price. Everything in magic has a price. There were human-made electronic devices available these days, so why waste magic on a simple thing like this?

I stuffed the clicker in my back pants pocket, not knowing what else to do with it, and ventured out into the hall. I noticed a tiny blue orb bobbing down the stairs. I recognized it as the spell Chester had used to contact Roman when we were with Paul in the underwater guest house. I held out my hand, as I remember Roman had done. It did a wobbly air dance in my general direction, erratically, like a round blue butterfly, then finally came to rest on my open palm.

As soon as it touched my skin, I heard Chester's voice. *Hello, young lady. This is Chester speaking. Make your way upstairs to the Library; got some information for you.*

I climbed the stairs and walked down the hall and into the library. Chester was sitting on his book, hovering in the air in front of a bookshelf, as he looked at the titles.

Without turning around he said, "Sit on down girl and make yourself comfortable. I've got some information for you."

I sat on a new buttery tan leather chair Roman must have purchased after the sub-demon attack. "What is it?" I asked.

Chester's book flew over to me so that mine and Chester's heads were on the same level as he replied, "Don't know yet, but got wind of something big happening. The high-level demons are all excited about a grand 'to do' coming up. Got 'em all in a tizzy."

I whistled inwardly at his announcement. The high-level demons, or demon-lords, are their ruling class and looked the most like us, even to the point of a rare few being able to have hybrid offspring, like Uncle Max.

"Oh, before I forget, I need to tell you I that I saw my Cousin Evika last night in a mirror. It looked like she was trying to contact me, to tell me something. I couldn't hear her, but at least it means she's still alive."

"Good. Good. Heard tell of the very thing, so your cousin's being held by demons in the mirror dimension for sure. Don't know the why of it yet."

"We have to get her out of there as soon as we can."

"Too dangerous. And don't you go saying *we* are doing anything, young lady. *We* are not going anywhere if *we* includes you."

"Please, Chester. I have to go! Evika is like a sister to me. She's my blood, my best friend. I can't just leave her there, now that I know she's alive." I felt tears well up in my eyes, overflow and run down my cheeks. To be so close to finding her but not able to do anything about it made me feel both helpless and frustrated. I missed her terribly. Just the thought of her alone in another dimension, surrounded by demons, made me cry harder. What was wrong with me? This was so not like me. Why break down now? I wiped at my face, ashamed of my weakness.

Chester floated over and patted me awkwardly on the shoulder. "There now, girl, stop them waterworks. Maybe we can do something. Let old Chester cogitate on it for a bit."

"Thank you!" I leaned forward to hug Chester in sheer relief. His book growled at me in warning. "I won't hurt him, book," I assured, and then I leaned over and gave him a light kiss on his soft textured cheek. Since the book didn't growl again, it apparently thought my gesture acceptable, but I could feel it watching me. How it did so without eyes was an unknown, but it could see me. I was sure of it.

"Why did your book growl at me? I hugged you before and it didn't seem to mind."

"Heh, who knows? Some days she just gets that way, don't you, old gal? She wouldn't hurt you none; I already warned her. Last of her kind, you know. Yep, the last of the Living Books of Xostoriatum."

I raised my eyebrows in surprise. "I thought stories about living books were just myths."

"No myth, here's the proof. She adopted old Chester so many years ago even Chester don't remember when it happened. Yessiree, she's been with Chester through thick and thin. No one knows why they pick someone or why they stay. When you get right down to it, doesn't matter. Just glad to have her."

"Why do you call it a she?" I asked.

He looked at me surprised, his wispy hair floating around his head. "Isn't it obvious?" Before I could respond, he made a shooing motion with his hand. "Alright now, you run off and keep busy. Old Chester has to do some figuring and talking to do. Shouldn't take more than another day or so."

"Can't we go now?" I asked in frustration.

"I told you to get that *we* business out of your head. *You* are not going anywhere. Master Roman would turn my old hide into a book cover if I let you go into a mirror to try to rescue your cousin."

I went still and cold inside at his words, blood draining from my face. "He would?" The dread must have shown on my face because I suddenly felt cold, felt my body pulling in blood from my extremities in response to my fear.

Chester shook his head and smiled. "No, not really, don't go looking like that. Now, Master Roman's father might have done it, but not Roman, at least not to old Chester." He made another shooing motion. "Go on now. See you tomorrow."

I walked out into the foyer and took a deep, relieved breath. I didn't know what to do with myself while I waited for the next meeting with Chester. Maybe I could visit Paul. I ran back into the library to ask Chester to open the door to the guest house for me, but he had vanished. Disappointed, I tried to work up some interest in exploring the house, but my mind was too occupied with the fate of my family and friends.

Thinking Chester may have gone back to his post in the little room down the hall, I went downstairs. The door wasn't locked. I walked into the dark room, barely making out Chester's chair and footstool from the hallway light. I ran my hands along the walls by the door looking for a light switch, but there wasn't one to be found. I turned to go when I noticed the room getting brighter. I turned back around. "Chester?"

A glowing rectangle appeared on the far wall. The glow subsided, replaced by the white mist I remembered.

"Chester?" I called out. Silence. I walked towards the misty doorway, unsure of what to do. "Paul?" Maybe he had found a way to open the mirror on his side.

As I looked into the mist, I thought I saw dark shapes moving around. Then a flash of red hair, and a woman's scream, making me jump. "Evika?" I ran forward, stopping on the threshold, straining my eyes to see into the swirling white. Another scream, more distant, moving away. "Evika!"

I couldn't wait. She was in trouble right now. I made up my mind and stepped through the doorway. The mist was thick, soft and as white as the interior of a cloud. Although I walked on solid ground, everything else was obscured. I might as well have been in a dream world.

I called out, "Evika!" but now there was only silence. Then I saw a flash of red to my left. I ran towards it, hoping I wasn't too late. I didn't even think about what might happen if I found her. First things first, as my grandmother used to say.

I don't know how long I ran through the mist before I had to stop. I was breathing hard; my heart pumping too fast, my chest in an agony of hot pain. "Evika!" Her name came out of my mouth in a whispery croak. I had lost her.

"No, no, no!" I turned around in a circle, trying to see the doorway, or some sign of my cousin, both of which, of course, were nowhere to be seen.

What was I thinking running in to the mist like this? I had no idea of where I was or how to get out of here. I sat down, dejected. I could breathe easier now. The ground seemed to be made of a substance resembling hard packed black clay, almost tar-like in appearance. I got to my feet, unsure of where to go, completely disoriented. I didn't even know from which direction I had run. Okay. This had to be one of my less brilliant moments.

I started walking in what I hoped was the right direction, berating myself with every step. Dark shapes flitted in and out of my field of vision, too far away, or maybe too insubstantial, to become clear to me. I heard occasional snatches of incomprehensible words strung together like water droplets on a spider's web, glimmering just beyond understanding. I wandered, lost in this misty place, with no points of reference, no landmarks to help me orient myself to somewhere, anywhere but this relentless fog. I was getting tired and thirsty, and my designer shoes were rubbing blisters on my heels and toes. I tried to see if I could mentally contact Tom, but couldn't make a connection.

I closed my eyes and reached down inside myself for the connections I had with Paul, and even Roman. The gossamer threads of energy, silvery green for Paul and blue-black for Roman, went spiraling out but didn't find the resonating auras they were searching for.

I stood still, exhausted from my efforts. I couldn't walk another step in these stupid shoes. Angry and frustrated, I yanked them off and hurled them into the mist.

"Ow! That hurt," a high-pitched voice squeaked.

I snapped my head towards the direction of the voice. "Who's there? Where are you? I'm lost. Can you help me?"

"Lost?" the voice again squeaked, sounding like a cartoon character.

"Yes! Please help me get out of here!"

"Why should I?" the voice replied.

I thought quickly, "A reward. I'll give you a reward for helping me!"

"Reward?"

"Yes. A big reward. Where are you? Can you come over here to me? I can't see you."

"You threw shoes at me. Why help you?"

"I didn't know you were there. I never would have thrown them at you on purpose. Please, help me." I was frustrated but desperate for help, and I fought to control my impatience.

"What are you? Maybe you want to eat me?"

"No, I would never do that!" What kind of person would want to know if I'd eat them, for criminey sakes?

I saw something shuffling towards me, a dark shape, squat and wide, about the size of a small wheelbarrow filled with dirt. As it came closer, I recognized it as a species of sub-demon. It had a jowly, porcine face rearranged somewhat to look cherubically humanlike. It had thick, bluish-gray, leathery skin, armor plated like an armadillo. Four incongruously thin legs, ending in cloven hooves, held up the bulky body, and two small, darker blue horns jutted straight up on the top of its head. It cautiously trotted closer to me, sniffing the air.

I squatted down, held out my hands, palms up, and tried to look as nonthreatening as possible. "See? I won't hurt you. Can you help me?"

"Where is reward?"

"I'll get it for you when I return to my dimension."

"What will you give?"

"What would you want for getting me home?"

"Have you cats? I had a most tasty cat a long while ago. Most tasty."

"Uh, no cats. How about a chicken or a leg of lamb?"

"These are tasty as cats?"

"Definitely *more* tasty."

"Reward with chicken and lamb, not just leg, but whole beast."

"Okay. The lamb might have to be in pieces, but it will be equal to a whole one."

"Then I will help for the most tasty treats."

I had never spoken to a sub-demon. I knew they were almost always carnivores, while the high-level demons usually feed off more insubstantial fare like emotions, auras, power, and souls. Most of the subs were not capable of human speech, and even if they were, they had a tendency to be of the maul first, ask questions later variety. I knew better than to trust it completely, but I was grateful to be able to have a chance of getting out of here.

The sub-demon turned and started trotting off into the mist, squeaking, "Follow," in its wake.

I hastened to catch up, barefooted, for fear of losing track of it. Now I wished I hadn't thrown my shoes away. "Hey wait, I want to get my shoes back."

"No time. Follow now." It didn't stop.

Oh well, at least the blisters weren't hurting as much this way. I jogged alongside the creature, surprised something so obviously not streamlined could move so fast and even gracefully.

"Hey, wait, I didn't tell you where I wanted to go." I panted.

"Not matter. Cannot go anywhere from this place."

We jogged along for a while, and I started to feel winded again. My throat still felt parched, and my mind kept conjuring up visions of waterfalls, icy pitchers of iced tea, and tubs of sports drinks foolishly wasted on the heads of team coaches.

"Wait, I have to stop for a minute." I stopped and bent over, hands on my knees, drawing in big gulps of air. The sub-demon I had mentally nicknamed "Squeaky" stopped to look at me.

"How long we wait?"

"I just need to catch my breath."

"Why? Did breath run away?" Then it snorted in laughter at its own joke. Great, I got a sub-demon with a lousy sense of humor.

"Have you seen another witch in here, one with long red hair?" I reached up and pointed at my head to make sure it understood.

It nodded its piggy human head, horns bobbing. "Ah yes, the loud, screaming one. Loud witch with red hair."

Evika knew how to throw a tantrum. That sounded like her! "Yes! I want you to take me to her first, then my home."

"Loud witch hurts ears. Demon lords hurt ones come near."

"She's my friend, my cousin. I need to get to her. Remember the tasty reward?

"Dead witch can not give reward," it said stubbornly.

"If you don't help me find her, I won't give you the reward."

It seemed to ponder for a moment, its moist blue snout twitching in agitation. "I take you to loud, red witch, but want more reward. *Two* chickens. *Two* whole-body lambs." It nodded its head at this request as if to emphasize its demands.

"Okay. Done. Now take me to my friend."

It made some squeaking sounds and hopped from its front two legs to the back ones in excitement. "Okay done. We go now," it said in its little high voice and trotted off again.

I resigned myself to jogging alongside it once more, but vowed to get in better shape when I made it back home.

The landscape of relentless white fog gradually began to give away to a dreamlike vista of black hills dotted with spindly white trees. Above the hills, a solid blanket of gray clouds covered the sky. What little light could filter through left the land in a perpetual twilight gloom. I felt like I'd lost my ability to see color. The cold, smooth ground became uneven, scattered with black rocklike chunks and long fallen branches from the deathly white trees. I watched the ground as we continued walking, careful of my bare feet, not wanting to step on the rocks. Closer inspection of the white bits revealed them to be bleached bones, some human-looking and some others of bizarre proportions. I looked over at Squeaky, who had slowed down, its head swinging from side-to-side nervously, moist blue snout quivering.

"Where are we?" I asked in a whisper. Even whispering, my voice sounded too loud in my own ears.

"Demon lord place."

"The red-haired witch is here?"

"Maybe here, maybe demon lords eat her. We see soon."

Shades of Hades! That thought had never occurred to me.

I had to believe Evika was alive, that coming here was the right thing to do.

After a few more minutes I realized what I thought were trees were the still standing remains of fantastical skeletons, rooted in the ground. They were somewhat dinosaur-like but with impossible looking joints and proportions. I became morbidly curious about what they might have been like alive and fleshed out. We walked until we came to the base of the closest of the dark hills. I saw an opening, like the mouth of a cave. Bones had been used to make a frame around it, and they had been covered in mud to hide their white gleam. Squeaky trotted up to the entrance, looking back over his shoulder to see if I still followed. A sudden unease wouldn't allow me to take those few last steps to the cave entrance.

Squeaky motioned with its head for me to follow, swinging it from me to the cave entrance. I wanted to go but my body wouldn't let me. It wasn't just reluctance anymore. My feet felt the ground soften, mashing between my bare toes like warm mud. I tried to lift my legs, but the mud sucked at my feet, clinging, tarry glue that covered my insteps. The mud obscuring the cave outline of bone fell away in gooey rivulets exposing an intricate lacework of calcified remains that formed patterns of arcane symbols. This was an elaborate trap!

Squeaky trotted back to me, tilting its head sideways and inspecting my stuck feet. "You cannot move?"

"No, I'm stuck! Help pull me out of this stuff." I reached out towards the sub-demon, but it danced nimbly away. "Come back here! I need to grab onto you."

To my surprise, it kicked up its hind legs and started to prance about in glee. Irritated, I motioned it over. "Stop it. I can't unstick my feet. Don't you understand? I need some help here?"

It stood just out of reach as I kept trying to get my feet out of the sticky mud. Every attempt seemed to make me sink lower. I started to get the cold feeling of trouble in the pit of my stomach.

Squeaky smiled grotesquely at me, revealing gleaming rows of sharp black teeth with extra long bottom incisors. Uh oh. The sub-demon's eyes were glowing red and drool had started dripping down at the corners of its mouth.

It said, "*You* are now my tasty treat."

Chapter Fourteen
Betrayal

It had led me straight to its own lair. I felt like a complete idiot to have trusted it, just like a lamb to the slaughter. The irony didn't escape me.

"What about the reward?" I reminded it desperately. "The reward will be much tastier than a stringy little witch like me. I can make sure you have lots of treats, a whole herd of sheep if you want."

"No sheep. Witches much tastier than sheep, much tastier than cats. Witches *very* tasty."

"Did you eat the red-haired witch?" I became sick with dread for both myself and Evika.

"No eating red witch," it said regretfully.

At least that was good. I renewed my efforts to free myself, but the mud had now hardened around my ankles. I felt like my feet were encased in solid stone or a block of concrete. Zul's horns! I didn't want to leave this life as a sub-demon's dinner entrée.

I tried to stay calm and remember those days at the cabin with Paul, practicing my magic. Adrenaline pumped crazily through my system, making it doubly hard to focus. I made myself go to the place inside me that held my power. I touched it and felt it grow, as I warily watched Squeaky start to advance on me. My ears inexplicably started feeling hot, but I ignored the burning sensation.

Just as Squeaky made its move, rushing forward, mouth wide open, black teeth flashing. My power flared to life, having found an intense focus. I brought up my left arm, palm out in a defensive move, as my power burst forth. The scattered bones around me started to move, but it was too late to prevent contact. Squeaky clamped its powerful jaws painfully down on my forearm. I grabbed onto its horns with my other hand to try to prevent it from pulling back because I knew those lower teeth would gouge out a chunk of my arm if it did. The bones rose in the air. I pushed with my mind and they shot forward like bizarre arrows, striking the sub-demon. Squeaky was so close to me I prayed I wouldn't get accidentally speared with the flying bones, particularly since my control was erratic and unpredictable.

Squeaky squealed in surprise and released my arm as the first volley made contact. A small rib bone had pierced one of its front legs, just above a hoof. It ran back a few feet so it could reach down with its mouth and pull it out. Despairingly, I saw the other bones had simply bounced off Squeaky's armored hide. I had to aim for the unprotected head and neck, if I had any chance at all. The smell of its own blood and mine seemed to infuriate the sub-demon; its face contorted in anger and bloodlust. The effort to hurl the bones at it had weakened me, and my ears and cheeks were hot and burning.

With my feet stuck in the ground I lost my balance and sat down hard. I heard a *click* sound and remembered the clicker Roland had given me. Glad the hardened ground didn't soften again to catch my hands I awkwardly rolled my knees and lifted my bottom up to take it out of my back pocket, keeping an eye on Squeaky the whole time.

Its eyes lit up dangerously when it saw my vulnerable position on the ground. Lowering its horns to point at me, it charged. I poured as much power as I could into the bones while pressing Roland's clicker rapidly, no doubt futilely. The bones rose up again and rained down on the sub-demon's head. I clicked a few more times, then threw the clicker at it. The bone arrows had weakened it but also made it angrier. Slashes covered its face, and sluggish black blood oozed out. The horns were about to gore me and I couldn't do a thing about it.

The impact knocked me backwards and my head bounced sickeningly on the hard surface, dazing me. I felt a searing pain in my upper right thigh. My knees pointed in the air, but the rest of me lay flat on my back. I could feel my life's blood spilling out of the wound in my thigh with every heartbeat. Did the horns hit an artery? I didn't have time to think about it because Squeaky pounced on me, going for my throat, for the kill. I tried to conjure another defense, but I felt too weak. I desperately wrapped both my arms like living shields around my head and neck and braced for the attack.

Instead of teeth, I felt a whoosh of air and a high pitched squeal from Squeaky. I saw him fly through the air, as a deep, male roar rang in my ears. I knew that roar. Roman had arrived. Relief flooded through me, overwhelmed me, and brought tears to my eyes. The blood loss had made me so weak I couldn't lift my head to even see what was happening, but I heard squeals, growls, bodies hitting things, and things hitting bodies.

Then the fight moved into my field of vision. A huge, tan wolf, the size of a Hellhound, held the blue sub-demon down by the throat while Roman pounded it mercilessly with his fists. Roman's face had changed into the nightmare visage I had seen when we were attacked in the library. I heard another whoosh of air, and craning my neck around, I saw Roland and Chester appear. Roland, holding a first-aid kit, stood for a moment taking in the situation, spotted me, and started running in my direction. Chester, riding on his book, joined the fight.

The book had lowered itself so Chester could get off of it to stand near the combatants, then it floated in front of him, apparently opening to a specific page because Chester looked down at the page and started to chant in a strange guttural language. He had a wand in his hand made of ebony wood, the handle encrusted in silver and gems. It surely had to be his major firepower as opposed to his everyday wooden chopsticks. Apparently I was correct because at that moment he yelled, "*Vislariumnia!*"

Roman and the wolf flung themselves off Squeaky as a bright flash of green flame gouted from the tip of Chester's black wand to hit the sub-demon's body.

From my vantage point on the ground I noticed the area under Chester's feet start to soften, and I cried out, "Chester, the ground will trap you!"

At my words, the book closed and zoomed under Chester, picking him up before the ground caught him. The green flames had now completely engulfed Squeaky, sticking to its body like napalm. The sub-demon's legs kicked franticly as it rolled around on the ground. Its frenzied, tortured squeals were coming out in a constant and ghastly torrent. I covered my ears to stop hearing those anguished screams, blood dripping from my bitten arm onto my face. Chester spoke one more word, and the sub-demon was consumed in a small inferno, rising twenty feet into the air and then disappearing. The only thing left was a smoking pile of grayish blue ash on the ground.

Roland had arrived by my side and pressed a thick pad of gauze hard on my thigh wound, trying to staunch the blood flow. Chester, Roman, and the wolf joined us. The pain was so intense I thought I would die from it. My eyesight faded, and I could hardly see. The world narrowed, as blackness closed around the edges of my vision in an ever-shrinking circle, and then it was gone too. The pain lessened, along with my vision, until it was just an annoyance as I floated semiconscious in the comforting dark. I heard Roman's voice telling me to hold on. Chester said something and my feet came free. It would have felt good to move them again if I had been capable of performing such a feat. A pair of familiar, strong arms lifted me as Chester chanted a series of musical vowels. I had a sense of moving through space, then breathed in the smell of sandalwood candles. We were back in Roman's room, and it felt like coming home. That bothered me for a brief moment, until I realized I couldn't see. I didn't know if my eyes were closed, or open and blind. I felt my body start to shut down.

Suddenly, I knew I now lay on the bed with people gathered around me. I felt the pulse of their auras, their bodies. Words floated in the darkness, *blood loss, too much, shock*. I knew I was in trouble, but it just didn't seem to matter all that much. My she-wolf poked her nose out and whimpered, searching for Tom. I felt him in his wolf form, and our energies briefly brushed together. His power flowed into mine, giving us some of his strength. Something was pushed between my teeth into my mouth; it dripped liquid, salty sweet and metallic. Blood? Yes, it was definitely blood, and as it flowed onto my tongue, it was absorbed by the very cells in my mouth. I didn't even have to swallow. Weird but cool, I thought dreamily. The gossamer threads of shimmering blue, my connection to Roman, slowly spun out of my body and latched onto his, drawing on his power. The wolves inside me—my she-wolf and Tom's wolf-nature—turned both their heads towards the dark energy and growled. I sent calming thoughts, healing thoughts, towards them and they lay down together, their golden energies entwining reluctantly with the blue. The blue and gold energies swirled around each other, separate and distinct but somehow not, growing in strength as they accepted each other.

But it wasn't enough. I tried to pull back, knowing instinctively that if I died, I might pull those connected to me down with me. I stopped pulling in their energy, but the flow continued. They were now pushing, giving me more. I tried to tell them to stop, but my mouth wouldn't work. Someone new had come in, someone with a familiar aura. I felt hands on my head and over my heart. A blanket of silvery green energy spread out from the hands, sinking into me, merging with the blue and gold. *Paul.*

As his energy touched the other two, all the colors faded

to white and expanded in a glowing mass that almost hurt to hold inside me. I could feel the power grow and intensify, from the top of my head to the juncture of my thighs. Pure white energy emanated from several points in a line down the center of my body. There was something familiar about them; I knew those areas. Then I vaguely realized they were chakra points, something I'd never really thought much about except as an interesting theory.

The energy flared out from my chakras, became a part of me, saturating every cell in my body. I felt like a container filled to the very top and a little beyond with water, the only thing keeping it from overflowing a delicate balance of surface tension. The pain in my leg and arm receded to dull aches, and then hardly even that. I felt renewed, whole, and alive. The energy slowly started drawing back in at the chakra points, the white separating into individual energies. Then those drew back until it left me breathless and tingling on the bed. I opened my eyes to see a large, tan-colored wolf with black markings lying at the foot of the bed, his tongue lolling out in a big, tired, wolfy grin. Roman sat on one side of me, holding a washcloth over his wrist. Paul sat on the other side, one hand still lying over my heart. Abruptly, Roman reached over, picked up Paul's hand and moved it off of me. I rolled my eyes weakly. I guess I was out of the woods; the guys were at it again. The wolf, who I now knew was Tom, sat up and growled at Roman.

"Cut it out, you guys," I croaked.

They all turned to me. Paul grinned widely, grabbing my hand. "Darling, we thought we were going to lose you," he said as he kissed my hand.

Roman snarled, "Wizard, I warned you."

This was too much. I struggled to sit up, feeling claustrophobic with all this maleness surrounding me, and Roland spoke up. "Gentlemen, please. Madam Cara should rest now to recover from her ordeal."

I looked over at him, grateful for his intervention. Chester hovered by Roland's side, sitting cross-legged on his faithful book, with a wide, knowing grin that transformed his face into a topographical map of time.

"You young roosters take your crowing out of here. Give the girl some breathing room," he scolded them good-naturedly.

The two men and even the wolf looked chagrined as they moved away from the bed.

"Wait. How is it possible all of you are here together?" I asked.

Roman gestured to the wolf. "The *were* came to the house saying he sensed you were in danger. He made his way past security to get to me. At first I didn't believe him; you were under my protection after all, but when we failed to locate you after a thorough search of the house, I had to think he might be right. Then Chester told me he detected unexplained mirror dimension energies from the Gate room, and I feared you'd been taken by whomever or whatever took your cousin.

"Why is Tom in wolf form?" I asked, as Tom couldn't answer me himself in his current state.

"He changed in the hope he'd function like a bloodhound and pick up your scent. You see, Chester opened a doorway so we could search for you, but the mirror dimension is vast, a world in itself. It would've been like trying to find the proverbial needle in a haystack."

"And Paul?" I asked.

Roman nodded, knowing what I meant. "I had Chester release him so he could help in the search. I knew he'd have your best interests in mind. He and Chester worked together, but nothing they tried could locate you."

"Then how did you find me?" I asked, puzzled. Tom had moved to the side of the bed and licked my hand. I scratched his ears.

Roland stepped forward. "If I may respond, gentlemen. It was the clicker, Madam. You clicked the emergency signal. I alerted Master Roman immediately."

Chester floated over so I could see him. "You had a mighty close call, young lady. The blue sub-demon has been luring victims to its den for centuries, near as we could gather."

"You mean all those skeletons were the sub-demon's 'tasty treats' as he called them?" I asked, horrified.

Chester replied, "Yep. The critters'd get stuck in the spelled ground traps. The demon could just take his sweet time killing and eating them. Hope in that order."

I felt queasy at his last statement and thought about all those skeleton trees dotting the hills and shuddered. I could have been one of them.

Paul spoke up, "Chester's clickers are a feat of wizard engineering. They worked even across dimensions. We were able to open a doorway right to you by using the clicker as a homing signal."

I looked at them all. Thought about how they had come to work together. "So how long was I gone?"

Roman sat on the edge of the bed and took my hand off of Tom's furry head to hold in his own. Tom bared his teeth in a silent snarl. Roman ignored him, "You were missing for five days."

"What?" I said, shocked by this news. "It felt like only a few hours."

Chester clarified, "Time works different in the mirror dimension, and not always the same each time. An hour there could be a year here or a week lost in the mist could only be a few minutes in this world. It's a very dangerous place." He gave me a significant look, his pale glass-green eyes glinting in the candlelight.

I chose not to respond to his look because I had done what I thought I needed to do. "So it's almost like being in the Fairie Mounds." I said, remembering stories of people who wandered into enchanted mounds for what they thought was a day, only to discover they had been gone years from their loved ones.

Chester nodded. "That's as good a comparison as any. Now you need to rest up, young lady. These men of yours should leave you be the rest of the night."

I shook my head. "One more thing. What happened with all of you?" I used my good arm to make a sweeping gesture that included the entire assemblage. "It sounds like you ended up working together to rescue me."

Roman sighed and ran a hand through his thick, dark hair. "With the *were* coming here, and with me not able to find you, I finally decided I needed all the help available. I thought these two—" He looked at Tom and Paul. "—would be useful, given their interest in your welfare."

Paul said, "We declared a truce of sorts. We all had a common goal. It didn't make sense to waste our energies fighting each other when we could put it to good use finding you."

I nodded, impressed. "Could you keep the truce going long enough to find Evika?"

Roman stood. "We can talk about that later. Don't worry about your friends. They're my guests and will come to no harm while you recuperate."

I smiled. "Good. Now I'd like a pot of mocha coffee, a big

pitcher of ice water, and a plate of cucumber sandwiches before I go to sleep."

Roland brightened, "Right away, Madam."

Chester chuckled, "Guess you're out of the woods, girl."

Paul gave me a wink, and I knew it was because of our now shared taste for cucumber sandwiches.

They filed out of the room, but I held onto Roman's hand to prevent him from leaving. "Roman, did you give me your blood?"

"Yes. It was the only thing we could think of to help save your life. You'd lost so much of your own."

"I know it was an emergency situation, but what will it do to me?"

"It'll give you strength and accelerate healing for a short time. My intention was to save your life, not to addict you."

I closed my eyes, exhausted by this conversation. Zul's horns! Now I had to worry about possibly becoming addicted to Roman's blood. I felt Roman get up from the side of the bed and heard his footsteps leave the room. I saw two charred and melted lumps of metal lying on the night stand. One had a small, clear bit of stone in its midst, and I realized they were the diamond earrings Roman had given me. I'd had them on in the mirror dimension. Were they the source of the burning sensation I'd felt on my ears? I remembered the sudden focus, the intensity of it. The diamonds must have become my power focus during the fight. I'd never heard of a witch who could do that; using objects as a focus was wizard ability. But I felt too tired to think about the ramifications of what it could possibly mean about my powers. I'd worry about it later.

Now, cocooned in blissful silence, I started to drift off to sleep despite all the thoughts running through my mind. I had one last thought about Roland arriving with the food and drinks I'd ordered, I hoped we wouldn't be too late to save Evika.

Chapter Fifteen
Strawberry Dreams

Amazingly, I could get out of bed the next day, albeit sore and a little wobbly on my feet. Sneaking a peek under the bandages I saw the bite mark on my arm was already pink, the twin gore wounds on my thigh were still tender but scabbed over and healing.

Roman came in and started talking to me without preamble. "*Cara mia*, I should have told you yesterday but you needed your sleep and I decided what I have to say could wait until today. I feel obliged to let you know this is the second time I've given you my blood."

"What?" I said in confusion. "That can't be. I'd remember something like that." I said, perplexed.

He looked away, into some inner place, his eyes unfocused, expression regretful with a touch of defiance. "It happened the night you refused to share my bed, saying you didn't want to wake up next to a corpse."

I kept quiet, the memory of what he'd done to me made me flush, my breath shorten, the core of me tighten with remembered pleasure. Oh yeah, my body remembered very well. He looked back at me, his silvery gray eyes familiar yet still startling against the black of his lashes. He ran his hand absently through his fall of dark hair. The way he did when nervous or upset, I realized.

"I was angry with what you'd said and afraid you'd still want to leave me, so after you fell asleep I pricked my finger and gave you several drops of my blood to bind us closer together. Even in your unconscious state, after the first few drops you suckled my finger like an infant with a bottle. The pleasure of your warm mouth pulling my blood inside you was painfully exquisite. It took every ounce of my willpower not to plunge myself into your body. I'd only intended to gratify you to the point you'd want to stay with me of your own accord."

No man had ever spoken to me like this. I felt both embarrassed and turned on by the memory of that night, and furious he had given me his blood without my knowledge or consent. The worst part was, it couldn't be undone.

I raked a hand through my hair, unable to handle all my conflicting emotions right now. I didn't know if I wanted to yell at him or pull him down to me and have sex with him, despite my injuries. I chose anger. "Get out. I can't talk with you right now."

"*Cara mia*, I . . ."

"Get out!" I yelled. Objects around the room started moving as my power flared with my agitation. The bed started shaking, and a vase full of flowers rose up in the air and started spinning, spraying water and flower petals across the room.

Roman walked to the door, turned, and looked at me. "If it means anything to you, I'm sorry. I wanted you to feel closer to me. I felt angry and hurt by what you'd said. I wasn't thinking clearly."

The antique clock I'd thrown at him before sailed through the air towards him. He again caught it, and tucking it under his arm, he closed the door.

How dare he? How dare he force his vile blood on me while I slept? I conveniently forgot that it was his vile blood that helped save my life a short while ago. My power tantrum had tired me out. I lay back on the bed, thinking of ways to get out of this house and away from Roman, and ways to bring Tom and Paul with me. I wondered if Chester would come with us. I pounded both my fists on the bed, hurting my arm where the sub-demon had bitten me. I hated that stupid magician! I don't care how much of his blood was inside me, I would leave this place and him as soon as I could. I needed to heal and get stronger. I needed sleep right now more than anything else.

I was tired, but couldn't sleep. My body felt wide awake even though I felt drained of energy. I got out of bed, determined to get Paul and Tom and leave. Limping into the closet, I went to my section to get something to wear. I had on a pajama set consisting of black silk shorts and a matching top with a mandarin-style collar, the whole set had an embroidered design of golden Chinese temple dogs and tiny stylized flowers. I couldn't go out dressed like this, even if the pajamas were beautiful.

When I got to the part of the closet holding my clothes, I found another thing to curse Roman about. Someone had taken all the pants, including the jeans, and left me with only dresses and skirts with matching tops.

"Oh! That undead son-of-a-Hellhound!" I was so angry I think my eyes actually crossed because I couldn't see straight.

I grabbed handfuls of the offending garments and threw them on the floor, then jumped on them. My wounded leg collapsed under me, so I ended up sprawled on top of the expensive piles of cloth, tears in my eyes from pain and rage. Did he think this would stop me from leaving? Who knows what went through that antiquated, chauvinistic mind when he ordered someone to do this? As I lay there, staring at the ceiling, it occurred to me how ludicrous this all seemed. How had my life come to this? I had gone from a basically carefree existence, no worries or responsibilities, going wherever my whims directed me. To binding a werewolf to me as my familiar—a big responsibility— to having a Nightkind magician think I was his *chosen* bride— or maybe just a version of my grandmother or something—to having somehow connected a wizard to me, a wizard who had risked his life for me and for whom I had feelings not yet fully explored. I had a missing cousin, a mysterious half-demon Uncle, and parents I hadn't heard from in at least a couple of months. All that and a bunch of weird demon things kept trying to kill me. Had I summed it up, or had I forgotten something? Couldn't I just hit rewind and make it all go away? The ceiling refused to give me any answers, so I sighed and sat up.

The bandage on my thigh was stained with fresh blood. I must have broken open the scab on my wound when I jumped on the clothes. Even though my injuries were healing at a miraculous rate, they were still tender. I had to be careful not to undo the healing.

I got up gingerly and started picking up the mess I'd made. It wouldn't be fair to let the servants clean it up since it wouldn't be Roman who was inconvenienced. I hung up the last dress, then sat on the soft leather ottoman. The bloodstain on the bandage had spread to a larger area. That ought to teach me to let my anger get the better of me.

Thigh throbbing and exhausted, I hobbled back to bed and lay down on top of the covers, pushing a pillow under my injured leg to elevate it, and finally fell asleep.

I woke up screaming from a nightmare where Evika had melted into a raging stream of blood. I looked around, panicked, expecting to see the torrent from my dream. There was no streaming blood, but I wasn't alone. Someone held me, rocking me like a child. It took me a moment to realize Roman had lifted me onto his lap.

He gazed at me, concern on his face and a frown forming

twin creases between those shining gray eyes. "*Cara mia,* wake up! You're dreaming. You had a nightmare."

I rubbed at my face with trembling hands. "Why are you here? Didn't I ask you to leave?"

Anger and hurt flashed across his face, then froze into a mask of arrogance. He lifted me off his lap and onto the bed. "I heard your screams and came in to see if you were alright. Obviously, you are, so I'll leave now."

He stormed out of the room without a backward glance. I raised my hand toward him too late, knowing full well he couldn't see the gesture, making it seem pathetic. I dropped my hand, disgusted with myself.

I lay back on the pillows. This time I slept without dreaming, or at least without remembering my dreams, if I had any, which was just as good.

Chapter Sixteen
Escape Plan

The next evening I woke up feeling pretty good. My arm didn't hurt much, although my thigh still felt tender. I went into the bathroom and cleaned up, put on some makeup and brushed my hair, noticing it had grown longer. After a moment's hesitation, I put on the engagement ring. I went into the closet and pulled out a silky, stretchy knit wrap dress. It had an appealing black-and-white print and long sleeves that would not only fit over but hide the bandage on my arm. I went to the mirror and looked at myself. I liked this dress on me. The deep V of the neckline brought attention to the curves of my breasts and the ties cinched my waist, emphasizing how small it had become. I'd lost weight over the last couple of months, the only thing I felt glad about without an accompanying sense of guilt.

All the shoes left in the closet had heels and I didn't think I wanted to try balancing on them with my hurt leg. I rummaged through Roman's things until I found his sock drawer. I pulled on a pair of black dress socks and pushed down the tops so they were around my ankles. They would have to do, even though the toes flopped when I walked. I pulled a black shoelace out of one of his shoes and used it to tie my hair back into a ponytail at the nape of my neck. I tied the shoelace into a bow and decided I was ready to go out and find my wolf and my wizard.

I walked out into the hall and up the stairs to the main floor. I'd only been to a couple of the rooms up here, the library and living room. I knew the kitchen was on this floor, too. A wooden staircase sinuously curved upward from the foyer leading to the upper floors. I decided to explore the second floor. It took a while climbing the stairs with my hurt leg, but when I got there, I saw a long hallway similar to the one where Roman's room was located. It had the same look, heavy on the polished wood. It was wide enough for small tables along the sides to display a variety of modern-looking bronze sculptures and large pieces of art glass. Paintings lined the walls in-between the rows of big wooden doors on either side of the hall.

I heard the sound of male voices drift down the hallway

and followed them to one of the rooms where the door had been left slightly ajar. I opened the door a little wider and peeked in. It looked like a game room, with a pool table that had a stained glass lamp hanging over it, and pool cues in a wooden rack on the wall next to it. In another area sat a grouping of sofas and chairs facing a huge television thin enough to hang on the wall. The last section of the room held a round table covered with green felt. The outer edge of the table consisted of trays holding poker chips. Six chairs ringed the table. Tom and Paul were sitting in the TV area talking to each other. The TV was turned off.

Relieved I'd found them so quickly, I walked into the room. "Hey, guys, making yourselves at home I see."

They both turned their heads towards me, looking surprised. Tom had propped his feet on a large ottoman that seemed to also serve as a table since a tray with two coffee cups sat by his feet. At my words he jumped up with a big grin on his face.

Tom ran over and hugged me before I could blink, picking me up off the floor. "Watch the leg!" I laughingly warned him.

He set me down carefully but kept an arm around my shoulders, as if he needed to keep touching me. Paul walked over, frowning at Tom's rambunctiousness, no doubt. But when he looked at me, he, too, had a grin on his face.

"Darling, should you be up and about yet? How do you feel? Here, let's get you off your feet."

Paul kissed my cheek and pulled me over to the sitting area with his arm around my waist. Tom had relinquished my shoulders with a good-natured shrug. I sat on one of the sofas, Paul at my side, and Tom sat on the ottoman directly in front of me. Tom picked up my feet and put them on his lap, grinning at the too-big socks.

"We have to get out of here." I said, sounding exasperated.

"For sure, babe. We were just talking about that when you walked in," Tom said.

"Yes, although I'll be sorry to not have Chester's knowledge available, I, too, believe we need to be free of Mr. Balthazar." Paul said.

After a few minutes of bringing each other up-to-date with our thoughts on how to escape, all three of us walked down the staircase to the foyer; even from there we could hear raised voices from the library—Uncle Max's distinctive bass and Roman's smooth baritone talking heatedly. At least I was pretty sure it was Uncle Max. We hurried down the hall and barged in without knocking.

Uncle Max stood at the sound of the door opening, spotted me and rushed over to give me a hug, strands of his long, blue-black hair getting in my mouth as I smiled. I brushed them away as we parted.

Roman didn't look happy as he growled, "Get away from her, demon-spawn."

Uncle Max stepped away from me, sighing deeply, and his pure black eyes glittered in agitation. "I told you I'm Cara's uncle, her Cousin Sonya's father. She's like my own daughter."

"Uncle Max, on my birthday, someone who looked like you was killed and may have had something to do with Evika's disappearance." Uncle Max gave me a sharp look.

"I thought you didn't remember what happened?"

"I still don't remember, but Roman was there. He told me about a man coming into the restaurant, someone I called 'Uncle,' and he looked like you."

I turned to Roman, "Is this the man you saw at the restaurant? The one you told me about?"

"It was someone who looked like the demon-spawn, but it's not this one," Roman said in a cool voice.

Uncle Max just stared at Roman for an uncomfortable moment, seeming to decide whether or not to believe him. He then looked at Paul and Tom, who were standing silently behind me, "And who are they?"

I turned around to looped my arm through Tom's and said, "This is Tom, my friend and, uh, familiar." Paul stepped up to stand by my other side. I looped my other arm through Paul's. "This is Paul. I met him on the plane to Aunt Amelia's house. He's been helping me control my craft. At the moment, we're all here as Mr. Balthazar's involuntary guests."

"Involuntary?" My Uncle turned toward Roman. I could tell his agitation level was rising by watching two small, black horns start to peek out of his hair. They tended to manifest with strong emotion. "You told me just a few minutes ago my niece agreed to be your fiancée of her own freewill."

Roman glared at me, then turned to Uncle Max, "She did."

Uncle Max turned to me, hiding his movement from Roman, and made a glowing sign in the air with his fingers, which immediately faded. "Cara is this true? You must be honest with me. I can't continue negotiating with this Nightkind without knowing the truth of your situation. If you're afraid to tell me, be assured I'll defend you no matter what happens. I won't let him hurt you or your friends."

I looked at Roman to see his reaction to our conversation. He looked confused. I found that curious.

Uncle Max smiled just a tiny bit. "The Nightkind can't understand what I just asked you. While my spell is active, it sounds like we're talking gibberish. Now tell me, my beloved niece, what in *Hades* is going on here?"

Even though I wasn't sure he was really Uncle Max, I took a chance and told him the whole story, well, the Cliff notes version, anyway. We drifted over to the sofa and sat facing each other, ignoring everyone else in the room. Uncle Max only interrupted to ask a clarifying question or two along the way, but mostly listened, his black eyes locked on me somewhat inscrutably. For the most part, I couldn't tell how he felt about everything that had happened to me and my friends. He would raise his eyebrows occasionally or look over to one of the men if I talked about them, like he wanted to be sure he got the right face associated with the right part of the story. Finally, I brought him up to date. He asked if I needed medical attention for the wounds the sub-demon had inflicted, but I assured him I was healing fine. His eyes had blazed at the description of what Squeaky had wanted to do to me, but he'd calmed down after he learned of its destruction.

"Uncle Max, where are my parents? I can't believe they haven't tried to contact me through all of this mess."

"That's part of the reason I came here today. I needed to see for myself what your situation with this Nightkind really was. I'll admit that Amelia already told me about your werewolf familiar and the wizard and the problems that arose in her neck of the woods. But no one knew you weren't still in Tahoe until I heard rumors about Roman becoming engaged to a young pretty dark-haired Augustine witch. I found it hard to believe you'd changed your mind about being with him." He patted my hand. "Of course it could only be you, my dear."

He paused and took a deep breath. "The spell disguising our conversation will only last a few more seconds, so I need to say this quickly." He took both my hands in his warm long-fingered ones. I gazed at his familiar unpainted black fingernails before looking up into his face. He peered into my eyes intently and said, "Your parents are both out of the country to stop a dangerous demon lord who's intent on regaining the power it had several hundred years ago. The Aztecs worshipped it as a god and sacrificed thousands of humans to it. Their culture included cannibalism, which was encouraged by their so-called god."

I opened my mouth to ask a question, but he shook his head and continued, "This demon-god, known by the name *Tezcatlipoca*, was generally considered the most powerful god. The god of night, sorcery and destiny. The word *Tezcatlipoca* means 'smoking mirror and it originally came from one of the forbidden mirror dimensions. *Tezcatlipoca* was also known as 'the Enemy' or 'the Enemy of Both Sides,' because it loved to cause wars. That's what we think it's planning to do—cause worldwide war so it can bring back its good-old-days of human sacrifice and carnage on a grand scale. Right now it doesn't have enough power, and a group of militant wizards and witches are trying to find the Caves of Dominion to reopen the Portal, a powerful energy supply. They've resurrected *Tezcatlipoca* because they plan to take over this world, or as much of it as they can."

"Come on, Uncle Max. You're joking right?" I said, trying to laugh but unable to do so. This was one scary bedtime story.

He shook his head again. "No, Cara, I'm not joking. We're nearly out of time to stop them, and as far as we know, only one kind of mage can stop *Tezcatlipoca*. A mage with special abilities called a Synemancer. You, my dear niece, are one of the first Synemancers to manifest since the time of the Aztecs, and from what we gather from the ancient records, it took a full coven of them to push the *Tezcatlipoca* back into its dimension."

I just looked at him, with my mouth hanging open. Well, it explained some things about my parents, and it verified what Paul's café owner friend had said about me. But how had Uncle Max known what I was?

Before I could ask the question, Uncle Max said, "I'm sure they've been behind the attempts on your life. They're trying to eliminate the threat to *Tezcatlipoca*. Your potential to become a mage has been a closely guarded secret in the family since the day you were born, even you weren't told in the event your powers never developed. We still haven't figured out how they knew about you."

Even though I'd been warned, I was still stunned to hear

it. I closed my mouth and couldn't think of a thing to say. Thoughts, memories, and emotions swirled around in my head. Strange things I hadn't paid much attention to in my childhood clicked into place. I shook my head. Tom came over and sat beside me on the floor, sensing my mood. I put my hand on his shoulder, sliding it under his mane of hair to the nape of his neck. Just touching his skin made me feel a little steadier.

"Can I do anything?" I asked reluctantly, when I really meant was, *What in Hades could I possibly do to help when I'm just learning how to control my power, I don't know how to use my familiar and I'm all confused about my love life!*

Uncle Max smiled. "That's my girl. Yes, we need your help, as well as that of your friends, and this will involve traveling." He swept the room with his dark gaze, looking at each man in turn, even Roman.

Apparently the spell had worn off because Roman stepped forward, fists clenched at his sides. "I won't allow my fiancée to leave me again."

I ignored him and turned to Uncle Max. "I want to believe you, but how can I? You might be an imposter." We all sat in silence looking at Uncle Max or maybe someone who was pretending to be him, wondering what to believe. I thought about what Sonya would say if she knew what was happening. Sonya! The Hounds! That was it.

"I know a way to tell if he's really Uncle Max." The group looked at me expectantly, and I said, "Jupiter and Archer would know the difference."

Tom smiled. "Yeah, those are awesome dogs. It was touch-and-go when I first got to Sonya's house. I thought I was going to be Hound chow for sure until they smelled Cara on me. That stopped them long enough for Sonya to come out and tell them I was okay. By the way, your cousin is majorly babealicious," he threw in, even though it was completely off topic. I frowned, and he quickly got back on track, saying, "Anyway, I guess she figured out who I was from talking with Cara. She also said the Hounds sensed something like a Cara-essence inside me, more than her scent."

Uncle Max only nodded, although he had raised an eyebrow at babealicious. "It would be a good way to prove who I am. Hellhounds are quite particular about who they accept. But we'll need to go to Sonya's house. It would endanger people to bring the Hounds here."

Roman made an angry slashing gesture with his hand. "I haven't agreed to this." I turned to Roman, impatient with his high-handed dictatorial ways, but careful with what I said next because I knew I'd have to convince him in order for him to let us leave his house.

"Roman, it's the only way I can think of to make sure it's really my uncle Max sitting here. If he is, then what he's been saying about me, my parents, the demon lord, and everything is true, and I have to know. If you really want me to start trusting you, then you'll let us do this."

Roman looked into my eyes for a long moment and sighed. "Very well. I'll have Lisette bring the limo around. I don't want to risk you entering the mirror dimension after what happened last time. I also want to bring Chester."

Glad to have the old wizard come with us, I just nodded. Inside, I was terrified. How could I defeat the demon-god by myself when it took a whole coven of synemancers to exile it in the past? I could barely protect myself much less fight a superpowerful demon. But, according to Max, I was the only one who had a chance of doing so. I wasn't ready. I didn't have enough control over my power. But, everything and everyone I loved would likely be destroyed if I didn't try. I had to try. There was no way out of it if I wanted to be able to live with myself.

Well at least there was one silver lining. A little bubble of happiness lifted my mood when I thought of seeing my cousin and the Hounds soon. I missed them. I had another happy thought. Sonya and I wore the same size shoes and most of our clothes could fit the other, even though I was bigger on top. I could change into jeans and athletic shoes while we were there. At least I'd be more comfortable and feel better prepared to do whatever needed to be done.

Lisette, the chauffeur, turned out to be a beautiful female Nightkind. I wondered why Roland hadn't mentioned her when he gave me a rundown on the staff. She had long, lustrous auburn hair and matching eyes with an exotic look, tilted up at the corners as if she had Asian blood in her background. She wore a black pants suit, white shirt, black tie and matching gloves, and a cap. Somehow, the outfit looked sexy on her. She announced the car was ready and stood with her hands clasped in front of her until we were all out the front door. As we filed past her, I noticed she winked at Tom.

We rode most of the way in silence. Roman had produced a cell phone and let me call Sonya to warn her of our arrival and bring her up-to-date. She sounded overjoyed to hear I was alive and well and seemed just as happy to hear Tom was safe. They must have really hit it off the few days Tom stayed with her.

The long black limo was a tad crowded with the seven of us piled in it. I counted Chester's book as a person, so to speak, as it seemed to want its own seat. I still couldn't get over the wonder of Chester's book every time I saw it.

Chester decided to entertain us with stories about him and Henry Ford joy riding in the first Model T. How Henry finally banned him from the workshop when he figured out his autos tended to have more mechanical difficulties in Chester's presence. Chester's face showed his disgruntlement at that part of the story. I had noticed that Lisette looked alarmed when Chester came floating out to get in the car, and now I knew why.

We drove over the Bay Bridge. I looked out the window at the bridge lights reflected in the bay's shimmering, dark water. Lisette veered towards the left onto the freeway leading to Berkeley, and soon we exited onto a street that took us up into the hills. Lisette had decided to go up Marin, one of the steepest streets around, so we slid on the leather seats towards the back of the limo every time she stopped at a stop sign. I kept thinking the limo would slide back into the car behind us before we could move forward again, but I should have known she would drive with preternaturally professional skill. We managed to wind our way through a series of narrow streets to park directly in front of Sonya's house without a single mishap.

Sonya had turned her porch light on, frosting nearby shrubs and trees with golden highlights. By contrast, the shadows were black and ominous. There was a new moon tonight, and the streetlights on this block were not working for some reason. Two of the shadows in her front yard elongated and separated from the surrounding blackness, their forms coalescing into animallike silhouettes. I knew with certainty no other animals in this world could glide with such lethal, boneless menace and silence as the Hounds. I could feel a big smile grow on my face, but given the circumstances, I tamped it down ruthlessly. If this man wasn't my Uncle, he might not survive the identity test.

I looked at Uncle Max, or the man who looked like him, and said, "You go first. Everyone else stay in the car."

I looked around and they all nodded, even Chester, who squinted out the window at the shadows while idly patting his book, which was ruffling its pages in agitation or nervousness, I didn't know which.

Uncle Max shrugged and opened the door. As he started towards the front door, the two shadows approached him, low to the ground, with heads down, red eyes glowing in the dark. As the giant black Hounds approached the half-demon, they moved closer to the porch light. I could see the play of thick corded muscles sliding smoothly under their black velvet fur in a way that emphasized their unearthly origins. He stopped a few feet from the front door and seemed to be talking to the Hounds. They both immediately stood up from their crouched positions, ears perked forward. As I watched, they opened their mouths in big doggie grins as they moved against Uncle Max's hands, begging for scratches.

I let out a breath I hadn't realized I held. "It's okay. He's really Uncle Max. Tom and I will go next, then Paul, Chester, and finally Roman and Lisette."

The curtain on the front window moved so I knew Sonya had been watching. Now, she opened the front door and ran the few feet to her father to give him a hug. Tom and I got enthusiastic welcomes from both Sonya and the Hounds. My face dripped with Hound slobber by the end of their greetings, and I coughed a little from their sulfuric breaths. We finally got them to sit obediently. Sonya had her hand on one Hound, Uncle Max on the other while Paul and Chester cautiously ventured from the limo. Chester held his book firmly in his hands. After some wary sniffing, the Hounds accepted Paul. Chester they loved immediately, rolling over on their backs for him, begging for belly rubs, which he gave them with a dry chuckle. Chester's book, which had been emitting a low, nearly inaudible, growl at first, now purred softly. Uncle Max was so surprised by their reactions I thought his eyebrows and widow's peak would merge together.

Okay. The last ones were Lisette and Roman. As Roman stepped out onto the curb the Hounds leapt up and faced him with twin growls, exposing their long, gleaming white, razor-sharp teeth. The short fur on their backs stood straight up, and their eyes blazed bright red, almost enough to cast a glow on the cement walkway in front of them. Roman growled back, his body moving into a defensive posture, ready to fight if he had to. Lisette exited the car, ready to come to her Master's assistance.

As I watched the Hounds approach, it occurred to me that if they killed Roman, I'd be free of him. But the thought of Roman forever gone didn't produce a feeling of relief. Instead, it caused a sense of profound desolation. Despite how high-handed and irritating he could be, we were connected. I knew instinctively that severing our connection would be far worse than putting up with him. My feet felt weighted down as I made myself move forward, putting myself between Roman and the Hounds.

Roman tried to shove me behind him while muttering furiously, "What are you doing? Get to safety!"

Well, hell. There he went getting all protective, and damn if I didn't find it endearing. "Roman, they won't hurt me." I turned to Jupiter and Archer, talking my usual baby-talk way to them, "How are Auntie Cara's little sweetie-Hounds? You're such good boys, aren't you? Aren't you? It's okay. These are Auntie's friends. Yes they are. Be nice, now."

I reached out to the Hounds. They stopped growling to come to me, but they eyed Roman and Lisette suspiciously. I put a hand on each of their heads, more than twice the size of mine, and scratched behind their soft ears. The fires in their eyes dimmed a little in contentment, looking more orange than bright red in the darkness. I recognized it as a good sign.

In a sotto voice, I said out of the side of my mouth, "Roman, Lisette, slowly offer the backs of your hands for them to smell."

Roman hesitated, "I happen to be quite fond of my hands, thank you."

I rolled my eyes. "Just do it. Or are you not as fond of the rest of your body?"

He looked at Lisette, who had inched around the back of the limo, ready to pounce. I thought it beyond being a loyal servant to risk her life for Roman, but Nightkind relationships are just . . . well, different. She nodded at him to indicate she was ready, and he slowly extended his hands. The Hounds inched forward to sniff them. Jupiter sneezed after getting a snoot full of Nightkind scent, spraying Hound nose juices on one of Roman's hands. An expression of disgust crossed his face but he didn't move. Archer's back hair started to rise again as he sniffed, so I said, "its okay Archer. These are a *good* Nightkinds." I hoped Archer didn't notice I kind of choked on the word "good."

"Cara," Roman's said, and his voice sounded dryly concerned. "You do know, don't you, that you have an expression on your face that looks as if you just took a big bite of sour lemon?"

I gave him a "what did you expect?" shrug but tried to smile for Archer. The Hounds glanced at me, then back at Roman.

Jupiter tentatively wagged his tail and I praised him. "Good boy, Jupiter!" His tail wagged harder in his happiness to have pleased me by not eating the nasty man and woman.

Taking his cue from his brother, Archer sniffed loudly then plopped down on top of my foot and started licking his privates, ignoring Roman and Lisette completely.

I looked at the two Nightkinds and grinned. "You've been accepted, Roman, Lisette. Come on, everyone, let's go in the house. Archer, get off my foot you big ox!"

Archer stood to free my foot, then he and Jupiter followed me into Sonya's house. Roman followed last, wiping his hand on a white handkerchief. It had his initials embroidered in black thread in the corner. I snorted to myself at his fastidiousness. He'd have to get over it if he was going to be around the Hounds, and he'd have to be around them if he wanted to be around me.

We all settle in Sonya's comfortable living room which was full of hand-crafted art and textiles. I sat on the sofa facing Sonya's big wall mirror. Roman sat on one side of me and Sonya sat on the other side. Tom sat on the arm of the sofa by Sonya. With his massive head resting on my lap, Jupiter snuffled between my legs. He looked so hurt when I tried to shoo him away that I gave up and let him stay, pulling my dress down under his muzzle. At least I knew the Hounds didn't have ticks or fleas, vermin that somehow make it onto them die as soon as they try feeding on the Hound's sulfuric blood.

The rest of the group found seats, except Lisette, who stood by the front door, keeping a wary eye on the Hounds.

Roman had moved as far from Jupiter as he could, looking unhappy in the corner of the living room. "Must that creature be here with us, Cara?" It's unseemly to allow it to be in that position."

I just turned to look at Sonya in silent "aren't men funny?" communication. Was Roman jealous of a Hound?

Sonya lifted her eyebrows as Roman tried again. "Cara, I must insist. Can't your cousin enforce some discipline with her animal?"

Okay, he was going to be a pain. I saw Sonya's face darken and headed off the confrontation at the pass. "Jupiter, down boy," I said, with a final rub under his chin. He puffed a sad little waft of sulfur breath and dropped to the ground, head between his paws. I propped my feet on his broad back, using him as my personal living footstool and turned to Roman. "Is this okay with you?"

As he nodded, a movement to my right caught my attention. Chester hovered on his book, eyes crinkled up, looking like he wanted to burst out laughing. Archer stood by his side, tongue hanging out, watching the group.

Uncle Max cleared his throat as a way of focusing our attention on him. "Very well, now that I've established my identity and you know I'm who I say I am, I need to give you important information. After which we will need to move quickly."

He had all our attention as he continued, "As I told most of you before, a group of *Tezcatlipoca*'s followers are trying to find the Caves of Dominion to open the Portal. It's imperative that no one ever open the Portal again. It's too dangerous, too much power for any person or group to have. We've achieved a precarious balance of power in our adopted world between humans, indigenous magical beings, and Portalkind. The demon lords make plenty of trouble on their own, but not enough to throw off the balance. But bringing in an all-powerful demon-god could change this world in ways that would be too horrible to contemplate."

Roman stood. "Why didn't anyone know about this before now?"

Uncle Max held up his hand, and the Hounds had lifted their heads to stare at Roman when he stood, their orange eyes becoming a fraction redder. "Mr. Balthazar, please sit down. I'm sharing our latest intelligence with you from Solange Augustine, Cara's mother. House Augustine is leading the current defensive. They have already informed Cornelius Balthazar." Uncle Max looked at Roman. "I'm afraid he declined to join the effort, saying one demon lord wouldn't be a direct threat to Nightkinds and he didn't want to commit resources. The Fae are undecided, both courts."

"So, it's up to the witches and wizards to fight?" I asked.

Uncle Max frowned. "Yes, it appears that way."

"Tell me more about what a Synemancer can do," I urged, wanting to know what I might be capable of, despite the cold lump of fear that formed in my stomach. I desperately wanted to run and hide somewhere but knew that wasn't an option. Not when so many human and supernatural lives were on the line. It sucked being brave. I couldn't give in to the fear that wanted to close over me, hold me in a tight grip that would freeze my body and mind. I tried to pay attention to what my uncle was telling us, me, about my abilities.

"It's a modern word, meaning someone who can pull energy from several sources to create something altogether different and more powerful than each individual power. It's very much like a Mage, but different in that a Synemancer binds energies to them to ensure an unbroken power chain. In order for you to be a true Synemancer, you'd have to bind others of power to you." He paused and regarded me intently. "You do know it is strictly forbidden to bind unwilling people, and frowned upon even if they're willing? You haven't done that, have you? I mean except for your familiar?"

Well put like that . . . "Uh, maybe." I said, surprised that Amelia didn't tell him about the others.

Uncle Max looked at Tom, Paul, and Roman in turn. He breathed out and paled even more than normal as he gasped, "Not *all* of them?"

"Uh, maybe?"

Unfortunately, Tom decided to come to my defense. "Hey, dude. Like I was totally willing. I wanted to hook up with Cara the first minute I saw her at the airport."

Paul also seemed to think it was the right time to confess. "The binding was unexpected, but I was a more than willing participant." He looked embarrassed as though everyone knew *how* we had bonded.

From the stormy look on his face, Roman had obviously guessed the catalyst of my binding with all of them. I could feel my face grow hot and red as he stared at me. I glanced at Sonya who had a funny little smiley-frown thing happening that looked to be just a hair away from some bigger emotion I couldn't decipher. She was either going to laugh or cry.

I felt I needed to say something to her, so I leaned over and whispered, "*It just kind of happened by accident. I didn't do it on purpose!*"

Uncle Max kept his face carefully neutral. "I see. Well, although this revelation doesn't change our plans, I have to warn all of you that we really don't have much information on *Synemancy*. There are, of course, references to Synemancers in the ancient texts, but no teaching tools or information about how it all worked. New mages apprenticed with experienced ones to learn their craft. A few mages are in existence, but none I've heard about are true Synemancers. We're in unknown territory here. You're connected in a way that probably hasn't been seen in hundreds of years."

I opened my mouth to say something, but Uncle Max held up his hand. Right now we have to concentrate on our most pressing problem, which is getting to the Caves before *Tezcatlipoca's* worshipers can open the Portal."

Tom spoke up. "Does anyone know where the Caves are? I thought they were destroyed by the original mages. Some people even think that the Portal origins theory is a myth to explain the presence of supernatural beings on our world."

"The Caves are quite real, I assure you, but their existence is a closely guarded secret known only to a very few individuals." Uncle Max glanced curiously at Tom, the first human familiar he'd ever seen. He seemed as surprised at Tom's question as he would if one of the Hounds had suddenly asked a question about algebra.

"Who knows where they are?" I asked.

"That's what your parents are trying to find out." Uncle Max replied.

I sat, stunned, and thought about all the things my parents had kept from me. It explained my overly protected childhood, and all the strange things happening now. I wanted to be angry, but all I could muster was a chilling numbness. My lighthearted, carefree existence had slipped away and I'd never get it back. I didn't want to go off and fight demons in some strange country. I didn't want to be a Synemancer. I'd never asked to have three men bound to me, like weights around my ankles. I stared at the large, ornately framed mirror Sonya had hanging on her living room wall, not really seeing it, but for some reason my eyes kept drifting to the bottom left corner. The figures carved on the frame drew my attention for no particular reason I could fathom. The fantastical creatures, some scary, some whimsical, had fascinated me for years.

I sat up straighter and squinted at a particular carving only a couple of inches tall. I got up, climbed over Jupiter, and walked up to the mirror to see the carving better. I squatted on my haunches and looked at it closely. Zul's horns, it looked exactly like the lizard-ape thing that had attacked me and Roman at his house!

"Cara?" Tom said, like he'd been trying to get my attention.

I ignored him, gesturing to Roman to join me. "Roman, look. It's the lizard thing that attacked us."

He got up from the sofa to join me, bending down and peering at the mirror frame. "Yes, it looks like a representation of the same type of sub-demon."

"What are you doing, Cara?" Uncle Max asked, sounding annoyed. "We have to leave here and go to your parents. Time is of the essence. We don't have the luxury for you to look at a wood carving right now."

I ignored what he said but asked him, "Uncle Max, are these carvings of actual demon types?"

"I suppose so. What difference does it make? They're just decorations."

"It's just weird that I never realized that before now. Where did the mirror come from?"

"It was a birth-gift from me to Sonya's mother. After Sonya moved into this house, my wife wanted her to have it."

As I continued to look at the frame, a movement caught my attention. The head of one of the wooden demons turned to look at me with malignant little gold eyes. I let out a startled yip and fell backwards onto my bottom.

I looked up at Roman from the floor. "Did you see that? The figure . . ."

Before I could finish what I was saying, Roman scooped me up and stood holding me in his arms on the other side of the room. Jupiter jumped up, growling at the mirror's frame, and his brother joined him. In another moment the whole frame started to writhe with carvings coming to life.

"Uncle Max, what's happening?" I gasped.

Uncle Max jumped up shouting, "It's a spell. Somehow the protective wards have been breached. Everyone get away from the mirror!"

Several of the tiny demon carvings had popped off the frame and were running towards us. One with bat wings, looking like a dollhouse gargoyle, flew around our heads. A Hound yelped as another carving sank sharp little teeth into its foreleg. The Hound snapped it up in his powerful jaws and bit down with a satisfying crunch. Pieces of gold-covered wood fell to the floor. Roman put me down to swat at the flying gargoyle, and more of the carvings jumped off the frame. The floor was now covered with the tiny figures. The huge frame must have had hundreds, if not thousands, of depictions of demons carved into it. The diminutive figures had teeth, fangs, claws, tentacles, horns, wings, and other things I couldn't even get my mind to identify. Every little face looked intently murderous. Shades of Hades, *preserve us!*

At the first sign of trouble, Lisette had tried to open the front door, but she'd had no success for some unknown reason. Roman looked up from the swarming demons and yelled, "Lisette, protect Cara! I'll try the door."

The beautiful Nightkind woman leapt over dozens of demons to stand in front of me. Roman went to the front door, but he too couldn't open it, either. He hurled himself against it with his preternatural strength with no visible effect. "I can't open the door. It must be spelled. This is a trap!"

Everyone in the room fought the miniature horde. Little gold figures were climbing up Tom's pants legs, biting and clawing at him. As soon as he'd fling them away, more took their place. Uncle Max picked up a wrought iron plant stand, took the aloe vera plant on it and threw it at an advancing three-inch tall Minotaur, a demon with a man's body and a bull's head. The Minotaur caught the plant and threw it back, hitting Uncle Max in the temple. He staggered, a cut opening on his head. Blood flowed down the side of his face. He managed to keep his grip on the stand and smashed it with all his might into the living room window. The stand bounced off the glass as if it hit a solid wall of rubber, the window glass actually bowed out for a second before springing back into a smooth, untouched pane. The impact of the bounce-back threw Uncle Max to the floor where a swarm of demons, the Minotaur in the lead, climbed on him, most going for his head, drawn by the scent of blood.

Chester and Paul were shooting green flames at the demons from small wooden wands. I knew Roman had taken away

Paul's own wand so I wondered if Chester had given Paul one of his chopsticks. Several of the tiny figures were engulfed in green flame, running around in circles as they burned into blackened cinders. Sonya had conjured up a personal body shield and backed into a corner. Archer stationed himself in front of her, protecting her from the attackers. Jupiter, his eyes blazing red, tore into as many of the demons as he could reach, crunching them between his sharp teeth into lifeless splinters of wood. Uncle Max had managed to regain his feet and began to weave a spell to break the window, but every time he drew a symbol in the air, a flying demon would erase it before it could activate.

I stomped on the demons that got past Lisette. She grabbed them, breaking them in two with her bare hands. A flying demon dive-bombed me, going for my throat. Lisette tried to grab it, but only managed to deflect it from its original target. It latched onto the top of my shoulder with sharp teeth and claws. The pain felt excruciating as it tore a dime-sized chunk out of my flesh, gibbering with delight as it gulped it down. I screamed, trying to pull it off of me. Its claws were half-inch needles both on hands and feet and all twenty were sunk to the hilt in my skin. Lisette snarled at the demon on my shoulder and reached towards it. It bared its bloody little teeth and released me, jumping out of reach of her hands. The same demon hovered near the ceiling then shot straight at the Nightkind's chest, too fast for her to catch it. It came at her like a diver plunging into a pool, hands over the single horn on its forehead, wings folded tight against its body to make itself into an aerodynamic projectile. She flew backward at the impact, almost doubled over at the waist. Her face registered surprise as she looked down at the wound in her chest, a pair of clawed demon feet the only thing showing against the white of her shirt. Then she started to cave in on herself, her skin turning gray and crumbling away. The thing had pierced her heart with its wooden body and killed her as effectively as a stake would have.

Horrified, I screamed again as she collapsed into a pile of dust on the floor at my feet. I clutched the wound in my shoulder and looked for Roman in a panic to warn him about what had happened to Lisette. I spotted him by Uncle Max. They stood back to back. Several of the flying demons were circling around Roman's head, darting in, inflicting a wound and darting away before he could catch them. His face and neck were covered with little bites and cuts. Tom fared even worse; the demons swarmed over him, clinging to him like golden leeches, inflicting as much damage as their diminished size would allow.

I reached inside myself to pull on my power, desperately throwing out tendrils of my aura to connect with those bonded to me. I could almost hear the psychic click of the connections as I became infused with streams of different energies. Tom's wolf's golden energy felt animal hot; Paul's pulled from the living green earth; and Roman's of cold darkness. They coalesced to become a pure shining core of power inside of me. The pain in my shoulder faded as I gloried in the power. I gathered it up into a pulsing ball, letting it feed and grow until I felt that my skin must be stretched into a thin diaphanous membrane barely containing the shining essence. I concentrated on the demons only; I didn't want to hurt my friends and family.

When I was ready, I yelled, "Take cover!" I sensed rather than saw larger bodies throwing themselves behind furniture. And then I loosed the energy in a blinding bright burst that radiated out from the center of my body in concentric circles of light, consuming the magic that had been animating the demons and my power blast fading as it hit the spelled walls.

I looked around the room. Lifeless little wooden statues littered the floor. "Everyone okay?" I asked.

Tom had a hold on Jupiter and they came out from behind a chair. Chester's book must have flown him into the kitchen because he came floating in from that direction. Sonya had curled up behind Archer. She looked shaken, but managed to smile a little. Roman ran over to me and started running his hands over my body, looking for injuries.

I slapped him away halfheartedly, my energy drained from the exertion it had taken to blast the demons. I looked around. "Where are Uncle Max and Paul?"

As everyone looked around, I spied Uncle Max crouched over Paul's prone body, partially hidden by a small wooden bookcase he had shoved away from the wall to act as a makeshift bunker.

Uncle Max looked up, saying, "Paul's alive, but weak. The energy Cara pulled from him took the last of his resources. He'll need to rest and recuperate for several hours."

I took a step toward Paul, concerned. A sharp sting on my ankle made me look down. A winged serpent had bitten me. The damned thing was still alive. I cursed as I stepped on it, breaking it into pieces. Then, as I watched in horror, several more figures began to stir.

"They're reanimating! We have to get out of this house." Uncle Max drew a symbol in the air that activated the mirror "The mirror dimension is our only way out. We have to go. Now!"

He grabbed one of Paul's limp arms, hooking it around his neck. Tom limped over to help Max. I went to Sonya and held out my hand. She stood shakily and took it. Her big brown eyes were a little glassy as we ran towards the mirror together.

She looked over her shoulder at the room, then tugged at my hand, bringing us to a stop before we reached the mirror, "Wait! My babies! Jupiter. Archer. Come to Mommy!"

The two huge Hounds came bounding up to flank us as we stepped into the mirror. I saw Roman and Chester close behind—Roman stomping on demon figures and Chester blasting them with a scorched-looking chopstick.

All of us finally stood in the white mist on the other side of the mirror, looking at each other. I took a deep breath which made my head spin. My shoulder throbbed from the bite and my ankle felt like it was on fire.

I bent over to inspect it and saw angry red lines radiating from the two tiny puncture wounds. "Chester, could you look at my ankle? On a da demonshs . . ." My mouth wouldn't form the words. My tongue felt swollen. Why's it getting darker in here? I wondered. The mist became so thick I could barely see anyone. I tried to go to Chester but somehow instead of moving forward I was walking sideways, bumping into Sonya. *That's strange. Huh. Let's try that again.*

I started forward and found myself looking up into a big furry face with bad sulfur breath. Jupiter licked my face and whined. How did I end up on the ground? I tied to sit up, but I couldn't move. Hands lifted me, every touch burning my skin. *No! It burns! Put me down!* I screamed silently. As hard as I tried, no sound escaped my lips. Another agonizing moment passed then a cloud of pink smoke drifted around my head and I inhaled the scent of strawberries that had me floating on a soft, pain-free cloud. *Oh, all right now, much better,* I thought, just before I passed out.

Chapter Seventeen
The Jungle

In my dream I was a little girl, sick with fever, lying in my bed at home. My mother put a cool compress on my forehead with gentle hands, chanting a healing spell in a soft, low voice. I wanted to open my eyes and see Mom, tell her I missed her, but my eyes just wouldn't cooperate. So I lay there and listened to the familiar chant I remembered from long ago. Soon it would be Vernal Equinox and the celebration of spring. I wanted to get well so I could find the hidden treats. My basket was usually full before everyone else's even though I caught Cousin Evika cheating by using a divining rod. We had a big fight over that. I said it wasn't fair for her to use a rod. She said it wasn't fair I was so good at finding hidden things, that she had to use something to help her or I'd end up with all the best treats. I said it wasn't *my* fault the hidden treats called out to me so I could find them. That shut her up, but she looked at me funny the rest of the day. I ignored her by asking Sonya to invite me over to her house so we could play with her Dad's Hounds.

I heard a man's voice. Dad? No, someone else. I knew the voice, liking it and not liking it at the same time. It made me feel all deliciously shivery, but annoyed, too. He sounded worried as he talked to Mom. Mom sounded worried too. I wondered what they were so worried about. But I felt too sleepy to think about it. Mom's healing chant always put me to sleep. So I just let myself fade into the comforting darkness, feeling safe and cared for.

My awareness sprang full blown from unconsciousness. No soft transitions. No gentle sliding from dreams to waking life. Like a bucket of ice water in the face. My eyes still closed, every muscle in my body tensed, ready to fight or run away, preferably the latter. I've had enough fighting to appease whatever female equivalent of machismo I might have had in me. I was ready to pack up my toothbrush, hair dryer, and best jeans and move to a different country as quickly as my legs could carry me. Disappointingly, my legs decided they liked it here where they could be couch potatoes, imploring me to tune the television to the Potions channel.

I finally opened my eyes and struggled to sit up. The dark was so complete I closed my eyes and opened them again to make sure my eyelids worked. They did. I lay in utter darkness and silence. Where was I? Where did everyone go?

"Mom?" I queried hesitantly. Had she been with me or was it just a dream? My voice echoed over and over, as if I were in a huge cavern. I giddily stifled the urge to shout "echo!" just to hear it, like a kid. What was wrong with me? I didn't know what else might be in here, so I couldn't even think about shouting.

For a moment, I thought it might be a good thing I couldn't see anything. But then the fear of the unknown dark took over. The fear came from the reptilian portion of my brain, the part that lived near the brain stem and liked survival, hoping to pass on my genes to some future generation one day. Unfortunately, that thought reminded me of Roman and his "offspring" plans.

I patted the area around me and discovered I sat on a soft mound of cloth, probably blankets. On further investigation, my fingers encountered the cool hardness of stone underneath the cloth. My legs still wouldn't work, but I stretched my arms out farther around me, hitting something softish to my right. It felt like a person lying on their back.

I rolled over on my stomach and pulled myself over to the person, using my elbows and forearms. Not as easy as it sounds without the use of my legs. I felt around for a head, found it, patted a bristly cheek. His skin felt cooler than I expected, even given the coolness of this place, and his body felt stiff. I pulled my hand away, startled. Then a thought came to me. I ran one hand over the body, holding myself up with my other arm. The well-developed but perfectly still chest and flat stomach were familiar. Indeed, I knew that chest well by now—Roman in his daylight-challenged mode, the lack of breathing perfectly normal, if creepy. Ha, fooled me once, but you can't fool me twice.

Well, at least I wasn't alone, even if he wasn't much help right now. And we must be in the real world, as opposed to the mirror dimension, with sunlight shining somewhere for Roman to be in this state. But why was it so dark? Were we someplace safe for Roman to sleep? If so, why was I here with him? *Oh no! What if he's turned me into a Nightkind?* Wait. I'm awake and he's not. Whew. Probably not changed. Either I'd have to wait until Roman woke up to tell me what in *Hades* was going on, or I could try to crawl out of here. In total darkness. With no clue in which direction to head. And I had to use the restroom or rest-rock, whatever. This felt so bad in so many ways.

I had no choice but to try to get someone's attention and take a chance on attracting the wrong kind of attention. "Hello! Can anyone hear me?" The echo said, "hear me...me...me?"

"Oh sure. It's always about you."

"You...you...you..." Said a teasing voice.

"Tom! Where are you?" I heard cloth rustling, footsteps walking towards me, hands patting my head and shoulder, then feeling me up. "Hey!"

"Sorry, too tempting. Besides, now I know you're okay."

He squatted beside me, warm and solid, smelling wonderfully of sun-warmed maleness with an undercurrent of wolf. I leaned into him. "Where are we? Why is it so dark? I can't see a thing."

"We're in a cave. Your Uncle took us through a mirror portal to a place where he says your parents were located. I think we're in a different country. It's all jungle out there. Oh, yeah, we put you in here because the Nightkind dude had to suck out the poison in your leg, and we didn't know if you'd make it. I guess we hoped that if you croaked, you'd at least come back as a Nightkind. Better than dead."

"Gee, thanks." I paused and frowned. "I don't think I'm a Nightkind. I'm awake and Roman isn't. And I can't move my legs. You'd think I'd be healed if I turned into a Nightkind."

"Yeah, probably. You feel alive and you smell alive. You don't have that weird Nightkind smell. I'd say you're definitely still the hot, live witch we all know and love. And, babe, that is like crazy good news." He choked out the last part, as if he were on the verge of tears. He wrapped his arms around me, hugging as much of me as he could gather into his arms, burying his face against my neck. "I was so afraid I'd lose you," he mumbled into my hair, his breath hot on my skin.

My she-wolf stirred sleepily, rubbed against his wolf energy reassuringly, then walked around in a circle, curled up, and went back to sleep. He took a quick, shuddering breath. As he let it out, his shoulders shook silently and I felt my neck getting wet. I wrapped my arms around him and just held him, realizing the depth of his attachment to me. I wished I could see his face. No sooner had I thought it, than a little orb popped into existence over our heads, emitting just enough light for us to see each other's faces. Now why couldn't I do that sooner?

Tom pulled his head away from my neck and looked up. "That's cool," he sniffed, smiling, turning his head to wipe the wetness on his face on the sleeve of his t-shirt. "Come on, I'll take you outside. I can see pretty well in the dark. That's why I volunteered to be on 'Cara alert' outside the cave, but your little light'll make it easier."

He lifted me up from his seated position and stood easily, making me marvel at werewolf strength all over again. He walked for a couple of minutes, then he pulled aside a heavy black cloth to reveal a sunlit jungle.

Out of the silent, dark, coolness of the cave, the air felt hot and muggy and so alive. The sun was glorious. Golden rays filtered through a thick canopy of trees, illuminating and backlighting vibrant green foliage. Looking up, I saw shining specks hanging suspended in long tunnels of light, falling in patterns of dots and dashes, like nature sending us messages in codes of heated energy.

I lifted up my arms, reaching for the sunlight, as if I could hold it in my hands. Tom smiled at me. His eyes looked like melted copper, as a splash of light briefly illuminated them while we moved along a narrow dirt path into the bustle of a camp. I smiled back at him. I was alive, being held by my gorgeous familiar. Just for a moment, I felt good.

The air here felt thick, full of a complex miasma composed of flowers, plants, animals, humans, and magic. A wild undulating cry from some hidden creature washed across the encampment, triggering a cascade of responses from the surrounding jungle denizens. I'd never experienced this strong a presence of magic from a place; it permeated everything. This area had been saturated with it for so long it had become part of its very elemental molecular structure, down to the last speck of dirt, tendril of vine, insect, and animal who made their home here. Just breathing in the air, taking the ambient magic into my lungs, made me feel stronger.

I looked around me, wondering how people could go about their daily tasks so calmly when I wanted to go running into the heart of this place to let the magic fill me up. I imagined lying sheltered in a bower of green, eating sweet, exotic petals of fleshy blooms.

It called to me, and I started to squirm in Tom's grasp. "Tom, put me down. Can't you feel it?"

"Feel what?"

"This place, the air, the jungle."

"I don't feel anything except maybe too much sweat. The humidity is what gets to you. Makes the heat worse."

I hadn't noticed the heat after my first impression as we'd left the cave. It felt wonderful to me. Like a caress, it lay against my skin. My every movement caused the air to slide sensuously across my sensitive nerve endings. My she-wolf roused herself, stretched luxuriously, and sniffed the air. This looked to be prime hunting ground with trees and plants to offer camouflage, so many warm little bodies to chase and eat. She wanted to run, to smell all the delicious things out there. Tom's wolf responded to her. I felt him tighten his hold on me, felt the heat of his body, then felt his aura radiating out to mingle with mine.

"Oh god, Cara. What are you doing? I feel like I want to lay you down right here and make love to you 'til we both come screaming, but we're in the middle of a bunch of people. So stop it." As I wound my arms around his neck, he put his lips on mine and whispered into my mouth, "I mean it, Cara." Then he clamped his lips over mine and groaned.

My body tightened, grew wet, wanting him to do what he'd suggested. I felt drunk on the magic, on being held so close to a warm male body. I vaguely registered another presence, another aura drawn to my desire. Another pair of hands caressed my body, kissed the nape of my neck. I broke the kiss with Tom to see what I already knew, the other presence was Paul. He had a glazed look, like he didn't know why he was doing these things, as if his reason had been swept away on a tide of passion. He tried to take me out of Tom's arms, but Tom stepped back and growled. Then he looked at me and blinked.

I looked back and forth between them, saw the desire in their eyes, and I wanted them both, at the same time. The thought surprised me enough that I shook my head, trying to clear it. What was I doing?

Then my joy melted around the edges. I couldn't make the feeling last, had never really thought I could. Maybe was afraid to let it overtake me. I cleared my throat. I had to say something. "Hey, you guys. This isn't right. It's the wrong time; wrong place. Tom. Paul. Snap out of it."

"Whoa. Sorry babe. I got caught up in the moment," Tom said, embarrassed.

Paul looked shaken. "I couldn't seem to help myself. In the middle of a conversation, I suddenly had to find Cara. I just walked away in mid-sentence. I saw you standing here, kissing each other, and I wanted to join you. I don't know how far things would have gone if Cara hadn't said something. Strange, this is not like me, public displays of affection and all. But I swear I would have done anything she wanted me to do." Paul shook his head as if he could shake off the haze that had taken over his mind.

"Yeah, I hear you, but my wolf wanted her all to ourselves. No sharing the alpha female, dude."

Tom had turned his body sideways, like he wanted me out of Paul's reach. Paul's face turned red. I don't know what would have happened next because a maturely beautiful woman wearing khaki shorts and a black t-shirt came running up to us.

"Mom!" I cried.

"Cara!" She looked worried and relieved at the same time.

"Mom, I didn't dream you! You really were with me."

I held out my arms and Tom obligingly positioned me so I could hug her as soon as she reached us. Mom told Tom to bring me over to a large tent at the far end of the camp. Inside, a battered wooden table covered with maps and papers stood in the center. Around the tent's perimeter, scattered as if hastily dumped, were sleeping cots, folding camp chairs, and black metal storage lockers. A double lantern hung over the table from the tent's support pole. Protective wards had been drawn on the fabric of the tent at the four compass points. I could feel them, like a barely perceptible ambient buzz of white noise, soothing instead of annoying. I knew if something bad entered the tent, the buzz would quickly turn into a burning pain. I had heard it said this type of ward, when activated, felt like a colony of angry fire ants biting and swarming underneath your skin. Ugh.

I still felt like a glass full to the brim with the magic of this place. It made me a little woozy, dampened my inhibitions and made me want something, but I didn't know what. It had channeled itself into desire a moment ago, but now it sat inside me, eager as a pup to play, to be free. Tom set me down gently on the closest cot. I automatically reached to pull down my dress, but discovered I wore a pair of baggy shorts and a t-shirt. With all the sensations that had overwhelmed me, I hadn't noticed someone had changed my clothes while I was out.

The clothes I wore smelled of Mom's perfume. It would be just like her to bring her bottles of fragrance to a camp or war zone or whatever this place was.

I looked down at my legs. I had only been bitten on one of them. So why couldn't I move either leg? A bandage covered a good portion of my right lower calf; the flesh around the edges of the dressing looked red and swollen. I gently pulled up a corner of the taped gauze pad to take a peek. There were two sets of puncture wounds. A tiny one with less than an inch between the two marks. Around the bite a discolored area had blossomed to about the size of a silver dollar, and my skin had turned an unhealthy looking reddish purple. Now that I had started paying attention to the wounds, they began to hurt. Why does that always happen? I had no idea, but the serpent-demon's bite felt like someone was slowing stabbing my ankle with a hot barbeque fork. It shouldn't be this bad, should it? Tom joined Paul outside the tent and they wandered off talking in hushed tones to each other.

My mother came over and sat by my legs on the cot. She looked at the wounds with a frown. "We tried everything, even having the Nightkind drain the wound area and give you more of his blood, but we couldn't get it to heal completely. Your wizard friend, Chester, seems to think the thing that bit you had been specifically cursed so that its bite was lethal to witches. We're lucky you survived. It was touch and go for you, to the point we put you in the cave in case you *turned* with all the Nightkind blood in you."

All the Nightkind blood in me? Huh. I filed the comment away to think about later. "I was only bitten on one leg, so why can't I move the other one?" I asked.

"The poison had reached your lower back by the time you got here. It must have affected the nerves there."

I frowned, confused. "But why kill me? From what Uncle Max said, the demons want me to help them open the Portal."

"You may not have been the original target," my mother said. "The spell was on Sonya's mirror frame."

"Sonya? It may have been targeted to kill Sonya?" I gasped in disbelief. "But why kill her, and why kidnap Evika? Do you know what's happening, Mom?" I had this childlike wish that Mom would be able to explain it all to me, and then fix it, like when I had been little.

Of course it didn't happen that way. She just shook her

head as she said, "No, I don't know, but we are trying to find out. For now, though, I'm planning a healing circle for you tonight at moonrise."

Before I could respond, she reverted back to being brisk and matter-of-fact. Sometimes those sharp bristles on the outside made her soft inside part hard to detect. But that was Mom. "Cara, I have to tell you something. Dad and I both hoped—and dreaded—the possibility of you coming into your powers. We waited until well past the point when most witches manifested, but yours never did, so it looked as if it wouldn't happen, despite the color of your eyes.

"Eyes of Dominion," I muttered to myself, remembering what Chester had said to me.

"Yes, you were born with the Eyes of Dominion, with that distinctive gold band around your pupils. Your grandmother seemed sure you'd be a mage, I actually thought it was an old witch's tale to explain an unusual coloration that crops up in a family every so often." She looked uncomfortable as she confessed, her eyes darting away from mine.

"Why didn't you tell me?"

She shrugged. "What would have been the point? If it didn't happen, you'd be none the wiser, and wouldn't carry the burden of unrealistic expectations. If your powers did manifest, we could help guide you. That was the theory, anyway. How could we have known events would take place the way they have?" She had a defensive tone in her voice which quickly turned to scolding. "I can't believe you made a *werewolf* your familiar, and bound a *Nightkind* to you! Those were not good choices." She sounded surer of herself now that she was on the more familiar ground of me screwing up.

"Mom, I didn't *have* a choice. It just happened. I can't do anything about it now because it's done. If you had seen fit to tell me about all this, maybe I could have protected myself and the people around me. But now we'll never know, and I have to live with what happened, not you."

My mother scowled at me. "Don't be so self-centered, young lady. The whole family has to live with it. Like it or not, you will likely be a major power and have the family responsibilities that go with it. You're not a child anymore. You can't think just of yourself."

I lay back in the cot. This was the same old stuff that kept me away from home all these years. "Mom, I'm feeling pretty

tired and my leg hurts." You'd think that if I couldn't move my
legs I'd at least get the benefit of being numb, but noooo. Why
should I get lucky on this one? "Could you bring Chester to
me? He has some medicinal potions to help the pain." And get
me high enough to stop feeling so guilty I wanted to add.

"Oh, darling, of course. Here I was lecturing you while
you're in pain. I'm sorry." There she went, being all motherly
nice so I'd have to forgive anything irritating she might have
said. I sighed, that's family for you.

She scurried out, and a few minutes later Chester came
riding into the tent on his trusty book. He administered a healthy
dose of his wonderful pink smoke, and after getting comfortable
on the cot with pillows behind my back, Mom decided to let me
have visitors. What I didn't expect was the continuous stream
of people—friends, family, and people introducing themselves
for the first time. Tom, Paul, and Sonya sat with me most of
the day. Others told me it was hot and humid, but the weather
didn't affect me the way it did the others. Although I wondered
about that, I was glad I was spared the discomfort. Of all of
them, the heat seemed to affect Paul the most. Looking wilted
and uncomfortable, he sat fanning himself with a large leaf,
beads of sweat dripping off his nose. Sonya informed me the
Hounds were out in the jungle somewhere, presumably hunting.
Uncle Max had left the camp on some kind of reconnaissance
mission with Dad.

In the heat of the late afternoon, I fell asleep during a lull in
the visits, my leg throbbing, despite Chester's smoke. I wished
the human medicines would work on us because from what
I'd heard about the painkillers, I could use some right about
now. Our physiologies were enough alike for us to have kids
together, and medicines worked on us the way they were
supposed to about half the time. But the side effects when
they didn't work were often worse than the original ailment, if
not downright lethal. Taking an unknown human medicine was
like playing Russian roulette with half the chambers filled instead
of one, so the magical community still mostly relied on old-
fashioned remedies like healing circles, spells, and potions.

When I woke up from my nap, I saw stars. Not the cartoon
kind when you've been whacked in the head with an anvil, but
the *twinkle, twinkle* kind. I lay in the same cot which had
been in the tent. It, with me in it, had apparently been moved to
a clearing off to the side of the camp, near the cave and away

from the privies. Not that the privies smelled. Fortunately, someone in camp had spelled them so the, um, waste would sink deep into the ground and break down harmlessly into the local ecosystem. No muss, no fuss. Gotta love modern magic. But contrary to popular human belief, magic couldn't do everything and there was always a price to pay. The bigger the magic, the bigger the price. So it couldn't end all world hunger, clean up all human pollution, or bring peace and goodwill to everyone. In fact, it always seemed doing good took more effort than doing evil, like breaking something was easier than building it. That's why we had to stop the bad demons from bringing more bad demons into our world. If a drop of venom could poison a well, an endless torrent could make our beautiful adopted world a twisted, noxious hell to live in. I, for one, didn't want to let that happen, if I could help it.

My thoughts were interrupted by a cold wet nose, followed by a warm wet tongue. One of the Hounds had returned from hunting. I reached out to ruffle Jupiter's ears. His flickering Hound eyes were twin flames of orangey red in the dark. Shadows shifted and moved around me, revealing people from the camp. They must be here for my healing circle. I thought about Tom and he appeared silently by my side. He held a candle, bathing his blond hair in a warm golden glow that threw his handsome face into shadowed relief.

He smiled. "Hey babe, we're going to do the healing thing for you."

"Yeah, I figured that out. I must have been out of it because I didn't even wake up when you guys moved me."

He looked troubled like he wanted to say something but held it back. "What?" I asked.

"What?" he said back.

"What aren't you telling me?"

"What do you mean?" He tried to look innocent and almost succeeded, but not quite.

"Come on, spill it. I can tell you want to say something."

He looked around, and said in a sotto voice "Your Mom would kill me if I told you, but Shades of Hades, you should know. We're worried about you because the demon bite is getting worse."

I looked down at my leg, but I couldn't see in the dark, "Lower the candle, I want to see."

"It's probably better if you didn't."

"Tom. Do it. I have the right to look at my own damn leg!" He let out an exasperated sigh and positioned the candle so it illuminated my leg. The reddish purple discoloration had spread way beyond the gauze bandage so it now nearly covered the whole side of my calf from ankle to knee. I swallowed hard. He'd been right. I'd have probably better off not knowing.

"Tom! What are you doing? What did I tell you?" my mother's commanding voice barked from the shadows, making Tom jump in guilt.

"Sorry, Solange, but she wanted to see it. I mean it's *her* leg, you know?" He managed to sound defiantly apologetic. I must be rubbing off on him.

"Mom, don't blame Tom. I ordered him to help me see my leg." I said tiredly.

My mother came striding over to us. She wore a long white robe, one I'd seen her don many times in the past for serious spell work. Paul walked a step behind her, carrying a large, ornately carved wooden box about the size of a piece of carry-on luggage. He, too, was dressed in a robe, only his was gray. My eyes had adjusted to the candlelit darkness enough to see everyone gathering around us wore the same type of gray robes that Paul had on. Well, at least Mom didn't make them all go sky-clad. Those circles always embarrassed me. I never knew where to look when talking with someone. I'm actually a little prudish for a Druccan, which my family often teases me about. But hey, that's just the way I am.

"Darling, I didn't want you to worry." Mom came over and smoothed my hair back from my forehead and gave me a little kiss there.

"I know, but as you reminded me earlier today, I am not a child. I need to know what's happening so I can make my own decisions."

She patted my shoulder saying, "Of course, dear, you're a grown-up now." The words were fine, but the tone said, I know what I said, but you're really my hurt little girl and Mommy is going to take care of you because Mommy knows best and I'll pretend to treat you like a grown-up because I don't want to upset you, but you're just being silly.

I smiled at her, resisting the start of an argument. She'd need her focus on channeling the circle, not on being angry with me. Anger in a healing circle could mess things up, and I could have a healed leg but end up with hives or something.

Paul set the box down at the foot of my cot and came over to us. He winked at me over my mother's head so she couldn't see him. I immediately felt better.

I looked around for Roman. Shouldn't he be awake by now? It was dark. Tom guessed who I was looking for, because he said, "Your Mom said a Nightkind couldn't be part of a healing circle, so Roman and the floating old dude went off somewhere." I didn't know if that was true or Mom was just biased against a Nightkind, but it didn't matter. If Roman's presence distracted her, the healing might not work as well as it should, and from the state my leg was in, I couldn't afford anything going wrong.

I watched Mom bustle about, situating the participants into a loose circle around me. They all held either purple or blue candles, now all lit, to help call on healing energies from within themselves and from the universal life force around us. The night air felt mild, a relief from the daytime sauna-like heat. I could hear the sounds of nocturnal jungle inhabitants starting their serenades, and I inhaled deeply as a light breeze brought me the alluring fragrances of night-blooming flowers.

With everyone arranged to her satisfaction, Mom came over to stand at the head of the cot. "Just lie back and close your eyes. Open yourself to the healing. Let the energies lift away the poisons, let the light dissolve the discord in your body and mind to bring you into harmony and balance."

Her tone had taken on the singsong quality of formal wording. She stood silently for a moment, then started chanting the words for the healing. The people in the circle joined her, their voices low and soothing. I closed my eyes and let the voices wash over me, bathing me in soft, positive energy.

The chant sounded almost musical, with the words needing to be said in a specific tonal range to resonate with the proper energies. I could feel my body start to tingle, my legs especially. It felt wonderful, like being immersed in warm bubbles that effervesced around me, through me. The chanting grew hypnotic, permeating my entire consciousness until nothing existed but the rise and fall of voices and the swirling energies cleansing and healing my body. My mother became the focus as the others sent their energies to her so she could channel and release the power into me. She directed the flow to my wounds, keeping the balances and intensities exactly right. She stood as a shining tower of pure energy in my mind's eye, directing the flowing musical energies around her. This was her power, her strength. I realized this was where I was formed; the genesis of my own powers lay here, in her ability to pull and focus where others would be consumed.

And then I forgot all about her, about the people in the circle, about everything, as my mind and body floated, suspended in the astral plane. I looked down at myself, lying on the cot, at my mother and the healing circle. Their auras shimmered like northern lights against the dark ground and, for a moment, I couldn't tell if the sky was up or down. I could see a glowing thread connecting me to my body as I rose higher and higher into the cloudless night sky. I turned my face to the three-quarter moon, absorbing its cool light. I felt I must be shining like a new star, with all the energies building and swirling inside me. It felt peaceful here as I filled with tranquility and quiet vitality. I wanted to heal. I was tired of being hurt, and I flung my wish out in a wave of fervent desire. *Heal me. I want to be whole.*

As I floated, I became aware of two orbs of light drifting towards me. I felt no alarm at their presence; nothing to indicate I should be wary. They circled me slowly. It seemed one came from the heart of the jungle, and the other from the sky. As the orbs grew closer, I could see one had the golden glow I normally associated with *were* auras, and the other had an unusual swirl of rainbow colors, like a soap bubble, the shining hues merging and separating in a continuous dance of lights.

I ignored them, wanting to regain the peaceful feeling I'd had before. But they circled closer, darting within inches of me, then arcing away again to continue their orbit around me, forcing me to notice them.

What are you? I thought.

We came to your call, the golden orb said in my mind. It had a feminine tone and feel, like a little silver bell of a voice.

The rainbow orb pulsed brighter, a bass tone like a huge Asian temple bell, told me in a thought, *I came to your call . . . like to like.*

I didn't call you and I don't know what you mean by like to like, I thought, confused.

We heard you call, sang the golden orb.

You pulled me from my slumber, young mage, the rainbow orb seemed to grumble.

Go away, I'm trying to heal, I said to them, and made a

shooing motion with my astral arms, which caused me to spin slowly and float upside down.

From this angle I noticed the chanting had stopped. My mother had moved from the head of the cot to stand over my legs, her arms outstretched, palms down, to direct the energies into my damaged body. I wanted to see my leg wound, and at the thought, I started drifting down towards the ground. The two orbs followed me, as if they too were curious. I floated unseen by the participants to hover over my body and watch as the discoloration on my leg slowly receded. A strange, sickly green-black haze seemed to cover my lower body, and a stream of white light poured from my mother's hands into the haze, burning it away like the sun burns off fog. But the haze seemed to be renewing itself. As parts of it burned away, more of it would billow out of the wounds to reshape the areas the haze had lost. Although the white energy edged out the haze for now, it was a close call. I didn't know how long the circle could feed energy to my mother.

I looked around at the participants and saw on their faces the terrible strain it put upon them. Paul's eyes were closed, his face pale. I reached out towards him, then drew back quickly as something lashed out at me from his body. It looked the same nauseating, green-black bile-color as the haze. I recoiled in horror when I saw that a tentacle of dark energy had connected itself from Paul to my physical body on the cot, and that tentacle fed power to the killing haze.

Horrified, I thought, *Oh, no, not Paul!* Did he work for the enemy? Anguished, I flew up into the sky, then back down again. My heart ached from this betrayal by someone I cared for and thought cared for me. I tried to yell, to tell Mom about Paul, but no one could hear me. The two orbs spun around me as if sensing my anguish. The small golden one zipped down to Paul, seemed to look at the dark tentacle of power, then flew back to the rainbow orb. The two orbs touched briefly, and then both flew down by Paul.

They hovered for an instant, and then both zipped under his robe. I continued my attempts to get Mom's attention. Her face was tight with the effort to keep the energy flowing, to keep fighting back the haze. I could see her faltering. She slumped a little and took a step back, and her arms sank a few inches. She looked like she had to struggle to keep them positioned over me. As I watched her, a tear streaked down her cheek, and I knew she couldn't hold on much longer. The haze was starting to win the battle over me; the reddish-purple poison now covered my entire leg to my hip. I could sense my physical form weakening, the shining tether holding me to my body looked thinner now, ready to snap.

No! I wasn't ready to die.

Suddenly, Paul jumped out of the circle, beating at his robes and yelling. The others around him broke their meditations to look at him. He ripped off the robe and threw it on the ground, then stripped off his pants. They were on fire. As his pants hit the ground, a small golden object fell out of a pocket. I could see it was a miniature bull's head. A stream of green-black energy poured from its open mouth, supplying the haze with power.

Suddenly, a look of loathing came over Paul's face. He stared at the object as if a venomous spider had crawled out of his clothing. He grabbed a nearby rock and brought it down on the bull's head, smashing it to pieces.

The two orbs flew out from under his pile of clothes. They went straight to my still body on the cot. My mother had collapsed to her knees beside my cot, one arm flung protectively over me. The orbs flew in a spiral over my legs, then sank into them. I felt a jolt, a violent tug on the tether, and then my body spasmed. Mom struggled to her feet to hold my shoulders. Suddenly, I was sucked back into my body. I sat up, throwing off my mother's arms, eyes wide open. My legs were glowing from within, lighting the area around the cot. Two men had Paul by the arms, restraining him.

I heard the orb voices in my head. *Do not fear, we are healing you*, they said.

I could see the poisoned areas of flesh growing smaller, the infection dissolving in the glow. The energy of the circle reasserted itself, now unobstructed, guided somehow by the orbs to heal me. In a matter of seconds the glow faded to nothing leaving behind perfect, healthy flesh. I wiggled my toes and they worked! I moved my legs, and they worked too! I felt okay—better than okay. I felt wonderful!

Two depleted-looking orbs rose out of me and hovered. *Thank you so much*, I thought gratefully. They bobbed as if in reply and then winked out.

I swung my legs over the side of the cot and sat up. My mother threw her arms around me and gave me a hug. Then she turned with fire in her eyes to look at Paul. "Chain the wizard to a tree and set a warded circle around him. I'll interrogate him later." Paul struggled between the robed men. One of them said a word and Paul slumped, unconscious.

Tom and Sonya ran up to me, faces full of concern. Jupiter trotted over to the sniff the wooden fragments that constituted the remains of the bull head. He sneezed, then growled at the broken figurine. Like wolves, Hounds rarely bark, but they nonetheless have an amazing repertoire of sounds by which to express themselves. At this moment, Jupiter's growls held an element of urgency the three of us responded to.

Sonya said, "What is it, boy?"

Jupiter bounded to her then back again to the broken bull's head, snapping at it, eyes blazing red. His brother, Archer, chose that moment to come running out of the jungle, a piece of raw meat dangling from the corner of his mouth. Archer quickly gulped the meat down whole as he joined us. Jupiter sniffed, then licked, the blood off his sibling's muzzle before turning his attention back to the bull's head.

The largest intact fragment, containing the bull's nose and mouth, was moving. It inched along the ground like a hideous slug, gathering the scattered splinters of itself in its mouth. Each gathered piece incorporated itself back into the place it belonged, as if it were made of protoplasm instead of wood. At this rate it would be whole again in minutes.

Tom picked up a rock, raising his arm to re-smash the dreadful thing, but I held up a restraining hand. "Tom, no, don't. I think we need to do something different his time."

He looked at me, nodded and dropped the rock he held. It landed on the ground with a solid thud. I could feel the impact through the soles of my feet, and I realized it could have been classified more as a small boulder rather than a rock. Tom had handled it as easily as I'd handle a pinecone

The rush of magic again filled me up, making me giddy. The poison had left my system, allowing me to be open to this powerful place. Something bright zipped past my head, too large to be a firefly. Did they even live in this part of the world? It flew in a large loop around the camp then settled on my shoulder. It was the golden orb that had helped me heal. It looked brighter, recharged, for lack of a better description. It nestled in the curve of my neck, under my hair.

You're back! I thought at it. I got the impression of a

question mark from it, like it didn't understand.

You called, it sang to me in its silvery bell voice.

You healed me, and that's what I needed. You can go if you want. I release you.

It quivered under my hair, making my neck tingle. *You called, I am here, I am with you*, it sang, frustration coming through in its thoughts.

You mean indefinitely? Like from now on? I thought, suddenly alarmed.

Yes! It thought happily in a "the dense one is finally figuring it out" kind of way.

I looked down at the bull's head which grotesquely rooted around on the ground for more of its pieces. I took a deep breath and yelled out, "Mom, I need help here!" I took another deep breath. Would this nightmare never end?

Chapter Eighteen
Suspicion

"I don't know how that thing got into my pocket!" Paul sat red-faced, bound by loops of finely-wrought spelled chains. He sat in one of the folding camp chairs. The chains were wrapped cuttingly tight, trussing him securely to the trunk of a large, lushly foliaged tree, its high canopy lost in the darkness of the night. Someone had hung a lantern above his head, on one the lower branches. The light cast his face in harsh shadows, his eyes unreadable. His hair looked disheveled, clothes in disarray. "It must have happened at Sonya's house, when we were fighting the things that jumped off the mirror frame."

His voice sounded hoarse, like he had been shouting for a while. I tried to harden myself towards him in case it turned out he was a traitor, but I just couldn't believe he was guilty. I'd be able to tell wouldn't I? We were, after all, connected, bound by our very essences.

He looked at me with imploring eyes and I hurt with an inner anguish. My chest felt tight, as if I were bound by the cutting chains instead of him. He croaked from his dry mouth, "I could never hurt you, Cara. I adore you, you must know that! Please, please, believe me!"

"I don't know what to believe, Paul." I closed my eyes and shook my head. Someone came up behind me and I caught a barely perceptible whiff of expensive cologne layered over the dry tang of Nightkind. Roman put a hand on my shoulder, then slid it down my back and circled am arm around my waist.

Paul looked at us with resentment, renewing his struggles against the fragile-looking chains. "It might have been that monster standing there," Paul shouted. "He may have planted it to make it look like I had it all along. Why don't you question him?"

I stepped away from Roman and looked up at his impassive face. Roman returned my look, eyebrows raised. "What possible motive would I have in killing off my own *chosen* bride?" He frowned. "He's obviously trying to deflect everyone's attention away from him. The desperate act of a guilty man, I dare say."

A thrumming from the back of my neck made me reach under my hair, brushing my fingers against the golden orb. My hand felt like it had passed through a mild electric current.

The orb flew out and hovered directly above Paul's head. *Do you seek the truth from this one?* It sang to me.

Yes! You can do that? I thought back.

It can be shown to you, the silvery bell voice said. *What do you wish to know?*

I paused for a moment then thought back, *I want to know if this man brought the bull's head animorphia here to harm me. How did it get in his pocket?* I hoped I was asking the right questions. I had no idea how much this being of light understood.

The orb bobbed uncertainly. *This name you use is unknown; it is the evil wooden golem of which you speak?*

Yes, I thought, excited.

Very well, it sang. Without another thought it sank down into the crown of Paul's head.

I gasped, and Roman looked at me, then back at Paul, his expression puzzled. "What is it, Cara?"

I pointed at Paul, "Didn't you see it?"

He frowned at Paul, "See what?"

I could still see a small portion of the orb poking out from the chestnut hair on Paul's head. It shimmered and pulsed with light. How could anyone not see it?

My mother came over to stand by me, "What is it honey, did something happen? Is this too upsetting for you? Maybe you should leave this to us and go rest in the tent."

I swallowed. "Mom, do you see anything on Paul's head?" I asked, my voice coming out a little high and shaky.

She walked over to the bound wizard. "No, I don't see . . ."

She started to inspect his hair when Paul suddenly stiffened and threw back his head. His eyes rolled up to show the whites, and she jumped back from him, startled. "What's happening? Cara, are you doing this?" she asked in her commanding way.

I had no answer for her as I watched twin beams of light shoot out from Paul's eyes. I followed his line of vision. Just over our heads, the lights flattened out into an ovoid shape about a yard in height and double that in width. It hung suspended in the air, and images flickered there like we were watching an old-fashioned movie projection. I heard gasps and mutters from the other people in the camp.

The images from Paul's eyes were blurred, in tones of sepia, but as we watched they became clearer, although still retaining that peculiar coloration. I recognized Sonya's living room, with all of us fighting the mirror frame's *animorphia* creatures.

Tom, Sonya and the Hounds ran up to us. The Hounds growled, vicious white fangs exposed, staring at the tiny sub-demons running about in the projection. The fur on both the Hounds' backs stood up in ruffled ridges, and salvia dripped from their open mouths to the ground, and their breaths were filled with the nose-stinging smell of a freshly struck match. They watched the projection with their otherworldly eyes glowing red. Sonya gave their huge heads calming pats, telling them it was okay, not real. They seemed to understand, pushing their great bodies against our legs, their noses still wrinkled and their mouths open enough for tongues to hang out, but teeth mostly hidden. I staggered a step to the side as Jupiter sat on his haunches, too close to my legs. I continued to pat his velvety head.

I could barely bring myself to watch the images of me and my friends fighting for our lives, but watching it was easier than living it. I saw Lisette's demise when the sub-demon *animorphia* plunged into her heart. Roman had stepped forward reflexively as if to stop it. He caught himself, fists clenched, and his face arranged itself into one of impotent anger and sorrow. We watched as the battle scene narrowed down to Paul. He was obviously fighting for his life, but he still managed to watch the "me" in the projected scene, as he crushed, burned and battered the tiny horde. At one point a flying demon grazed his head, and he dropped to his knees to protect himself, batting at the horned creature diving at him. That's when I saw a little golden Minotaur run up to him, climb his pants leg, tear off its own head and stuff it into his pants pocket. The body fell lifelessly to the ground once its mission was complete. Paul, seemingly oblivious to the Minotaur's actions, managed to fend off the flying demon only to have to turn and fight a trio of horned and fanged horrors jumping up at him from the coffee table. As the lights blinked out, it seemed clear to me Paul hadn't known about the Minotaur's head in his pocket.

I turned and watched the golden orb rise out of Paul's head as he slumped over, unconscious. The orb once again looked faded, its glow dimmed to a faint glimmer as it slowly floated over to me to once again snuggle under my hair.

"Well," my mother breathed out, "If that was a true

depiction of what happened, I think we can give this wizard the benefit of a doubt. Let's untie him and get him onto a cot to rest."

As two male witches stepped forward to do as she asked, she whipped her head around to stare at me intently. "How did you do that, Cara?"

I could tell she was trying hard not to act as freaked out as she felt. There was an image to maintain as Head of the House, after all.

Before I could answer, I heard a deep male voice shout, "Zul's horns and tail, what was that all about?"

I swung around to see Dad stride out of the jungle, Uncle Max by his side. He wore khaki pants and a short-sleeved khaki shirt, stained dark under the arms and at the throat. A rifle was slung casually over his shoulder, and his short, graying, dark brown hair lay plastered to his head with sweat. Even with his face smudged with dirt, he looked as vital and strong as a man half his age, and his eyes positively shone with delight as he spotted me. He shrugged off his rifle and practically threw it at Uncle Max as he opened his arms for a hug.

I ran over to him and hugged him hard, sweaty and dirty as he was, smiling with relief the whole time because he was safe.

He gave me a little harder squeeze and released me. "I've missed you, kitten!"

"I've missed you too, Dad," I said.

"I wish we could just visit for a while, but there's no time." He looked over at my mother, his expression turning hard. "We found the way to the Caves of Dominion. From what we could gather, *Tezcatlipoca's* minions have been trying unsuccessfully to open the Portal, but it's just a matter of time before they succeed. We have to stop them before they figure out how to do it."

Mom came over and joined us, threading her fingers through Dad's. They walked hand-in-hand to the central tent, and Dad looked over his should at me, saying "Come with us, Cara. We don't have a choice now that we know they're close to opening the Portal. We'll have to move out in the next twenty-four hours, and there's a lot of planning we have to do before we leave."

Chapter Nineteen
Dangerous Influences

Some of the men took Paul to a tent to recover. It looked like he was innocent, but I couldn't quite shake the nagging suspicion I shouldn't fully trust him. I kept thinking back to how we met. Was it really a chance meeting on the plane? Why had he wanted to date me? Was he attracted to me for me, or for something else altogether? But then, would he have become my teacher, my lover, just to betray me? I wanted to say no, but men betrayed lovers all the time, didn't they? I'd been so sure of Paul's affection, so could I really have been so wrong? Then again, the orb had shown us it wasn't his fault, the sub-demon had planted its head in his pocket. Geez, who would have thought I'd ever say that phrase in my life? Planted its *head?* Shades of Hades, *my* head was starting to hurt!

I went looking for Chester to see if maybe I could get some of the medicinal pink smoke from him for my headache. I saw Tom and Sonya sitting together on a couple of camp stools in front of the equipment tent, Hounds at their feet, talking and laughing like two old friends. Sonya's eyes had a gleam I hadn't seen in a long time. Hmmm.

Tom glanced up as if feeling my gaze and waved at me. Sonya followed the direction of his gaze, and she waved too, but not before I saw a guilty look pass quickly over her face. She smiled and the look was gone, as if I'd never seen it. Well, well.

I ruthlessly tamped down a little spark of jealousy. I'd have to talk with her soon to tell her it was okay with me if she was interested in Tom. I'd never really wanted our relationship to be a physical one. He is my familiar and anything more was just too complicated. But then my life keeps getting more complicated by the day with no reason for me to hope it won't get messier. I just hate it when my life gets messy.

I let out a startled squeak when Roman appeared from out of nowhere to walk beside me. "Roman, don't do that! You nearly gave me a heart attack." I slapped at the arm he tried to wrap around my waist, moving away.

He just moved with me, smiling in an irritatingly indulgent way and kept walking, arm firmly in place around me. "*Cara mia*, you must know I wouldn't hurt you for all the rubies in the mirror dimension." I rolled my eyes as he continued, "I'm not pleased with this situation. I can't allow you to fight demons. How can your parents expect you to put yourself in danger? I won't tolerate it. I don't care about the portal or the demons. I tire of all this, and my business dealings are suffering from my absence. We need to return to San Francisco."

I stopped dead in my tracks and rounded on him. "Listen to me, Roman. I am going to help my parents defend my House and this world. It's the right thing to do. There is no way I can stand by and let more evil into the world if there's a chance I can stop it from happening. I'd never forgive myself—or you, if you stopped me." I stared into his eyes; they looked dark in the light of the campfires. Roman looked angry and frustrated with what I'd said.

"You promised to marry me, and I can't allow you to put yourself in danger." At my infuriated look he added with a slight shrug, "I'm willing to live with your anger as long as I have you with me."

His expression became stubborn. His lips compressed into a tight line, making his handsome face look more angular without the softness of his lips. He shifted his body so he faced me, and his hands gripped both my upper arms painfully tight, as if he wanted to shake some sense into me. I felt my stomach clench as a small fissure of fear went through me at the sudden realization that he really would try to take me away from this important mission. I knew that if he did, everyone in this camp would come to my defense. I didn't want to see anyone get hurt over his damned refusal to let me do what I needed to do.

Tom had walked up to us, scowling. "Hey, dude, take your hands off Cara."

Roman snarled, "This is none of your affair, wolf. Go away." Tom growled, crouching slightly. I could practically see the blond hairs on the back of his neck stand up. Roman turned his head to face Tom. "I don't want to hurt you. For some misbegotten reason my fiancé has forged a connection with you as her witch's familiar, and I don't want to harm anyone she cares about. But don't push me. Leave now or suffer the consequences."

Tom started forward but a slender, delicate hand on his arm stopped him. Sonya had joined us, bringing the Hounds with her. They sat behind her, watching us curiously, huge dark shapes with glowing red eyes.

Just when I thought things couldn't get more awkward I saw Paul running towards us. Chester flew right behind him, perched precariously on his book, one hand on his head in an effort to keep his reading glasses in place while the other hand clutched the edge of the book's leather-bound spine.

They both came to a stop beside Tom, and short of breath from his run, Paul gasped, "What's going on?"

I twisted in Roman's grip to look at Paul and said, "Roman doesn't want me to go on the mission." I turned to Roman and angrily spat, "I can't believe you don't understand how important this is! Evil demon lord causing global wars, bringing back human sacrifice on a worldwide scale, creating mayhem and *Zul* knows what else! What part of that scenario is okay with you? This is a deal breaker. If you stop me, I won't be your damned bride. I'd never marry a callous, coldhearted monster like you."

I paused, feeling so angry I could barely see straight. All the things he had done to me and to my friends came back to me in a roaring tide of resentment, and I said, "You're on my turf now and I don't have to put up with your high-handed, stupid, archaic Nightkind crap. I never want to have anything more to do with you!"

I would have yanked the ring off my finger if I wasn't still caught in Roman's steel-like grip. Uh oh, I thought, as the small, underappreciated rational part of my brain repeated the thought. *I was still caught in Roman's steel-like grip.* I stared at him, and like a glass of ice water, my anger turned to ashes in my mouth. His face was a mask of fury, his eyes pure silver. His face's pale, unnaturally luminous skin had pulled so taut over the bones of his skull that he was hardly recognizable. I had miscalculated the depth anger my words would cause. At that moment I knew without a doubt I was close to death. He might regret it later, he might even mourn my loss, but right now Roman stood on the shinning knife-edge of Nightkind blood-madness. That could send him into a killing rampage that might not leave anyone in camp alive. And I'd be his first victim.

From the periphery of my vision, I saw Chester slowly float around until he was about four feet off to the side of where I stood, and he said, "Just hold real still there, girl. Master Roman hasn't fed for days now, and his hunger is great due to blood loss from the battle with the sub-demons, and then feeding you after your injury. Then there's the magic in this place, which has to be playing havoc with him, and on top of that, you have these other men around you. He's not himself." Then to Roman, he said softly, "Master Roman, old Chester knows you don't want to hurt your bride-to-be. You're just a might hungry, is all. Let's go back to the City house so you can get the sustenance you need."

Roman ignored the old wizard, his full attention focused on me, his body trembling, and I knew instinctively he was fighting himself for control of the madness. I licked my dry lips and he focused on my mouth. The cold silver of his eyes began to bleed into black. I could almost see him start to channel his blood lust into something else. I heard buzzing whispers in my head. Was it the orbs or Chester? I couldn't tell. I shook my head. The voices were indistinct but annoyingly persistent. Roman filled my vision, my thoughts. His blood in me and mine in his, called to each other, and my body responded despite my fear.

Roman growled and brought his mouth down on mine in a punishing kiss. His extended fangs cut my upper lip as his tongue pushed inside my mouth. I opened my mouth wider to try to escape the fangs. He pushed even deeper, the taste of my blood making him crazed. He released my arms. One of his hands grabbed a handful of my hair at the back of my neck; the other pulled my hips in tight to his body. I felt the hard bulge of his erection as I struggled to breathe from his plunder of my mouth. I was drowning in him. Even through my fear, I felt my body respond to his passion, his lust. It was too much, and I tried to break free.

He tensed, breaking off the kiss, then put his mouth to my ear and fiercely whispered, "Struggling will make me completely lose control. Your fear and arousal are too intoxicating. They make me want to hurt you, bleed you, but they also make me want to fuck you, to make you never want to leave me."

"Roman, please." I whispered back, although it came out as a whimper.

"I *want* to please you, Cara, but you keep fighting me." His voice sounded low and deep and harsh, tinged with the madness I could still see on his face, in his eyes. "Don't you realize, you stupid little witch, how much I want you? You have bespelled me. I don't desire any other woman. I can think only of you. I *want* only you. I'm spellbound by your body, your fragrance, your blood, and your power, my infuriating *cara mia.*"

He was still balanced on the edge and I was balanced there with him. I somehow knew if he fell into the pit of madness he would take me with him, and there would be no stopping his rage from spilling out in a wave of destruction, hurting the people I loved, the people loyal to my House. As far as I could tell, no one else in camp had noticed our little group's deadly tableau. We were on the edge of the jungle, the thick canopy of trees crowding out the moon's light so that darkness concealed us.

The buzzing in my head grew louder, incoherent voices intruding until I thought I'd go mad with the noise. I reached up with a freed hand to clutch my head and realized that whatever was in my head was fading so I could think more clearly now. The noise receded until all I heard was a small clear silvery bell of a voice—the golden orb. But I still couldn't understand it. I saw a movement, a solid darkness against the moon dappled background. Behind Roman's back, Paul gestured to me and then pointed to Chester. I glanced towards the older wizard and sensed rather than saw that he had a wand out, ready to strike at his master. I wanted to tell him to stop, that Roman would never forgive such a betrayal. I opened my mouth to shout at Chester, but at that moment Roman tightened his arms, lifting me off the ground and biting my neck savagely. There was no preparation, no answering passion in me, only pain. I screamed.

The sharp pain of Roman's fangs faded as he sucked greedily at the wound he had made. My voice went silent, a pleasant lethargy stealing over my body as his magician's hypnotic venom entered my bloodstream. For some reason, I could now see more clearly in the dark. Tom had jumped on Roman's back, and I could hear the tearing of cloth, the sound of claws rending clothes as Roman's body jerked and twisted with the attack. And still he wouldn't release me. My blood and life were draining away with my consciousness. It'd be nice to just float away, like I did in the healing circle, but something wouldn't let me. The top of my head felt hot, pulling me back. The night became brighter—was it dawn already? *Would Roman stop killing me if the sun came up?* I wondered dreamily, as I gazed unseeing into the night sky.

The light above my head grew brighter and hotter until it burst into an incandescent strobe. At the same time, the intense green sizzle of a war-wand burst flashed across my field of vision. I instinctively closed my eyes tight, but even through my eyelids it was blindingly bright. Roman let go of me with a snarl and a shout. Without his arms holding me, I dropped to the ground in a boneless heap. Suddenly the burning light vanished, as if someone had flipped a switch, and the blessed darkness came back. I struggled to sit up, to open my eyes. I accomplished both to a degree, but flickering, amorphous, multicolored afterimages crowded my vision, so I still couldn't see what was happening.

I collapsed back onto the bare dirt and closed my eyes again, smelling the rich loam of the jungle in the ground beneath me. The afterimages from my punished retinas still vied for attention on the insides of my eyelids. I could hear shouts and footsteps of people from the camp running towards us, undoubtedly alerted to the scene by the impromptu fireworks display. The voices in my head were back. The golden orb's bell-voice stayed with me, but now the deeper gong-voice of the rainbow orb had joined it. They were trying to talk to me, to tell me what had happened to Roman.

The deep, rich tone of the rainbow orb took over the explanation in a series of images and thoughts. Roman had been seized by the blood-madness, but not on his own. A *push* from an outside source had tipped him from ordinary anger into the almost berserker rage of the blood lust that only Nightkinds can attain. It doesn't happen often, and it usually ends in the Nightkind's insanity, at which point he or she must be killed.

I was unexpectedly overcome by grief at the idea of Roman lost in the dark realm of blood-madness, that he would need to be killed like a crazed animal. My despair made it hard to take in any more of the orbs' thoughts. Yes, Roman tried to kill me, but according to the orbs, someone else had caused him to do so. Who would want to push him to the edge of madness to hurt me? I thought of Paul and the Minotaur head. Was he really innocent, or was there another enemy among us? Who could I trust?

My head spun with conflicting thoughts and emotions, as I felt hands lift me from the ground and carry me into camp. I told the orbs I didn't want to hear any more. I felt tired to my very soul and wanted to sleep for a week. A small part of me never wanted to wake up, the despair of suspecting that someone I cared about wanted to see me dead. I started to slip gently and gratefully into unconsciousness, shutting out the frenzy of shouts and activities around me, only to be jerked rudely awake by the orbs ringing loudly in my head.

You cannot leave. You must know, they sang.

Know what? I asked, thoroughly annoyed.

See. You must see, they replied, as my inner eyes looked on the scene I had just experienced, only now I was an observer, not a participant. Against the moon-drenched jungle night I saw the tall, dark silhouette of Roman holding my body tightly in his arms. Chester, on his book, hovered off to the side of us, sparse white hair standing straight out like a dandelion gone to seed. Tom had moved behind Roman, ready to spring onto the Nightkind's back. He had partially changed, his fingers tipped with lethal looking claws and his lips pulled back to reveal a mouth full of sharp teeth in a slightly elongated jaw. Paul started to recite an incantation of some sort, softly, barely audible, his fierce eyes belying the quietness of his voice as he focused on the two of us. I could see Roman open his mouth, the white glint of his fangs in the moonlight a moment before his savage, lightning fast strike at my neck. Thankfully, I felt no pain this time. I watched as he greedily drained my life's blood, his face contorted with fury, his eyes silver and black pits, merciless and cold as a snake's. This mindless animal wasn't the Roman I had grown to know, maybe even love. There wasn't a trace of humanity in him, apparently burned away in the flames of the madness. He was possessed and utterly out of control.

Like watching a movie in slow motion, I saw Chester raise his wand at the same time the golden orb flew out from behind my fall of hair to sit atop my head like a strange crown. The orb pulsed and glowed, its light growing brighter and, I knew from experience, hotter. It looked like a halogen light had been placed on my head, my body mostly in shadow, as it cast its harsh light on Roman and the others. I saw Sonya point a shaking finger towards Roman, shouting a command, fear and desperation in her eyes, and the Hounds leapt forward in perfect fluid synchrony, their eyes blazing red. Tom jumped onto Roman's back, tearing at him with his vicious claws, sinking his teeth into Roman's shoulder. But still Roman clung to me, his mouth fastened onto my neck, his body twisting to shake off his attacker. I could now see the color draining out of my face in the stark light of the orb. Chester uttered a word of power, causing a green blast to issue from the tip of his wand towards Roman. Simultaneously, the golden orb seemed to explode in light and heat like a magical incendiary bomb. I expected to see that we are all nothing more than charred remains, even though I already knew the outcome.

From out of nowhere, an odd rainbow-colored film snapped into place, covering everyone in what looked like giant body gloves, including the Hounds who had frozen in mid-leap. The one exception was Roman who shouted out something incomprehensible and released me a moment before he became encased in an opaque milky shell, which tore Tom off Roman's back and threw him several feet away where he lay stunned but not visibly injured. I could now see what I couldn't before. The rainbow orb had returned, and it flew wildly above us all, weaving a series of glowing symbols in the air that flashed and dissolved immediately. I knew it had produced the coverings. I just didn't know if they were meant to be protective or containing or, perhaps, both.

The rainbow orb still sang to me in its deep melodious voice, and I vaguely realized I was back in the present. I felt the orb sink into my solar plexus and spread itself like scented oil on water throughout my system, calming me, strengthening me. My own power surged up to meet this new thing, and as it did the rainbow melded with it. Connecting tendrils of energy shot out of me and plunged into Tom, Paul, and even Roman, who was still encased in his milky carapace. The rainbow orb directed the influx of powers with as much finesse as a conductor conducts an orchestra, each source a different instrument to blend and complement, soaring with the music of elemental energies. The orb then threw out its own tendrils, connecting us to every witch and wizard in camp, and then with the Hounds and all the animals of the jungle. Then it connected with the both the organic and non-organic yet living essence of the magical heart of this place.

Filled with life and energy, the orb and I, pulled in our connections. The orb disconnected from me and left my body with a promise of becoming my teacher in the mysteries of *Synemancy*. Surprised, I opened my eyes and sat up. The entire camp crowded around me. People shook their heads, as if they'd just woken up from falling asleep on their feet. The Hounds were at the foot of my cot, yawning and wagging their tails, eyes yellow with calmness. My mother looked at me askew, as if she didn't know who I was. Paul and Tom lay on the ground beside me, fast asleep. I looked over at Roman, standing statue-like, apart from us. The milky shell that had encased him had disappeared, and I had a moment of panic knowing he was free. But when he turned those gray eyes towards me, I could sense he was in control of himself once more. The madness had left him, but his face had become an immobile mask. I couldn't tell what he was thinking or feeling.

I looked away, not able to deal with him right now. I just felt relieved to know no one had died, including me. I wasn't sure what condition Roman might be in, but I simply didn't care right now. Even though I knew he'd been pushed by something to harm me, his attack changed something in me. There was now a part of me that was cold and emotionless. It was a deep, primal part of me I'd never known existed. And that part would be able to kill.

Chapter Twenty
Ziggurat

The next day, the camp made ready to move out. Roman had returned to San Francisco, but only after I threatened him with permanent encasement in the opaque shell if he didn't leave. What I didn't say was, even though he'd tried to kill me, I had feelings for him. How could I not like a man who paid attention to the things I liked, the way he comforted me, and . . . well, damn, even the way he pursued me, as if I was the most important, most desirable, woman in the world.

I held my breath to see what he would do. I didn't for the life of me know how I would make good on my threat to put him back in the shell if he didn't leave.

The two orbs, golden and rainbow, stayed close to me, hovering above my head everywhere I went. I felt like a kid with a couple of balloons tied to her wrist, but knowing they were there comforted me. Weirdly, since last night, people could now see the orbs. Roman had narrowed his silvery eyes at them suspiciously. He eventually decided it might be dangerous to stay with me in this place.

"Cara, I don't know why I went into the blood rage. I don't want to risk harming you again, so I'll leave now," he'd said.

I didn't tell him the orb had showed me he'd been under the influence of someone or something. The knowledge would have made him want to stay to find out what could do that to him, and, perhaps, make him an ongoing danger to me. I was happy when Chester offered to stay and help with the mission. Roman agreed, as did I, that we could use all the help we could get.

Naturally, Roman had to have the last word before he walked into the cave where Chester had opened a mirror dimension door back to the City. He vowed he would never stop trying to win me. The golden orb once more took up residence under my hair and seemed to go to sleep or hibernate or whatever orbs do when they aren't saving my witchy behind from disaster.

The camp was being broken down quickly and efficiently by a team who looked like they knew what they were doing. I noticed they used mostly manual labor and only a minimum of magic. A couple of the men had walkie-talkies that tended to go all static-y when Chester and his book floated nearby. After I told Chester to stay away from any of the equipment, I looked around for a spot where I could watch the camp but keep out of everyone's way. I sat on a tree stump, feeling useless as people rushed about carrying things, calling out orders, and generally looking like a colony of ants who had found an abandoned picnic lunch.

My mother had put Tom and Sonya to work and the Hounds were off hunting again. I'd heard Sonya warn them not to eat any endangered species. They focused on her with heads cocked, tongues lolling out. Jupiter blinked and looked at his brother who nodded back. Those Hounds were scary smart. I was glad they liked me.

Dad came over at lunch to sit beside me and brief me on "the plan." His and Uncle Max's earlier reconnaissance mission had yielded what they hoped was reliable information as to the location of the Caves of Dominion. Unfortunately, the only known way to get to them was located within a vast complex of connected underwater caverns in the Yucatan called *cenotes* that consisted of a 300 mile network of caves and tunnels. The locals called them the Rivers of Magic, which were once thought to be the gateway to the afterlife. I gasped at the magnitude of the search. It would be like finding *a wand in a thicket,* as the saying goes. But then Dad told me that, luckily, their informant had been able to narrow it down for them to a single hidden access point and had drawn a rudimentary map for us to follow.

Okay, this looked bad on top of bad. Not only did we have to find the Caves of Dominion and the site of the original Portal within the Caves, which by-the-way would be heavily guarded, warded, and who knows what else, by demons, but we had to get to the gateway via underwater caves, wearing scuba gear, and using a crudely drawn map as a guide.

"Dad," I said, "this is not sounding like a good idea. Besides, I've never scuba dived in my life! Is there some kind of spell to turn us into fish or something?"

"There might be, but no one here knows how to do something like that. And even if we did, you know transfiguration of a human is tricky. We'll also be underwater. If something goes wrong we won't have a safety net. No, this is the best plan we have. Donovan has scuba experience and he has all the equipment we need. We'll take an extra day so he can give you lessons before we dive for the gateway."

"Cousin Donovan? Dewlap Donovan?" I asked disbelievingly. "The cousin who tried to turn himself into a lizard when he was thirteen and ended up with floppy neck skin for a year? He's our dive expert?" I rolled my eyes. Here I thought Mom and Dad had a professional mission team to go save the world. Instead, we had volunteers from our extended family and a few allies from the House networks. "Doesn't anyone else out there think an insanely evil Aztec demon-god invading our world is, oh, I don't know, maybe a *bad* thing?"

"Frankly, the general attitude is that because Evika was taken, it makes this whole mess House Augustine's concern. She's one of ours, and each House takes care of its own. That's the way it's always been. I think the other Houses believe they can deal with one demon lord if we don't succeed, and they won't have lost any of their people in the process. And well, if we do succeed, then they won't have to do anything."

I was woefully ignorant of House politics. I was never interested in knowing the ins and outs of all that stuff, but I couldn't believe the other Houses wouldn't help. When had the Houses gotten so insular, isolated and selfish? I knew we'd all worked together during the Great Purge to save magic-kind. That was in General Portal History 101. What had happened? Had the intervening years and gradual, albeit reluctant, acceptance of us caused us to let down our guards? To turn our backs on our brethren in pursuit of money, influence, and power? Or could it be something more insidious and sinister? I shook my head. I didn't have the energy to guess why the other Houses refused to help. We'd just have to make do and hope to stop the demon somehow.

"As for your opinion of your cousin, Donovan's grown-up and matured since the unfortunate lizard incident. You'll be surprised when you see him" Dad said with a small smile.

Dad turned to me, his face now serious with regret and sadness in his eyes. "One more thing, Cara. We should have planned better, well, done a lot of things better for you. After we discovered that Evika's disappearance was linked to a maverick group of witches trying to raise the Aztec god, we should have told you everything. We knew there'd be a chance your power would manifest, but we thought you were too far past puberty, that you might not be a Synemancer. We thought a lot of wrong things."

He paused and took my hand in both of his. "I was away trying to find out how to get to the Caves of Dominion because we had heard Evika might be there, and your mother had her hands full pulling together people willing to fight. Your uncle Max was supposed to keep an eye on you. I know it's a poor excuse, but we were all so focused on these other things that, well, we just ended up not talking with you. We were wrong to keep you in the dark. If you'd known what could've happened you might have been able to handle how your abilities, er, attracted power sources to you and what form it would take."

Dad looked off into the jungle as he said this. His ears had pinked and he carefully avoided eye contact, as he let go of my hand to pat me awkwardly on the arm. What he meant was how I had bonded all these men to me. Oh well, he'd chosen to be part of the whole keep-the-truth-from-Cara conspiracy, so I didn't feel bad for him.

After the camp was finally packed up, we formed a caravan line to follow a narrow trail recently hacked into the living green mass of the jungle. The heavier items were being levitated by magic, and we carried our belongings in backpacks. I asked why we didn't have pack animals to help with everything, Dad explained we'd be leaving this part of the jungle and the animals would have to be set free without anyone to take care of them. It would basically be like hanging a "good eats" sign around their necks for the local predators. I nodded, ashamed I hadn't thought of that myself. It would have been cruel and bad karma to allow living things to die just for our convenience. I trudged along, careful to watch for tripping roots and poisonous insects. I wondered why my parents and those loyal to House Augustine were determined to stop *Tezcatlipoca* without the help of the other Houses. Walking the trail, thinking about the situation, I eventually could see why. It was hard enough for all of us, Portalkind, Nightkind, magic users, and humans to live here together without adding more evil to jam up the gears. The demons already here have left a pervasive taint around the edges of the general humanity, magic and non-magic alike. *Tezcatlipoca* would ratchet up the evil factor considerably. From what I'd learned about him so far, the demon-god would relish goading humans into initiating another Great Purge, turning country against country, neighbor against neighbor, and whispering dark thoughts into people's ears to bring about evil deeds on a grand level. Portalkind originally came to this world to fight side by side with the native magic users against the humans determined to wipe them out. After centuries, they managed to turn the tide of persecution and settle into an uneasy truce with humans. The witch inquisitors, preternatural being hunters and exorcists had decimated the magical populations, forcing the great Mages to open the Portal in the first place in an effort to find supernatural and preternatural allies in alternate dimensions.

That was ancient history. Things have improved in terms of equal opportunity and the like. It's not great, but better. They don't have public witch burnings anymore and staking a Nightkind only happens with a legal court order. Exorcists only cast out demons if it's determined it wasn't a consensual possession. The history of a people is a funny thing. It defines and teaches us, determines who we are and what we stand for. One major event can change everything. A curious string of events, thoughts, and deeds made it possible for my people to exist in this world. Another major event could cause us to cease to exist.

An object whizzed by my head, startling me from my brooding thoughts, the rainbow orb. I felt a burst of happiness at its return. The golden orb flew out from under my hair and circled around the larger orb like a bright little planet orbiting around a rainbow sun. I smiled as I walked along the trail behind Tom who carried a backpack that looked bigger than he was.

We marched all day, with only a lunch break and a quick reenergizing circle for the heaviest magic users. The air felt still, hot and humid. Plant-filtered sun beat down on us relentlessly. Although I longed for the relief of night, I worried the sun would set before we could get to our destination. The farther away from the camp we got, the less I could feel the magic heart surrounding the cave. Oh, it lingered, but the almost intoxicating power it radiated was starting to fade, and with it went my initial immunity to the heat. What had felt like a warm caress at the campsite had turned into a hot, sticky annoyance in this part of the jungle.

None too soon for me, the word came back that we were almost there. My feet ached in my borrowed shoes and my t-shirt was soaked with sweat. I would have given anything to be able to take a shower. I even guiltily thought about Roman's luxurious bathroom, which caused me to think about Roman. Those thoughts made my stomach hurt, so I stubbornly turned my attention to my surroundings. The pervasive dense flora of the jungle started to clear and the trail widened. I started to see vestiges of ancient stone markers and crude monoliths, carved with grotesque images oddly elegant in their raw intensity. The exact nature of the carvings was difficult to make out as masses of sinewy vines, dark green moss, and spider webs covered most of the huge stones. From what little I could see, the carvings looked to be of women and men in ceremonial headgear interacting with fanciful animals, wolflike in appearance on some stones and feathered dragons on others.

Over the tops of the heads of the people in front of me, I saw an incredible stone temple slowly rise out of the jungle. With each step closer, I became increasingly overcome with the magnificence of the structure. The sides of the pyramid-shaped building consisted of huge, terraced stone steps, each step taller than a man's entire body. I wondered how people got to the top and then saw that a long staircase, one with smaller steps a human could climb, spanned the front of the temple, or what I guessed was the front. The stairway was wide at the bottom and gradually narrowed at the top. I couldn't tell exactly, but it looked like a stone alter at the top. It consisted of four stone columns held up a carved stone slab.

The orbs both swooped down to nestle under my hair and started to vibrate with what I sensed to be agitation. This place alarmed them, made them uncomfortable.

What's the matter with you two? I thought at them.

The silvery ring of the golden orb answered me. *Bad priests spill blood, take lives here. Tezcatlipoca demands many sacrifices.*

There's no one here anymore. No priests. Look at the temple, it's totally deserted, and the people long gone. It's okay, you don't need to worry. I tried reassured in an effort to get them to calm down. Their vibrations against my sweaty neck were starting to give me another headache.

The rainbow orb acted uneasy and that surprised me. It seemed to be the more powerful, somehow more mature, one. The rainbow orb gonged deeply in apprehension, but I didn't couldn't understand its words. I saw a movement ahead of me. Tom had turned to face me, waving his hand at me to get my attention. I could see his lips moving, but with the orb's bass tones ringing in my head, it drowned out anything my physical ears could hear. The look on his face was amused irritation tinged with a certain urgency.

I thought at the rainbow orb, *Stop making that racket. I need to hear Tom.*

The orb-voice rang a single discordant *bong,* as if miffed by my request, and then stopped ringing. I shook my head and looked distractedly at Tom. "Yes? You wanted to tell me something?"

"Yeah, babe, you were totally spaced out. I've been trying to tell you we're going to set up camp at the base of the temple." He took a deep breath then said, "And it's close to full moon, so watch how you're feeling. You know, like if you feel like wolfing out or something tell me or Paul pronto." He paused and frowned. "Hey, you hearing me, babe?"

I looked in his direction, but didn't really see him as my stomach clenched at the thought of going through another horrible full-moon experience. Paul almost got hurt last time, and so did I. Either way, it was not a good thing. And, Shades of Hades, to have my mother and father see what happens to me? I had so many emotions, not the least of which was embarrassment and fear of hurting someone, then more embarrassment, and finally dread. But on the other hand, I had a whole group of wizards and witches here with me this time. Maybe someone could help me not "wolf out" as Tom put it. When we got settled I'd have a talk with Mom. There was so much about having a familiar I didn't know. Like, why did I channel Tom's wolf? Other witches don't turn into cats, owls, dogs, or whatever species their familiar was. Why did I go all wolfy?

"Babe, you with me?" Tom said again.

"Oh, sorry, Tom. Yeah, I heard you. I guess I'm just tired. Thanks for the warning." I smiled weakly at him.

He put an arm around my shoulders as we walked side by side to the camp site being set up. I was fond of this man, my familiar, and I looked up at him. He had pulled his blond hair back into a ponytail and tied it with a strap of thin black leather. Strands had worked their way loose and stuck to the sweat on his face. His copper brown eyes looked bright and alert despite the miles he had walked with the heavy backpack. Again, I was struck by his boyish good looks, as I gazed at the muscular column of his neck as it curved into his strong jaw line. My she-wolf stirred, as if in response to my thoughts. She wasn't conflicted about her attraction to him. As far as she was concerned, this young alpha male seemed just fine to mate with, assuming, of course, that he proved worthy of her. I couldn't stop a small, playful growl from escaping my lips as I breathed in his enticing musky male scent.

He responded immediately with an answering growl, pulling me in closer to his body, his eyes becoming heavy lidded as he sniffed me in return. "Oh babe, don't do this to me. We have to help set up camp."

He'd whispered the last sentence so close to my lips that I felt his breath, hot and smelling of the spearmint gum he had been chewing. I couldn't resist the urge to kiss those soft-looking lips, surrounded by dark blond stubble. Just a little kiss, I said to myself as I moved forward the inch needed to reach him. The moment our lips touched, I felt a jolt of power flow between us. My she-wolf sprang out from me in a blazing stream of energy to meet his wolf. Their energies intertwined, metaphysical fur brushing against metaphysical fur, the dynamic of the two powers amplifying each other and causing a chain reaction of passion and magic. I clutched at his shoulders, digging my fingernails into him as we kissed. He groaned, then growled, pushing his tongue into my mouth. And I got his gum.

It startled me, and I pulled back and spat it out, watching the grayish blob land in a spider web. A big black and yellow spider scuttled to it and wrapped its prize in silky threads, rotating the gum with its front legs until it turned into a wad-shaped cocoon. I looked at Tom who looked at me, then at the spider. We both started laughing at the same time, and the wolves slowed their energy dance, finally stopped and separated, sliding smoothly back into us

"That was close. We shouldn't do that this close to the full moon. Lesson learned." I said.

"Yeah," Tom agreed halfheartedly, "but it sure is bitchin' when it happens." He grinned.

I barked out a laugh, "No pun intended?"

"Huh? Oh yeah, she-wolf, bitch. Got it. No pun intended, babe, but hey, you're no bitch. For real, you are the coolest, hottest, most awesome witch ever. How many people could have gone through what you have and still be able to laugh? Not many."

"Come on, you'll make me blush. Let's help get this camp

set up."

    I took his hand and we walked along the trail leading to the stone temple, fingers clasped, our hearts just a little bit lighter for now because I knew that soon we would be fighting the demon-god and some of us would lose our lives in the battle to come.

Chapter Twenty-one
Final Preparations

Mom stood near the temple stairs, talking with a dark-haired young man wearing horn-rimmed glasses. I noticed he stood eye to eye with her because she didn't have to tilt her head up to look at his face. It only took me a moment to tell who he was. The years since I'd last seen him hadn't changed him all that much. Regardless of what my father thought, my Cousin Duncan still looked like the slightly-built geeky cousin I'd known before. As I approached them I surreptitiously glanced at his neck, curious to see if he had any vestiges of his infamous dewlap. There wasn't.

"Hey, Donovan good to see you." I waved at him as I got closer. He turned to look at me, raising his hand automatically in answer to my greeting.

"Cousin Cara, how're you doing this morning? Were you able to get some rest last night? I thought you were going to fall asleep in your dinner plate and we'd have to save you from drowning in your mashed potatoes." He smiled good-naturedly at me. I saw a glint of bright green behind his glasses and remembered his emerald colored eyes were the same color as Evika's. He came from her side of the family.

"Yeah, I could barely keep my eyes open." I walked over to them and hooked my arm through my mother's saying, "Would you mind if I interrupted? I need to talk with Mom for a minute."

Mom looked a little annoyed but Donovan nodded. "Sure Cara, no problem. Hey, it really is good to see you again. Maybe we'll have time to catch up later on, after, well you know, this is all over." He looked up at the temple, frowning as he said the last part, obviously thinking about what we were about to do.

"Thanks, Donovan. I'd like that." I didn't say any more, although I thought, *if we both survive.*

Mom turned to me after we walked away a few feet away from the temple. "Cara, what is it? There's so much to do right now for us to get ready. Can it wait?"

"I don't think so. I need to ask you about these orbs that keep following me around." I pointed my index finger upward to a spot over my head to where the gold and rainbow orbs floated.

She looked up, following my pointing finger, and her gaze lingered there for a moment. "Yes, the spirit lights. I've never seen anything like this happen to a member of our family."

"Does that mean you *have* heard of orbs attaching themselves to people?"

"Yes." She looked away, into the jungle, uncomfortable.

"What aren't you saying? Is it something bad?" I knew her well enough to tell when she held something back. Well, at least I thought I had until I discovered she'd been hiding a really big secret from me all my life.

"Cara, I just don't know what to say. I need to talk with your father and some others, scholars of magic, those in our society who study such things."

"What do you mean 'such things? What are you afraid of?" I asked, getting agitated.

She gave me an angry look, saying too loudly and sharply, "I'm not afraid of my own daughter! What a question to ask!" She rubbed her eyes with the heels of both hands, looking tired. "I'm sorry Cara. There are stories of spirit orbs attaching themselves to people with certain, well, propensities."

"What kind of propensities?"

"The kind I don't want you to have, if you must know."

"Just tell me. Straight out. What is it about the orbs that you're worried about?"

"I can't tell you right now. I don't want to tell you something that may not be true or will just worry you for no reason. Just wait until after we take care of this demon problem and I do some research."

I was so frustrated, I wanted to scream. "Mom, you're driving me crazy! You hint I may have certain 'propensities' that are probably bad, but you won't tell me what they are. How am I going to deal with the orbs and everything else if you keep important information from me? I have no idea why all these people and things keep attaching themselves to me or me to them. You decided *not* to tell me I might have the potential to become a Synemancer, which it seems has happened, and look at the consequences of your decision! I have a werewolf for a familiar, a Nightkind who's obsessed with me, and a wizard who may or may not be an enemy agent, but who is connected to me regardless of his loyalties. And now I have two spirit orbs following me around, for *Zul's* sake! Why do you keep hiding things from me? Don't I have the right to learn anything you know that might help me figure all this out?"

She gave me an irritated frown. "You do have the right on one hand, but frankly, you may not on the other. I can't tell you more than that. You'll just have to wait. I don't have the time to stand here and answer all your questions. We have to prepare for a fight. People, *family*, might die before the end of it. Do you understand that, Cara? We might have to ask our family and friends to make terrible sacrifices so everyone else in the world won't have to suffer. We're fighting for our way of life, for our future, for all the good things in this world that should not be destroyed and lost forever. You have to think beyond yourself. The problems of one witch do not outweigh the devastating evil that prepares, even as we speak, to gain unthinkable power from the Portal." She turned and walked away without as much as a backward glance.

I felt like she'd punched me in the stomach. I grabbed my middle with both arms and bent over. Tears started rolling down my cheeks, and I wiped at them ineffectually with the backs of my hands. My nose dripped. I sniffed. I didn't have anything except my shirt to wipe it with. She didn't understand what I was going through—or didn't want to understand. This felt like my childhood all over again. I felt alone, confused, sick at heart. We still didn't know for sure what had happened to Evika. Dad had told me this morning that there was a good chance she was alive and held prisoner by *Tezcatlipoca*. His intelligence source had told him the demon-god's followers had a captive Augustine witch. So, whether it was really Evika or some Augustine distant cousin, who knew? On top of all the selfless stuff about saving the world, my own private agenda included getting one of my favorite cousins and best friends back safely as priority one. Sonya was my other cousin-slash-best-friend and I was going to do everything I could to make sure she stayed safe. I sniffed again. As soon as I finished having this little breakdown, I'd find Tom and appoint him as Sonya's personal bodyguard. Sure, I still felt sorry for myself, but I had things to do.

I straightened up, wiped my face and blew my nose on the inside of my t-shirt and went to find Tom and Sonya and another t-shirt.

* * * *

"No, I don't need a bodyguard!" Sonya crossed her arms

stubbornly. "Besides, I have the Hounds. You can't get better guards than that."

"Babe, you need me with you. I'm like your familiar, you know?" Tom stood next to Sonya mimicking her stance but in a more masculine way. "Back home I spend more time in the water than I do on dry land. I could really help in the diving department. Your Dad told me the group going to the gateway is small because everyone needs to be able to dive. It's the only way."

I frowned. "Yeah, he said I'd have to get some instructions today. He said he'd send someone over."

Just as I finished speaking, I saw Donovan walking towards me, carrying scuba equipment. Oh, great, Dewlap was going to be my diving instructor. He had an awkward gait as he walked, somewhat bandy-legged, like a cowboy whose legs had grown used to curving around a horse's body. He smiled as he saw me, tried to push back his glasses as they slipped down his nose, but because of the equipment in his hand, managed to just knock them askew.

"Hey, Cara," he called.

"Hey again, Donovan. So you're my dive instructor?" I said back.

"Yeah, your father wants me to go over everything with you. Once we're in the cave system, there won't be any chance to surface. I just hope we have enough air in the tanks to get us there, even though we have a couple of guys hauling extra tanks."

I turned to Sonya and Tom, who looked like they were trying to sneak off before I could wring promises out of them. I jogged a few steps to catch up with them. "Hey you two, I'm not finished with you yet." I called over to Cousin Dewlap, "Just a minute, Donovan, I have to tell these guys something."

"Tom, you have to promise to take care of Sonya," I insisted. "I just can't lose her too."

I gazed into his eyes, focusing on making my request a command. He blinked quickly a couple of times and slowly nodded. Sonya glared at me, then at Tom.

She grabbed his arm and shook him. "Snap out of it! She's making you do her bidding as her familiar. You're a human, so you can push back."

Tom ran a hand through his hair, combing long blond hair away from his forehead with his fingers. "Whoa. It was like she hypnotized me or something. I just suddenly thought doing what she said sounded like the best idea ever." He grinned at me. "Oh, babe, you're one sneaky witch."

I glared at Sonya. "Thanks a lot for ruining my familiar. What good is he now that he knows he can question everything I tell him to do?"

She gave me a guilty look. "Come on, Cara. You know he should go with you. Like I said, I have the Hounds, and everyone who can't dive is going to camp here. I'll have a lot of people around me. You won't, and I've overheard people talking. The dive's going to be dangerous. For some reason, your mom thinks it's essential you go, and I would feel much better if you had Tom with you. Actually I'd feel great if you didn't have to go at all, but that's not the reality."

She looked at me pleadingly with her big brown eyes, and I felt my resolve start to melt around the edges. "You know I won't forgive you for this," I said resigning myself to the inevitable.

"Yes, you will," she said, give me a little crooked smile.

"Maybe, but it'll take a long time and a lot of chocolate." I went over to her and hugged her tight. She hugged me back, just as tight.

"That's hot," Tom said a little breathlessly.

Sonya and I released each other and both of us swatted at Tom at the same time. He jumped nimbly out of the way, laughing. Damn those wolf reflexes.

I walked back to Dewlap, who looked bemused by the scene he just witnessed. "Come on, Cuz. Teach me how to scuba dive" I said.

It took all day, but after listening to Donovan give me the basics and trying on the equipment, I thought I'd be able to manage. *Cenotes* diving was different than cave diving or open water diving. I wouldn't have to worry about coming up too fast from the depths because the *cenotes* were not very deep. About halfway through my lesson I stopped calling him Dewlap in my mind. He was good. Despite his appearance, he turned out to be an experienced diver and a patient teacher. He explained that because we were doing a cavern dive, we'd be using the same equipment used in open water. The *cenotes* were naturally occurring limestone caverns where rains, over the course of millennia, had worn away the rock to create underground lakes and tunnels filled with fresh water. He told me that cave diving has to be approached differently because its deeper, with no natural light. In the *cenotes*, there were a series of natural openings that would provide light along the way, and we had flashlights for particularly dark sections. By the time we finished, I was as ready as I'd ever be, given the circumstances. I wished we had a pool or pond handy so I could practice in water, but that's the way it goes.

After my lesson, I saw Dad walking across the camp and flagged him down. I'd been thinking he should be able to tell me about the orbs. But before I could, he called a meeting of the most senior witches and wizards who'd be diving to discuss strategy for the approach to the Caves. I noticed Chester and Paul were included, but I wasn't. Tom and the Hounds had left to hunt, and Sonya sat with her father and a group of female witches preparing charms for us to carry with us on the dive. My orbs—I'd started to think of them as "my" orbs—had flown off somewhere. I'd asked Chester earlier if he could open a mirror dimension door into the cave because it would make things so much easier. He'd shaken his head, saying he'd need to have the coordinates or someone he could connect with at the other end for him to do so.

Once again, I didn't have anything to do and felt totally left out. I hovered on the periphery of Dad's little think-tank group of seven people and tried to eavesdrop. They were sitting on camp stools in a circle, heads down, murmuring things I couldn't make out. Occasionally one or two of them would lift their heads and look at me, then rejoin the conversation. I sidled closer until Dad saw me and made a shooing gesture with his hand for me to go away. I kicked at a vine at my feet, feeling about six years old and the big kids wouldn't let me play with them.

I huffed over to the temple, deciding to look around. Muttering under my breath, I barely looked at the worn stone slabs, carved within an inch of their lives with blocky yet intricate patterns and figures. It made me uneasy because the carvings reminded me of the mirror in Sonya's living room. But none of the stone figures looked ready to pop out and attack me, so I kept moving around the base of the temple. The jungle vegetation grew in a green mass so dense towards the back side of the structure it looked as if I'd need a machete to get through.

I started to turn around when I saw a movement in the

bushes. I tensed, knowing there might be predators out here. A pair of little black, shining eyes peeked out at me. A tiny brownish-gray monkey sat partially hidden, eating what looked like a fig.

I squatted down smiling. "Hello little monkey. Oh yummy yum, that's a tasty looking fig you've got there. Yes it is." My voice had risen about an octave of its own accord, and the words came out as soft coos, like when you talk to babies or puppies. The monkey stopped eating to blink at me. It looked adorable. I inched closer, talking softly. The primate blinked its button eyes at me once more, and then turned its attention to finishing its snack. I got within five feet of it when something large and fast snatched it away. The monkey disappeared with a tiny scream.

I fell back on my bottom, scrambling away. Shades of Hades, what was that? The jungle and the shadows hid whatever had taken the monkey. I got to my feet and started backing away. I didn't know if running would just cue whatever lurked out there into thinking I looked like prey. I backed up until I felt the stone of the temple against the heels of my shoes, then sidled sideways as fast as I could while still trying not to look like I was running away.

Suddenly, I heard a high-pitched chittering sound that sent chills up my spine. It didn't sound like anything native to this jungle. The chittering began to form into words. "Commina leettle weetch," it said.

That tore it. I turned and started running as fast as I could back to camp, screaming at the top of my lungs for someone to help me. I heard it behind me, a series of rapid thuds on the ground that sounded like a herd of things running towards me . . . or something with multiple limbs. My last thought made me run faster, even though I got winded and had a cramp forming in my side.

I had roamed too far from the camp for them to hear me. I tried not to give in to my panic, even as I stumbled, falling face down over a piece of carved stone. I turned over to at least see what creature was going to get me and wished I hadn't. It looked as big as both Hounds put together. It was the deep red of a boiled lobster and had an insectoid head and a long, thin body from which dozens of long limbs served as legs, making it look like a cross between a spider and a centipede. The front part of its body curved up into an "L" shape so it could use its two front legs like arms. Those "arms" ended in sharp-looking pinchers shaped like malformed hands, and they both reached towards me. The mouth mandibles dripped blood, and a small furry hand dangled off one side.

This monster looked to be some sort of sub-demon, and as I watched it, it chittered, swung its head and deftly caught the monkey hand, swallowing it whole. My stomach roiled, but this was no time to get sick. I focused on escape, thinking wildly of what I could do. It had tried to talk to me, so it must have some rudimentary intelligence.

I held up a hand, palm out, thought about the monkey and pulled my hand closer to my body, still giving the "stop" signal as I yelled, "Wait! What do you want?"

It hesitated, tilting its insect head to one side, as if it was thinking, "Waant leettle weetch. Keelll leettle weetch for master." It seemed to look at me questioningly, "Why leettle weetch much hard to keelll?"

"But why do you want to kill me?" I asked, stalling for time while franticly trying to concentrate enough to let Tom see what was happening. And where in Hades were the orbs?

"No talk more leettle weetch. Keelll now."

It advanced on me with pincers and mandibles open wide. I noticed a symbol carved into the carapace of its thorax. It looked like the same symbol branded on the first sub-demon that had attacked Roman and me, and again on the crab shells on the beach in Santa Lacuna. All these sub-demons must have been sent by the same spellcaster.

"Tell me who sent you!" I yelled, trying to push as much persuasive power into my voice as I could.

It stopped inches from where I knelt on the ground clutching a piece of stone I planned to use to at least give it a headache before it ate me. It did its odd head tilt again, apparently thinking about whether it would answer my question or just chow down. It swung its head around towards me, and I raised the stone, ready to swing at it. Then it started talking, "Leetle weetch baad for deemoon loords. Eyeees oo doomeeneen, keelll poortaal deemoons."

Could it be saying "Eyes of Dominion?" Wasn't that what Chester had said about me when I met him at Roman's house? That he knew I was an Augustine witch because I had the Eyes of Dominion? My mother had said something about my eyes too.

"How can I kill portal demons with my eyes? I don't understand."

It swayed its head towards the temple then back to me. "Maasteer says keelll. Noo taalk."

It opened its maw wide again, aiming at my head, and I envisioned it snipping off my head like a gardener pruning a rose bush. I screamed for all I was worth while reaching into the core of my power, willing it to manifest. Three dark blurs appeared at the edge of my vision as I put everything I had into slamming my piece of stone into the sub-demon. I felt the stone hit something solid and a sound of broken glass. The sub-demon reeled back. I saw I'd put a crack in its shell precisely on the etched symbol. The blurs flashed in front of me, and three large figures launched themselves at the demon insect. The Hounds and Tom in wolf form had come to help me.

The sub-demon let out a long, undulating cry of exaltation just before the three canine-shaped animals slammed into it. "Nooo, mee freee, nooo keelll!"

Realization struck as I stood up, yelling. "Don't kill it! It won't hurt me now! I freed it from its master!"

Tom's wolf body did an almost impossible midair turn so he hit the sub-demon with the side of his body instead of ripping into it with his fangs. He crashed to the ground with a yelp, staggering to his feet almost immediately to face the enemy. The Hounds both changed their trajectories, bouncing off the demon's back with fluid grace and landing on the ground on either side of it, heads down, growling, their eyes flaming bright red even in the sunlight. They were ready to attack if the demon even twitched in my direction. The weight of the huge two Hounds bouncing on its back had flattened its entire body to the ground. A couple of the legs looked broken, but the rest worked to move the demon backwards in an undulating motion towards the jungle.

It made a kind of bow to me with its upper body, "You noo keelll thiis oone. Leetle weetch goood. Baad maaster inside waateer stones. Yoou say *K'tak*, thiis one come to leetle weetch." It reached around with one of its pinchers and cut off a claw from one of its many legs, throwing the piece at my feet. With that, it plunged its head into the ground, which parted like water to engulf the huge body in a matter of seconds.

Water stones? I repeated as I eyed at the temple speculatively. Was the demon lord inside the temple? Tom had trotted over to where I stood and sniffed at the sub-demon claw. He wrinkled his nose and sneezed, then put his head under my hand so I could scratch his ears. The Hounds also wanted some attention, not about to be upstaged by a mere werewolf, so I spent the next several minutes obliging my saviors. It was least I could do.

My arms were tired from all the scratching, petting, hugging and thanks given in baby talk to the three beasts. I knew Tom wouldn't be offended by my silly talk, and the Hounds loved it. The two identical brothers sat grinning at me with tongues lolling, then turned and melted back into the jungle as if they had never been here with me. Tom stayed.

After a brief rest, I gingerly picked up the claw. It looked to be about three inches long and was as smooth and sharp on one end as a polished horn. I wasn't sure why the creature had given it to me, but some inner instinct told me it was important and I should keep it. With a resigned shrug, I looked at Tom and asked him if he wanted to change back, but he shook his head. Apparently he thought his wolf form was better suited for guarding me as we walked back to camp.

As we drew close to camp, I decided I needed to talk to Chester and ask him why my eyes were called "Eyes of Dominion" and how I could kill portal demons with them, assuming the sub-demon had really known what it was talking about. If I could use my eyes as a weapon against the Aztec demon, I'd want to know how to use them. And if I could do that, then I could protect everyone else, maybe even end the battle before it began. But I also thought if I couldn't do it, I'd probably be the first to die.

Chapter Twenty-two
Angel of Death

Tom and I made our way back to camp. I had put the demon claw in my back pocket, not sure what else to do with the thing. The camp was in a frenzy of activity, and Paul came running up to us looking harried, his dark hair falling into his eyes. When had his hair gotten so long? I suddenly realized it had been weeks since we had first met on the airplane.

"Where were you?" he asked, his voice short with irritation. "We've been looking all over for you. Come on, Donovan has your gear. We're leaving in an hour."

I started to tell him about the demon attack when Tom pushed against me with his big furry body, causing me to stagger sideways a few steps. I looked down at him, "Hey, what's that for?" He looked at Paul, then me, then back at Paul. I got a strong thought from him he didn't want me to tell Paul. I frowned at him and he whined, licking my hand. "Okay, okay, but you better have a good explanation when you can talk again."

Paul had been visually scanning the camp but now turned back to me, "Did you say something?"

I shook my head, "No, just talking to Tom." Paul distractedly glanced at Tom who sat on his haunches trying to look as innocent as a giant-sized wolf can look.

We all turned our heads as we heard someone call my name. Donovan walked rapidly towards us. "Cara. Paul. Tom? Come along you lot, we have loads of things to do before we go." He waved us towards him and the three of us obediently followed him.

Donovan led us to a spot at the base of the temple. There were about thirty people there, men and women, sorting through piles of scuba gear, shoving masks, regulators, flippers, and other things I couldn't identify into black mesh duffel bags. Donovan pointed to the equipment, "Paul and Tom, pick out your gear and pack it in a bag. Don't forget, Paul, you'll need your wand and anything else you want with you for casting spells and who knows what else. Tom, would you change back to human form now? But for Zul's sake, not out here. Go in one of the tents. The last time you changed in the open the women and a couple of the men were so distracted that work stopped for a several minutes. We don't have time for that sort of thing at the moment." He said this matter-of-factly, like a scientist making an observation about some strange animal behavior.

Tom opened his mouth in what looked like a wolf laugh and trotted off towards a tent. He came out a few minutes later, bare-chested, zipping up a pair of worn cutoff jeans. A few people still paused in their work to give him appreciative once-overs. I rolled my eyes but felt secretly smug that this yummy golden werewolf was mine. I immediately felt guilty for the thought. He was mine, so to speak, because I had bound him to me. He would never be free of me.

He came over and put an arm around my shoulders, as if he knew my thoughts. And maybe he did. I didn't ask. Instead, I put my arm around his waist and leaned my head against his chest, closing my eyes for a moment. He wouldn't be here if it wasn't for me, and I knew this would be a dangerous mission. We were going up against some very bad demons, the kind that didn't play around, the kind that would keep you alive just to make the terrible torture last a little longer so they could enjoy it just a little longer.

I opened my eyes and looked up at Tom, seeing a young man with a life ahead of him. "Tom, you don't have to go with us. This isn't your battle."

He tightened his arm around me and brought his mouth to my ear, his warm breath stirring my hair as he whispered, "I go where you go. You are part of me, *leetle weetch!*" He said it like the insect demon had, and I turned to give him an earful when he started tickling. I slapped his hands away, laughing. Damn. I guess he was going on this suicide mission.

Donovan paired us up by Scuba experience, the least experienced, me for instance, was partnered with someone with lots of experience. My partner turned out to be a tall, almost feminine-looking man with delicate features, high cheekbones and long thick hair a shade more beige than white. In contrast to his androgynous looks, his body looked definitely male, with wide finely-muscled shoulders narrowing to a trim waist.

Although his appearance was very different, he reminded me of the security guards at Roman's house. Something about the way he moved, the way he seemed to survey his surroundings, his, well, serious *vigilance*, screamed either soldier or enforcement. His told me his name was Azrael. Either he had cruel parents to name their son after the Angel of Death, or it was a nickname. My money was on the latter, and if I was right, it wasn't one of those opposite joke monikers, like a really big guy everyone called Tiny. No, the cold steely look in his pale blue eyes told me Azrael probably had earned his nickname. I didn't want to know how. I would, however, make another bet that someone—probably Mom or Dad—had assigned him to be my bodyguard, not just a dive partner.

Azrael was also a witch. I found that out when he checked the fit of my mask and other equipment and brushed my face with his fingers. Our auras flared on contact and it felt wonderful. His energy spread warmth and comfort over me like a security blanket. My power liked him—a lot. It wanted to lap him up like cream from a bowl. Tendrils reached out from me, twinning around his power in an almost caress, delicately merging with patient precision. His power felt mostly bright, with dark purple currents running throughout; those currents were no doubt the dangerous side of him.

He grabbed my shoulders and pulled me to him, wrapping his arms around me protectively, like we were being attacked. "What's happening?" he demanded, his breathless voice betraying his confusion.

"My power, uh, likes you." I think I said it out loud, but I wasn't sure. He nodded like that explained everything.

He laid his cheek on top of my head and just held on. I sensed the people around us had stopped their preparations to watch us curiously. The witches and wizards in the group could probably feel our powers merging and growing. Azrael's power manifested big and strong, like his physical form, but it was also protective of me, again, just like he was. He could have tried to break out of our connection, maybe causing pain or injury to me or both of us in the process. But he wasn't spooked or even all that surprised, and his power didn't try to lash out at me to protect itself from being absorbed. It made me think someone may have told him this might happen. And if they had, did he volunteer for the assignment of being my partner?

I couldn't think about it anymore. The powers were calling me; they danced around us, merging and growing. I had done this with a Nightkind, a werewolf, and a wizard, but not with my own kind. This was nice. No this was incredible. Our mingling auras slid across our bodies like hundreds of soft fingers, brushing our skin, almost tickly, almost sexual. We were on a bright precipice. I felt his hands rubbing my back, up under my t-shirt, skin to skin. Yes, I needed to feel his skin. I slipped my hands under his shirt, and as my hands touched his fever-hot skin, the "almost" exploded into pleasure. He groaned deep in his throat almost choking it out as he tried to resist his feelings. But they could not be denied, I knew my power a little better now, and it wanted what it wanted. And right now, it wanted Azrael, wanted his bright and dark power, wanted his body, maybe even his very soul.

This last thought should have alarmed me, but it felt too delicious, too intense, to resist. I felt his control start to crumble; he bent down and captured my lips, thrusting his tongue into my mouth without any preamble. I met his kiss eagerly, sucking at his tongue, exploring his mouth the way he explored mine until I wanted more than his tongue inside of me. I didn't care if a group of people watched us, or if I had just met him, or that we didn't have time. I didn't even care that my parents and friends were here. My power took over and it had no social conscience whatsoever. I moaned into Azrael's mouth, pushing my lower body against his. He immediately grabbed my bottom with one hand, picking me up off the ground, grinding his hips into the core of me. He was hard and swollen with need. I wrapped my legs around him, bringing my shorts-clad intimate parts in contact with his shorts-clad erection. We rubbed and pressed against each other, our mouths still connected, our powers forming a nimbus around us, shafts of raw energy pulsating out in waves.

Azrael's dark currents ebbed and flowed, then I felt them consolidate into three distinct streams. One connected with my power, feeding it like it was a hungry baby bird, and it greedily took in his energy, filling itself. The other surrounded my heart like a shield, and the third, the largest, thick and powerful, entered me at the point where our lower bodies met. It felt exactly like Azrael had entered me with his body. It pulsated inside me, growing larger, then it lessened, then grew again, as if his physical body pushed in and out of me. The current felt so big and powerful that I had a moment of panic. I wanted to escape the strength, the intensity of it. I released his mouth, throwing my head back, hands on his shoulders, arms extended, back arched, trying to pull away. He tightened his grip around my waist, preventing me from moving away as his power expanded all three currents at once. My pleasure exploded in waves of exquisite sensation. I heard Azrael shout out, saw his neck taut with straining muscles, and with a last punishing grind of his hips, his knees gave way and we dropped to the ground together. As we fell, our powers pulled back into us and, once again, I felt the now-familiar exchange of our auras. Some of Azrael was in me and another small piece of me stayed in him.

I couldn't move. My muscles were useless, my bones liquid, my mind numb. Great Shades of Hades and Zul's horns, I'd done it again, and my parents and friends had watched! I hoped the ground would open up and swallow me, but no such luck. Where was a nice, distracting, rampaging sub-demon when you needed one?

Azrael still held onto me, arms around my waist. My legs were both still wrapped around him although one of them was going numb because he lay on top of it. I'd have to move soon. I'd even have to open my eyes and face my mother and everyone else. I whispered to Azrael, "Can you move?"

His breath smelled of vanilla as he whispered back, "In a minute. Zul's horns! They warned me, but I didn't realize . . . how could I know?"

He slowly untangled himself from me and stood, taking me with him. I lay cradled in his arms like a child, and as tempting as it was to just let him take care of me, I told him to put me down. Actually, it surprised me he had the strength to pick me up. I mean, after what he, uh *we*, went through just now, I'd have expected him to be as limp as a noodle.

As soon as he set me on my feet, I looked around. The area had been cleared of everyone except Mom, Sonya, Tom and Paul. I took a step back, but Azrael pulled me to him as if I'd fall if he didn't hold onto me—or maybe that he would fall, who knows?

I pulled away, wanting to face Mom on my own. She glared at me. Her arms were folded tight against her chest as she said, "Caravier Augustine, you and I have to talk. Right now." Uh oh, she'd used my given name. I was in big trouble.

* * * *

The rest of the group had geared up and were waiting by the time I left my parent's tent. Some of the men gave me speculative sideways glances; the rest appeared to be particularly fascinated with the local flora. Azrael and I were still teamed up as we walked the short distance to the temple steps. He had changed into a wet suit that emphasized his triangular body from broad shoulders to narrow hips. I silently slipped my wet suit on over a swimsuit my mother had given me to wear while we were in the tent. I tugged it up over the lump of demon-claw I had taken from my shorts and tucked into the front of the swimsuit, not knowing what else to do with it and not wanting to leave it behind. Azrael reached over and took my left hand, and I immediately pulled back. He looked a bit exasperated as he pointed to the diamond ring on my hand. I hadn't even realized I still wore it.

"You can't wear that on a dive," he said, and handed me a long steel chain, the type that usually held dog tags. I smiled at him, shrugging in apology as I took the ring off and secured it onto the chain. I looped the chain over my head and tucked it into my wet suit. Hey, it was a major piece of jewelry and I wasn't going to leave it here in the jungle where it would go unappreciated. It fleetingly occurred to me that *I* wouldn't be able to appreciate it if this mission wasn't successful, but decided if I thought about *that* I wouldn't be much help at all to anyone.

Ahead of us, the temple rose up into the solid blue of the sky. Now that I was going inside, it seemed immense. Off to the side of the stone staircase was an opening in the wall where a seemingly solid block of stone revealed a doorway. It's existence had been hidden by the carvings around it. Most human scholars believed these temples were solid structures without the secret tunnels and chambers the Egyptian pyramids possessed. They were wrong. They just didn't have the means to detect the multidimensional magical elements used to create the maze of intricate passageways that honeycombed this particular ziggurat.

Led by Donovan, we filed one behind the other into the narrow, dark passageway. Each of us had our flashlights in hand and loaded packs on our backs. None of us spoke. We seemed to walk a long time on an ever steeper downward slope, the walls growing cooler and damper as we descended. I heard a sound and slipped on the wet stone as I turned my head sharply. Azrael steadied me with a strong grip on my upper arm.

"Did you hear that?" I asked him.

"Hear what?" he replied. His voice sounded overly loud in the silence.

I heard ringing bells, one silvery sweet, the other a deep gong, the tones somehow sounded desperate, pleading. My orbs! They were in trouble!

I turned to Azrael and Tom, who was right behind him. "Come on, the orbs need me!"

Without waiting for their responses, I ran down a side corridor, Donovan shouted for us to stop or we'd get lost. I didn't care. The orbs had saved my life more than once and now they needed me. Azrael and Tom were right behind me as I ran, following those bell-voices down the twists and turns of the stone passages, the urgency of the orb-cries overriding my fear of getting lost.

I was breathing hard with the weight of the pack and the limited air supply in the tunnels. I turned left then left again and ended up in a high walled chamber, light and air coming from somewhere up above, the builders of the temple must have designed the room to supply air and light. I glanced around at the walls that were great slabs of smooth rock. I was standing in a rectangular area about the size of a football field, as I searched for the orbs, I saw ingenious polished disks of metal angled to reflect tiny pinpricks of sunlight so they illuminated the room. At the far end was a large statue of a demon standing on an obsidian pedestal which was submerged in the center of a dark pool of water surrounded by a low, circular stone wall. This was no sub-demon. It had the typically humanoid shape of a demon lord. I saw ancient portal-witch runes inscribed in the rock wall. There was no discernible source for the water in the pool, but there had to be one to replenish it or the pool would have dried up long ago. Part of the chamber's floor had been torn up, the raw dirt of the jungle beneath exposed.

As I approached the statue, I saw the orbs huddled in one corner of the chamber's ceiling. Their bell-voices had stopped calling me once I'd arrived here. The runes on the wall around the pool started to glow. Tom shouted a warning a moment before a stone slab slid vertically from the ceiling to cover the doorway, sealing us in the room. I ran to the doorway and pushed against the rough stone, my efforts useless against the thick, solid piece of rock. Azrael and Tom pushed at it with me, their muscles straining against the incredible heaviness. They both finally stopped.

Azrael had fine beads of sweat on his forehead from the effort, and he shook his head as he said, "That stone must weigh several tons. No way we can move it." Even Tom, with his werewolf strength, couldn't budge it. He looked at me with resignation in his eyes, as if to say he was sorry although he had no reason to be. We were trapped, and it was my fault.

The orbs flew down to me, circling my head before flying back to their corner of the ceiling. The silvery bell-voice of the golden orb kept chiming in my head, no words, just a string of chimes, like an alarm, as if it had forgotten how to talk to me.

"What is it? What are you trying to tell me?" I said aloud. I heard a splash as something fell into the pool of water. I looked into the pool but saw nothing in its inky depths. Another splash made me look at the statue, and I saw a small piece break off and fall into the pool. The statue's face started cracking, pieces of it falling into the water below. The runes glowed brighter, looking like lines of firelight in the darkening room. We must have been in the tunnel longer than I thought because I watched sunlight fade into twilight.

The eyes of the statue were now gone and where they'd been, I now saw red demon eyes with split pupils looking at me. I screamed running back to the men. "The statue is alive! I saw its eyes look at me."

Azrael and Tom ran to the edge of the pool and looked at the statue. Azrael cursed as more of the statue cracked and fell away, revealing the rest of the demon's head that had been under the stone. It had dark reddish-purple skin, the color of cooked beets, with the texture of fine sandpaper. The head was finely featured and leonine in appearance, with four delicate horns on its head, each about two inches long and as thick as a finger. They were the same shade of red as its skin.

When the last of the rock fell from its head and neck, it turned to stare directly at me and spoke in a language I didn't understand. The rainbow orb hovered briefly above it, and the demon lord rolled its eyes upward and scowled. The orb then flew to me and nestled on my shoulder, touching my right ear. The demon spoke again and suddenly I could understand it.

It said, "...*Angel of Death shall protect thou Eyes of Dominion, wolves lie at thy feet, who is loved by ones who know death but know not the grave, learned ones shall gather to teach thee mysteries of the craft, a triumvirate shall be born who shall draw mystic forces unto itself, demonkind shall bow to the triumvirate or suffer the oblivion of the Eyes...*" Then it repeated the same message again, not big on syntax, but I got the message.

Tom and Azrael stood by me, looking questioningly at me and the orb. The demon had to be talking about me, maybe even to me. It had to be. Could the triumvirate be me and my cousins? My parents used to jokingly call the three of us the Triumvirate of Terror or TOTS for short, when we were little witches. I ran the message over and over in my mind, and then I gasped. He couldn't really be saying what he was saying. All this could *not* have been preordained. I was *not* destined for this . . . well, whatever this mess was. No way!

I covered my ears, shouting, "Stop it! Stop it!"

Azrael pulled one hand away from my left ear and asked, "What is it? Is the demon hurting you somehow? What's it saying? Can you understand it? Look at me, damn it! Talk to me!"

I pulled my arm free from his grasp and ran to the other side of the room. "It's talking about me. *Me* . . . my life . . . the people I have bound to me. . . my cousins, or maybe . . . Oh, I don't know!"

I ran to the side of the pool, and leaning over the wall I shouted at the demon, "Are you talking about *me?* If so, stop it! I don't want to hear any more."

At my order, it stopped. I was so surprised I nearly fell into the water. Holding onto the edge of the wall, I fell to my knees and stared at the demon-lord. More rock had fallen away, revealing a barrel chest and arms and long, six-fingered hands. On its left hand, it wore a ruby ring.

The demon lord focused its blood-red eyes on me and said, "I have waited for you little witch." The term oddly reminded me of the insect sub-demon earlier. "I have waited here for you for these past millennia, to prevent the prophesy from being fulfilled. It tells of a witch child with Eyes of Dominion. You shall not live to doom demonkind."

It bowed its head to me in a kind of salute, saying, "You are very hard to kill. I spelled the Nightkind to kill you, but it did not happen. I sent my insect servant to kill you, but you freed it instead. We took from you the memory of your manifesting power on the eve of your twenty-first year of life, but your power sought and bound the prophesied ones even without your knowledge. I am the last defense. The sentinel of the Cave of Dominion."

I turned toward the blocked doorway as I heard a blast.

The others must have found us and were trying to free us from this chamber.

Tom looked at me and said, "Its Paul."

I didn't ask how he knew; I just took his word for it. I turned back to the demon, watching as the rest of the stone fell off it like the petals off a dying flower until it revealed the demon in all its red glory. It was naked, definitely male, and most frighteningly, apparently very glad to see me. The black water of the pool swallowed all the stone pieces with no sign that they had ever broken its surface.

The demon shook one last piece of stone off a clawed foot and leapt off the pedestal to land within less than an arm's reach of me. Azrael and Tom sprang in front of me. The sunlight faded completely, but the runes still burned brightly. Azrael crouched down and lashed out with his foot, knocking the demon off its feet. Tom immediately climbed onto the demon's back, bringing one of its arms around to the back, and holding the arm with both hands, Azrael jumped on its back, tore off his backpack, took out his diving weight belt and started to bind the demon.

Tom grit his teeth with effort and said, "Azrael, hurry up. He's a strong one."

Tom suddenly arched his back, head thrown back in pain, and I yelled, "Tom! What's wrong? Is the demon hurting you?"

"Moon. Full," he grunted. I saw the light from outside had turned silvery on the metal disks making it appear as if a full moon was in the sky. But there was a three-quarters moon in the sky tonight! The reflections must have the effect as a full moon on werewolves! Tom convulsed again, his body changing, fur growing on his face and hands. The last convulsion caused him to loosen his grip on the demon before Azrael could finish tying it up. It screamed in triumph, then the demon snarled, revealing a mouth full of sharp pointed teeth. It sprang to its feet, throwing both Tom and Azrael off its back, and jumped into the air to hang from the stone of the ceiling by its clawed feet.

With its eyes full of fury, the demon spat, "I have waited since before the Great Purge and the summoning of Portalkind to this world. We had led the earth demons to influence and twist the minds of the weak humans of the time, made them afraid of magic folk. Made them kill for us. We would have had dominion over the earth but for the interference of those meddling Mages. Over the years we were able to destroy nearly all the Mages, but one managed to escape and fall in love," it sneered, "with a portal witch. Together they produced their blighted brood. Your ancestors, little witch, but you will be the last Augustine Mage."

With that the demon jumped on top of me so fast the men couldn't move to block it although they stood right beside me. The demon latched onto my throat with its sharp teeth. The pain of its bite seared like fire, and the saliva burned like acid. My body convulsed. I couldn't scream as its jaws slowly crushed my windpipe and vocal cords. I weakly, ineffectively, hit at it with my puny hands. I was suffocating, and I couldn't concentrate to tap into my power. My hands both went to my neck to try to pull the demon off me, even while knowing that if I did, it would take my throat out with it.

Then I felt something move, to vibrate, on my chest. It was the insect-demon's claw. I instinctively reached for it, managing to unzip my wet suit enough to grab the now furiously vibrating claw. As surprised registered on its face, the demon loosed its death-grip on my neck just a fraction to swipe at my hand, causing the claw to fly out and bounce against a wall. I saw the reflection of it in one of the metal disks as it landed in a small patch of dirt where the stone floor had buckled. I felt my she-wolf stirring, whimpering, trying to rise, but too weak, even with the false full moon calling. My vision darkened around the edges. I couldn't breathe, scream, cry. All I could see was a circle of black. I'll never know why, but I suddenly recalled what the insect sub-demon had told me, and I called out in my mind, *K'tak!*

Beneath my back I felt the ground rumble. I heard blasts at the doorway, as the remainder of the group tried to get to us, and the sound of falling stones. I saw Azrael and Tom pounding, biting, tearing at the demon on top of me. And then the earth exploded from beneath us all. A loud chittering sound filled the chamber. Something wrenched the demon lord off of me, its arrival surprising the demon lord enough that my throat didn't rip away with it, but I still couldn't breathe. Unholy screams echoed in my ears as drops of acid blood burned my skin. Tom, in wolf form licked the blood from my face, burning his tongue, but he kept at it until I pushed him away. My she-wolf tried to rise again, and this time Tom's wolf energy merged with her, helping her. I felt cool air enter the chamber as the group outside managed to blast open the door. Then I felt Paul by my side, lending me his power. Azrael knelt beside me, chanting a spell and using his body to shield me from the fight still raging on the other side of the chamber. It was odd how I took all this in even though I was suffocating. I had to breathe soon or I was a goner. Someone pushed some type of tube into my throat, one more pain, no greater than the others, but suddenly I could suck air into my lungs. My vision started to clear and I saw the rainbow orb fly out of the chamber as sweet, sweet air filled my lungs. The golden orb settled onto my chest, flattening out, covering me from my jaw to my stomach. I felt my she-wolf grow stronger, and realized the golden orb-skin was magnifying the wolf essences flowing between Tom and me.

I could feel the change starting to take hold of me. My aura reformed, becoming wolf-shaped, and I rejoiced. I would be free from this weak human form, free to run and hunt, no worries, nothing to think about, only to feel the wind, smell the night, and feast on flesh and blood. The she-wolf energy built, ready to burst out of me in splendid transformation. With my entire being, I wanted to be transformed. Without warning, someone pulled the tube out of my throat. I could now breathe without it. Then a cold, dark slap of energy shook me, prevented me from changing.

No! I snarled at it, warning it away. *Let me be*, I growled, my growl turning into a whimper as the energy held me in my human form. I recognized the shining dark blue aura. Roman. His presence was preventing me from becoming my she-wolf. I tried to lash out at him, but another presence, calm and strong, muffled my attack on Roman. But it didn't matter; the wolf energy inside of me had been enough to start the healing process, and now my bound ones poured their strength into me, my power taking the many streams and forming them into a rope of energy stronger by far than any one of them on their own. This, then, was my power manifest. This bringing together of other energies, binding them, bringing them to another level beyond anything they could have achieved alone.

I became aware of the ongoing battle between the demon lord and *K'tak*. My energy rope snapped out like a whip and ended the struggle between the demon lord and his former minion. The red demon literally vaporized so no trace of its body remained. The insect-demon was barely alive, but its wounds were too severe and it died soon after its former master's demise. This battle was over.

I directed what energy I had left back into me, I fought the darkness pressing in on me. I couldn't leave my friends and family to fight without me. But I didn't have the strength to fight the darkness and it wrapped its black velvet cloak around me as I felt myself fall into its depths.

Chapter Twenty-three
Cave of Dominion

We were still inside the stone temple, in a cramped dark passageway. After the dust settled, so to speak, I was awake and alive with only a crisscross of small pink scars on my throat to show for the demon lord's attack. I couldn't see them without a mirror, but that's what Paul told me. My friends and family gathered around me and told me what had happened. When I summoned the sub-demon with its claw, it came up through the ground and went straight for its former master. At the same time, Paul and the rest of the group outside the chamber door had managed to break through to help us. The rainbow orb had flown to Chester at the campsite and somehow managed to convey to him that I needed Roman. Roman in the meantime had a feeling I was in trouble and desperately tried to get another wizard to open a mirror dimension gateway for him to get back to the jungle cave. Luckily one of his business associates had his own house wizard who opened a gateway for him, using Chester as the homing signal.

Once again, it all felt too overwhelming, I didn't know if I had the strength to keep going. I wanted to go back to my childhood room, get into bed, pull the covers over my head, and sleep forever. But my thoughts of childhood evoked memories of playing with my cousins, of them defending me against the bullies who made fun of my lack of ability, loyal cousins who were my closest friends. I mustered up what little energy I had left. I wouldn't give up. We had to find Evika and prevent the demons from opening the Portal. Still, I felt so tired. These last few weeks I'd been closer to death more times than I wanted to think about. I'd had more embarrassing—and pretty cool and exciting—incidents with men than I'd ever had in my life. And what was the deal with my parents? What had they been thinking when they'd decided to leave me ignorant about everything? I hoped there'd be time for answers later. First, we had to survive.

The smell of the dead demon permeated the place; it coated the back of my throat and seemed to sink into my very pores. The disgusting rotten meat, sulfur, and jasmine smell would stay with me a long time. Too bad being vaporized didn't eliminate the awful smell the demon lord left as a parting gift.

Azrael held me against his chest, whispering soothing sounds against my hair, his long legs flanking mine as I half-sat, half-lay in his lap on the hard stone of the passageway. Tom had changed back to his human form. He told me Azrael and Roman had a brief tug-of-war over my unconscious body after I healed enough to be out of danger, and Azrael had won. I arched a brow. That was interesting.

I glanced over at Roman who stood against the wall directly in front of me, looking cool and detached, impeccably dressed in black water-combat gear, eyes fainting glowing silver in the dim light. He had learned about the demon lord's attempt to spell him into killing me, so he now wanted to join our little army. I couldn't imagine how he'd convinced my parents and the others to let him join us.

When I met his gaze, he immediately came away from the wall to kneel beside me. "*Cara mia*, I would never again hurt you. Spell or no spell, I promise you. Say you believe me." He took my hand and kissed my palm.

I felt tears sting my eyes. Before I could answer Roman, Chester and the orbs raced down the tunnel towards us. Chester relayed that the rainbow orb had told him the black pool in the chamber was a shortcut to the Portal gateway. I turned my attention to the news, ignoring Roman's question because I didn't know what to say.

Donovan volunteered to check it out. He shrugged into the straps of his scuba tanks and jumped in the pool, reemerging a few minutes later to verify that it did go directly into a part of the *cenotes* that would lead to the gateway. It was time to go. We all suited up and, one by one, jumped into the pool's opaque black water. I had a moment of initial fear when I couldn't see anything, but then the world became a beautiful watery blue. Breathing with the respirator, I turned around to see where I had come from. It looked like a dark shadow on the wall of the submerged cave. No one could have guessed it was a gateway to the temple pool. These new surroundings were otherworldly, with white limestone spires, ripples made of stone, and other formations that looked like partially melted statues in one area, and fairy castles in others.

Little white, eyeless fish swam around us, their internal organs glowing inside translucent bodies. They were pretty in a bizarre way. They nipped at our exposed skin, not really hurting, but annoying. I made a "shooing" motion with my hands, which made them swim away, but they returned immediately. For the first few minutes I felt dizzy, but it passed quickly. Now I felt wonderful. I'd survived another demon attack. Hurray for me! And I get to watch these fabulous fish.

The school of iridescent white fish started to swim around me in precise synchronized formations, fashioning intricate geometric patterns with their little bodies. I clapped my hands together, enchanted and delighted by their strange behavior. It seemed hilarious. I tried to laugh but the respirator was in the way. I pulled it out of my mouth so I could enjoy the show, to let my laughter ring out. I took a breath and water started to fill my lungs instead of air. That was so funny! I'd tried to breathe water, what a super funny thing to do! I laughed and choked. All the while the little fish swam around and around in their pretty formations.

I felt someone grab my hair. *Hey,* I wanted to say, *let go of me. Can't you see I'm enjoying these hilarious little fish?* Roman pushed my respirator back into my mouth and held it there, shaking his head at me. Sure easy for him, he didn't have to breathe the same way I did. A magician could make his body go into deep hibernation mode even while awake and moving. He held up a card with writing on it. "Fish bites = hallucinations" it said. That was also funny! I coughed out the water in my lungs even as I tried to grab at the fish, wanting to save some for later. Maybe when we got to Evika I'd make them bite her and we can have a laugh together.

I looked around me and saw several of the other divers playing with the fish. A few divers floated motionless in the water, respirators out of their mouths, smiles fixed on their faces. The little fish were nipping at their hands and cheeks, eating tiny bites of them, blood spiraled out from the wounds like translucent red ribbons in the still water. The sight shocked me out of my fish-bite-induced euphoria.

Roman, without the need for oxygen tanks, had more flexibility and speed than the rest of us. He swam around pushing respirators back into people's mouths and hooking each person by turn to a long nylon rope. The fish bites seemed to have no effect on him as he swam with incredible strength, pulling at least a dozen of us farther into the cave, then down a tunnel, away from the school of fish.

We lost two people to the hallucinogenic fish. The rest of us sobered up within minutes of escaping them. Apparently, victims had to have a steady supply of whatever substance was in their bites to stay in the altered mind-state they produced. Fortunately, we didn't lose anyone I knew well or was related to. Selfish, I know. I'd feel guilty later, but right now I felt relieved.

I don't know how long we swam, but my arms and legs were getting tired and felt much heavier than when we started. I needed to rest, but pushed myself to keep up with the group. Even tired as I was, in some ways I would liked to have had the leisure to enjoy these fascinating surroundings. Well, without the little killer fish, of course.

We swam through areas of darkness that shifted into areas filled with shafts of bright sunlight from openings far above us. In those caves the water plants flourished and we moved through miraculous upside-down green forests of long trailing roots. We swam through liquid rainbows, the sun refracting inside the water, as if thousands of tiny prisms infused it. And on we swam for what seemed like miles until the group stopped at Donovan's signal.

We were at the gateway. It appeared as a pool of water within the water of the cave. The liquid there looked heavier, like a silvery spill of mercury on the limestone floor. We all gathered around in a group to read Donovan's instructions, written on a white board attached to his belt. We were to get ready to face anything as soon as we went through the gateway. The wizards pulled out their wands, and the witches closed their eyes to silently recite their incantations, focus their energies. Tom gave me a "thumbs up" sign. Roman just floated there, unhindered by equipment, looking like a fashion mannequin lost at sea.

We went in teams. My parents went in front of me, after which Azrael and I headed down to the pool together. He held my hand as we plunged head first into the gateway. At the last minute I felt someone grip my other hand. I looked over to see Roman beside me.

We emerged in a pool of water located in an enormous dry cave. It had a gradual stone slope leading out of the water and into the cavern. There was air here, and we cautiously took off our masks. All around us blazing torches sat in metal holders attached to walls of solid crystal. We had finally arrived in the Cave of Dominion. I don't know what I expected, but it wasn't this eerie, deserted silence. I'd thought we'd have to fight our way through a throng of demons, or armed mercenaries. But all that greeted us was the glitter of reflected flames in the cave's translucent white and pale yellow crystals.

"Welcome," a woman's voice rang out.

Most of our group still stood ankle-deep in water, reluctant to venture into the cave. We looked around us as her voice echoed up into the darkness above us. Evika emerged from one of the many openings in the cave wall. At least it looked like Evika. She had my cousin's long shining red hair, her face was the same perfect pale oval I'd always envied, and her familiar green eyes were shining like they, too, were made of crystals. But her face looked remote and devoid of the animation and life that was her personality. She wore an odd, slimy-looking black body suit, and as I watched her, I could see a reddish network of pulsating veins running just underneath the blackness. The living ooze that was *Tezcatlipoca* covered her body from ankle to throat. She still wore her familiar around her neck—the thin translucent green of her stone snake topping a wide gold collar. On the collar was etched the symbol I had grown to hate and fear. The one I'd seen on the sub-demons who'd tried to kill me.

Watching as the realization dawned on my face, she laughed. "Yes, our dear cousin, what you perceive is correct. We sent the lower demons to kill you once we had become one with the living god *Tezcatlipoca*. There was another vessel, a male. It was weak and gave out quickly, so another was necessary. This witch's body is strong with her powers."

"No!" My mother stepped forward, one arm reaching out as if she could touch my cousin from where she stood at the water's edge. My father held her back, disgust and horror on his face. Another figure joined Evika from the darkness behind her. It was her father, Levititus. He smiled at us in greeting, as if we had come for afternoon tea, not to stop this demon from plunging the world into war and carnage.

My father stepped back, splashing the water at his feet, "No, Levi, not you. You told us about the gateway. You were our source of information about the Portal."

Levi smiled sadly, "How else could we get you all to come to us? To bring your precious Cara and her little male harem of bound ones? Did you really think your no-talent daughter would be witch enough to rule House Augustine?" Watching them speak to each other, I realized how much Uncle Levi looked like his half-brother, Max.

I turned to Roman and whispered, "Was he the person you saw in the restaurant on my birthday?"

He studied the man standing in the torchlight, talking to my father. "It could very well be. They have the same dark hair, pale skin. But the eyes are different. Your Uncle Max has the demon eyes like I saw, but this one has human eyes."

Then I saw ooze cover Uncle Levi's eyes like tarry tears. "How about now?" I said to Roman.

He nodded, "Yes."

Uncle Levi turned to me. "I see you've figured out I was the "Uncle" who came to the restaurant. What you didn't realize was I didn't die in the blast; some poor waiter had that honor. No, the great *Tezcatlipoca* took me to serve at my daughter's side when she rules House Augustine."

At his words, Evika looked at him and casually backhanded him across the face. He flew in the air, hitting the sharp projecting crystals with a moist thud, shock on his face.

Evika smiled coldly and turned back to us, "Let us correct our dear pathetic 'father.' We will rule this part of the *world* as we once did, with thousands of human sacrifices offered to our dark glory. The death and blood and exquisite cries of pain shall ring throughout hell on earth again. Who cares about one insignificant witch *House*?"

Levi was still alive, blood bubbling from his mouth; probably a broken rib had punctured a lung. He crawled towards Evika, "No, I didn't bargain for that . . . you were . . . to rule House Augustine."

Evika leaned down, her lush lips pressed together in a pout, and caressed her father's face before grabbing the front of his shirt with one hand and hurling him violently against the wall again.

He struggled to speak, more blood flowing out of his mouth as he looked pleadingly at my parents and me. "I thought . . . I could control it . . . wanted Evika . . . to take her rightful place. I never meant . . . for it . . . to go so far." He crumbled to ground, an awful gurgling sound issuing from his mouth, and then he lay still on the cavern floor, eyes open but unseeing.

Evika tilted her head to gaze at her dead father, a beatific smile on her face, before turning her attention back to us. "There is one more little thing we need to do, dear cousin, before we can open the Portal. We will have to eliminate the supposed danger you pose to our new kingdom. Some silly demon prophesy about the Eyes of Dominion. Stupid, really, but the masses must be appeased. We know you don't have the power to light a candle, much less stop us from our great purpose. Tsk, tsk, Cara is such a disappointment. Isn't that what you told our mother many years ago, Solange?" My mother started, as if caught in a lie. She looked at me with a mute apology in her eyes.

"Yes, Cara, see how she doesn't deny it? How could *you*, little no-power thing, rule House Augustine?" She rolled her eyes toward the ceiling and nodded. "The one who owned this body feels love for you, her cousin, even though this love would not benefit her. How very sad, then, that when we use your blood to open the Portal, she might feel a loss. Ah, well, there you have it. Just as well I now control this form." Evika ran her hands across her stomach and breasts in pleasure. "We are female in this incarnation; there are intriguing possibilities to be explored."

My mother shook free from my father's grasp, "Evika, I know you're in there somewhere! Look at what the demon did to your father! Now, fight it. You have to fight it!"

Evika looked over at her father's crumpled body and a hint of sanity surfaced in her eyes for just a moment

"Now!" My father shouted.

While Evika was distracted, our group had stealthily taken up positions to her right and left sides. At his command the wizards pointed their wands at Evika and, in unison, green battle flames shot from the tips. The witches, Azrael included, started their incantations. Glowing symbols formed in the air, and frost started to cover the ground and the crystals on the walls behind my possessed cousin.

Evika screamed as two voices issued from her mouth, one human and one inhuman. She lowered her head, glaring at her attackers, with the green nimbus of wizard-fire dancing around her frost-rimed body as she became a creature of fire and ice. She raised her arms and smiled, as if to revel in the power thrown at her. I squinted in the brightness of the spells being cast. When the attack stopped, Evika still stood. She threw back her head and laughed like her old self, unrestrained, full-throated.

Then she lowered her arms and looked at us through her lashes, purring, "Now it's my turn." She made a sign in the air.

At her signal, dozens of demon lords, sub-demons of every description, and a few witches, wizards, and humans, came pouring out the darkness. I was gripped with a deep sense of dread as I realized our little group couldn't possibly fight them all. I grabbed Tom's hand on my right and Roman's hand on my left. Azrael stood in front of me a little off to the side, and Paul, I knew stood in back of me. If ever there was the time for my power to manifest, this was it.

As if they instinctively knew what I planned to do, the men moved marginally closer to me, as if they were of one mind. I marveled at that, but didn't have time to think about it. The horde approached too quickly.

If I looked at the bloodthirsty demons rushing towards us it would be all over, so I closed my eyes to focus inwardly on my power and to prevent panic from freezing my mind before I could do what I needed to do. I felt the diamond ring tucked inside my wet suit grow warm. I reached down, farther and stronger than I had ever consciously attempted before, and the ring became almost unbearably hot. I struggled to keep my concentration and focused it through the diamond. My she-wolf was also there, curled around the core of my power like a guardian as she raised her head with a snarl, ears pricked forward. As I called to my energy source the she-wolf stood and grew in size until in my mind, her head grazed the ceiling of the cavern. My power snaked out tendrils of my essence and found the bound ones around me. Their auras blazed as we merged, and the colored streams of pure energy wrapped around each other familiarly. They knew each other, and now this merging seemed natural. I could feel each one of them separately, and yet they were all a part of the greater power rising inside of me. I forgot my physical body as my inner awareness spread throughout the cavern, searching, seeking what was there.

I discovered that the orbs had also joined us, somehow using their very selves as shields to protect us. How long they could do this, I didn't know, and I couldn't think of it while the indescribable beauty of the entwining energy streams took my breath away and brought tears to my eyes. The power was building, until I felt I would break open like an overripe fruit. My skin felt thin, fragile—hot and cold at the same time. I opened my eyes and saw the cave as a kaleidoscope, as if I were inside the crystals looking out. The crystals began to resonate with the diamond-focused mass of energy strands I held in my body. The crystals rang clear and pure as each of the millions in the cave started to vibrate in sympathetic harmony with my power.

The demons reacted first. The sub-demons stumbled and fell, grotesque bodies seized with uncontrollable shaking as they writhed on the ground, causing the ones behind them to trip over their prone bodies. The demon lords held their hands over their ears, faces contorted in pain. As the demons fell around them, the humans and magic users among them looked around in confusion as they found themselves in the forefront of the charge. A few aimed wands at our group, but we were prepared and blasted them first, and seeing their comrades' fall, the rest turned around and ran back into the darkness of the caves. Evika's face became a mask of fury as she ordered her minions to keep attacking. Some of the demons tried to crawl towards us, and I poured more power into the crystals, the sound rising to ear-splitting levels. Some sub-demons increased their shaking to the point that they were vibrating in tune with the crystals as their bodies liquefied into steaming pools of slime. The black ooze covering Evika's body twisted and squirmed, as if in pain. She looked at her fallen troops, then straight at me and started to run towards us. She either leapt over the bodies littering the floor between us, or used them as stepping stones as she made her way closer to us.

I called out, "Evika, stop. I don't want to hurt you!" She kept coming, not bothering to answer, as if she didn't hear me.

Tom had fallen heavily to his knees beside me; I was draining the men's energies. I couldn't keep this up much longer or I would kill them. I had to stop Tezcatlipoca.

I focused on Evika, not my cousin but the hideous ooze that was the demon-god clinging to her skin. I knew instinctively that was what had to be destroyed. I pulled on the power inside me and concentrated on the ooze. The crystals' song changed, rose to a higher pitch than I would have thought possible. My vision split into a million crystalline images of Evika, all running closer to us, her long red hair flying behind her. I felt heat and power rise behind my eyes, and an incandescent blast of energy shot out from them, magnified by the diamond burning on my chest. It enveloped Evika's body.

She stopped running and stood transfixed by the blast, body stretched taut. She stood on the toes of her bare fee, back arched, mouth open in a silent scream. A thin string of green disengaged from around her neck and fell to the ground. Her familiar! Its usual green eyes were covered in black slime; it too had been possessed. Then the ooze surrounding Evika's body started to burn, dropping to the ground as fine black ash. When it was gone, The demon-god Tezcatlipoca was gone too, and Evika slumped forward and crumpled in a naked heap.

My power was fading, exhausting its resources. I trembled with fatigue and my eyes burned, so I wasn't prepared when Paul flung himself at me, causing us to both crash to the ground. He cried out in pain, and I saw a flash of translucent green. Evika's snake had been coming for me, but Paul shielded my body with his and took the bite instead. He writhed on the ground in agony, his flesh slowly starting to crystallize into green stone. I could feel my attachment to him cut off like a thrown switch. Roman pulled the snake from Paul's shoulder with his bare hand, throwing it to the ground and stomping it to pieces.

I reached for Paul from my position on the ground, as the entire cave started to shake and crystals began falling from the ceiling and walls. But before I could touch Paul, Roman pulled me to my feet. Anguish welled up inside my chest, a dark deep pain, squeezing my heart. I cried out in sorrow and loss for my teacher, my friend, because I knew he was dead. My power drained out of me until it released the men who had fed it. The ringing of crystals stopped. I heard Azrael curse. Roman stood silent, but his face looked too pale, his cheeks sunken. He bent down and helped Tom to his feet. Shaken, I looked around. What was left of our group looked to be still intact. I knew I should be grateful for that, but my grief for Paul nearly incapacitated me. I fell to my knees cradling his stone-hard body in my lap, hot tears falling into the half-open eyes in his statue-like face. Uncle Max ran forward and lifted Evika up in his arms as more of the cave started to fall around us, yelling that we had to leave or we'd be trapped in here.

A part of the cave's wall, about the size of a doorway, melted then reformed into a solid, smooth reflective surface. The surface rippled. Something emerged from the mirrorlike stone. It was a big leather-bound book carrying a small wrinkly brown man with a shock of wispy white hair and two enormous black dogs. Chester and the Hounds!

Chester looked at the scene in front of him and shook his head before gesturing for us to come to him. "Better get over here, if you want to get out of this cave alive." The Hounds leapt into the midst of the hideously deformed demon bodies, opening their huge mouths to howl eerie battle cries that echoed throughout the cavern. One of them reached into the mass of slime and flesh to pull out a weakly struggling wizard who had been trying for one last blast at our group. Before I could stop him, the Hound whipped his head savagely from side to side, breaking the man's neck. The other Hound had gone deeper into one of the side tunnels and now dragged a body by one bloody leg into the main cavern. I could see from here the body had no head.

I yelled, "Asher, leave it! Come here!"

A huge chunk of rock cracked off from the ceiling behind us and fell into the water, splashing our whole group. That got us moving. Asher dropped the body and bounded towards us, licking the blood off his muzzle on the way. Jupiter followed close behind his brother. Roman picked up Paul's petrified body and slung it over his shoulder.

"Run to the mirror!" he yelled at me. We all started running towards Chester's makeshift mirror portal as tons of rock and crystal rained down in the final collapse of the Cave of Dominion, destroying any possibility of anyone trying to open the Portal again. I just hoped we could all make it out of here before it was too late.

Chapter Twenty-four
Home

Three months have passed since the battle with the Aztec demon-god. I remembered that after we'd emerged from the cave through Chester's mirror-dimension portal, I'd taken stock of our group. Roman had set Paul's body on the ground and covered it with a blanket. He'd offered to arrange to take Paul back to Santa Lacuna. Evika had been in shock, although physically unharmed. We'd gotten another blanket so she could cover herself. All traces of the demon had been gone from her, but she'd still had to deal with the fact that she had killed her father and that he had allowed *Tezcatlipoca* to possess her body. All for what? For her to become the head of House Augustine? I would have handed it to her myself, if it had been up to me.

Soon after we got back to Berkeley, Evika's mother, Marissa, arranged for both she and Evika to go to a clinic in Europe for therapy sessions with a very good witch psychologist who used spells, potions, and cognitive therapy to help her patients cope. Marissa had needed counseling too because she hadn't had any idea what her husband had tried to do and had been devastated.

Sonya offered to have me as a roommate, but it took some fast-talking to convince her to let Tom, Azrael, and the orbs to move in too. Sonya's father, Uncle Max, had her house totally cleansed by a team of reputable fairies to eradicate any leftover bad resonance from the anamorphic mirror-frame-demons-attack-spell. She also installed a new living room mirror slash mirror dimension portal with a nice modern, plain titanium frame for her father's visits and for the Hounds to use to hunt in other dimensions. It must have cost a small fortune, but everyone knows titanium can't hold a spell, so it was worth it. I refused to use it. I was not going to risk getting lost in the mirror dimension again.

Tom and Sonya have hit it off really well, so I guess we will just wait and see where all that is headed. Roman has mostly stopped being so impossibly high-handed and is now trying to "woo" me, as Chester put it. He keeps sending me obsequious little men in dark suits carrying cases full of diamonds for me to choose a replacement engagement ring.

Sadly, I fried the original into a little charred lump of melted metal while destroying *Tezcatlipoca*. I tell Sonya to send them away before they can open those cases. Hey, I know my limits when it comes to jewelry.

Azrael's a little scary, but he's trying hard to adjust to living with two female witches, a couple of spirit orbs, and a werewolf. I suspect my father told him his new assignment was to be our bodyguard, which is okay for now. I still have nightmares about all the things that have happened, so truth be told, I feel safer with his big, solid presence in the house. With him, Tom and the orbs we're pretty well protected.

And the orbs, well, the orbs do whatever orbs do, I guess. They disappear most of the day, but like to talk to me in the evenings, telling me about their past lives. Their amazement over modern life is hilarious. Things we take for granted, like television and off-the-shelf potions, just throws them for a loop. The rainbow orb especially found it hard to accept that the general human population knows about us and hasn't tried to kill us all in our sleep. It still can't believe we are a part of society now. The Hounds particularly like the golden orb. They play chase with it all over the house. How we'll get those paw prints off our white ceiling, I'll never know.

I'm still a mess over how I feel about my "bound" men. Tom is my familiar, so of course I think he's wonderful. I miss Paul terribly. He taught me so much and I really think I was starting to love him. Roman is, well, I don't know what he is, except my stomach does flip-flops when he's around. I hate to admit I kind of admired the heroism he displayed during our ordeal. If only he wasn't such a Nightkind, always being so intense and irritatingly bossy. The other thing I have to get used to is Azrael's intense awareness of me. Sometimes I'll catch him staring at me in a particularly unnerving way, like he wants to eat me up with chocolate sauce. I'm not at all sure how I feel about Azrael. Regardless of how I feel about any of them, I guess they're mine. We are, after all, connected no matter what happens.

I still have a lot to learn about my powers and why I'm so different from other witches. My mother has started running a personal campaign to make me accept my responsibility to House Augustine, and despite everything that has happened, still refuses to tell me about the ramifications of having spirit orbs. I now try to avoid her whenever I can get away with it.

The latest news is that Tom got a call from Aunt Amelia this morning. She told Tom he and I have to come back to Santa Lacuna. There's some kind of big trouble brewing with the werewolves and we are both needed there. She also hinted that Etienne, the French werewolf who had given us trouble at the picnic, was to blame and that I might be the actual bone of contention. So it seems I'll have to pack my suitcase again, just when I thought I could settle down for a while. It'll be hard to see the little town without thinking of Paul. On the other hand, I always have enjoyed the California coast this time of year.